THE FOREVER GARDEN

ΙΥ

The Forever Garden

ROSANNA LEY

QUERCUS

First published in Great Britain in 2023 by

QUERCUS

Quercus Editions Ltd
Carmelite House
50 Victoria Embankment
London EC4Y 0DZ

An Hachette UK company

Illustration on page ix by Studio Page

A CIP catalogue record for this book is available
from the British Library

HB ISBN 978 1 52941 356 4
TPB ISBN 978 1 52941 358 8

10 9 8 7 6 5 4 3 2 1

Typeset by CC Book Production
Printed and bound in Great Britain by Clays Ltd, Elcograf S.p.A.

To Meriel, with love

The love of gardening is a seed that once sown, never dies . . .

Gertrude Jekyll

If I had a flower for every time I thought of you, I could walk through my garden forever.

Lord Alfred Tennyson

The Forever Garden

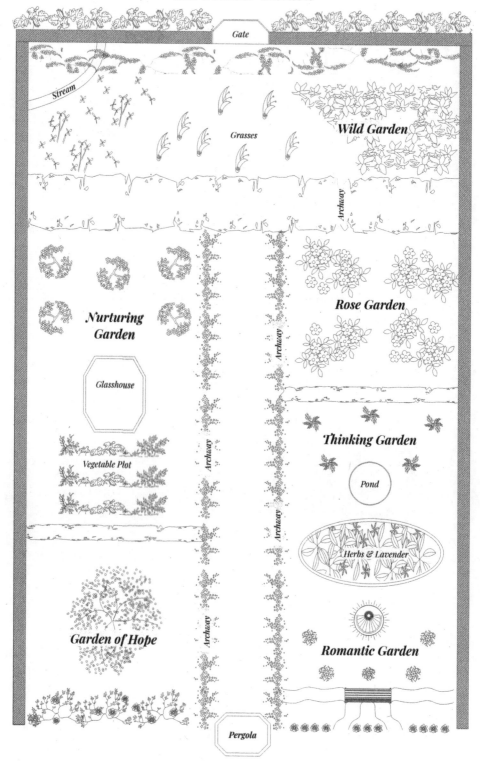

Gate

Stream

Grasses

Wild Garden

Archway

Nurturing Garden

Rose Garden

Glasshouse

Thinking Garden

Pond

Vegetable Plot

Archway

Herbs & Lavender

Garden of Hope

Archway

Romantic Garden

Pergola

CHAPTER I

Lara

Italy, March 2018

It wouldn't be long now.

Lara held on to the edge of the stone balustrade. It was very warm for spring and she felt a little dizzy. From this spot on the terrace, she had the best view of her Italian garden – the garden she had created long ago in her new home in the Valle d'Itria, Puglia, just as soon as she'd been able.

So many years had passed. It had been difficult at first – adjusting to Italian ways, learning the language, feeling such a stranger to it all. But despite the hard work, she had found a sense of peace here at the *masseria*, a sense of peace still rooted here, despite the frequent visitors they now welcomed to the farm. She had been young, there had been plenty of time to adjust to her surroundings and she had been so very desperate to escape.

Recalling that desperation, Lara found herself gripping the stone balustrade so tightly that her knuckles turned blue-white with tension. The feeling wasn't new. *Breathe*, she told herself. *Don't think of it now. It was so long ago. It's over . . .*

She was grateful. Because she'd needed to leave England so badly, because of all the joy Italy had brought her, she would always be overwhelmingly grateful – for her new home, for everything.

Lara focused on a statuesque cypress tree on the far left of the row lining the back of the garden. If she concentrated on one static object, one definite shape, the dizziness would pass. And from the tree . . . the rest of the garden swam into focus.

It was surrounded by dry-stone walls, to protect the fig trees, the pomegranate and the more vulnerable of the citrus. The garden was divided into seven small but separate sections – that much had been important – and Lara had worked on the perspective, so that when standing on this terrace, the viewer could look over, through, beyond, be visually connected and hopefully appreciate the overall symmetry, the way the garden blended with the farm buildings and the landscape of the olive grove and hills. Thus far she had not strayed from her mother's vision of an Arts and Crafts garden. This garden was an echo of the first, but it was certainly not a replica – how could it be? This Italian garden was very different from the garden of the past, the garden Lara had left behind.

Creating it, even while she worked hard with the rest of the family in the olive grove from which they made their living, had been a solace. The planting, the laying of stone pathways and the small pond, the selection of a crumbling stone urn here, a delicate sundial there, had brought order to her mind and made her feel more at home. Most of all, it had allowed her to remember her mother's walled garden in Dorset.

Remember, yes. But Lara had never been able to go back.

How could she go back? It was impossible. She had always known that if she left, the garden would be lost to her forever.

'Mamma?'

Lara turned around. Her daughter Rose stood framed in the doorway. She was tall and fair just as Lara had been before her hair turned grey and she'd begun to stoop and hobble around like some elderly *nonna*. Well, now she was an elderly *nonna*, she reminded herself. She was ninety-seven years old and, indeed, also a grandmother to Rose and Federico's daughter Beatrice. *Beatrice* . . . Ah, now, there was a girl who made Lara's breath catch in her throat for so many reasons.

Much as she loved Rose, Lara had always wished they were closer, whereas Bea . . . Grandmother and granddaughter shared so much more than a love of gardening. Like Lara, Bea was a dreamer. The bond between them ran deep and true.

'Yes, darling?' she said to Rose.

Lara had never quite understood her daughter, perhaps that was it. Even now, as Rose stood poised in the doorway as if unsure whether to dash forward onto the terrace or whisk back to attend to some task in the kitchen, there was an elusive quality to her daughter's green eyes that Lara had never been able to quite fathom.

'Should you not be resting, Mamma?' Rose came out onto the terrace. But she barely glanced at the garden and so she wouldn't have noticed the way the warm afternoon sunshine created a yellow heat haze around the tops of the olive trees beyond. Instead, she tutted (Rose tutted rather too frequently in Lara's opinion), took her mother's arm and led her gently back to the chair she'd been sitting on before.

Like a rag doll, Lara found herself thinking. 'I'm not tired, Rose,' she said. Though she was. Her eyes were aching with

3

the effort of taking everything in and oh, it was so bright today. Her mind was aching when she thought of Dorset – which she still did so often – of the house and garden there and everything that still needed to be done. And her heart was aching because she knew she didn't have long left on this earth and she really didn't want to say goodbye to the family she loved.

'So you say. But come.' Rose was calm but firm.

She eased Lara into the chair and adjusted the cushions to support her mother's neck. She was a good girl. She seemed more settled now too and Lara was relieved. That was what she wanted – for everyone to be settled before she left them.

That was why she simply must consider the Dorset business . . . How she hated to leave ends untied. The promise she'd made to her own beloved mother before she died had been made more years ago than Lara cared to remember. Nevertheless, a promise was a promise and perhaps it wasn't too late to see it fulfilled. But how? Lara was far too old to go back to Dorset now – she could barely make it to the end of the olive grove. She couldn't ask Rose or Federico – they were much too busy here on the *masseria*, especially since Federico had converted three of the *trulli* on the farm to take paying guests and Rose had to cook and clean for them.

Then there was Bea . . . But how could she deprive herself of her granddaughter for what might be the final summer of Lara's life? Besides, Bea was working now, building up her horticulture and landscape gardening business. She was making contacts, finding new clients; she was already somewhat in demand. Her granddaughter had a bright future in front of her, Lara was sure. So how could she uproot her and send her to Dorset? Lara found herself chuckling at her own pun. No.

It was impossible. The chuckle turned to a frown. There must be another way.

'Why are you frowning, Mamma?' Rose smoothed Lara's hair from her face. 'What do you have to worry about, hmm?'

'Oh, nothing. *Non importa*. Take no notice of me.' Lara picked up the book she'd been staring at earlier. She couldn't remember either the plot or the characters, but it didn't seem to matter as much as it once had.

She was reluctant to confide in Rose. It was a time in Lara's life that was painful to revisit and keeping silent was a hard habit to break. But if things were to be sorted, then she would have to tell someone the truth, painful though it might be. She had told Bea stories of the garden when she was a little girl, but she had made them into fairy tales, thinking perhaps of the sweet afternoons when Lara had climbed the roots of the wisteria, over the wall and into the woods beyond. To tell the whole story, though, that seemed a daunting task indeed.

Unlike Lara and Bea, Rose wasn't a dreamer. Her daughter wanted everything to be clear-cut and organised. If Lara was supposed to be resting after lunch, then Rose expected her to close her eyes and do exactly that. Rose wasn't one for gazing sightlessly into space and letting her thoughts wander; she was unlikely to lose herself in contemplating the beauty of the landscape around them. Lara glanced up to take in the dark and intense green of the cypress trees outlined against the canopy of blue sky. Her daughter would say she didn't have time.

'Good. I'll make you a cold drink then, shall I?'

'*Grazie*, darling.'

'And I'll get your hat.'

'I'm sitting in the shade,' Lara remonstrated.

'Even so.' And Rose disappeared through the doorway.

Always doing something, thought Lara. It was quite exhausting, just watching her. Why did Rose work so hard? Of course, there was the *masseria*; there were the guests, the cleaning and cooking that was demanded of her. But it was more than that. Lara's gaze drifted out towards the garden once again. It was almost as if her daughter was forever trying to atone . . . But for what, she couldn't imagine.

Lara supposed that when Rose was young, she had rather let her go her own way. It was a reaction, she knew, to what she, Lara, had gone through. Not her childhood – no, that had been happy enough – but after her mother's death, that was when it had begun. Lara had been obliged to fight for her freedom and so she knew more than most that freedom was a precious gift – and the gift she'd always wanted to give her beloved daughter.

She knew that others – not least her own husband – had sometimes doubted the wisdom of her liberal parenting. She'd caught the occasional frown from Eleanora or one of the other family members that seemed to forever fill the Romano home on the other side of the olive grove. They would speak, too, in a fast Italian that Lara had not yet got to grips with back then. Not unkindly, for the Romano family were far from unkind; they had welcomed Lara into their midst without question; they had always tried to make her feel as if she belonged. But sometimes, Lara had sensed their disapproval. The way that Lara brought up her daughter . . . it was not the Italian way, and so, for them, it was certainly not the right way.

Lara was determined, though, that Rose should not have a strict upbringing. She wanted Rose to feel unburdened by rules, free to experiment (at least, up to a point – she didn't want her to get into trouble, naturally). Lara trusted her daughter, as a young girl, as a teenager, to choose the right pathways. More than anything, Lara wanted her to be free to climb and ramble, just like the wild rose in the Dorset walled garden after which she had been named.

Lara closed her eyes. *Allora.* There had been that time when Rose was a teenager, but their daughter had come through that and probably learnt from it too. She pushed a memory away. There were so many memories cascading through her mind now that she was old – some good, some bad. They appeared, they disappeared; there wasn't room for them all these days, something had to go. But in the end . . . Lara hoped she did not have too much to reproach herself for. Rose was married – happily, she was sure – to Federico Romano no less, which was so much more than Lara and all the rest of the two families had dared to hope for. There had been undeniable losses – but then there was Beatrice.

'Here you are, Mamma.'

Lara opened her eyes and looked up in surprise. She hadn't heard Rose come out again, so deep in thought had she been. Or was she sleeping? She really wasn't sure.

'Thank you, darling.' She took the juice with a trembling hand.

'Are you feeling okay, Mamma?' Rose looked concerned. She placed a hand on Lara's forehead.

'I'm perfectly well.' Lara put down the juice, the glass rattling ominously on the tiled tabletop for a moment before it found its balance. She took Rose's hand from her brow and held it. 'You are happy, aren't you, Rose?' She searched her daughter's face for the clue she needed.

Rose's expression moved so speedily to a reassuring smile that if Lara had blinked, she would have missed it. She didn't blink, though, and so she saw it — a deep sadness in her daughter's eyes that shocked her.

'Rose?' she whispered.

'What a question! *Certo.* Of course I am.' Rose moved the footstool (was that a chance for her to look away?) and gently lifted Lara's feet so that they rested on it.

'You're sure?'

'*Sì* . . .' Rose laughed. 'Honestly, Mamma . . . What has brought this on? Too much sun?'

Lara shook her head. Though sometimes the sun could help you see. 'I'm here, you know,' she said.

'Here?'

'If you ever need to talk.'

'Oh, Mamma.' Rose had already moved to one side. Now she was examining the leaves of the lemon tree just in front of the terrace, checking for pests, no doubt. In the last few years, Bea had begun a tradition of planting a trough of strawberries and pots of peppers and tomatoes alongside, so that the fruits were all handy for picking — no need for a greenhouse here. And for Lara, more than any ornate fountain, piece of statuary or line of cypress trees, it was the simple lemon planted in an old clay pot that most symbolised the Italian garden.

'I may be old,' Lara said. No one could argue with that. 'But I can still listen, you know. Perhaps even help — if you needed me to.' *I am still your mother,* she wanted to say, *even though it is now you that is nurturing me.*

'Help?' Rose glanced back at her. She looked fond and affectionate but not as if she needed help. She was, she had always been, very capable. Nevertheless. Lara was certainly old and canny enough to have learnt to look below the surface now and again.

8

'With anything that's bothering you,' she clarified. Because she knew she hadn't mistaken that look of sadness. Was it the old loss that her daughter still mourned? Or was it more than that?

'I am fine.' Rose took some scissors out of her pocket and snipped off an offending leaf. 'There is nothing wrong. Nothing at all. Please do not worry so much, Mamma.'

Do not worry so much. Lara sipped the cool orange juice. If only. This knowledge that there wasn't long left had taken up residence in her mind and she knew she must pay attention to it. She must find out what was making her daughter sad. And she must decide what to do about Dorset, about the house and the walled garden. And only then, she realised, could she be at peace.

CHAPTER 2

Bea

Italy, March 2018

Bea was working in a garden in Ostuni, a city whose tumble
of whitewashed buildings rose high on a hill above the sea
of olive trees in the Valle d'Itria. The clients were kind and
pleasant and, even better, had given Bea free rein to design the
garden she wanted to design – with certain provisos, of course.

Everyone had provisos and it was her job to establish the
clients' needs and desires first off, even when they didn't themselves know what those needs and desires might be. *Especially*
then. Even so . . . it was the best thing, Bea reflected, when a
client trusted you to do the job.

She paused to survey the landscaping. The garden was long
and rectangular and she'd broken it into connecting pockets,
using the plants to define the spaces. Stone paths led to two
long, scented pergolas draped with honeysuckle and orange
trumpet vines to provide privacy and create shady, welcoming
and sensuous areas for outdoor seating. The pathways would

give a sense of journey as they drew the garden walker around the rest of the space, with smaller pebbled paths of light and dark stones leading to the central parterre of box hedging and the stone pool and fountain. Most Italians adored proportion and symmetry, but there was room within *la ligne* for artful invention, for history and for emotion – in Bea's opinion at least. Traditionally, the Italian garden was never merely a grouping of plants; it was a pool of ideas reaching beyond its boundaries into a realm of philosophy, myth or poetry – if that wasn't too fanciful a notion, she thought to herself. And here, Bea intended to be sensitive to the surrounding landscape. Ostuni was a labyrinthine city and she wanted this garden to reflect that quality.

A terrace of cool pale stone stretched the full width of the villa; this Bea had decorated simply with terracotta pots crammed with geraniums, fragrant bay and a lemon tree. Wooden trellising supported dark pink bougainvillea, which would climb up the white walls with a splash of vibrancy intended to give impact to the back of the villa. Stone steps led down from the terrace past a prickly pear and a walnut tree and these added a little trick of perspective and invited exploration – she hoped.

The white city of Ostuni, known as *La Città Bianca*, with its tangled alleyways, steep staircases and crumbling arches, was also a coastal town, being only eight kilometres from the Adriatic Sea, and so she had kept the colour palette of her planting bold and simple. The complexity of the garden was provided by the symmetrical pathways, the neat box hedging at its best when viewed from the terrace or back windows of the house, and the mosaicked stone. And the history lay in the small half-hidden grotto and the stone pool and fountain – these being the only structures that had existed in the overgrown garden when she began. The fountain especially had taken a lot of work, but it was a vital element; the cascading water brought music to the garden after all.

This was her final week and Bea was working alone, though she had employed some labour for the earlier and heavier jobs. Now, she was adding some finishing touches — training her climbers, clipping back the geometrical box hedges, laying more gravel, planting up the rest of her pots and urns. Making it as perfect as it could be. Imagining how it would be used, exactly how it would make people feel.

'Beatrice? Could you come up to the house for a moment, *per favore*?' Signora Milella's voice from the direction of the terrace interrupted Bea's daydream.

Bea's mother always said that she didn't know how her daughter got any work done, she spent so much time with her head in the clouds. Nonna, though . . . Bea smiled fondly at the thought of her beloved grandmother who sadly was now so frail. She understood that sometimes it was the dreaming that got the best things done.

'*Sì. Certo.* I'm on my way, signora,' she called back.

Some last-minute change of mind perhaps? Bea got to her feet from where she had been kneeling at the base of the pergola. She brushed some loose earth from her jeans and pulled off her gardening gloves as she made her way up to the house. Or perhaps the signora had made her a cool drink — she could do with one, it was surprisingly hot for March. Bea fanned her face with her gloves as she reached the steps leading up to the terrace. She would have to water the plants in extra carefully if they were to take quickly to their new surroundings here.

Signora Milella was waiting for her on the terrace. She

took in the sight of Bea's muddy boots. 'Let's chat out here.' She waved at some people in the house. 'Come through,' she called to them. 'Come and meet Beatrice and see what she has done for us.'

Bea's heart sank. She wasn't unsociable, but she was working and she didn't relish small talk. Her father was fond of pointing out that it wasn't very Italian of her and this was certainly true. *It must come from your mother's side of the family*, he'd say, rolling his eyes good-naturedly. He was only teasing. He adored Bea's mother and anyway, Rose was sociable enough; it was Bea who was the 'quiet flower' as Nonna called her, the solitary one of the family.

The signora bustled over to the door, speaking to the three people standing on the threshold. According to Bea's grandmother, Bea had always been the same. Nonna had told her she used to play alone for hours with her toy animals and, later, Nonna would find them in her garden – elephants, giraffes and the rest, who had kept Bea happily occupied all morning with whatever activities and stories she had conjured up for them. Now it was plants, she supposed. But, she reminded herself sternly, she had a business to run and this kind of networking was a vital part of it.

The older couple were accompanied by a younger man who was about her age and rather attractive. Bea quickly glanced away. If only she wasn't looking quite so, well, earthy. And were there sweat marks from her armpits visible on her faded T-shirt? She kept her hands stuck firmly to her sides just in case.

'Meet Beatrice Romano,' Signora Milella said to the couple. 'Our garden designer.' She smiled. 'Bea, I am happy to introduce you to my good friends Signore and Signora Leone.'

Bea returned the smile. But she wasn't yet accustomed to

being called a garden designer. Had she earned the title? She wasn't entirely sure. 'I am very pleased to meet you,' she said.

'The pleasure – it is ours.' The signora gave a little nod but her eyes were appraising.

'*Grazie.*' Although it was nice of Signora Milella to want to show off her garden and Bea's talents, this was the part of the job that made her feel uncomfortable. Secretly, she'd rather like to get on with her planting – after that cool drink, that was.

'*Prego.*' Signora Leone gestured proudly to the young man beside them. 'And this is our son Matteo.'

Bea turned towards him. It would certainly be rude not to return eye contact.

'*Ciao.*' He stepped closer and, to her surprise, kissed her on both cheeks, a greeting usually reserved for those who might have met at least a few times before. Bea felt the stubble from his jaw slightly graze her skin. He smelt of *agrume*, of citrus and cedarwood. His hair was thick and dark, his eyes a rather shocking navy blue. His smile was confident and his look was direct – friendly, maybe even a bit more than friendly.

'*Ciao.*' She kept her voice casual. He was quite something. But men like this one, *allora* . . . In Bea's limited experience they were usually best avoided.

He touched her arm. *More physical contact* . . . 'It looks amazing.' And he finally stopped staring at her for long enough to allow his gaze to scan the garden and presumably ensure that his compliment was justified.

'Thank you,' she said again. '*Grazie mille.*' She glanced across at the view of the landscape beyond the garden. It was impressive. The house was situated near to the ornate Ostuni Palace, on the higher reaches of Corso Vittorio Emanuelle, which ran around the perimeter of the old town, and so this terrace overlooked the *centro storico*, clusters of pine trees and hazy olive groves beyond merging into a wide strip of sea on the horizon. From here, Bea could easily make out the white and pinky-beige profile of the fifteenth-century Gothic cathedral standing serenely at the peak of the white city, the gentle blue sky above. And she hoped she'd made this garden special too – to make 'practical logic meet beauty' as one of her tutors used to put it; the aim of any fine Italian garden.

'You have done a brilliant job. Has she not, Mamma?'

His mother was smiling at him fondly. '*Sì*,' she agreed. 'She has indeed.'

Was Matteo an only child too? Bea wondered. She suspected so. Bea would have liked siblings for companionship, for sharing, even to take the parental pressure off from time to time because when she was younger her mother had always wanted to be in full control of her daughter's life . . . But the brother that she might have had was taken from her parents at birth, and Bea suspected that her mother couldn't bear to take the chance on having another child. She couldn't blame her. It must have been heartbreaking.

Signora Leone looked to her husband who gave a little nod.

'And so,' she said to Bea. 'Are you very busy right now?'

'*Allora* . . .' Bea realised that she was still clutching her gardening gloves as if for protection. Really . . . She should have at least put them down when she greeted these people. 'I have a few small projects in hand,' she said. 'But nothing major.'

'*Bene*.' The signora beamed. 'And you are finishing here soon, is that so?' She looked from Bea to Signora Milella for confirmation.

'Yes, yes,' the signora reassured her friend. 'Though Bea will be coming back to keep an eye on things. Right, Bea?'

'Oh, yes, of course.' This garden – like every garden she worked on – felt like her baby. Bea wanted to continue nurturing it and watching it grow.

'But not every day?' Signora Leone asked.

'No.' Bea shook her head. 'Not every day. Otherwise, as I said, I have a few other clients, some ongoing jobs . . .' It sounded as if the signora had something big in mind, and Bea was still building up her business, so of course she would accept – but not too eagerly.

After she'd completed her degree, Bea had done some work experience at various public gardens in the areas of Bari and Lecce in Puglia. After that, she'd worked for another company based in Brindisi, labouring, planting and fulfilling someone else's designs. Then eventually, when she'd felt ready, she'd set up her own business, Giardini di Beatrice Romano - Beatrice Romano's Gardens. She still lived at home, so her expenses were low; she'd managed to procure a small bank loan and her parents had helped out with some savings. Their family had never been wealthy, but the olive farm did well enough and Bea's father had always taken on extra building work to help them get by and afford the occasional luxury. Since the *masseria* had opened its doors to visitors, with the farm stays, they had done better still and her parents had been able to set some money aside to help Bea with her plans.

It was early days. Things were going well so far, but a new client would be more than welcome.

'I will get us some drinks.' Signora Milella smiled graciously as she left the terrace for *la cucina*.

'We live in Polignano a Mare.' Signora Leone took Bea's arm and spoke quietly, confidentially.

'Yes, I know it well.' It was an upmarket and charming town

on the Adriatic coast, a cluster of whitewashed buildings built on limestone cliffs overlooking the turquoise waters and sea caves and only half an hour's drive or so from Bea's own home near Locorotondo in the Valle d'Itria.

'We run a restaurant there,' the signora added. 'Our terrace is a little . . .' – she grimaced – '. . . tired, and we want a revamp, a new concept for the coming season. Perhaps you would come round and see it?'

They weren't giving her much time if they wanted something for the season which was already almost upon them, thought Bea. Over her shoulder, she saw Matteo grinning. He gave her a thumbs up and she couldn't help smiling back at him. He was quite a charmer.

'*Certo*,' she said. A job was a job and she would check it out first before she told them how much or how little she would be able to achieve in a few months. 'When would be convenient? Next week perhaps?'

They fixed a date and Bea was glad to see Signora Milella returning with a tray of homemade lemonade.

After her drink and as soon as it felt polite to do so, Bea asked them to excuse her. She wanted to get back to work. They were all pleasant enough, but there was so much more she had to do in the garden in a relatively short time and she wanted to get on.

For the next half hour, she continued working on her pergolas, training the vines to achieve the effect of a simple and casual drape of flowers and leaves that actually took a lot of effort to achieve. The honeysuckle was already blooming, the blossoms frothing cream, yellow and pink and scenting her fingers as she teased and persuaded their vines to do what she required.

17

Bea only felt truly herself when she was designing a garden or, better still, in it, walking around to survey the mood of the place, digging the soil, tending to plants, weeding or snipping or trailing. Her back and shoulders sometimes complained – she often took a hot bath in the evenings and she kept up with her daily stretching and yoga, aware that she hadn't chosen the easiest of career paths.

But the rewards more than made up for it. To be outside, in the fresh air, in the elements. To hear birdsong and to feel at one with nature. To nurture plants and watch them grow, to witness a garden coming to life, changing with the seasons and evolving into a relaxing space, a tranquil space, a liberating and healing space – indeed, whatever kind of space was required. A garden was a living being full of the living beings that made it their home – birds, animals, insects, yes, and humans too – and a garden could make you feel alive. These thoughts and sensations, these daily joys, made every ache and pain worthwhile.

Bea twined the last of the honeysuckle around the pergola and checked the trumpet vine. She had chosen *Campsis grandiflora* because although it was vigorous and would be flowering by mid-May, it was not as invasive as some of its cousins. This variety would provide a vivid sunset-orange spectacle of blooms with golden-yellow throats which would mingle with and take over seamlessly from the honeysuckle. And when the orange trumpets stopped growing, there would be pretty seed pods to ensure that the pergola's interest went on.

By her feet were some pots of thyme, which she'd been pushing in between the gaps of the path so that it would scramble over the stone, blur the hard edges and be crushed by footsteps which would send its scent wafting into the air. Bea breathed in deeply, relishing the lemony fragrance.

She had been inspired to study horticulture by her grandmother. Not just by the Italian garden that Nonna had created which had been Bea's playground as a young girl, but also by Nonna's stories about another garden, a garden in Dorset, England, where Nonna had lived as a child. Bea had loved to listen to her grandmother spinning her stories about that garden – an Arts and Crafts garden, Nonna had told her, which stood for traditional values of honesty, simplicity and appreciation of the beauty of nature – and about a girl who was saved by her love of the garden which became her sanctuary. Bea had been spellbound.

Was Nonna that girl? Bea suspected that she was. But why had she needed a sanctuary? Bea didn't know the answer to that one. But she did appreciate how a garden could save you. How a garden could make you feel free.

Bea sensed something. It was unsettling and out of place. She flicked her gaze upwards. 'Oh.'

Matteo Leone was lounging against the stone wall of the little grotto. Bea had discovered that shady grotto, grown over with weeds and grass and neglected for many years. She had gently cleaned the crumbling stone and restored it into an original feature of the garden. There was a little figure inside, a cherub, and if Bea had the time, she would have loved to find out more about the history of the piece. But that wasn't her job. Her job was to create the garden. And then like a surrogate, she must hand it over to the care and emotions of the client – apart from her weekly maintenance visits, that was.

'Ciao again.' He shot her a disarming smile. It seemed, she thought, to be his speciality.

Bea pulled off her gardening gloves which were somehow making her feel at a disadvantage and got to her feet. She swept the strands of hair that had escaped from her ponytail away from her brow with the back of her hand. '*Ciao*,' she said. 'Can I help you with something?' It was rude of her perhaps, but she didn't much want to be disturbed.

He didn't reply at first, just continued to survey her coolly. 'What made you choose it?' he asked instead. He leant forwards as if it were important for him to know.

But know what? Bea was still standing by the pergola. But he couldn't be referring to the orange trumpet vine surely? 'Choose what?'

'Gardening,' he said. 'What made you choose it for a profession?'

Bea felt herself bristle. 'When I could have been someone's PA, do you mean? Or a . . .' – she flapped her gardening glove around as she tried to think of stereotypical jobs for women – '. . . nursery school teacher?'

He shrugged. 'Or a lawyer,' he said. 'Or a politician . . . whatever.'

Obviously, he knew nothing about her, but she took his point. Attractive men put her on the defensive, they always had.

'I like gardens,' she told him. Obvious but true. 'I like how they can make people feel.'

'And how do they make people feel?' He took a step closer.

'How do they make *you* feel?' she countered.

He laughed. '*Touché*. Let me put it differently.'

'*Va bene*.' She waited.

'How do you design a garden to make a person feel a certain way?'

That was the question – he had it in one.

'Answering that would make up an entire thesis,' she said. It certainly wasn't something she could explain in a few minutes. 'But it's one of the elements of my job that interests me the most.'

He nodded. 'And to continue on the personal note . . .'

'Yes?' Bea felt her stomach give a slight lurch. He'd shown himself already to be the kind of man who didn't take long to get personal.

'How do *you* like to feel in a garden?'

Was he teasing her? She glanced away. His eyes were blue enough and intense enough to be even more disquieting at close quarters.

'Peaceful,' she said. 'I like tranquillity in a garden. It should be a space to relax in, somewhere to chill out.' That was part of it, at least.

'It shows,' he said.

Bea was surprised. 'In what way?'

'In your eyes,' he said.

'In my . . . ?'

'In your expression. The way you look when you're touching the plants.' He pointed to the thyme she'd been planting at the edge of the stone paving.

What exactly had she given away? And for how long had he been watching her in the garden? Bea gave a little shrug of her own. 'I do enjoy my job,' she agreed. If that was what he was saying.

'Hmm.'

Bea frowned. Why had he come down here anyway? To look for her? To inspect the garden? Was he bored with the conversation on the terrace perhaps? 'Why do you ask?' Bea was curious. She'd only just met him and so she knew almost nothing about him, but she had to admit, she was drawn to finding out more.

He sat down on the stone bench under the pergola and stretched out his denim-clad legs as if he owned the place. Bea looked away. He felt like an intrusion into something quiet and peaceful she had constructed here. And yet . . .

'I envy you,' he said.

She was surprised again at that. And he hadn't really answered her question. 'What for?'

'You know what you want,' he said. 'You know what you love doing. Where you need to be. All that.'

Ah. Bea considered his words. This was unexpected. Who would have guessed when she came here today that she'd be having an intimate conversation with a man she couldn't help but feel attracted to? It was true that she'd always known what she wanted to do. Even as a girl, she'd learnt the names of most of the flowers and trees, often found herself thinking about which plants should go where in a garden and what they would add to the overall picture and mood.

'You are right,' she told him. 'But it was easy for me. Being in a garden always makes me feel good.' She gazed out towards the parterre that made up the heart of the garden. 'And it has been scientifically proven now. Something to do with the patterns of the leaves and the structure of the bark of the trees. They affect your mood.'

'Is that so?'

Bea gave a little start at the irony in his tone. She'd almost forgotten who she was talking to there. 'It is true,' she said staunchly. 'Gardening is excellent for your mental health.'

He eyed her intently. 'Perhaps then I should work for you as a labourer when you come to work on Mamma's garden,' he said.

Really his mood was very up and down. 'If I do it,' she said primly. 'Nothing has been agreed.'

He raised an eyebrow. '*Va bene*,' he said. '*If* you do it.'

Bea hesitated. 'And why do you need to improve your mental health?' she asked him. 'If that is not an intrusive question?' It was hard to take him seriously, but she sensed that there was something more, buried behind his teasing bravado. 'Is it because you do not know what to do with your life? Or has something happened to make you sad?'

At this, she had clearly cut too close to the bone because he jumped to his feet as if stung. 'My life is entirely mapped out,' he said. 'But you need not worry about me. I am in a privileged position.' His mouth twisted. 'And nothing has happened to make me sad.'

'Good.' At least she thought it was good. Though having your life mapped out for you, privilege or no, wasn't necessarily desirable. But he was smiling again so perhaps he was still half joking after all.

'Though I would be sad not to see you again, Beatrice Romano,' he said.

'Oh.' Bea wasn't sure quite how to respond.

He came closer so that she could smell that cedarwood and citrus on his skin again. He took her elbows in his palms and leant forwards. One kiss, two, three, side to side, all on the cheek, all signifying nothing – other than the actions of a man who was probably just another Italian flirt.

'And why is that?' she asked him, refusing to feel unsettled.

'Because, Beatrice,' he said, fixing her with another stare from those very blue eyes. 'You are a breath of fresh air.'

CHAPTER 3

Lara

Italy, March 2018

At dinner, Lara and Bea were sitting quietly while Rose and Federico were having one of their spirited conversations about how many visitors had been booked to stay at the *trulli* this season and whether this was a good or a bad thing. Rose seemed to want the visitors – she was forever planning how they could attract more people – but at the same time, with every booking, her anxiety appeared to grow.

'All the guests have reserved dinner that night,' she was saying to Federico. 'Is it too much? Should we get help in, do you think?'

Lara thought back to the day she had first arrived here in Puglia. Everything had felt so strange; even the farm buildings were unfamiliar: the distinctive conical *trulli* – traditional stone huts with thick whitewashed walls and pointy roofs apparently built using a prehistoric building technique of drywall construction that was still used in the region today. And now

24

the very same *trulli* had become the unique selling point of Puglia. There was even a town nearby, Alberobello, which drew visitors in their thousands as the *centro storico* was constructed entirely of *trulli* – some still inhabited, some given over to souvenir shops and some sadly gone to ruin.

Federico twirled his pasta around his fork. 'It is up to you, *cara*,' he said.

Which was fair enough. After all, Rose was the one who would be doing the cooking. But Lara knew full well that Rose sometimes wanted – or needed – Federico to make the decision for her, or more accurately, she wanted him to show that he understood just how much work there was to be done. Relationships were very complicated sometimes.

Sure enough, Rose sighed. She put down her fork, got to her feet and began clearing away with rather more ferocity than necessary.

'What?' Federico asked her.

But she didn't answer; only stacked some empty serving dishes and took them over to the drainer.

Federico looked at Lara and Bea. He spread his hands, clearly perplexed.

'It is a lot of work for Mamma,' Bea put in.

'Yes, I agree.' But despite her words, Lara smiled fondly at her son-in-law. She loved Federico, had loved him from the moment she'd met him, as a black-haired toddler, when she first came here and the Romanos had taken her under their generous wing.

Since her birth, Federico had always seemed to want to protect Lara's little girl. When Rose was a baby, sleeping in her pram in the shady part of the terrace, he would break off from his games to watch over her, running swiftly to alert Lara

25

if the baby so much as stirred or cried out in her sleep. When Rose was old enough to toddle around the garden, he would play with her, always patient, spending as much time with his young friend as he did his older brothers and sisters and his peers from nearby farms and the village.

And as they both grew older . . . Lara watched him now as he ran his fingers through his thick dark hair, now grey at the temples; his skin was deeply lined, tanned and weathered from so many days working in the sun. For a while they had been inseparable.

It had been the greatest hope of both families that the two young people would fall in love, and eventually marry. But although Federico had always appeared happy with the idea, Rose had seemed to think of him more as a brother. *Let her go her own way* . . . This had been Lara's refrain back in those days. She shook her head at the memory. Not always wisely, as it turned out.

Because young Rose *had* gone her own way and with consequences.

'I am confused,' Federico groaned. 'Did I not say . . . ?'

'Mamma and Bea understand.' Rose was back at the table, hands on hips.

'But . . .' Federico began.

'*Certo*, you should have someone come in to help prepare the food when you are busy,' Lara said.

'And to serve and help clear up afterwards,' added Bea.

'Indeed, yes.' Lara patted her daughter's arm as a slightly mollified Rose leant over to collect the empty pasta dish. 'You are not a slave to this business, Rose.'

'Naturally, she is not a slave.' Federico looked affronted. 'I would never expect her to be a slave.'

26

'We know that,' Lara soothed. Really, both these two were so prickly sometimes.

'We do not even need to have the tourists.' Federico hit his chest for dramatic effect. 'Why have them here at all?'

'For the money we need to live on?' Rose suggested dryly. 'And you have converted the *trulli*. Why do that if you do not want to have people staying in them?'

'It is not that I do not want them. It is simply that . . .' He tailed off. As usual, Federico had got muddled by his own argument – or by Rose. And so it would always be.

Lara exchanged a complicit glance with her granddaughter. They both understood how Rose should be handled, but much as he loved her, Federico had never quite got the hang of it, and so Rose and Federico's discussions would always take the same circuitous and often tempestuous paths.

But although she had not fallen in love with Federico in quite the way her family had hoped she would, Federico had always been there for Rose and ultimately, thankfully, Rose had seen the light. Friendship was an excellent basis for a life together, in Lara's opinion. And despite Rose's early miscarriages and the trauma of the stillbirth of the child she had carried full-term, they had survived the losses and emerged stronger than ever with the birth of their beautiful daughter Bea. Or at least – and Lara thought again of the sadness she had seen in her daughter's eyes the other day – they had *seemed* stronger than ever, and she had *thought* Rose had put it all behind her.

'Oh, well, I will manage, I suppose,' Rose said now. She glanced down at Lara's plate. 'Mamma, you have barely eaten a thing.' She tutted.

'It was delicious,' Lara assured her. 'But you know . . .' She didn't need to finish the sentence. Rose must realise that she no longer had much appetite for food. She still had an appetite for life, for her family, for her garden. But food . . . She had very little hunger for that.

'You must eat,' Rose told her.

Lara saw that her daughter had a tear in her eye so she patted her arm again. It made her feel so guilty. She tried, God knows, but . . .

'You must keep up your strength.' Rose turned abruptly away.

Lara knew that now she should change the subject. 'It's such a lovely evening.' She looked out of the window wistfully. 'I think perhaps—'

'Would you like to take a short walk in the garden with me, Nonna?'

Bless the child. She always knew.

'I'd like that very much.' Lara smiled at Bea. At this, her granddaughter was immediately up and out of her chair to help Lara to her feet.

'You sit down, Mamma. I'll finish the clearing up when I get back,' Bea told her mother.

'No, no, my love, you have been working hard all day. It is fine.' Without further ado, Rose whisked the last of the plates from the table.

Lara suspected that her daughter actually quite liked doing it all herself. But Rose also needed to be appreciated. Lara raised an eyebrow at Federico who was now peeling a tangerine.

He nodded.

Lara took her granddaughter's arm. Best, she decided, to leave them to it.

★

Once outside, taking the stone steps from the terrace down to the garden, her hand tucked in the crook of her granddaughter's arm, Lara felt Bea's body relax. They were so alike; they could both breathe more freely in the open air.

'Hard day, darling?' she asked her. It was still mild outside, but even so, Lara had tucked her wrap around her shoulders. These days she felt the cold so much more; she needed something to take the edge off and the feel of the soft fabric around her shoulders was comforting too.

They both paused at the bottom of the steps to take in the scent of the small perfume garden which Lara had planted strategically right by the house. The jasmine climbing up the trellis was now flowering in clusters of white stars and Lara breathed in the familiar heady fragrance she never tired of. The parma violets too had been in bloom since late winter and were now at their best, shaded by the terracing for part of the day, blossoming in shades from pale lilac to deep purple, their delicate, sweet fragrance mingling with that of the jasmine, hanging softly in the evening air. Lara had ensured there would be a different perfume emanating from this spot all year round but this was possibly her favourite season – spring, traditionally a time of hope and new beginnings.

'Not really,' Bea said. 'A good day, I think. Finishing touches, you know?'

Ah, yes. The finishing touches were always a pleasure and often the most rewarding. Lara nodded. 'And what were you doing today?'

They continued along the garden path. When Lara had first begun work on creating this garden, she had found some old iron hoops rusting among the weeds. These she had restored and they now supported the white fragrant climbing roses.

After the rose bed came the water garden (a small pond with water lilies, yellow irises and papyrus). Then came the rock garden created from the limestone of the area with bright red African daisy succulents surrounding an old stone lion basin that Lara had found at Ostuni market. And to their left, the figs and pomegranates were positioned for shelter against the dry-stone wall. Everything in the garden had its part to play.

Bea began to chat about the plants in the Ostuni garden – she was always happy to talk horticulture and Lara loved to listen. But there was something different about her grand-daughter tonight. Lara focused not on her words, but on her face. Although she had been quiet and thoughtful at dinner, now Bea was animated; there was a buzz about her, an extra sparkle in her dark eyes.

'It all sounds wonderful,' Lara assured her. She paused to peer into the water, which was dim but active with pond life, she knew, ready to spring to the surface over the next month or two – literally, in the case of the little frogs and toads.

'I will take some photos tomorrow,' Bea said. 'I need some anyway for the website and then you can see everything that I have been doing.'

'Everything?' Lara teased.

'Everything.' Bea squeezed her grandmother's arm in response to the tease, but Lara knew there was something more. And if she couldn't find out now at her age, then when could she?

'So, nothing else happened today?' she asked. 'Nothing out of the ordinary?'

'How do you mean, Nonna?' Bea was all innocence.

'Nothing especially interesting?' Lara stopped walking to scrutinise her granddaughter's expression. 'Nothing significant?'

Bea laughed. 'Well, something came up,' she said. 'Nonna, you know me so well.'

'Oh? What sort of a something?'

'Maybe another job.'

'Good news then.' Lara had great faith in Bea's talents but everyone had to start somewhere and Bea needed to get her name known, to carve out a reputation.

They continued walking past the prickly pears, aloe vera and agave – positioned here because they were so good at storing water and therefore needed little care and attention – towards the secret garden. Naturally, Lara had included a small *giardino segreto* – how could she not?

'Shall we go through?' Bea asked.

'Just a peek,' Lara said. She could rarely resist. It wasn't strictly secret – there was a visible but narrow path which wound between the patch of natural Mediterranean scrubland of broom, juniper and myrtle, and for this they had to move into single file.

As it was so warm, some of the wildflowers were already coming into bloom: there were primroses peeking from the shade of the scrub and budding poppies, camomile and cornflowers threaded through the grasses.

Lara gave a little satisfied sigh. She had done everything that she wanted to do. It was undeniably almost time. She could feel it, shimmering on the edge of her world, a sense of passing.

'Nonna?' Because just as she knew her granddaughter rather well, Bea knew Lara. '*Va bene?* Are you tired?'

'I am, *cara*,' Lara admitted. She was always tired.

'Do you want to go back to the house now?'

'I think so, yes.'

They retraced their steps along the path. 'Tell me about

this new job.' Lara wanted to listen to the melody of her granddaughter's voice; it had always chimed so well with the springtime, with this garden.

Bea explained about the couple she had met at Signora Milella's, about the restaurant they ran in Polignano and the terrace garden she was going to see. But Lara, tired as she was, still sensed there was something Bea wasn't telling her. And this new terrace, charming though it sounded, did not seem to be quite enough to account for her granddaughter's mood.

'And?' she asked, when Bea had finished.

'And?'

Lara stopped walking once again. She raised an eyebrow at her granddaughter. She didn't need to say that she was still waiting.

'Oh, well, their son was with them. He came out to talk to me in the garden.'

'Ah.' So there was a son; that might explain it.

'Ah, nothing, Nonna.' Bea laughed. 'You know I do not have time for men.'

Lara turned to face her. 'Darling.' She took her hands. 'Trust me. Gardens are important but there should always be time for love.' Because if there was anything that Lara had learnt, it was about the importance of love.

'Love?' There was a wistful expression in Bea's eyes now. '*Certo*, it was different for you and Nonno . . .'

Lara said nothing. But Bea was right. It was a long time since Lara had lost him and at times things hadn't been easy . . . She repressed a sigh. The past had always been there, often threatening them both. But they had overcome so much. And perhaps now she might somehow find him again?

'And Mamma and Papà.' Bea gave a cursory glance towards

the house where Rose and Federico might be raging at one another or passionately kissing – who could tell? 'But I have my business to think of.'

'*Allora*, you do, yes, of course you do.' Lara turned and tucked her hand in Bea's arm once more. 'And all that is vital, yes. But . . .'

'But what, Nonna?'

The walled garden in Dorset flickered into Lara's mind. The more time that went by, the less likely it seemed that she could put things to rights. And yet she had to. She had to find a way. *Love and gardens* . . . How could she even consider asking Bea to put her life on hold? 'But there is such a thing as creating a balance.'

They smiled at one another, on the same wavelength as ever.

'And what is he like, this young man who made an impression on you?' Lara asked her. 'Good-looking? Charming?'

Bea put her head to one side. 'Yes and yes,' she said. 'And he probably knows it.'

Lara patted her hand. 'But you like him,' she said.

'Yes and no,' Bea replied.

Lara caught her granddaughter's eye and they both laughed. Lara shouldn't worry about her; Bea was more than aware of the complexities of love and life.

'He seemed a bit sad,' Bea went on. 'He asked me questions about gardens and how they make people feel.'

She must have loved that. Lara smiled. But at least he sounded interesting and they hadn't talked about the weather. 'And when you go and work for his mother, maybe you will see him again, hmm?'

'Perhaps,' Bea conceded. 'I am going to see the terrace on Tuesday and then we will see.'

'Yes, we will see.'

'Oh, Nonna, you are such an old romantic.'

Old most definitely, Lara thought as she leant on the stone balustrade of the terrace. But was she romantic? Once, perhaps.

She had been so naive. Then there was the war and all the difficulties it brought. And then . . . She let her thoughts drift. And then, of course, there was Charles.

CHAPTER 4

Lara

Dorset, May 1945

'But, my dear Lara . . .'

'Yes?' Lara blinked up at him, distracted from her task of cleaning the rhubarb stalks she'd just picked from the garden – the first crop of the year. Some she'd cook up today, some she'd distribute to the neighbours.

He was looming. Tall, rather distinguished – fair hair, moustache, well-groomed – and smiling, always smiling, as he leant towards her.

She turned off the tap, put her hands on the edge of the kitchen sink and straightened so that they were more on level terms. The tart, earthy scent of the rhubarb hung in the kitchen.

Lara was still both tired and reeling from yesterday. It had been a long day and night of celebration and, of course, it was all wonderful. Tuesday the eighth of May 1945 would go down in history and the day had been declared a public

holiday – why wouldn't it? Hitler was dead, there was uncon-
ditional surrender and Europe was now victorious and free. It
was almost impossible to believe after all this time, but it was
really true. Lara was thrilled; everyone was thrilled. There had
been such excitement – it seemed to fizz in the very air like
thousands of bonfire night sparklers all let off at once. People
were shouting, laughing, crying. Flags and bunting bedecked
the buildings in Bridport town centre. People were dancing
in the street, hugging complete strangers, celebrating as one.
But David wasn't there. So how could Lara be as happy as the
rest of them?

'You must have guessed how I feel about you,' said Charles.

For a moment, Lara didn't take it in. What was he saying?
She was confused. Charles? Charles didn't talk about feelings.
He was rather a cold fish, but more like a helpful uncle than
a . . . than a . . . Well, what *was* he saying? She looked away,
scrubbed with her fingernail at a piece of earth still stuck
to one of the rhubarb stalks. 'I don't understand. What do
you—'

He leant in closer; she could smell the tobacco on his breath,
and something greasy like shoe polish. 'Lara,' he said. 'You're
such an innocent. But you're what, twenty-five? Can you
really be that naive?' And he smiled once more, fondly, as if
her naivety was actually perfectly charming.

Oh, my goodness . . . Lara pulled back. She was worried he
was about to kiss her. She found herself looking at his mouth,
though she didn't really want to. His teeth were white and
even. She reminded herself quickly that Charles had always
been kind. *An innocent?* She didn't feel innocent. Her father's
death, her passion with David, the war . . . Some days she felt
ninety, not, 'Twenty-four,' she told him.

36

'Twenty-four then.' Charles's face now wore the benevolent expression she was more used to. 'Don't be scared, Lara,' he said. 'There's nothing to worry about. It's all right.'

Was it, though? Lara wasn't so sure. She was still scrabbling to make sense of it all. 'David,' she said. Charles had clearly forgotten about David.

They'd never met. Charles had come into their lives four years ago just after David had enlisted. Charles's sister Marjorie lived in the same village as Lara and her mother, not far from Bridport in Dorset, and Charles had moved in with her. He always bemoaned the fact (to anyone who would listen, and most of the women certainly did) that he was unable to join up himself.

'I'm young enough,' he'd told Lara and her mother the first time they'd met outside the newsagent's, and Lara remembered him standing more upright as if good posture could indeed strip away the years.

'I'm sure.' Lara's mother Florence had smiled back at him – she'd thought him the bee's knees right from the off.

His words meant he was under forty-one and unmarried, Lara realised. She knew the rules as they all did. The army had tried at first to spare those with someone to come home for, but of course in the end, they all had to go if they were young enough and fit enough.

'I have a bit of trouble with the old ticker, though, that's the thing.'

'Angina?' Her mother's expression became sympathetic.

'Exactly.' He'd always had a charming smile. Her mother had been charmed; Lara could tell. And Lara didn't like that. Her mother, she felt, shouldn't be charmed by anyone bar Father. 'But if I can help out, then I will,' Charles went on.

'The name's Fripp. Charles Fripp. So, if there's anything you need . . . any problem . . . just say the word.'

'Oh, super. That's awfully kind of you.' Her mother had been a pushover.

And Lara remembered thinking, even back then, *All very well, but what does he want from us – this man who's suddenly appeared in our lives offering to help out if there's anything we need? He must, mustn't he, want something?*

Her mother, she soon concluded, when his visits became more frequent. Her mother was a widow and a beautiful one at that with her high cheekbones and her intelligent grey eyes. They all had to make do during these times. But Mother always looked so elegant in her simple day dresses with the puffed sleeves and nipped-in waists; she was a keen needlewoman and could make the plainest fabric sing.

But Lara's father had been dead only a year, and Lara couldn't bear the thought of it. It was too soon. Much too soon. Always would be too soon, come to that. And it wasn't Mother he was interested in, she realised now. Perhaps he never had been.

Charles stepped closer. He took hold of Lara's arms gently. Her sleeves were rolled up because of cleaning the rhubarb and she could feel his palms under her elbows, the skin slightly moist. In contrast to her mother, she seemed to spend most of her time at home in overalls or slacks – they were so much more practical for the garden.

'I know David hasn't written to you for a long time, Lara.' Charles spoke slowly, quietly, as if this was necessary for the significance of his words to sink in.

'Letters don't always get through.' But Lara didn't immediately pull away from him this time. So many young men had died . . . But she would have heard, wouldn't she, if David had been one of them? They'd never much liked her – but still, his grandparents would have let her know. And she would have felt it. Lara was sure she would have felt it.

'It's difficult to accept, I know.' Charles continued as if she hadn't spoken. 'But you have to be realistic. We can't cling on to all our dreams. Now that the war is over . . .' He let his words hang.

'He'll come back.' Because if she said it out loud, it might happen. And this was one dream that would have to be torn away from her; she was never going to voluntarily let it go.

Charles sighed. He released her arms. 'I admire your faith, Lara, my dear,' he said. 'I really do.'

'I love him,' Lara said. And if she loved him so much, he'd come back, wouldn't he? He had to.

He'd been eligible for call-up at the start of the war, but because his grandfather relied on his labour, he was considered to be in a reserved occupation and for this, Lara was overwhelmingly grateful. But his grandfather had to apply for his deferment every six months and with so many of his peers joining up to fight for their country, Lara could tell that David was getting restless.

At first, little had seemed to change in West Dorset – even some of the earlier evacuees had been sent back home again. But later, air activity began to increase: German bombers were bombing somewhere almost every night, while searchlights streaked the sky in an attempt to pick them out and shoot them down. Even Bridport was bombed by a plane returning from a raid on Yeovil, emptying its load on the town in 1940 – several people had been killed. It was during the Battle of Britain that same summer that David finally made up his mind. He had to go, he told Lara. He couldn't live with himself otherwise.

Their last evenings together were so special.

'Be strong, Lara,' David said to her on that final night.

She had tangled her fingers through his thick dark hair and tried not to think of all the lonely times ahead. Of her lover marching into war; or worse, lying dead in some bleak field somewhere, never to return. 'Come back to me, David. You will, won't you?'

And then he had kissed her instead of answering her question, because it was something he couldn't have known, couldn't ever promise. And it had seemed to Lara that even his kiss had tasted of parting.

'Yes, yes.' Charles looked irritated now. 'Well, you're young.' As if that had anything to do with it. He shot her a look of reproach. 'But I have tried to help you and your mother, you know.'

Which was true. 'I know,' she said. 'And we're grateful.' Without Charles, Lara and her mother would have had a much harder war. He had often appeared with little luxuries they couldn't have hoped to get hold of otherwise: a packet of biscuits, coffee, stockings and lipstick. Goodness knows where he got them from. Lara's mother had warned her not to ask, in case the gifts stopped coming. They were aware, too, that Charles did similar favours for some of their neighbours in the village. Sometimes their local grocer held things 'under the counter' – they'd got hold of evaporated milk and cocoa this way – but no one wanted to push their luck. The black market was illegal after all and anyway, if others had to suffer rationing, then they should all be in it together. But it was tempting . . .

Before the war, and some of the time during it too, Charles

had worked as a travelling salesman, so Lara supposed he had contacts all over the place. Lara and her mother had given back what they could – fresh eggs from the hens, vegetables and fruit from the allotment – because over the last six years they had used their large garden to grow produce that would help the small village in West Dorset to survive. Digging for victory, as the government called it; nearly everyone was growing something edible in their garden, no matter how small.

In return, some of the villagers had helped out, doing bits of gardening and picking crops whenever they could. Elizabeth from next door was particularly good at dashing out first thing to shovel up the steaming manure left by the milkman's horse with her coal shovel and leaving it by the back door for the veg garden. There was usually fish brought in from West Bay, and plenty of milk and rabbits for a hearty stew. Everyone did their bit if they could. That was what happened in times of trouble, Lara reminded herself. The spirit of patriotism had brought them together and Charles had made himself integral to that.

He'd helped them out when anything had gone wrong in the house too; when a drain was blocked or the cooker stopped working, Charles always seemed to know how to fix the problem – or he knew someone who did. As an able-bodied man in the village he seemed to be capable of sorting out many people's problems. He sometimes dropped by Lime Tree House for a few hands of gin rummy in the evening or even just to sit with them and chat or listen to the wireless. The entire village seemed charmed by him, Lara thought. But although he was helpful to everyone, he had his favourites and she and her mother had always been two of them – more so as the years went by.

'I thought it was Mother you were interested in,' she blurted now. Not that Charles hadn't behaved as a gentleman and Lara had always known, deep down, that Father was Mother's one and only. She still wandered into the attic studio where he had worked and looked around as if she might find a part of him there. When they lost him, Lara had been compelled to support her mother through her grief whilst somehow managing to also cope with her own.

Father had been their sunshine, their laughter, their fun. Lara was an only child and back then, it seemed, a blessed one. They had been happy. Father painted his portraits – and was quite successful at it too – while Mother created her Arts and Crafts walled garden at Lime Tree House, which she had inherited from her parents. When the stroke killed Father – that was when everything changed.

Lara had heard the story of this house so many times but never tired of it. It had been built during the heyday of the Arts and Crafts movement in the second decade of the 1900s by Mother's parents, Lara's grandparents, whom regrettably she'd never known. They had wanted a low-roofed, gabled house made of rustic and local stone with a large garden and glasshouse (and an indoor bathroom, of course), and planned the project so that everything outside would harmonise with the house. According to her mother, this was very important. Heavily influenced by William Morris – whose wallpaper design adorned their sitting room – the Arts and Crafts movement harked back to a pre-industrial time of simplicity and utility.

'People were proud to work on the land back then,' Lara's mother had told her on more than one occasion. 'And in traditional crafts too.'

It had all sounded rather nostalgic to Lara and she had said as much, but her mother had shaken her head. 'On the contrary, my dear,' she had said. 'Arts and Crafts ideas opposed the rigid artifice of Victorian design. The movement was subversive. By rejecting the prevailing values of the time, you could even say it was at the very vanguard of modernism.'

Lara didn't fully understand what she meant. But she did understand how much her mother loved the house and garden.

Now, she glanced warily towards Charles.

'Don't be ridiculous, Lara.' Charles softened his words with a light laugh. 'Naturally, I'm very fond of your mother . . .'

But equally naturally, it would be the daughter you would rather have. Lara completed the sentence in her head. How old was Charles anyway? Mid-forties by now, she guessed. Around her mother's age and twenty years older than Lara. She repressed a small shudder.

'I know I'm a bit older than you,' Charles added. 'But perhaps you need to be looked after, hmm?' He seemed almost wistful now and this made Lara feel bad. Had she encouraged him? She was sure not. She liked to think that she was part of a breed of newly independent women. She worked, she looked after the house, she'd done her bit with the evacuees they'd had billeted with them at various times during the war and she'd cared for her mother on the bad days.

'I'm sorry, Charles,' she said stiffly. 'I never knew . . .' – she hesitated – '. . . how you felt.' And she still didn't. It all seemed mad. There had been no spark, no hands brushing, no meaningful words spoken. No wonder she hadn't cottoned on. Thank goodness at least that he hadn't mentioned the word 'love'.

Charles nodded as if she'd said something that satisfied him.

43

'Think about it, Lara,' he said. 'Wait a while longer if you must. Talk it over with your mother by all means.'

Lara stared at him. 'But . . .' *David*, she thought.

'And then you can give me your answer. When you've thought through all the practicalities. When you're ready, dear girl. I'm not going anywhere.'

'Answer?' As he bent his head, Lara couldn't help noticing the sparseness of the fair hair on his crown.

'To my proposal,' he said. 'The war has ended, Lara. Everything's different now. We all have to begin again. I'm asking you to marry me.'

CHAPTER 5

Bea

Italy, March 2018

Bea stood on the terrace of the Leones' restaurant in Polignano. Its position – perched on the limestone clifftop just above one of the famous panoramic viewpoints – was perfect. Half waiting, half hoping for Matteo Leone to appear, Bea felt that she was standing on a dizzy edge – of the cliff, of the atmospheric *centro storico* of old churches and whitewashed houses, of adventure perhaps.

There was no sign of him yet, however, although Signora Leone had already given her a harassed greeting and told her that she would be with her in two minutes. 'Take a look around, Beatrice,' she had suggested, and so that was what Bea was doing.

First, she contemplated the view – of Cala Porto, Polignano's small pebble beach and the aquamarine waters of the Adriatic Sea. The beach was surrounded by these cliffs and one could dive from here; the town was famous, in fact, for its cliff diving;

the Red Bull diving competition held every year attracted huge crowds. Even Bea had attended, purely as a spectator, of course; she could vouch for it being an exciting event.

She tore her gaze from the turquoise sea and looked around the garden area of the dining terrace. This place was even lovelier than she'd expected . . . The limestone paving was natural and would provide an excellent foundation. And the colours of sea and cliff created a dramatic contrast; a perfect backdrop for planting. But the terrace was as tired as Signora Leone had indicated, and it seemed almost criminal to Bea that it didn't offer any similar charm or beauty to the intoxicating view to be seen below.

She glanced up expectantly as the door opened, but once again, it was the signora who stood there. *Allora.* Her appointment had been with Matteo's mother. Matteo had intimated that he would see her too, but more fool her for allowing herself to be disappointed.

The signora came to stand beside her. 'Do you have an immediate idea of what can be done, Beatrice?' she asked.

Hmm. Almost any planting would be an improvement. The terrace was in need of colour and it was in need of life. 'If you could give me an idea of budget?'

Bea's first thought, though, was of culinary herbs, their fragrances wafting in the air, mingling with the ozone and the smell of delicious food from the restaurant kitchen. Rosemary, sage, mint, thyme, oregano, bay and basil . . . They would all do well here, and if – as Bea believed – their herbal scents could help repel mosquitoes, this would be appreciated by the diners, for sure. Furthermore, the herbs would be in keeping with the wild grasses and thyme she had spotted growing from the crevices of the cliffs opposite. Since this was a terrace, and a working terrace at that, which would often be full of people, the simplest solution would be to fill the edges of the space with pots, troughs and urns that could, if necessary, be moved around to accommodate the seating.

She glanced down again to the white houses squatting on the steep shelving of the creviced limestone cliffs, their balconies ablaze with pink and orange bougainvillea. And then once again, her gaze was drawn irresistibly out to sea. Day cruisers were cutting a foamy path through the water and the waves were breaking onto the white pebbles. It was an idyllic scene. The water was so clear that she could see the rocks on the floor of the ocean, the colour shifting with the shadow of the limestone cliff above.

Bea pondered. Some structural plants definitely – cacti tucked away at the back would produce bright and brilliant flowers in high summer and maybe a yucca; anything green and spiky would take the heat. Trailing plants in the window boxes on the outside of the high white railings would create an arresting flow down the white walls. And small drifts around the edges would also serve to echo the shape and movement of the tide. Since the chairs and tables were made of wood and wrought iron, it would make sense to use the same materials to achieve a sense of harmony.

'I think . . .' The signora named a figure which was generous enough.

'That should do it.' Bea was now considering what materials she would have to buy – the town had a powerful history and attracted upmarket tourism; everything must be of the highest quality. But materials should be old and rustic – using the limestone that was so much a part of the natural landscape. And what could be nicer than cultivating herbs, to be seen and smelt by the diners, that had also been used in the cuisine they were sampling?

'Good.' Briskly, the signora rubbed her hands together. She was more businesslike here on her own territory, thought Bea. 'Then let us have coffee and discuss things in more detail.'

They sat at a corner table, a waitress brought them espressos and Bea sketched out a few initial ideas in pencil on the drawing pad she'd brought with her, to show the signora where her plans were heading and to make sure she was on the right track with what the signora was trying to achieve. Fortunately, they seemed to be in broad agreement. Signora Leone liked the idea of the herbs and of the terrace becoming their kitchen garden as well as the impact that the more colourful planting would provide. 'It is different,' she said. 'It is unique.'

Bea was sure this couldn't possibly be the case, but she kept this thought to herself. 'Perfect,' she said. 'I'll do some thinking and draw out some detailed sketches and plans.'

'This is so exciting.' The signora put down her cup and pushed it to one side. 'I am so grateful to you for helping us and at such short notice too.' She eyed Bea expectantly. 'When can you start?'

Bea didn't need to check her diary. 'I can do the drawings in the next few days,' she said. 'And I might pop back sometime tomorrow if that's okay — for a bit more inspiration?'

'Sì, sì. Excellent. And then?'

'And then, if you approve, I could make a start on the work next week,' Bea told her. 'I can't come every day — I have a few other commitments — but perhaps Monday to Wednesday?' She guessed that the terrace would then be at its quietest. The season wasn't yet in full swing but it was already warm and it wouldn't be long before this restaurant and everywhere else in Polignano was heaving. This was a popular town for day-trippers, she knew; they'd soon be crowded on the *logge* balconies gasping at the sight of the crashing waves below, visiting the limestone caves in the tourist boats and filling the *cornetterias* in Polignano's historic centre.

'That is wonderful.' The signora beamed. She got to her feet, a clear signal that their meeting was over. 'Then I shall not keep you any longer. I know you are busy.'

'Yes. Thank you.' Once again, Bea couldn't help but wonder where Matteo Leone was this morning. She'd been thinking about him more than she'd like – revisiting his blue eyes, his wide smile. She shook her head in frustration at herself. *Come on, Bea.* Like she'd told Nonna, she didn't have time for men, especially ones that had been spoilt, as she suspected Matteo Leone might have been.

Bea shook hands with the signora, assuring her that she'd see her the following day. Taking a final glance at the breathtaking terrace view of the beach, the Monachile Bridge and the crystal water – it would be a picture-perfect place to be working, at the very least – she took a deep breath of the salty air and began to descend the worn stone steps to the street below.

'Beatrice, wait!'

She heard his voice and looked up. '*Ciao*, Matteo.' He stood on the terrace above, dressed in jeans, boots and an open-necked shirt. And he looked even sexier than before. *God help her* . . . She waited.

He bounded down the steps to where she stood. '*Ciao*.' He kissed her on both cheeks and once again she caught the scent of him – just as before, that hint of cedarwood and citrus. '*Mi dispiace.* So sorry I was not there to say hello,' he said, his voice soft, almost intimate. 'I had something to sort out in the office.' He gestured towards the restaurant building.

'There is no need to apologise.' Bea smiled. 'You work here too then?'

'Yes.' He glanced up at the building and she saw a glint of pride. It was clearly a family affair. 'Beatrice . . . there is something I want to ask you.'

She adjusted the bag slung over one shoulder. 'Ask away.'

'*Va bene*. Shall we walk?'

'Why not?' Though that presumably wasn't the question he'd wanted to ask. Polignano was such a pretty place and she hadn't been here for a while. True, there were other things she should be getting on with, but she'd parked outside the *centro storico* anyway and half an hour or so wouldn't hurt.

She followed his lead as they headed down the alley, deeper into the old town. Vines clung to the walls and red geraniums and white lilies tumbled from window boxes. Architects and builders had been clever with this town, Bea found herself thinking. The natural curve of the rock could create a balcony here and steps down could be cut into the limestone there. It was faithful to itself. Although the houses were whitewashed, there were panels of exposed honeycombed stone on some of the buildings, a reminder of the history, the beginning. The houses here were three-storey, home also to artists and craftsmen selling paintings, leather goods, jewellery from shops that were like little caves on the ground level. And the stone wasn't white at all, she realised. It was a kind of whitish, pinkish greige.

'You know this town?' He was watching her take it all in. 'I was born here. But the beauty, it still gets to me, you know?'

Bea nodded. She knew. 'I live on an olive farm just outside

50

Locorotondo,' she told him. 'So yeah, I've been over here quite a few times.'

'Ah, the green gold . . .' He kissed his fingers. '*Benissimo.* That is great.'

'Mmm.' It had its moments and Bea loved the tranquillity of home. Her father's family had been farming and pressing the olives for seven generations – they had even preserved the underground mill used way back in Roman times when the big stone wheel was the grinder, pulled by donkeys, in conditions that would certainly not be tolerated today. Thankfully things were very different now. Bea was proud of the legacy of the *masseria* even though she'd chosen a different pathway for her own career. Fortunately, there were plenty of cousins to take on the mantle her father wore so proudly. She had no doubt that the olive farm would live on for generations to come.

Bea ducked behind Matteo as the street narrowed still further. She liked the way he walked, his stride loose and free, and the way he continued to talk to her over his shoulder, pointing out some interesting carving on a wooden door, then a delicate fan-light, then a coffee shop that sold particularly good pastries. Bea didn't doubt it – she could smell the rich scent of them in the air.

'What did you want to ask me?' she said as they passed the faded pink façade of a building with worn green shutters and a rusty wrought-iron balustrade. Some things became simply more beautiful with age, she thought.

'I have a day off tomorrow.' He paused and glanced across at her.

'That is nice.' *And?* she thought.

'And I wondered if you wanted to . . . *passare il tempo* – hang out for a bit?'

She blinked at him. He certainly didn't waste any time. Had

51

their brief encounter reached the hanging out stage without her even noticing? 'I will be working,' she said. 'Sorry.' She repressed the small pang of regret.

'Here in Polignano?'

'On the drawings and plans for the restaurant terrace, yes,' she said. 'I'll be coming back tomorrow to measure up – and to think.'

'To think?' He smiled. 'I bet you do a lot of that, hey, Beatrice? Thinking?'

The narrow street opened out into a small piazza. On one corner stood an old *palazzo*, to the left was the cathedral. Bea gave his question due consideration though she knew that once again he was teasing. 'A fair bit, yes.'

The smile became a disarming grin. 'See the mechanical clock?' He pointed.

Bea looked up. 'It is unusual.' The hands were verdigris, there were black Roman numerals, and she noted the little shrine on the bell tower and the incredible detail of the stonework above the windows.

'Rococo,' he said. 'The facade, that is.' And then, without missing a beat, 'I could speak to her.' He put his head to one side, waiting.

Bea frowned. This man had a habit of jumping subjects. He was disconcerting, to say the least.

'My mother, I mean. She would not mind. There is no pressure, is there? One day off could not make that much difference, could it?'

He was very persuasive too. They walked on past the little bars and cafés in the square. Bea was aware of the buzz of conversation around them, music wafting from a bar, soft footsteps on the limestone floor. 'What do you say?' he pressed.

It had been a long time since Bea had taken a whole day off. Nevertheless, this was a professional engagement and she didn't want him speaking to his mother before she'd even begun the work. 'No,' she said. 'I am afraid I will be too busy tomorrow.' Was she trying to put him off? She wasn't sure. Right now, her feelings were ambivalent. She was attracted to him, yes. She'd been thinking about him a lot, yes, yes. But . . . He was unsettling. He was the type of man who could disrupt your life, who could change things out of all recognition. The question was: did Bea want that?

But he only gave a little shrug and pointed to another building she should take notice of, as if he didn't mind at all. Was the subject closed? Bea wasn't sure whether to be relieved or sorry.

At the Porto Vecchio, she thought that he would leave her – she was hardly encouraging him after all – but to her surprise he touched her elbow and guided her to the right. 'Another impressive *palazzo*,' he said. 'The Pino Pascali.'

Privately, Bea thought it looked more like a prison looming above them with iron grilles at the windows, but she decided not to say. Had she hurt his feelings? 'Sorry,' she said instead, not quite sure what she was apologising for.

He turned to look at her. 'Your work is very important to you, I remember.'

At least he hadn't taken offence. They passed a massive church on their right. *Chiesa del Purgatorio*, she read and grimaced. The skulls and crossbones were beautifully carved out of the old stone, but they were hardly a cheery motif.

'I wanted you to see the poetry.' He pointed to some steps. 'You know about the poetry, *sì*?'

'*Sì*.' She knew. The story was that the poet had moved to

53

this town thinking it would inspire his writerly ambitions. He wrote poetry all over – on walls and steps – not just his own, but verses he admired.

'Guido Il Flâneur,' murmured Matteo.

'Mmm.' That was what the poet had called himself, fancying himself perhaps an equivalent of Baudelaire's French wandering observer of modern life. 'You admire him?'

'He was free,' he said. 'To express himself, to wander . . .'

'Yes, I suppose he was.' And Guido had certainly achieved some degree of fame. Bea looked across at the man beside her. Matteo had told her he envied her. He'd told her his whole life was mapped out for him – did that mean the restaurant? she wondered. But despite this, he had an air of carelessness about him – certainly as far as work was concerned. Was he really so accustomed to getting his own way? Was that it? Had he led a charmed life?

As they too wandered on, past overhanging balconies and wide wooden doors, down tiny winding alleyways that were more like tunnels carved in the pinky-white rock, Matteo seemed to be considering his next move. 'And are you working tomorrow evening too, Signorina Romano?'

'No, it will be too dark.' She was flirting with him, Bea realised. And what's more, it was fun.

It was easy, she found, to lose her sense of direction here in the old town, but the man by her side seemed to know exactly where he was going. He spoke a friendly greeting to the artist painting in the street, to a girl watering plants on a balcony, to the elderly *nonnas* shredding aromatic mint leaves from their stalks as they sat side by side in the narrow shady street.

They walked on until once more they arrived at the Porto Vecchio. And once again, instead of taking his leave, he gestured to her to pass through the doorway before joining her on the other side. 'Then I will take you out to dinner.'

He was very sure of himself. 'Is that an invitation?' Because it sounded more like an assumption.

'Yes, Beatrice.' He gave a mock sigh. 'It is an invitation.'

She smiled, unable to resist. 'Then I accept.'

'Good. I know an excellent place to eat not far from where you live.'

'Oh?'

He named a *masseria* that she'd never been to, though she knew it had a good reputation.

'That sounds lovely.' And what harm could it do? He was not even a client, not really. *And even if . . .* Enough. She pointed. 'I parked over by the statue,' she said. It was rather famous. It encapsulated the figure of the singer Domenico Modugno, who had given the world the song 'Volare'.

'I will walk with you.'

Bea asked him a little more about his parents' restaurant as they strolled side by side through the busy piazza and onto the bridge where tourists lingered, capturing photos of the famous view. Bea glanced down at the white shingle beach – Lama Monachile was actually the mouth of an extinct river spanned at the end by the Roman bridge.

'I am very happy,' he said.

'Happy?' The smells of tomato, garlic, olive oil and focaccia from a nearby *Focacceria* filled the air and made Bea's mouth water.

'That you will be doing the garden for us.'

She gave him a sidelong glance. 'I am looking forward to the challenge,' she said. And looking forward to seeing more of Matteo . . . ? Well, of course. He was an attractive man and she was only human.

55

'*Bene.*'

The strains of 'Volare' could be heard from a passing tourist bus and they shared a smile. Domenico hadn't only been a singer, he was also a passionate advocate of human rights and Polignano was obviously proud of him. His statue stood, arms outstretched towards the town, singing his heart out and everyone who came to see him wanted a picture of themselves adopting the exact same pose in front of him. Bea had to admit, it was one of the most striking statues she'd ever seen, three metres high, she guessed, and cutting quite a picture with the backdrop of the rocks and sea behind.

'And for the dinner?' he asked. 'Shall I pick you up at home? Or would you prefer to meet at the restaurant?'

Bea thought quickly. If she said at home, then she'd have to introduce him to the family and she wasn't sure she was quite ready for that, or the questions that would ensue. Nonna was bad enough. 'At the restaurant is fine,' she said breezily. It would also mean she'd have to stay sober enough to drive back – which could be a good thing.

'As you wish.' But his eyes darkened and he seemed annoyed. Once again, his mood had changed. He was mercurial. Bea could imagine that you would never know exactly where you were with a man like this.

'There's my car.' She pointed again. 'Thanks for walking me. The *centro storico* is lovely.' Which seemed like a ridiculous understatement but she guessed he would understand.

'*Prego.*' He inclined his head. 'You are very welcome.'

'Until tomorrow then.'

Once again he touched her arm and Bea felt a spark of anticipation jump inside her.

'Until tomorrow.'

She watched him as he strode away, back towards the restaurant which she could just glimpse on the cliff edge beyond. And as she watched, without turning around he lifted a hand in a goodbye wave, clearly not needing to check that she was still standing here watching him. Bea shook her head in despair. *Like a lovestruck teenager . . .* She would have to watch herself with this one, she thought. He was tricky.

CHAPTER 6

Lara

Dorset, May 1945

The following morning, Lara didn't have to go to work and she knew the time had come to muster up her courage. She had heard nothing from David's grandparents and there were things she needed to know.

She tied a silk scarf under her chin, pulled her bicycle out of the shed, swung her leg over the pedals, smoothing her skirt onto the saddle in one practised movement, and set off down the driveway lined with the lime trees that had given Lime Tree House its name.

The Curtises lived more than ten miles away on the farm where David had worked before the war, where he had been brought up by his grandparents who leased it as tenants from a local landowner. It was quite a way, but Lara knew that she should have made this journey before now. She'd been busy, of course; had her hands full with the house, work and her mother. But when she'd met them before David went away, she'd found David's grandfather gruff and dour and she'd been a bit scared of him, to be honest. His grandmother had been marginally friendlier, but Lara had felt that they resented the time David was spending with her; time that would have been better spent looking after things at the farm, no doubt. They certainly made it clear that they disapproved of the relationship. Perhaps they thought them too young? Certainly, they would have preferred him to choose a farmer's daughter.

Even so, she was sure they would have let her know if there had been news of David. He'd told her of their deep-rooted kindness, the simplicity of their lives, how hard it had been for them to lose their only son, David's father, to the First World War, where so many men like him had died in the trenches. Lara knew that their generation had all imagined there could be no other war after the horror of that one.

But, not so. And now? What would happen now that this terrible war was over?

At the end of the drive, she turned into the lane. In the front basket sat a small spring cabbage – fresh, green and only picked from the kitchen garden this morning – a bunch of spring onions, white-paper skins glistening, and a few sticks of pink rhubarb.

She'd written, of course, when she hadn't heard from David, to find out if they'd had any news – in fact, she'd written several times – but she hadn't heard back. And she hadn't pursued it further. Lara supposed that part of her had been too frightened to try to find out the truth.

Lara pedalled hard against the wind, noting the trees that were in bud, almost ready to blossom, the fuzzy star-like blooms of the blackthorn and the clusters of pale primroses and shy violets peeping out from the grassy banks and verges, as she pushed on by, her eyes watering, her hair escaping from the confines of the scarf and streaming behind her in the wind.

She spotted red-haired and buxom Mrs Stone from the post office coming through her garden gate with her daughter Dorothy, still dressed in the plain black buttoned coat she'd been wearing all winter, and she took one hand from the handlebars to wave to them.

'Good morning, Mrs Stone! Dorothy!'

'Good morning, Lara! And such a fine one too.' They were both beaming. Everyone was still full to bursting with the excitement of the news of victory, with the possibilities of it all, the hope. And yet at the same time, some people Lara had seen in the last day or so had worn almost bemused expressions, as if they couldn't quite believe it. And if it were really true, if war had indeed ended, then what now?

Charles, thought Lara. An image of his face yesterday in the kitchen as he leant closer, as she thought he was about to kiss her, sprang into her mind and she banished it with a shudder. She hadn't spoken to her mother yet; Lara didn't want to worry her unduly. First, she needed to see David's grandparents, find out what they knew. Then, she hoped, she would have some ammunition behind her against Charles's assault.

Oh, my heavens . . . Lara almost stopped pedalling. She was even thinking in war-like terms. She had to stop this. She had to remember, Charles was a good man who had helped them out many times over the past years. And so, Lara must be kind when she told him how impossible it was. Lara could never marry him. Because Lara was in love with David.

Even the skylarks singing as they hovered overhead and the lambs gambolling and bleating in the fields bordering the lane seemed to be aware of the celebrations. Even the cowslips growing around the fences and the dry-stone walls. Even the sun poking through the high wispy clouds above seemed to be shining on a different and happier world. And if Lara could get some news of David – some good news, that was – then she would be ready to truly celebrate too.

She smiled as she recalled the first time she and David had met at the agricultural fair. It hadn't been long since Lara's father had passed away, and it was the first local event she'd attended, dragged along by her friend Alice who had been determined not to miss the opportunity of eyeing up the local farming lads.

Lara hadn't wanted to leave her mother, but she'd insisted she go, had told Lara that she would be happy alone, just sitting in the garden. *Her mother and her garden . . .* Lara knew she would be spending the time thinking of Lara's father, but at least her mother's Arts and Crafts garden, which she'd created herself, with the help of Joe, their old gardener, was bringing her solace.

Lara had needed to get out. The atmosphere in the house – of grief and desolation – was hemming her in. She felt guilty even listening to the wireless. She'd adored her father; she missed him more than words could say. But she was young. She needed to distract herself from her grief somehow, otherwise she felt in danger of drowning in it.

And at the fair, she'd met David. Tall, dark and rangy, looking rather smart in the black jacket and tie that all the farmers tended to wear at the agricultural fairs, he was leaning casually against the fence and – she realised immediately – he was staring at her.

'That boy . . .' Alice had noticed too.

'Uh-huh.' Lara took her arm. 'Don't look.'

61

But of course, it was too late. David nodded to the girls and, half turning, he whistled to his sheepdog. It was a very distinctive sound. The dog came running and when David turned back, grinned at her and touched his cap, Lara couldn't resist going over. Just to stroke the dog, she told herself, who had a gorgeous silky black and white coat. But that meant she had to speak to the boy.

'Hello,' he said. 'I haven't seen you here before.'

As if he'd have remembered, she thought. She looked up shyly. 'I haven't been here before.'

'Ah.' He laughed. Lara liked the sound. 'That'll be it then.'

'Yes,' she said.

He fidgeted. Lara felt herself smiling. She liked his nervousness too. The fact that it – she – mattered.

'David Curtis.' He stuck out his hand; a brown, hardworking hand.

'Curtis?' Lara was trying to think if she knew anyone around here of that name.

'My grandparents run a farm in Lodestock.'

She knew the village although it was some miles away. 'Lara Gray,' she said. 'It's nice to meet you.' She looked down at the dog who was nose-butting her hand for more stroking. 'And your dog.'

'Rex.' His hazel eyes were warm but appraising. He was young – maybe a year or two older than Lara – but he had a look about him as if he had seen something of the world.

'You live with your grandparents then?' she asked him, just to make conversation.

He gestured towards the field scattered with buttercups and she saw a man in his sixties or so, with another dog like Rex, shepherding a small flock of sheep into a pen. 'That's my grandpa.' He hesitated and then seemed to come to a decision. 'My father died right at the end of the war – he'd been on leave only a few months before. My ma passed on a few years later.'

Lara saw the sadness in his eyes, but it wasn't a raw grief; he must never have known his father and his mother must have died when he was still very young, she realised. 'I'm sorry.' She took a little breath. 'My father died recently too. It's . . .' – she faltered – '. . . hard.'

He reached out then, a gesture of solidarity, she supposed, and rested his fingers gently on her wrist. It was a small thing. But again, it meant more than that.

They only talked for a few minutes more. Lara could see Alice kicking her heels and looking impatient from where she stood a short distance away and anyway, David Curtis was glancing over towards his grandfather and she guessed that he had work to do.

'I'd better go.' She gave the dog one last pat.

'He's taken to you,' David said. He cleared his throat. 'Um, I was wondering . . . maybe you might come walking with me one Sunday?'

Lara met his worried look. She liked that too. 'Yes, that would be nice,' she said.

'All right.' His brow cleared. 'Next week?'

She nodded and told him where she lived.

He raised his eyebrows and she knew what he was thinking. Theirs was one of the grandest houses in the surrounding area; he was probably wondering if Lara was too hoity-toity for the likes of a farm labourer. She hoped it wouldn't put him off.

But he only smiled. 'I'll come for you then,' he said. 'In the afternoon?'

'Yes.' Lara walked quickly away before she betrayed any

63

emotion. She didn't want him to know how her heart was thumping against her ribcage, how that short conversation had left her almost breathless. There was something about him. Something that pulled her in and made her scared at the same time.

'You dark horse,' Alice said when she caught her up. 'What did he say to you?' She took Lara's arm and the two girls began to walk away.

Lara turned around. He was standing still, watching her. He waved and she waved back. When she turned to face front again, she was grinning, and it was the first spurt of joy she'd felt since her father had died. 'Nothing much,' she said.

At that moment, she hadn't wanted to share. She had only wanted to hug the thought of David Curtis in close to her like a secret.

'Are you going to see him again then?' Alice was curious, and from the little pout on her face, probably a bit jealous too.

'Maybe.' But of course, Lara knew that she would.

The evidence of the war was so much more obvious here in Bridport, Lara found herself thinking as she cycled down East Street. They'd escaped the worst, but there had been a bombing here a few years back that had demolished several houses – she glanced across at the sad remains of the buildings as she cycled past. Lara had seen billeted soldiers here when she'd come into town and she'd heard about the fundraising processions taking place during Spitfire Week or Salvage Week when everyone went out collecting metal from everything from aluminium cooking pots to iron railings to make aeroplanes, designed to help the war effort.

Oh yes, Lara thought as she cycled on, there had been a

great spirit here, everyone supporting each other. Somehow, they had managed. Everything delivered to Bridport came by rail and was then loaded onto horse-drawn drays for delivery to various shops and businesses. The twine factories had gone over to making camouflage material. Everyone had done their bit. And although most of their time went into the war effort, in one way or another, there had still been the rare opportunity for fun. There were still the pubs and the cinemas, Lara had been to the occasional dance and, of course, as locals, most of the time they were even still allowed to go swimming in the bay.

When she eventually got to the farm, Lara dismounted and leant the bike against the side of the low-roofed house. She was out of breath and relieved to have reached her destination. She straightened her jacket, rather crumpled from her journey, and took in her surroundings. Things didn't look good. The place seemed deserted, there were no animals in the fields nearby nor in the cow stall David had helped his grandfather build a few months before he went away to war, and she could see a pane of glass broken in the front barn.

Lara took a walk around, but there was no evidence anyone even lived here any more. She heard the distinctive call of a cuckoo in the distance and the echo of the cry made her shiver. 'Mr Curtis?' she called. 'Mrs Curtis? Is anyone here?'

But the emptiness of the place only mocked her.

Lara's shoulders slumped. She wheeled the bicycle back to the lane and looked around. *What now?*

A tractor was coming up the lane, so she stood back to let it pass. But the man driving it stopped to address her. 'You looking for the Curtises then, love?' he asked her.

'Yes.' Lara glanced at the cabbage, onions and rhubarb in the basket on the front of her bike. 'Do you know where they are?'

She should have come over before, she thought again. She should have been braver. They were David's family and she felt she'd let him down. There were no excuses, not really.

They've gone,' the man said. He shook his head sadly.

'Gone?' As in moved away? she wondered.

'Passed on,' he clarified. 'Mrs C. went first and then Joe a year later.' He regarded Lara curiously. 'Did you know them well, my lovely?'

'Not really,' she admitted. Even so, the news of their death was another punch of shock to the belly. It seemed like one more connection to David broken and lost.

'Sorry to be the bearer of bad news,' the farmer said.

'Are you a neighbour?'

'Yep.' He touched his cap. 'Ours is the next farm down the lane.'

'I see.'

'Were you just visiting then, may I ask, or . . . ?' He let the question hang.

Lara looked up at him. He seemed friendly enough. He might know something. 'I'm a friend of David's,' she told him. 'David Curtis, their grandson.' Because how could she call herself anything other than a friend? It wasn't as if they were engaged or anything and so much time had passed. As Charles had said, it had been a long time since David had written to her; almost a year. Lara didn't want to contemplate the reasons why. Even if he was still alive, he might have forgotten all about her by now. And with his grandparents dead, would there be any reason for him even to come back here?

'Ah, David. Oh, yes. Nice lad. Well then.' The man frowned. 'I see.'

'Do you know if they heard from him? Or anything about him?' Lara asked. 'If he's well? If he's alive? If he's . . .' *Coming home*, she wanted to say. But words failed.

The farmer took off his cap. 'They'd already passed when the news came,' he said.

'News?' Something leapt alive inside her.

He shook his head. 'I'm sorry, my lovely,' he said in his gentle voice with the strong Dorset burr. 'It wasn't good news, y'see. There was a telegram, I heard.'

'A telegram?' Lara whispered.

'David Curtis was missing in action and nothing heard since,' he told her. 'Poor lad. Seems that he's missing, presumed dead.'

Presumed dead. The words rang on in Lara's head. David. Her sweet David. 'I understand,' she managed to say. She had to get away from this man; she had to be alone. 'Thank you for telling me.'

'And nothing's been done with the land, as you can see for yourself. You wouldn't think a new tenant would be hard to find. Damned waste.'

'I . . .' Lara stumbled as she turned to walk away.

'Are you all right, love?' He looked about to get down from the tractor.

Lara held up a hand to stop him. She didn't want any witnesses to how she was feeling. 'I'm fine,' she said. 'Thank you. Goodbye.'

She wheeled the bicycle down the lane away from the tractor, scooted a few yards and swung her leg over onto the pedal. Downhill now, between the elm trees that lined the lane, where the rooks built their nests every spring. Downhill and with the wind, hot tears spilling. So that was why David had stopped writing to her. She had hidden from it for the past year, but now she knew. David was presumed dead. She had lost him forever.

CHAPTER 7

Lara

Dorset, May 1945

By the time Lara got home, her tears had dried although her heart was still aching. This was the true price of war, she thought. All the lives lost, all the love. And that was only a small part of it.

She put her bicycle away in the shed, straightened, and took a deep breath. She would speak to her mother and tell her about David. It had been so long since she had seen him – four what had seemed like never-ending years since he was deployed to Europe – and yet Lara had felt his presence close by so many times . . . In her thoughts, in her dreams, standing right by her when she was doing some mundane task: weeding the vegetable patch or cooking up the apples. Watching over her almost. And he had written, at least until a year ago, he had written.

But even if David had gone forever – Lara left the shed, shutting the door behind her – she would not marry Charles. She didn't love him; she could never love him and however much they needed help to pay the bills . . . Lara was confident that her mother – who had married the love of her life – would say the same. She wasn't the sort of woman to prioritise practicalities over affairs of the heart. Even now, at the end of this costly war.

But Lara must talk to her and make sure that this was the case. She ran into the house, unbuttoning and shedding her jacket on the way. 'Mother?' But of course, she wasn't here. She would be outside – wasn't she always? – in her beloved garden.

Lara went through to the bright and airy sitting room. The oak furniture and flooring had been made by a local carpenter and the large inglenook fireplace featured work by another local craftsman in its use of hammered pewter. The beams of the roof were exposed, which seemed to lend a sort of structural authenticity to the house, and the chairs were deep, comfortable and ready to sink into, covered with fabrics of olive green, mustard yellow and deep crimson that complemented the flowery wallpaper. There was also a cushioned window seat where Lara liked to sit and look out into the walled garden – but there was no time for sitting now . . .

She flung open the French doors that led onto the veranda. And there she was . . . Lara watched her for a moment. Beyond the pergola, already cloaked in yellow and cream honeysuckle and dark purple clematis, her mother was seated in her favourite place on the bench in the Romantic Garden – which wasn't as romantic as it had once been, being filled with as many vegetables as Lara, her mother and Joe had managed to cram into the flower beds. Many of the more established perennials had been put into pots and left outside the greenhouse and the original garden of romance was now a sight more practical, with its wigwam of runner beans, rows of salad leaves and beetroot.

Needs must, as Lara's mother had come to say rather more often in recent months. It had been a long war and they had tried to do their bit by providing fresh vegetables to as many local people as they could. But Lara knew how desperately her mother longed to turn the garden back into the one she had created, her own mother's original vision.

Sadly, Lara's grandparents had never been able to bring that vision into fruition, being two of the casualties of Spanish influenza that winter in January 1919, and after their deaths, their daughter Florence and her new husband Jack – Lara's parents – had moved in. Lara's mother's aim was to fulfil her own mother's ambition for the garden and during Lara's childhood, this was exactly what she had done. She'd made her mother's dream come true; her vision a reality in a garden destined to last forever.

But something made Lara pause, instead of rushing out to speak to her mother at once. The way she was sitting perhaps? Her mother's expression as she gazed out towards the lavender and the garden beyond?

The garden was divided into seven sections – the seven levels of spiritual elevation, her mother called them – designed to invite exploration and to create a seamless flow, a journey, from one to the next. This sequence of outdoor 'garden rooms' planted with traditional perennials for natural beauty offered the opportunity for privacy and reflection and each had a distinct personality designed to complement the others. *Seven different rooms to dream in . . .*

As a child, Lara had taken it all for granted; as an adult she could only admire. And somewhere along the line, she had fallen in love with all this, her childhood home and the walled garden that was an integral part of it.

Mossy stone steps led down from the veranda to the Romantic Garden with its central stone sundial, herbs and lavender and twin paths through to Mother's Thinking Garden which included silver-leafed foliage plants, white blooms and a pond lined with grasses that rustled pleasingly in the wind. It was a garden conducive to reflection and privacy; Lara had come upon her parents here on more than one occasion, sitting contentedly together on the bench under the small pergola dripping with white wisteria. This was how she always pictured them.

Back on the central avenue, a yew arch led to the colourful and fragrant Rose Garden and a final archway revealed the Wild Garden. On the left were Mother's Garden of Hope with its springtime blooms, the Nurturing Garden and greenhouse, and the orchard, which Lara supposed was the seventh garden. At the back of the Wild Garden was a wooden gate leading to the outside world, the woodland beyond.

Lara took the steps down from the veranda to the Romantic Garden, passing under the sweet-scented pergola. 'There you are.' She went to sit beside her mother on the wooden bench and glanced across at the arrow of the stone sundial. The air was fresher now; it would be a cool night ahead reminding them that summer wasn't yet here after all.

'Hello, darling.'

Her mother's face was so pale. She was still looking out towards the lavender parterre that rose behind the herb bed. In a few weeks' time the lavender would bloom, and the scent would fill the Romantic Garden all summer long.

Lara adjusted the blue cardigan that had half slipped from her mother's shoulders and took her hand. She was wearing a pretty dress in cream with a round embroidered collar.

But the collar seemed looser around her neck. And for how long had she been sitting out here alone? 'Are you all right, Mother?'

'Oh, you mustn't worry about me, my dear.' Her mother reached out, brushed an imaginary web from her face – or so it seemed. Had she been thinking about Father again?

'We'll get it back to how it was.' Lara looked around at the dark-veined leaves of beetroot, the runner bean shoots winding up the bamboo canes, the crisp green of the early lettuces.

'Yes.' She patted Lara's hand. 'But not yet. There'll be rationing for a while longer, you know. Things won't suddenly become easy.' She frowned.

Lara knew she was thinking about the unpaid bills. About how they were going to keep the house going. And she was right, none of it would be easy. Lara had tried to hide it from her, but her mother was far from stupid. She knew and Lara knew that they were broke, that the house was eating up their meagre funds. 'We'll manage,' Lara said staunchly. That's what people did. That's how they had all survived this war. They had pulled together and pulled through. But perhaps not David, she reminded herself. And Lara would have to face that. Everyone had lost someone. But all these years . . . She had just hoped that it would not be David.

Lara had finished her year's secretarial training just before war had been declared and she had managed to keep her first job at the Savings Bank. She didn't earn much, though. How would that ever be enough – unless she could find a better job or get a promotion? Was that likely? Probably not. Women's work might be more highly valued than it had once been – especially when it came to secretarial skills – but Lara feared that promotions would not be two a penny.

'Darling, you know I adored your father.' Her mother turned to her, eyes suddenly bright. 'But as we're both aware, he was completely hopeless with money.'

'Yes.' Lara had indeed worked this out for herself. Her father had earned his living as a portrait artist — a good one, if the portraits of Lara and her mother hanging in the hall were anything to go by. But he'd enjoyed life and life was for living, as he'd often said. Which meant — as far as Lara could make out, for she had taken over the household accounts after his death when her mother couldn't cope with them — that money was not for saving but rather for spending.

Consequently, after his death, they owned the house and its contents, but very little else.

'And I can't sell the house.' Her mother seemed to be following the line of Lara's thoughts. 'I simply can't.'

'I know.' Lara thought of all the vegetables they were growing, the fruit in the orchard, the hens clucking about in the Wild Garden because they hadn't known where else to put them, the jam she could make using their own berries and plums and their meagre sugar rationing, the extra typing she could do. She thought of David. And she thought of Charles. But there must be another way.

'But . . .' Her mother shook her head in despair.

'Mother . . .' said Lara. She must tell her about David. Lara wanted to say the words. She wanted to lay her head on her mother's shoulder and weep. But 'presumed dead' wasn't the end of a story, was it? 'Missing' — that was the important bit, that was the bit that was known and true. David was missing — but he could be in a POW camp somewhere. Italy perhaps, because that was where he'd been deployed to, last Lara had heard. And so, he could — couldn't he? — come home.

74

Her mother let out a deep sigh. Her mind seemed to be elsewhere. 'I have something to tell you, my darling.'

Lara gave a little start of surprise. *And me you*, she thought. 'What is it, Ma?' she whispered. In the breeze, she caught the wistful scent of the rosemary and the thyme. She didn't like the expression in her mother's blue-grey eyes and she couldn't help but notice that she looked wearier than ever, her skin paler, her arms thinner. The cream dress made her look more fragile, more vulnerable. Her mother had lost weight – they had all lost weight – but it was more than that. Lara suddenly knew that it was much more.

'I'm not well.' Once again, her mother patted her hand. 'And so, you must be brave, my darling.'

'Brave?' Lara stared at her. What was she trying to tell her?

'Yes. You must be brave, because I will have to leave you. I don't want to . . .' She gripped Lara's hand more fiercely. 'But I must.'

'But why? What do you mean? What's wrong with you? Mother?' Lara hated the panic that was rising in her chest. She hated this conversation. For a second, she almost hated her mother. Was everyone she loved going to leave her? Was that it?

'I have cancer.' She took another breath and met Lara's gaze full on. And Lara saw it there – the illness; the cancer that would take her, as if it were even now just lying there in waiting. 'I saw the doctor earlier, while you were out. He said it was time to tell you.'

'No.' Lara didn't think she could hear this. It was too much. Especially after learning that David . . . 'No,' she cried.

'I'm so sorry, my darling.' Her mother took Lara in her arms and then she was holding her close, so close that Lara could feel the thinness of her, the bones almost jutting through her skin, and Lara was weeping into her shoulder and she could smell the scent of her — geranium and lavender — and she was crying for her mother, for David, for herself. Crying as if she was already quite broken.

CHAPTER 8

Bea

Italy, March 2018

Bea was nervous as she got ready for her date with Matteo Leone. What should she wear? They were going to an upmarket *masseria* but on the two occasions they'd met so far, he'd been wearing jeans and . . . She stared at herself in the mirror. Surely Bea wasn't his type? She'd always thought herself a solitary sort of a person. Different things were important to her – the world of nature, her gardens, space in which to reflect. He seemed much more worldly, not like her at all.

She chose a simple black dress and gold jewellery. She fastened the delicate chain with a cross given to her by her parents around her neck. She twisted her hair up and put on dangly gold earrings and black strappy shoes. The truth was, Bea didn't go out very much – mainly family celebrations and drinks and casual suppers with friends – and she wasn't sure she knew the rules. She'd had a few boyfriends, of course – local lads, who like her were connected to farming families.

But nothing had ever become serious – perhaps because Bea had always been focused on her career, her gardens. Bea stopped in the act of applying her lipstick which was a rather 'out there' scarlet. Was it too much? What was she thinking? That this would become serious? Who was she kidding? She was sure it wouldn't. *Only* . . .

In the end, she accepted a lift from her father to the *masseria*, despite knowing that he offered it not so much out of thoughtfulness but more so that he could catch a glance and maybe even have a word with 'this mysterious Matteo' as her parents had been calling him ever since she'd told them about her date.

'He is not mysterious.' Bea had rolled her eyes.

'He is until we meet him,' her mother had replied.

Bea had exchanged a despairing look with her grandmother. Why was she even surprised? If her parents had their way, she wouldn't be allowed to see him until a full interview had taken place.

'You look nice,' her father told her when they were in the car heading towards the restaurant. He glanced critically across at her. 'Hmm,' he added.

Hmm? 'Thanks, Papà.' Bea looked out of the window. She knew this land so well – the narrow winding lanes, the crisscross of dry-stone walls, the terraced orchards, the vineyards and olive groves. *Trulli* houses built of layered limestone were scattered around the fields and agricultural plots, so integral to the landscape here.

Her father began humming, which wasn't a good sign. Bea waited for the inevitable.

'This *masseria* you are going to is an expensive place, you know.' He shot her an eloquent parental look and arched an enquiring eyebrow. *And this is your first date?* he might as well have asked.

'I do know that, Papà, yes.' She'd had reservations about it herself. Nevertheless, she was certainly looking forward to it . . .

Her father drove on down the narrow road, the increase of his speed on the tight bends her clue that he did not feel comfortable. 'So, does he have money, this Matteo?'

Bea sighed. They were passing another olive farm, where a worker was clearing the red-brown earth of weeds and under-growth. Her father beeped the horn and lifted his hand in a wave. 'About time,' he muttered under his breath. 'That land should have been cleared weeks ago.'

Bea gave a little shake of her head. Her father believed that every olive farm in the region should be run exactly like his own. 'I have no idea of his financial status, Papà,' she replied. 'I have only just met him, you know.'

'Eugh.' Her father made a noise low down in his throat, which meant, she knew, that he was not impressed.

She tried again. 'His parents, they run a nice place, a res-taurant in Polignano, I told you.'

Silence. Bea glanced out of the window. The sun was set-ting and the sky was streaked with red and gold, making the landscape glow. Fig trees, vines, prickly pear . . .

'But Matteo himself – I have not asked.' It wasn't exactly the first question you put to someone when they invited you out to dinner.

'Hmm.'

Bea knew what was coming.

'Take this.' With one hand on the steering wheel, her father pulled some banknotes out of his pocket and practically threw them at her. The car veered crazily over to the other side of the road but fortunately nothing was coming their way. 'You might need it. He might expect to go *alla romana*, to go Dutch. Who knows what he might expect? You know what I am saying?'

Bea knew, but she didn't want to get into that. And she didn't want a confrontation, not now, so it was easier to take the money. 'All right. Thanks, Papà.' Though she also knew she'd be giving it back to him in the morning. Beatrice Romano's Gardens was only in its first stages as a business, but she had enough to pay for her own dinner if needed and she didn't want to encourage her father's belief that he still had to look after her all the time.

At the crossroads, her father braked suddenly and turned to her. '*Prego*. You may think you are grown-up but you remain my daughter, *sì*?'

'Yes, Papà.'

He turned and accelerated, drumming his hands on the steering wheel now. 'And when dinner is over. When you want to come home – which is the same thing, yes? – then you call me and I will come to pick you up. Whenever it is.' Another parental look. 'But not too late, okay?'

'*Va bene*.' Bea was faintly surprised he hadn't decided to wait for her all evening outside the *masseria*.

In the event, he did stay outside until she had gone in, greeted Matteo who was waiting for her at the bar and come out again to shoo him away. The sky was already darkening into dusk.

'He is here then?' Her father peered behind her, almost as if he was hoping Bea had been stood up, she thought.

'He is here. And I am fine, Papà. So, please go.'

Back inside, she smiled at Matteo who was looking pretty dapper in a dark jacket, chinos and leaf-green open-necked shirt. 'Sorry,' she said. 'I was going to drive myself but my father offered to give me a lift.'

'It is fine. And you look beautiful by the way, Beatrice. *Bellissima.*' He led the way back over the smooth paving slabs decorated with little jewelled stones to their table which was laid with white linen, shining cutlery and gleaming glasses, lit by a white candle and decorated with a vase of wild spring flowers.

Nice touch, she thought. Maybe she should add that idea to the Polignano terrace design. Cut flowers would look so pretty on the wooden tables.

'He is very protective of you, your papà?'

'You could say that, yes.' Both her parents always had been. As a child, Bea hadn't minded too much; as she grew up, it was sometimes irritating, sometimes quite reassuring to feel so sheltered. She wasn't the type of girl who liked to party and it had never been much of an issue. But now . . . Bea appreciated their concern, but she was perfectly capable of making her own choices about the men she dated – or more often, didn't date, she thought, suppressing a smile.

'But this, you know, is a good thing,' Matteo said.

Bea supposed that he was right. She loved her father and she really didn't mind so much that he wanted to protect her.

The waiter brought their drinks and read out the menu for the day. Each evening, he explained, the bill of fare differed, depending on seasonal availability and the chef's personal decisions; this was a tasting menu and each course would be accompanied by a glass of a wine, considered a perfect pairing. Bea was excited – she'd never come to a place like this before, though Matteo was probably more used to it, being the son of restaurateurs and clearly a bit of a foodie.

She liked the atmosphere in here too – the lighting was subtle with an amber warmth and the tables were spaced far enough apart to preserve the diners' privacy. Bea glanced around. The restaurant was full but still seemed spacious. The walls were of the palest limestone, rising up to a vaulted ceiling, and there were tall glazed green and brown olive storage jars by the doorways and antique agricultural tools providing a reminder of the building's history.

As the courses and drinks started coming, she and Matteo began to chat about their lives. He told her some more about the family restaurant. His father was head chef. It had always been his father's dream, he said, to own such a place.

'And your mother?' Bea bit into the little slice of salted bread served with rosemary and wild onion pâté. Mmm. It was salty, fragrant and delicious.

Matteo leant closer, confiding. 'Mamma, she likes to be in control.'

Bea caught a note of the citrus and cedarwood on his skin. Along with the food and the dry white wine served with this course, it was a sensory overload. She hoped Matteo was half joking. 'What does she control? The restaurant? Or is it you and your father, you mean?'

His blue eyes gleamed. 'Everything,' he said. 'At least, everything she can.'

Bea made a further mental note not to cross Signora Leone. So far, her new client had been the epitome of charm, but Bea could sense a flinty strength behind it. Matteo's mother would be friendly enough when it suited her. But if something didn't go her way . . . Bea gave a little shiver. She would be *formidable*.

'Are you cold?' Matteo was all concern. He had already ensured that Bea had the best seat at the table and he had explained the intricacies of some of the dishes on offer.

He was, she thought, the perfect gentleman. Or so it seemed . . . She shook her head. 'No, I'm fine thanks.' She took another sip of her wine. Matteo was drinking too, she noted. She hoped he wasn't expecting her father to drive him back to Polignano – if that was where he lived. That wouldn't go down so well with Papà.

Matteo was spreading more of the fragrant wild onion pâté onto his bread. 'In fact, Mamma does the restaurant books and takes care of the staff and all the administration.'

'And you?' she asked. Because so far, he hadn't said too much about himself. 'What do you do?'

'In the restaurant?' He touched his lips with the white linen napkin.

Bea nodded.

'Officially, I am front of house. Welcoming people, organising the tables, making sure the food comes out to the diners on time.'

'And unofficially?'

'Ah, well.' He pushed his plate to one side and smiled at the waiter who was bringing another course of fried stuffed zucchini flowers which he placed carefully on the table in front of them. 'Grazie.' Matteo thanked him and turned back to Bea. 'I am the general dogsbody, you could say.'

Bea couldn't imagine that somehow. 'You never wanted to be in the kitchen?'

'Not really.' For a moment he gazed away from her, over her shoulder, as if lost in thought.

What was he remembering? she wondered.

'That was what my father wanted – for me to follow in his footsteps.' Matteo took the tongs and dished two perfect little crispy golden flowers up onto Bea's plate.

'*Grazie*. But you weren't interested?'

He shrugged. 'It was not my thing. Any interest I had in cooking disappeared the moment he started ordering me around.'

Bea laughed. She could imagine Matteo as a young boy, eager to please his father perhaps, but wanting to be praised, not criticised. It had been different for her with her love of gardening, apparently inherited from her grandmother. Nonna had nourished it as you might a plant itself, but she had never taken Bea's passion for granted, nor tried to control it. Nonna had taught her much of what she needed to know and given Bea her own patch in the garden to experiment with.

'Do you get on well with your father now?' she asked lightly. She tasted the zucchini flowers which were cheesy and garlicky – a little bite of heaven.

'Well enough.' He popped a flower into his mouth whole and nodded approvingly. 'But he is not easy. He expects to get what he wants. And if he does not . . .' He pulled an expressive face.

'He has a temper?' And what about Matteo? she found herself wondering. Did he too expect to get what he wanted?

Matteo laughed. 'Papà is very fiery, yes. When I finally summoned the courage to tell him I was not bothered about learning all his precious chef's secrets . . . Let's just say it led to a big row and *la cucina*, it got very hot indeed.' He fanned himself with his hand.

Bea chuckled. But that must have been hard for his father, she thought. She took another bite followed by a sip of the floral-scented wine. Though to be fair, it must also have been hard on Matteo, to be pushed into something he had no interest in or flair for.

'So, I guess in the end, I will assume my mother's role.' Though Matteo didn't look overjoyed at the prospect. 'When I take over the restaurant, I mean.'

It sounded as if that was a foregone conclusion and Bea wondered if he'd ever had any different ambitions 'But you like food?' Bea gestured at the next plate that had appeared as if by magic on their table. Artichokes cooked in sweet wine with orange honey, if she recalled correctly. *Mi Dio*, she thought. The food here was something else. She glanced around at the other diners who somehow all seemed more accustomed to this sort of luxury than she. The presentation of the food and surroundings of the *masseria* had all been done to such a high standard. The place was not just atmospheric, it was exquisite,

'*Sì, sì,* I like food.' He eyed the plate appreciatively.

Yes, she had assumed this to be the case. 'Enough to be happy about taking over your family's restaurant one day?' It was perhaps a delicate subject, but Bea wanted to get to the bottom of what Matteo might really want.

'Of course,' he said and once again his expression changed. 'It is my family's life. And I am the only son.'

'I see.' So his mother was controlling, his father was fiery and Matteo's future was mapped out for him. She was getting the picture. He didn't have to say more. But where would a relationship fit in?

Over the next courses of pasta with ragout, meatloaf with thyme, spring salad – goodness, the food just kept on coming – Bea told him about her family and the olive farm, about how her grandparents had come over from England and built a life here.

'So, you are half-English?' He twirled the wine around in his glass.

'Yes.'

'I thought there was something . . .'

She put her head to one side and regarded him curiously. 'What do you mean?'

He put his hand over hers as it rested on the white linen tablecloth. 'You are different, Beatrice,' he said.

Like a breath of fresh air, he had told her before, she remembered, after their first encounter. It had felt a bit soon for him to be saying such a thing when he hardly knew her – but nice anyway. Everything about their relationship felt a bit soon, though, when she came to think about it. The intimate way he had kissed her cheeks when they first met, the random seriousness of their initial conversation, his easy assumption that they would see each other again, even this first date at such a special restaurant.

But Bea pushed this thought aside too. She was getting way ahead of herself. It was crazy to worry about things like that at this stage. Matteo was just that sort of a person – a rushing forwards sort of a person – while Bea tended to hang back a little. Perhaps that would make them compatible – they could balance one another out.

'I don't think so much about being half-English.' Though even as she said this, Bea wondered if it was true. She did think about her English connections, about the land Nonna called home. She had often wondered about that other garden too . . .

'What are you thinking, Beatrice?' He gave her hand a squeeze before letting go.

Bea took a sip of the musky red wine they were now drinking, a Susumaniello from the local region. She wasn't quite ready to tell him about Nonna's garden. 'Oh, just about my grandmother,' she said. 'Her stories.' Fairy tales really, about a girl and a garden. But fairy tales that must surely be grounded in reality. In which case – why had that girl needed a sanctuary? she wondered, and not for the first time. Was there something she had needed to escape from?

'I cannot wait to get to know you better.' Matteo's voice was warm and low. Bea could feel it caressing her senses like silk. 'Though already I feel I know you.'

Bea almost laughed. She had always considered herself a rather secretive person. But she didn't laugh. His voice was too seductive for laughter and she wasn't sure that he would appreciate it. She dared to meet his intent gaze.

'Tell me, when we first met, did you feel it too?'

Bea raised an enquiring eyebrow though she thought she knew what he meant.

'The connection.'

Had she? She had certainly felt something. An attraction. A sense of being taken somewhere way out of her comfort zone.

'I always know,' he said.

'Always?' Bea spoke lightly. It made her wonder about Matteo's relationship history. Should she be worried? But at the same time, she was cross with herself. Perhaps he wasn't even talking about relationships. Why did she always have to question everything? Why did she always have to notice the small stuff that other girls let go? Like that slightly arrogant tone he had, that air of being used to getting what he wanted. Why did she have to overthink?

'Always,' he repeated.

'Yes,' she said. Because she had kept thinking of him. Connection or not, Matteo Leone had been very much on her mind.

★

The evening flew by. They'd eaten so much, drunk rather a lot and talked a great deal. Bea was heady with it. Matteo and the door he'd opened was showing her the prospect of another life, one that was intense, sensual, exciting.

Matteo took care of the bill while she went to the bathroom and stared at herself in the gilt-framed mirror. Who was this wild-eyed girl? Some of her hair had escaped from its confines and now hung in tendrils around her neck framing her face. Her skin was flushed and warm to the touch, her mouth was smiling, her eyes were awake to something she hadn't experienced before: something new, something delicious that lay ahead.

'My God,' she whispered to herself.

Back outside, as they left the *masseria*, Matteo waved away her efforts to make a contribution to their dinner. 'Naturally, not,' he said firmly. He took her arm and steered her outside. 'I invited you, remember?'

'Thank you.' Bea decided to give in gracefully. 'But I should call my father.' She groped in her bag for her mobile.

'You do not have to disturb him,' Matteo pointed towards the road where a taxi was waiting a short distance away. 'I booked a cab, as you see. We can drop you off first, do not worry.'

He seemed to have thought of everything. 'Then . . .'

'Beatrice.' He pulled her gently to one side so that they were sheltered from any passing glances by a tall and sturdy pine tree. But there was no one else around and certainly no one could see them from the road. It felt as if they were quite alone.

Her back was flat against the rough bark of the tree. She could feel its sharp ridges and she could smell the resin like bitter honey. 'Matteo.'

He bent towards her, Bea lifted her face to his and his lips brushed hers, tender and inviting. The charge was utterly compelling. She pulled him closer. He pressed hard against her then, his hands holding her face, his lips more demanding now.

The longing pulsed through her, sweeping away all thoughts other than a single desire. The kiss swept into another, then another and in seconds his hands were on her breasts and hers were under his jacket pulling at his shirt so that she could touch his skin.

'Beatrice.' He let out a little groan and at last they dragged themselves apart, both breathless and staring at one another in the moonlight.

Bea had never felt this way before. She was in shock. She couldn't believe how much she wanted him.

'Not here,' he said.

'No, *certo* not here,' she agreed. And not now. Surely it was too soon?

'We should get in the cab,' he said ruefully.

'Yes.'

She straightened her dress and he straightened his jacket. She took his arm and they made their way to the waiting taxi. Bea would have some explaining to do to her father, but she couldn't bring herself to care.

'That was nice,' he murmured in her ear as he held the door open for her.

'So nice,' she said. *Oh, my goodness* . . . Nice was hardly the word. What would have happened if she and Matteo had not been in a public place? Bea shivered. And she realised that her grandmother was right. There were definitely other things to life apart from gardening . . .

CHAPTER 9

Lara

Dorset, February 1946

Lara followed Dr Barnes out of the room and closed her mother's bedroom door softly behind them. 'How is she, Doctor?' she asked.

The doctor shot her a sympathetic glance from under thick charcoal brows. He was in his mid-sixties with a shock of white hair and he was kind enough, calling in most days in his worn-out suit, carrying his battered black leather doctor's bag. But they both knew there was not going to be a miraculous recovery. Lara's mother was fading away. Every time Lara looked into her blue-grey eyes, they seemed paler; every time she held her mother's hand, it seemed lighter, more insubstantial.

'Bearing up in the face of the inevitable,' he replied. 'How are *you*, though, Lara?'

'Oh, I'm fine.' She ran her fingers through her hair, which she knew needed washing. She wasn't fine. She was exhausted.

She didn't want to admit that leaving the house to go to work was a release from this – tending to her mother's needs, watching her grow more ill with every day that passed – but actually, it was. At work, she needed to clear her mind so that she could listen carefully to dictation and write quickly, the little squiggly notes of shorthand. And so that she could type – because then she must focus on the job in hand, the click-clack of the keys, the dring of the ribbon, the words on the paper. And not think about her mother, about David.

'You have to look after yourself too, you know.' He was writing out a prescription and turned to give her a stern but kindly frown.

She nodded.

'Do you have help with her still?'

'Yes.' Elizabeth from next door came in every day, bless her, and other women from the village popped over from time to time to visit and see if they could do anything to help. And then, of course, there was Charles.

Lara had to admit that Charles had continued to be good to them. He brought delicacies that he thought might tempt her mother to eat – occasionally even oranges and a few bananas; fruit that had become an untold luxury, that they'd hardly glimpsed during the wartime years. Mother had been right: there was still rationing, though things had eased. As for Charles, he helped with practicalities in the home, he even sat with her. In fact, he was one of Mother's favourite visitors.

'Hmm. Well, you must keep up your strength.'

'Yes.' She couldn't give up work, though. Where would they be then?

Dr Barnes handed her the prescription for more painkillers. 'Will someone fetch this for you?'

'Oh, yes.' Lara put it on the hall table. Charles would be over later. She knew that he would see to it and sometimes, just sometimes, she acknowledged to herself how blissful this felt – to have someone to lean on.

'I'll call in again tomorrow,' the doctor said.

'Thank you.' Lara never asked him how long he thought her mother had left. She didn't want to think about it, couldn't measure out the time remaining in that way.

After he'd gone, Lara slipped back into her mother's room. She refilled her water glass and held it to her mother's dry mouth for her to take a few sips.

'You're a good girl,' her mother said as she sank back into the pillows.

Stay with me then, Lara thought fiercely. *Don't leave me.*

'And loyal too,' her mother said.

'Loyal?'

'To David.'

They sat quietly. Lara let David's name sink into the space between them. She still missed him. She still waited for him every day, but she'd heard nothing. She'd even made enquiries of the authorities, but the answer was always the same: *missing, presumed dead*. It was an awful presumption to have to make of anyone, but of course, in the war there had been so many instances where a body couldn't be found or identified. Lara shuddered.

It had been nine months since victory had been declared. Despite that victory, Winston Churchill had been replaced as prime minister by Labour's Clement Attlee and atomic bombs had been dropped on Japan. Some things were the same but many things were changing – there was rebuilding and supposedly there was reform. She'd even heard talk about nationalisation, which would apparently save the railways. But there was still plenty of food rationing and it took ingenuity and time that Lara didn't have to create nourishing and different meals that might tempt her mother to eat.

Lara couldn't think of any other reason why David wouldn't have come home in all this time, wouldn't at least have written. And so, she knew better than anyone that the 'presumed' would one day soon have to be scratched from her mind. Because David was dead. He had to be.

'But I'll be gone soon,' her mother said, after a few minutes had passed.

'Hush, Mother.'

'And I want to know that you'll be looked after.' She seemed to sink even deeper into her pillows with the effort of talking, the concern.

Lara took her hand and held it gently in her own. These days, her mother's body seemed so fragile that Lara worried that even the act of touching some part of it could lead to it bruising. 'I'll be fine, Ma,' she said, as breezily as she could manage. 'I can look after myself.'

Her mother gave a little shake of the head. She spoke and Lara had to lean forwards to hear. 'Everyone needs someone.'

'Well, my someone's lost to the war like half the other lads.' Lara blinked back a tear. 'So that's that.'

Her mother spoke again, a faint whisper.

'What's that, Ma?'

'Charles?' she said.

Lara sighed. She had told her mother about Charles's proposal nine months ago, though anyway, she probably would have guessed. Every time he came here, Charles looked at Lara as if he wanted to speak out. But he said nothing, just as he'd

93

promised, though he was always solicitous, always there. Lara had told her mother about David too, about his being missing, presumed dead, that same afternoon in the Romantic Garden when Ma had told her about the cancer. And they had wept together.

'I don't love Charles, Ma,' Lara said now. She was grateful to him. But surely that was different?

Her mother gave her a wise look. 'It's up to you, my darling,' she whispered. 'But he's spoken to me, you know. He can look after you. And remember that sometimes it's not just about love.' She closed her eyes; Lara could see how much energy these simple words had cost her.

She put a light hand onto her mother's forehead and smoothed a wisp of hair from her face. *Not just about love?* Lara pondered this. It was, though, wasn't it? If you didn't have love, what else was there? She thought of her parents. Her father might have been careless with money, he might have squandered precious funds he should have saved, but they'd been happy, she knew; they'd experienced love. Did her mother regret it? Did she wish they'd never met, never married? Lara couldn't believe that this was true.

And she thought of her all too short-lived passionate love affair with David. When he left for war, she was so miserable that she'd thought she would die. She hadn't, though. Instead, she had survived, she had made it through this war and now she was on the other side. Without love, yes, but . . . Was it better to have experienced the love and the loss – or not? It was all very confusing.

How long was she going to wait for David?

Her mother was resting now, so Lara retreated to the sitting room and curled up on the window seat, her thinking spot.

She knew that her mother did not want Lara to lose Lime Tree House and its walled garden. The place meant so much. And she wanted Lara to be cared for too. But . . .

Lara was still wearing her utility suit, her normal workwear; there hadn't been time to change. A pile of darning lay on the cushioned seat beside her, but she couldn't bring herself even to look at it. Instead, she stared out into the garden. Her mother had worked so hard on it. It was the dead of winter, but soon spring would be here again and the plants would return to life. And what about Lara? Was her mother right? *How long can you wait for a man who is already gone?*

She was still sitting there twenty minutes later when Charles came into the house, tapping lightly on the back door to announce his presence, before letting himself in. Already, Lara thought, he seemed to belong here.

'Lara?' He came into the room and walked up to where she was sitting curled foetus-like against the olive and crimson cushions. She should get to her feet, be polite, offer him a drink or something. But she was just too plain exhausted.

Could she do it? Could she throw herself into his arms and mourn what she'd already lost and what more there was to come? Could she let him hold her? Could she let David go at last? She blinked back a tear. 'Thanks for calling in, Charles,' she said.

A brief disappointment seemed to shadow his face and then was gone so fast she wondered if she'd imagined it.

'How is she today?'

'The same. The doctor's been. He's left another prescription.'

'Do you want me to . . . ?'

'Would you?'

'Of course.' He hesitated. 'I'll just pop my head round to say hello, shall I?'

'Yes,' she said. 'She'd like that. Though she might still be sleeping.'

'I'll be quiet.'

Lara let out a small sigh as she turned away to look out into the winter garden. It was dusk and the light was dimming. As she watched the sky, she saw a flock of starlings darting, swooping, creating their complex and intricate patterns as they flew past, on their way to roost. A murmuration, wasn't that what it was called? The pattern became delicate as lace as the group moved away, beyond the garden, out of sight. And then . . . they were gone.

CHAPTER 10

Bea

Italy, April 2018

The past three weeks had tumbled by, spinning Bea this way and that until she hardly knew where she was.

Like her, Matteo was busy, but unlike her, he worked what he called unsociable hours, so when he had a day off, he wanted them to spend it together. 'What could be more natural?' he said, as if them not being able to spend time together was Bea's doing, not his. Then he'd laugh and she'd laugh with him – and usually capitulate.

Sometimes this was fine. Other times she had work commitments and he didn't always understand.

'Let it go, Beatrice,' he would say, a hint of exasperation in those blue eyes. 'Live a little. Who wants to be alone and hiding away in a garden every day? Take some time off now and then. Where is the harm?'

Bea tried to silence the inner voice that had always made her want to work hard. But she knew that the garden was where she belonged. And she never felt alone there, though it was true that sometimes she did indeed use her gardens to hide away in. But Matteo was probably right. Why not have a little more fun? All work and no play was never a good thing.

So, Bea tried to fit everything around Matteo and when he was free – it seemed easier that way. She wanted to see him and he was great company; he made her feel truly alive as if she was breathing different and more vibrant air from the air she'd always breathed before. But sometimes when they parted, she felt drained. He was lovely, but he could be overwhelming. With Matteo in her life, somehow it seemed as if the rest of that life was in danger of fading so far into the background that she would forget to attend to it at all.

Bea hadn't found her usual sense of peace working on Signora Leone's restaurant terrace. From midday till four there was a steady stream of lunch-goers, who often stopped to comment on what she was doing. It was gratifying that they were interested . . . But Bea also needed alone time in which to think. And then, she never knew when Matteo would appear, released from his restaurant duties for a break or perhaps simply slipping away when he got the chance. He was always surprising her – she would feel strong arms sliding around her waist as she was busy potting an oregano plant or a rosemary bush, he would steal a kiss on the pretext of bringing her coffee, and when all the customers had finally gone home, he would lure her down to the beautiful limestone beach, Cala Porto, with a late packed lunch from the restaurant.

'Your mother . . .' Bea would say, glancing at her watch.

'Oh, forget my mother.'

But of course, she couldn't. His mother was Bea's client after all. His father too, though the signore was kept busy in the kitchen and rarely made an appearance on the terrace unless it was to meet a certain diner with whom he might have an acquaintance or to be congratulated on the quality of the lunch.

But all this meant that Bea couldn't form the same relationship with the terrace as she usually would with a garden she was working on. She couldn't find the oneness, the understanding of precisely what was needed, the sense of fulfilment in her task. She was used to being solitary; this was a very different experience.

As for Signora Leone, however, she seemed delighted with what Bea had done, even recommending her to another client. But sometimes Bea would catch Matteo's mother looking at her in a certain way and she'd wonder – was she the kind of girl Signora Leone wanted for her son? Matteo had said his mamma was controlling. Did that mean she wanted to control Matteo's life? He had certainly implied as much during their first conversation in the Ostuni garden. And if so . . .

Matteo – so bold, she thought; so fearless – was far from reluctant to meet her parents and he was so confident and charming that he made an instant and positive impression on Bea's entire family – even the Romanos from the other house who just happened to be passing through when it was known that Bea's young man was about to come calling. He brought Bea chocolates and her mother and grandmother flowers and even her super-protective father started referring to him as 'one of the good guys', which was, Bea had to admit, quite a relief.

Naturally, Bea was flattered by the attention – what girl wouldn't be? It was all so new, so exciting, so different. Matteo whisked her off to fancy restaurants and cocktail bars. He took her out in a friend's yacht one gloriously sunny day when she really was supposed to be working and for a long drive down to a nature reserve on the south coast. Bea was getting a taste of another life and she was exhilarated by it. For the first time ever, she felt as if she was basking in the sunlight – and it was the sunlight radiated by Matteo Leone.

Three weeks into their relationship, he bought her a silver necklace, the pendant a delicate filigree stalk of lavender crusted with tiny buds of amethyst.

Bea gasped. 'Matteo. This is too much. It's not even my birthday.'

'Nothing is too much.' He kissed her, a soft brush of the lips that left her skin prickling with desire. 'You are such a shy flower, my Beatrice,' he said. 'I would like to dress you up and show you off to everyone. I want to see you bloom.'

They were in his flat, a small annexe attached to the restaurant in Polignano. Bea always felt a bit uncomfortable there, knowing that his parents were close by, either in the restaurant itself or in their rooms above, but it didn't seem to bother Matteo in the slightest. Sometimes she wondered how many other girls he had brought back here. Sometimes she just didn't care.

The first time they made love had been here in this bed, after Bea's first full day of work on the restaurant terrace. She had known it would happen. Those feelings she'd experienced after their dinner at the *masseria* had increased in their urgency since then, and when Matteo invited her in for a drink (*and a shower if you like*, he had added with a knowing smile; after all, she had been hard at work clearing the terrace all day) she'd known exactly what she was walking into.

In the event, they had showered together, sharing wet kisses, exploring one another's soapy bodies, before wrapping themselves in white fluffy towels and collapsing in a tangled heap on his bed. Since then, they couldn't get enough of one another.

Now, Bea turned, so that Matteo could fasten the chain. The little head of lavender glittered. 'It's beautiful,' she said.

'So are you.' He kissed her neck.

She turned back towards him. He was like a magnet for Bea; she'd never known a relationship like this – physically, it was all-consuming.

'*Grazie*, Matteo,' she said. 'Thank you so much.'

He stroked her hair from her face. 'I am falling in love with you, Beatrice,' he said.

Oh. She stared at him. She was taken by surprise – it seemed so soon.

'Do you mind?' he asked softly.

Bea shook her head. But she couldn't quite bring herself to say the words back to him, the words she knew he was waiting to hear. Was she too falling in love? She supposed that she must be. That was what it was – this feeling, this electric connection between them. But it was all so fast.

She reached out a hand and curled a lock of his dark hair through her fingers. Every time she touched him, the intensity of it zinged through her. She was way out of her comfort zone. When he was close to her, she could hardly catch her breath. She had been catapulted into another world, but did she really belong there? Would she still be able to find the peace and tranquillity that was so important to her? Or did being in love with Matteo mean that she would have to change?

In love . . .

He tilted her chin and kissed her long and slow. Bea smelt the familiar scent on his skin and she felt herself melting inside.

'I love you too,' she said. Why harbour doubts when everything was this good? This was what mattered – this connection between them. And everything else . . . *Allora*, it would all come right in the end.

CHAPTER II

Lara

Dorset, April 1946

Lara was planting the perennials out in the Romantic Garden. Spring had well and truly arrived and although she would still be growing some vegetables this year, it was time, she'd decided, to bring these plants back home.

It was an appropriate job to be doing on a day like this. The sun had warmed the earth since winter and dried it a little after yesterday's short sharp showers so that it crumbled easily, and the sky above was a promising silver-blue with puffs of cloud passing by. There was a certain monotony about the task that felt pleasing too, she thought, as she wheeled the barrow down to the greenhouse, eased the plants one by one from the pots where they had been living a claustrophobic existence for the past six years, loaded them into the barrow, and took them back to the Romantic Garden, to soak in deep buckets of water while she prepared the ground.

Lara could do this all day if she wanted to. It was Sunday,

she'd had no desire to go to church this morning – if God could wantonly snatch away everyone she loved, then why should she bother to pray to him? – she didn't have to work and there was no one to cook for, not any more.

She let out a sigh as she drove the spade into the bed. Her beloved mother had passed away six weeks ago, the ghastly paperwork and practical arrangements that inevitably followed death were more or less done, and now it was a question of survival – or at least, that's how it felt. She pushed deeper, felt the blade slice cleanly into the damp earth. Not just Lara's survival, but the survival of what was left – her mother's much-loved house and the garden she had hoped would last forever.

Lara was wearing her sturdy green wellington boots and the overalls she often wore for gardening. She shovelled out the earth for the planting hole. The robin who claimed this garden as his territory hopped closer in the expectation of worms. Lara smiled and nodded to him to go ahead; she could see that there were plenty.

She rested quietly for a moment, leaning on the spade, breathing in the scents of freshly dug earth and sap. Sometimes it was too much. Sometimes she felt as if she had lost too much. First her father, then David, now her mother too. There had been no news of David and over time, Lara's breath had stopped catching in her throat when she thought of him. It had been naive of her to ever imagine that there would be news. Now, almost a year after the end of the war, Lara had finally accepted that he'd gone. In her heart, she had said goodbye.

The robin hopped closer in his pursuit of a bigger and juicier worm and Lara observed the way he stayed constantly alert for predators; continually watching, eyes darting, head turning. But he was brave. She looked past the stone sundial and up at the house, at the small-paned windows and red roof tiles, the satisfying use of local wood; the pleasing way that the rafters extended beyond the roofline to form the veranda and the terrace. None of that Arts and Crafts simplicity or utility was worth a fig, though, if she couldn't manage, if she couldn't pay the bills. But at that moment a ray of sunlight caught the stained glass in the panel above the French doors and the effect was so beautiful, so theatrical and unexpected, that she almost gasped.

Lara straightened her back and continued her task. She was planting echinacea and verbena with drifts of erigeron daisies intended to form a romantic haze of pink and white in front of the lilac buddleia. Harmony in nature, she reminded herself. That was what the Arts and Crafts garden was all about: shapes, colours and scents that worked together like a symphony. She'd been left alone to carry on, but she could do it. She still had a future and she must stay positive. She still had the house; she still had the garden. She didn't have the friends around here she'd once had; she hadn't had the time, she supposed, to keep up with them, and since the end of the war some people had already left the village looking for work in bigger towns. But she'd made a promise to her mother, and she would keep it.

It had been very near to the end. Lara had been sitting by the bed and her mother had suddenly gripped Lara's hand with surprising strength. 'The garden,' she said. It was the day before she passed and she had seemed different; stronger, filled with some strange kind of adrenalin.

'Don't worry about the garden, Ma,' Lara had soothed. She knew what was on her mother's mind. 'Just rest.'

Her mother's eyes briefly flashed defiance. 'Nothing to do

but rest,' her expression seemed to say. 'The garden,' she whispered again. 'She wanted it to last forever.'

Lara smiled. 'I'll look after the house and the garden,' she told her. 'I know how important it all is to you. You told me the story, remember?'

Her mother strained forwards as if she were trying to sit up.

'It's all right, Ma.' The doctor had said it wouldn't be long. He'd suggested they move her to the local hospice for her last days, but Lara knew her mother would rather be here in her own home at the end.

'Lara. Do what you need to do.' There was a new note, almost an imperious note in her mother's voice. What did she mean? *Do what you need to do?*

'I will, yes,' Lara said. And she was aware in that moment that she was making a promise.

The next day, Lara's mother was gone.

'Lara!'

The sound of her name being called jolted Lara back to the present. Her arms were aching, she realised. She pushed her hair from her face with a hand that was, she saw too late, smeared with mud. She looked up. 'Hello, Charles.' She gave a little wave.

He was standing by the open French doors and now the light was catching his fair hair and giving him a heroic look that she'd never seen in him before. He must have let himself in, she supposed, and gone through the house looking for her. She didn't keep the back door locked during the day; they never had.

Charles had been as frequent a visitor after her mother's death as he had been before. Was he still interested in Lara romantically? She supposed that he was, though he never really showed it. But maybe practical help spoke louder than mere words and romantic gestures? He had been particularly supportive when Lara's mother died, and she knew he would have done more if she'd let him; she sensed that he rather wanted her to let him take over. But Lara had felt that it was her responsibility and Charles had seemed to respect this.

'How long have you been out here working?' He clicked his tongue and made his way down the stone steps. 'All morning, no doubt.'

'Probably.' She shrugged. It was easy to lose track of time. It was a relief.

'Lara.' Suddenly he was standing much closer to her than usual and the tone of his voice had changed. She noticed that the robin had flown away.

So, this was it then. She steadied her breathing, looked up at him. 'Yes, Charles?'

'You have dirt on your face.' He took a white handkerchief from his pocket, shook it out of its neat folds and wiped the mud away. The gesture was so kind, so tender, that she felt tears threatening to come, those tears that she battled to keep at bay at work, but which would arrive, suddenly, when she was least expecting them. She found them overwhelming, exhausting, but also cathartic.

'Thank you,' she said.

He held her gaze. 'It's time, Lara, my dear,' he said.

'Time?' Though she knew.

'To consider what you will do next,' he said.

'I'm working,' she said, choosing to deliberately misunderstand him. She didn't want to be forced into making a decision, she still wasn't sure that she was ready. 'I need to get

107

the garden back to how it was before the war just as Mother wanted. And then—'

'I'm talking about us,' he said. The sunlight was no longer lighting up his hair in that heroic way and there was a cool determination in his pale eyes that rather scared her.

'Us?' Her shoulders slumped. There was, she saw, no getting away from it.

'I still feel the same about you, Lara,' he said. 'Even now, almost a year since we last spoke of it. You must know that.'

'Yes.' Though she had wondered. Was it possible that you could love someone and yet never touch them, never hold them, never kiss them? Could you want to marry someone without all that?

'I know I'm older than you.' His voice was soft. 'But I can look after you. That's what I'd like to do.'

Lara had always prided herself on being independent. Her parents had encouraged her to do her secretarial training. 'So that you have something to fall back on,' her mother had said. 'So that you can look after yourself.'

But Lara was no longer sure that she wanted to look after herself. It seemed daunting. Actually, after all she'd been through, no matter how positive she was trying to be, she rather longed to be looked after, now that she'd been left all alone.

'I can ensure that you are able to stay in this house.' He made an expansive gesture that seemed to take in everything that Lara was fighting for – the house, the garden, the memories. 'You will never have to leave.'

This was what Lara needed to hear. She didn't exactly know Charles's circumstances, but she did know that she couldn't leave. She'd made a promise to her mother on her deathbed, after all. Lara gripped on to the handle of the spade for balance.

She thought of the pile of bills she was gradually working through, the desperation.

Charles dropped to one knee on the gravel. Lara stared at him. This didn't seem like him at all. He was so fastidious. Was it a sign of the strength of his feelings perhaps?

'Once again, I am asking you to marry me, Lara,' he said. 'And this time, I need an answer, I think that's fair.'

Lara hesitated. It was fair, of course it was fair. What other man would have waited so long?

'If you don't want me,' he said, 'I will walk away and I won't bother you again.'

Lara thought of the house she could barely manage and the garden that required a restoration she couldn't do alone. She thought of David, who was never coming back, and she thought of her father and the attic studio that had been left empty of painting and of life since he'd been gone. Finally, she thought of her mother. *Do what you need to do.*

Lara took a deep breath. 'Yes, Charles,' she said. 'I will marry you.' This was what she needed to do. Because it seemed she no longer had a choice in the matter. Because Charles had been so kind to them and he had waited so long. Because she simply could no longer do it alone.

CHAPTER 12

Lara

Italy, April 2018

Lara was sitting on the wooden bench by the pond in her Italian garden staring at the water-lily. The pink-white bud was swelling with every day that passed, its leaves speckled, glossy plates floating flat on the water. But soon, she knew, the flower would burst into bloom, its marmalade centre surrounded by pastel-perfect petals shimmering on the surface of the pond.

'Mamma! Mamma?'

Lara stirred. It was Rose, rushing around as usual.

'Down here, darling,' Lara called. She lacked the energy at this precise moment to rise from the bench, though as she heard Rose's footsteps she managed to sit up a little straighter.

'Oh, Mamma, I thought you were on the terrace.' Rose was frowning. 'You really should not be coming down here on your own, you know.'

When exactly had their roles reversed? Lara wondered. When had she stopped looking after Rose, stopped feeling responsible for her daughter's welfare? When had Rose started doing those same things for her? Lara still worried for her daughter, though. She always would.

'I *was* on the terrace,' she said, trying not to sound like the child she wasn't. 'And I can still manage the steps alone.' On a good day, that was. 'I came down to watch the water.' Water allowed your thoughts to drift. It was the shimmying of it, she supposed, for it was never still.

'You should have told me before you went off wandering.'

For a moment, Lara was swept back to that other time and she gave a little shudder. But it was all right. This was Rose, just Rose.

Her daughter stood, hands on hips, obscuring Lara's soothing view and looking more harassed than ever. Her fair hair had loosened from the twisted knot she often wore and her eyes were red-rimmed as if she hadn't slept well last night. What might have kept her awake? Lara wondered.

'You mustn't worry, Rose,' Lara said. 'I'm fine.'

Rose tutted. 'But you know, Mamma, you are not steady on your feet and—'

'Stop.' She'd had enough. What use was it being alive if you couldn't so much as wander down to your garden if you felt like it? Where was the freedom in that? And it crept into her belly – something slow and dark that she hadn't felt for a very long time. Lara closed her eyes.

'What is it, Mamma?'

Lara struggled to regain control. She opened her eyes again. Rose was staring at her, biting her lip, looking as if she might cry. 'Sorry, darling.' She wanted to say so much more.

Rose blinked at her. 'What do you mean? Stop what?'

'Sit for a moment.' Lara patted the bench next to her.

'Oh, Mamma.' This was much more Rose's known territory. 'You know I do not have time to sit around and—'

'You work too hard, darling,' Lara said. 'You push yourself too hard.'

'But—'

'Take a breath. Take a break. Take time to . . .' – she hesitated – '. . . look around.' Lara did what she was advising her daughter to do. She looked around at the spring bulbs already flowering, the trees that were in delicate pink and white blossom, the row of cypresses lining the avenue and separating her Italian garden from the olive grove. She looked up at the sky too which was a clear spring blue, deepening away from the sun.

'Look around?' A spark of irritation lit her daughter's eyes. '*Allora*. So, if I do that, then who will sort the laundry and prepare the dinner, Mamma, hmm? Who will clean *la cucina* and chop the vegetables and make the beds in the *trulli* ready for the next lot of guests?' She paused for breath, but it wasn't the kind of breath or pause that Lara had been meaning. 'Do you have any idea how much there is to be done, Mamma?'

'*Sì*.' Yes, she did. She heard Rose talking about it and doing it all day long every day, which was precisely her point.

'Well then.' But despite herself, Rose sat down with a plop, as if once down she might never get up again. Lara knew the feeling.

Cautiously, she took her daughter's hand. 'I worry about you, Rose. You know, sometimes you should slow down, that's all I'm saying.' Or she would burn out. Lara thought of the sadness she had glimpsed in her daughter's eyes. What was it? She was already like a candle flame flickering. Lara wanted her to burn bright, straight and strong.

For a moment she thought she had her.

Then Rose pulled away as she so often did. 'I am fine,' she said. 'Honestly, Mamma. I will be fine – as long as I get everything done.' She jumped to her feet. 'But if I do not get on . . .' – and for a moment she looked so lost that Lara's heart went out to her – '. . . then I will not be fine at all.'

Lara couldn't fault the logic. 'Rose . . .'

But already she was off, down the path, up the steps. 'Later, Mamma.'

Later, later . . . There was always later. There wasn't, though, quite so much of a later, at least not as far as Lara was concerned.

She might have dozed off, because the next thing she heard was her granddaughter calling. It seemed to be a day for it. 'Nonna! Nonna! Where are you?'

This time, Lara struggled to her feet to wave and Bea, who was standing on the terrace, shielding her eyes from the late afternoon sun and looking down onto the garden, ran to greet her.

'Hello, darling.' They hugged. 'Just back from work?' Lara wasn't sure what the time was, but the sun was dipping low in the sky. She shivered.

'I've brought your wrap.' Bea tucked it around Lara's shoulders. 'Have you been out here all afternoon?'

'Oh, no, only an hour or so. Perhaps more.' Time had flown away as it always did these days. It was such an elusive concept. Once, time had hung so heavy on her hands. Your entire life you thought you had so much of it. And then all of a sudden . . .

'And you?' She looked at her granddaughter properly. Bea hadn't been at work, she realised, although it was a weekday. She wasn't dressed for it in her lemon and grey stripy dress, white plimsolls and denim jacket.

'Bea's eyes gleamed. 'I went out with Matteo this afternoon.'

'Ah.' *Another day off,* she couldn't help thinking. It was funny how Rose couldn't stop working, while Bea . . . Bea had always been so dedicated to the gardening business she was building and yet now . . . She seemed to be losing her focus. Lara shook her head at her own inconsistency. Apparently, she was never satisfied.

'He has gone to work now,' Bea said. 'And he will be working a late shift. I have a lot on tomorrow. It's hard – fitting things in, you know?'

Lara knew. 'You really like him, don't you, darling?'

Bea smiled. 'I do.' Her face was still flushed from their meeting; she seemed like a different girl. Perhaps, thought Lara, this was the girl she was supposed to be.

'And you, Nonna?'

'Me?'

'Do you like him?'

'Oh, he's charming. Yes, I like him.' Lara chuckled. Though that hardly mattered. 'He's very . . .' She hesitated.

'Full on?' Bea laughed. 'I know. I feel as if he has taken hold of my life and turned it upside down. In a good way,' she added quickly.

'That's nice,' Lara said doubtfully. Though it sounded uncomfortable.

'Yes, it is.' Bea turned her attention to the pond.

How convinced did she sound? Lara wasn't sure. 'It must be very seductive,' she murmured.

'Yes.' Bea laughed again.

She was happy and that was all that mattered. But Lara also noticed a bluish weariness around her granddaughter's eyes. First Rose, and now Bea. Was she trying to do too much?

Was she playing too hard? Lara couldn't blame her and she was young. But at some point, something would have to give.

'What does he think about you running a gardening company?' Lara trod carefully.

'He thinks it is an amazing thing to do.' Bea looked thoughtful.

'But perhaps not when he wants you to do something else,' Lara said. A little tartly perhaps, but she was old, she could get away with it. And sometimes one couldn't see the truth even when it was slap bang in front of you. After her own experiences – well, she thought, let's just say that she could recognise the danger signs.

Bea giggled. 'You are right, Nonna,' she said. 'Matteo does like to have his own way. But he is proud of me. And you must not worry. You know how important the gardens are to me. And the business too. I won't let anything threaten that.'

'Good.' Though having observed the dynamic between them, Lara guessed that Matteo Leone might have something to say about that too.

'And now, perhaps I should take you inside,' Bea said. 'It's getting a little chilly, don't you think?'

'Yes, it is.' And she felt so tired. Lara suppressed a sigh. The time still didn't feel quite right, to speak to Rose and Bea, to work out what to do about Dorset. Especially now that Bea was involved with Matteo Leone. But soon, she told herself. It would have to be soon. Because she knew she couldn't afford to wait for long.

CHAPTER 13

Rose

Italy, April 2018

It was a few days later and Rose was getting one of the *trulli* ready for the next guests who would be arriving tomorrow. She thought back to the conversation she'd had with her mother the other day. Mamma really had no idea what was involved. Everything had to be just so. The rooms must be spotless . . . *Sì, sì.* Every last corner. People weren't satisfied with anything less than the best linen, gleaming surfaces and a bottle of local wine in their welcome pack.

She smoothed the bedcover one last time and arranged the cushions artfully on top. It was not all bad, of course. In fact, it was satisfying when people wrote about the blissful and authentic experience they'd had coming here to Puglia, to the Romanos' *masseria*; such praise made it worth the work. And work, after all, was what Rose did best. Sometimes she worked to feel that she was doing something worthwhile. Sometimes she worked to forget.

Satisfied with the bedroom, she moved to the bathroom for one last inspection of the basin and mirror. The complimentary toiletries were placed in a little woven basket with a cotton flannel and the obligatory shower cap. Rose gave a little shake of the head. Even if they hadn't made use of them, guests tended to pop the toiletries into their luggage and take them home. Which was also, she supposed, a compliment of sorts.

She could understand the attraction of the *trulli* even though to Rose, the squat conical buildings were commonplace. They were made with thick walls to protect their inhabitants from the hot summers here in Puglia and to keep the interior mild in winter. Federico had once told her they were originally a form of tax evasion – some rich landowner encouraged his workers to build them and if anyone came to investigate, the key stone could be removed and the *trullo* would collapse so that no evidence remained. Not that Rose had ever seen anyone try it . . . But the story explained their unusual shape and this gave them their character. Inside, the wooden deck could be used as additional sleeping space and there was a little fire used for both heating and cooking in the old days. Outside, rainwater drained easily from the roofing stones, while the walls were decorated with the traditional symbols of protection or good luck.

Rose was especially busy today as Matteo Leone was coming to the *masseria* for dinner – another thing to worry about.

'What can we give him to eat?' she had asked Federico last night as they got ready for bed.

'Oh, who cares?' Her husband was not in a helpful mood. 'You are a wonderful cook, my love. Whatever you cook, it will be *squisito*, exquisite.' He smacked his lips in appreciation.

'Hmm.' This didn't make Rose feel any more confident. She felt that Federico was dodging the issue.

'And besides, you have decided already, *sì*?'

'Yes, of course.' She would hardly be considering the menu for the first time the night before. Food must be purchased. Preparations must be done. This all took time.

'Of course,' echoed Federico. He knew her. He knew she'd been thinking of little else for days.

He drew her towards him and nuzzled her neck, clearly imagining that the subject was closed.

Rose pushed him away. 'Not now, Fedi. I am thinking.' She loved her husband, but she would not be put off the subject that was occupying her mind.

Federico sighed theatrically. 'Of what are you thinking, *cara*? Of food, when you should be thinking of love, hmm?'

Rose couldn't help laughing at his desolate expression. 'I can only think of love when I am relaxed,' she informed him. She went into the bathroom to remove her make-up.

He followed her. '*Cara*, you are never relaxed.'

Didn't she know it? Rose avoided her own eyes in the bathroom mirror. If it wasn't the housework, it was the cooking; if not the cooking, then the olives, or her mother . . . Not that Federico expected her to play a large part in tending to the olive trees – they were his babies. He could talk for hours about the irrigation, the pruning and the clearing of the grass to prevent bacterial infection, not to mention the harvesting and production. She rolled her eyes. It was hard to stop him, in fact, once he got going on the subject dearest to his heart.

But they had expanded. Now, there were the *trulli* too, which had proved more time-consuming than Rose had estimated. Perhaps she shouldn't have taken it on – this business of tourism. But she had been concerned. How would they manage when Federico was too old, too tired or too decrepit to manage the olive grove? They should, should they not, have something else up their sleeves?

And tourism, it had come to Puglia in a big way; Rose had witnessed this in the *masserias* and towns all around – the tours and the tastings that proved people wanted to know how they lived in this region of southern Italy, how they worked, how they grew and prepared their food. The Romanos could be a part of that. It was more work, yes. But it was also another step towards security.

And security – a feeling that she couldn't be harmed, that she was safe – was one of the things that Rose was searching for.

'But this evening I am even less relaxed than usual,' she countered, applying her cream cleanser to her face.

Federico put his hands around her waist. 'What can I do to help?' he purred. 'How can I make you relax more?'

'Go through the menu with me,' said Rose.

'What?'

'So, for *antipasti*, I thought *Bombette della Valle d'Itria*, chickpea *sformato*, stuffed zucchini, pitta *rustica* with onion and perhaps also *parmigiana di melanzane*.' Rose removed the cleanser with a face cloth and rinsed it under the tap.

'A lot of antipasti,' he murmured. 'But mmm, very good.' He passed her the towel.

'Then the pasta.' She told him what she had planned as she patted her face dry. 'Then lamb.'

'*Mio Dio*,' he groaned. 'You are killing me, Rose.' He clutched at his stomach. 'So much food!'

'But it is Bea's chance.' She turned to face him. 'Matteo is from a good family.' *Va bene*, she admitted it, by 'good' she partly meant they had money, but not only money; there was ambition, success, a chance for Bea to have some of the nicer things in life.

Federico pulled a face. 'Sì,' he agreed. 'But they are a long way from marriage, are they not? And it is more important for her to be happy, yes?'

'Of course. But she can have both.' She moved in closer and he wrapped his arms around her. He smelt of the tang and bitterness of the olives and the earth; he always did, no matter how often he showered. 'And I think it is serious between them. She is happy, do you not think?'

'Yes.' He stroked her hair. 'It seems so.'

'And he is a nice boy.'

'Yes.' With the other hand, he cradled the back of her head. 'He seems a very nice boy.'

'So that is all good.' Rose couldn't believe it, but what he was doing to her head and her neck was making her feel relaxed at last.

'It is very good,' Federico murmured. 'And you have the menu sorted, my dearest. It all sounds wonderful.'

'Grazie.' Rose nestled in closer.

They had both always been very protective of Bea. Rose had needed to know where Bea was and with whom – particularly in her daughter's teenage years. Because Rose wanted to be sure that Bea would not follow in her footsteps, make the same mistakes that Rose had made, have the same regrets. As for Federico, he was Italian – being protective was in the blood.

Bea, though, had not rebelled like Rose. She was very different – so quiet, so dreamy, a girl who seemed happy with her own company and with nature. But Bea was also determined. Rose was proud of what her daughter had achieved so far – in creating her own business and making a go of it too. But more important than that was finding love and happiness with the right man. And having a family – Rose would love to have grandchildren. And so, tomorrow evening was important for Rose and for them all. She wanted it to go well.

'How are you feeling now, my love?' Federico crooned. He had slipped down the straps of her chemise and was kissing her shoulder.

'Better,' she said.

'Then perhaps we should go to bed?' He drew away and took her hand.

'Perhaps we should,' she agreed. 'We need to get some sleep. It will be a very busy day tomorrow.'

Now, in the *trullo*, Rose smiled fondly as she thought of her husband. She had grown up with him. He was like the older brother she'd never had, and when she was younger, it had never occurred to her to think of him in any other way. She knew he was devoted to her, she'd always known, but selfishly she'd taken that love for granted.

Rose crossed the flagstones over to the window of the *trullo* and gazed out beyond the little white chapel where the family and workers used to pray together back in the old days, towards the olive grove where Federico would be working as he worked every day. Every season had its jobs, and different kinds of oil must be harvested and produced in their own way. Some olives were encouraged to fall into the nets by a systematic shaking of the tree, some were left to fall naturally. Young October olives were strong and intense enough to be used for the *bruschetta*, the soup, the roast beef; others that came later were light and fruity and ideal for the salad dressing.

But that was further along, after the oil had been bottled

and was ready to use . . . First, it was important, Federico always said, to give the trees due care and attention. If you treated a tree right, he claimed, that tree would repay you in full. An olive tree was immortal – you might think a tree had died because there had been no regrowth for years, but then suddenly – *Caspita!* – you would see young shoots which would go on to bear new fruit. Rose knew that as well as her husband did. It was the way of the olive.

As for care and attention . . . Rose sighed. She hadn't treated Federico well in those days; she had never deserved him. And yet . . . he had stayed steadfast and true, just waiting for her to come round to his way of thinking.

She hadn't, though. Rose shook her head. She had lost the plot. She had strayed far from what should have been her right path and had paid the consequences ever since with the losses she had suffered, with the guilt that still sat heavy on her shoulders, the shame that still burnt. She couldn't shake them off, no matter how hard she worked. Bea had been born and she thanked God for the gift of her daughter, but as for the rest . . . Rose had been punished and quite rightly. And she was still haunted by the secret that she kept. *If Federico knew the truth . . .*

Federico had been like a shining beacon that had brought her back to sanity. It had not happened suddenly. She had come back to her family, back from Cesare, and slowly she had come to appreciate them more. Federico had been patient. He had not put pressure on her but once again they were friends. And then one night as they stood outside in the moonlight, after a family dinner, he had said something to make her laugh, and she had turned to look at him and that was the moment when she realised that her feelings had changed.

After that, there was no going back and Rose didn't want

to go back. She grasped at his love with all her being, returned it with all her heart and that love had been there for her ever since. She was fortunate indeed. And yet it still came between them – this knowledge of what she had done, the pain that she had inflicted – because Federico knew nothing. And if he did know . . . Rose couldn't help but worry that his feelings for her might change.

She heard the sound before she saw the reason for it; it broke her from her reflection and reminded her that she must get on. A man on a scooter was driving towards the house, taking the bend too fast. One of their workforce, no doubt.

But instead of heading off towards the olive grove, the man parked his scooter near the house, got off and sauntered up to the front door, pulling off his helmet as he went. He had a very cocksure attitude, Rose thought. And there was something about the way he walked . . .

She stiffened. *It couldn't be . . .*

He turned and looked around, continued up towards the house.

Oh, my God. Rose put her hands to her flaming cheeks. She had dreaded this day. She had prayed it would never come. She didn't know what he wanted, but he was here and that was enough. And now . . . Now, she had nowhere to run.

CHAPTER 14

Lara

Italy, April 2018

During the family dinner that evening, Lara was aware that she was zoning in and out of the conversation. It was a treat to listen to Matteo's banter and to watch her granddaughter glow. But . . . she remembered what Bea had said about Matteo turning her life upside down, about his wanting his own way. *Oh, for heaven's sake* . . . She placed her fork carefully on her plate. Nobody was perfect. But was he too charming to be true? And what in heaven's name was wrong with Rose? Tonight, Lara's daughter was jumpy as a cat on a hot tin roof.

'Mmm.' Matteo smacked his lips together appreciatively. 'This pasta is very good, signora. *Buonissimo.*'

And it was true – the *orecchiette* (literally 'little ears') – with *ricotta forte* and fresh tomatoes was soft, thin and perfectly shaped. It was a simple pasta, made with just durum wheat and water – no eggs – and even Lara had managed some.

'Oh, Matteo. You make me feel ancient. *Per favore*. Please call me Rose.' She smiled back at him.

But was there an edge of panic to that smile? Lara wondered.

'*Va bene*. Rose then. I am very grateful to you all for inviting me.' And he gave them a little nod, almost a bow.

'Can I offer you a top-up, young sir?' Federico, in jovial mood, splashed more wine into Matteo's glass and then pushed the bottle towards Rose's end of the table so that she could help the others.

Matteo held up a hand, though much too late. 'I am driving. Which is a shame as the wine also is very good.' He beamed at Federico.

'It is, is it not? A Mandurian Primitivo. Very powerful.' He held up a fist and flexed his biceps, with a guffaw at his own jesting.

'One of my favourites,' Matteo said sadly.

Federico gave an expansive shrug. 'Then stay the night, why not?'

Lara caught the look that passed swiftly between Bea and Matteo. She suppressed a chuckle. Of course they were sleeping together. Why wouldn't they? They were in love, this was 2018, it was perfectly natural and she for one harboured no objection.

'*Sì*, why not?' Though Rose cast a glance of surprise her husband's way. Lara too was surprised. Federico seemed to have transformed from overprotective parent into broad-minded liberal overnight.

'We have an empty *trullo* tonight, do we not?' Federico continued. 'So, drink up, my boy.'

Clearly then her son-in-law had not had a personality transplant after all. Lara gave a little shake of the head. She knew what was coming next.

125

'But you know it is ready for the next guests,' Rose remonstrated.

Fair enough. She was the one who had to prepare the rooms.

'*Allora*. Where else then?' Federico spread his hands. 'There are no other spare rooms.' His brow darkened as he caught the drift of everyone else's way of thinking.

'It is fine, really.' Matteo pushed his glass away, though with evident reluctance. 'I do not want to put anyone to any trouble. I will drive back home. *Non importa.*'

'But we have the room in the *trullo*.' Federico had the bit between his teeth and his mood had shifted. He had never been an angry man, but like many Italians in Lara's experience, he was volatile and his emotions ran close to the surface. 'Is it so much of a problem, Rose? I will help you change the sheets in the morning if you like?'

Rose flushed.

Lara felt for her, she really did. Federico didn't mean to be unkind; he simply did not understand. It wasn't only a question of changing the bedding. There would be a lot more work. Federico was usually *simpatico* but now he didn't seem aware that he and Rose could be heading for another row. Lara had noted how quickly the level of wine in his glass was going down.

He certainly looked defiant as he pushed Matteo's wine glass back towards him. 'Really,' he said. 'It is not a problem. We Romanos have always been hospitable, and we always will be.'

Abruptly, Rose got to her feet to clear the dishes.

Lara could not deny the Romanos' hospitality – it was legendary. Hadn't they taken her in all those years ago? Hadn't Federico's mamma and papà provided them with food, lodging, work when they had nothing? She leant closer to Bea who was on her right. 'Perhaps Matteo could simply *pretend* to sleep in the *trullo*?' she suggested in a whisper intended for her granddaughter's ear alone.

Bea spluttered into laughter. Her father shot her a suspicious glance but before he could say anything, Matteo changed the subject in that slick way he had. *Smooth way*, Lara chided herself; she was too critical, just as protective of Bea as Bea's father was, in her own fashion. Anyway, the subject was closed. Matteo was staying the night and hopefully, the *trullo* would remain pristine and ready for the next guests.

Rose began to dish out the main, her signature dish of baked lamb layered with potatoes, tomatoes and parmesan, flavoured with garlic, bay leaves and rosemary and cooked very slowly in the oven. The fragrance of the herbs and the meat filled the kitchen where they were all eating at the big farmhouse table by the window. Lara knew that Rose had been worrying that this dinner could not possibly compare with the food Matteo would be accustomed to – as prepared by his father, head chef of Ristorante Leone in Polignano. But she had no need – Rose had excelled herself this time.

'*Grazie*.' Federico put a gentle hand on Rose's arm as she served his food. 'But, *cara*, I meant to ask you before. Who was it that visited this morning?'

Rose visibly blanched and a fork she'd been holding clattered onto the table. 'What?' She pulled her arm away. 'I do not remember a visitor.'

'Ah, yes.' Lara entered the conversation and they all turned to look at her.

'Mamma?'

'The man on the scooter, do you mean?' Lara asked innocently. She had seen him. He had talked to Rose for several minutes outside the front door and then ridden off. Lara hadn't much liked the look of him. Was he a salesman perhaps? But would a salesman be riding a scooter? Probably not.

'A scooter, sì.' Federico nodded. 'One of the men mentioned it.'

'Oh, yes.' Rose seemed very flustered again. 'Him. He was looking for work.'

'Why did you not send him to me?' Federico took another slug of wine.

'I knew you were not looking for anyone right now, Fedi,' Rose replied. 'And you were busy.' She shrugged. 'So, I told him, no.'

'I can usually find some work for the right man,' Federico said. There was a discernible note of challenge in his voice.

'Perhaps Rose didn't think he was the right man.' Lara hadn't intended to intervene again but Rose seemed to need help and if she couldn't help her own daughter . . .

'Exactly.' Rose threw her a grateful look and Lara was glad she'd spoken up. 'There was something about him . . .'

'You cannot be too careful with casual workers.' Matteo joined in now.

'You are right there.' Federico relaxed and tucked into his lamb. 'Mmm.' He smiled at Rose. 'Excellent, my love.'

'We take on extra staff during the summer,' Matteo went on. 'They claim to have experience, but . . .' – he made a gesture, a baffled shrug – '. . . often they have no clue about customer service, which is an important part of the dining experience.'

'Sì,' Federico agreed. 'Naturally so.'

Lara thought back to the early days when she had first arrived here in Puglia, and discovered the reverence in which olive groves and the olive oil they produced were held. Especially here in the Valle d'Itria – a valley of limestone dominated by the silvery-green foliage of the olive tree and red-clay soil, some trees so gnarled and ancient it was hard to comprehend. They grew so well here; Federico often boasted that Puglia had over sixty million trees and produced more olive oil than any other region of Italy. During the poverty of wartime, it was the olives as well as the tomatoes and wheat, also part of their agricultural economy, that had kept many families from starvation.

Coming from England so soon after the end of the war, Lara had never tasted olive oil before – a fact which came as a shock to the Romanos. For them, the bread they baked and the olives they harvested were integral to every meal.

Lara remembered her first taste – mopping up the golden liquid with a piece of bread, her senses truly blown by the simplicity, the layers of flavour. The oil was bitter and yet grassy; it held salt, pepper and something smoky that she couldn't place. It was as fresh as an apple but silky on the tongue with an aromatic aftertaste. Lara was immediately hooked. And that was a good thing – because the olives were to become her livelihood too.

Shortly after, Rose brought in dessert, a *pasticciotto*. It was a crowd-pleaser, the recipe passed down by Eleanora Romano to her daughter-in-law. The outside appeared to be a flaky crust. But when you took a bite, there was the surprise – a creamy custard filling, made even sweeter with black cherries. Lara thought that she might manage just a little.

Federico produced a dessert wine that he'd been saving for a special occasion, he told them.

'And *certo*, this is a special occasion.' Matteo raised his glass. '*Grazie mille* – to all of you.'

'*Prego!*' They all joined in the toast. Lara realised at this point that both Federico and Matteo were quite drunk. This was unusual for her son-in-law, though she had no idea about Matteo. She just hoped that he would be able to find Bea's room tonight without making too much noise on the way.

'Though perhaps we must start persuading Beatrice to dress for a special occasion when that occasion demands it.'

A small silence greeted Matteo's words. Rose glanced at him in astonishment, Federico seemed confused and Bea merely looked down at her empty dessert plate. Surely, he was joking, thought Lara. Why hadn't her granddaughter simply laughed it off? Lara frowned.

'Bea looks beautiful,' she said, aware that she was intervening yet again. 'Just as she always does.' Under the table, she searched for her granddaughter's hand and gave it a squeeze.

'Of course you are right.' Matteo laughed as if it had all been a joke and Federico laughed with him now, clearly relieved.

'I was working late,' Bea said.

For the first time, Lara noticed that although she and Rose were wearing dresses, Matteo was looking rather dapper in dark jacket and trousers and even Federico looked smarter than usual, Bea wore jeans and a simple silk top. She still looked lovely, though.

'I guessed that, *cara*, when I saw the leaf in your hair.' Matteo leant forward and brushed it away.

Bea smiled.

'You want the girl, you get the gardener,' Lara said, quite sharply she realised, as they all turned to look at her again.

'*Sì*. I understand that, signora. And I am very proud of her.' Matteo was all smiles again. He leant closer to Bea. 'It is because I am so proud of you, my love,' he said, 'that I want you to shine.'

130

Then perhaps she is not the right girl for you after all. Lara didn't say this aloud, though. She just squeezed Bea's hand again.

'It is okay, Nonna,' Bea said softly. 'Do not worry. He is only teasing.'

But Lara did worry. It was the tone of his voice. It had taken her back to another life, another man, but with the same tone of voice. Perhaps she was being oversensitive. Perhaps she was even imagining it? But she didn't think so. Matteo had consumed rather a lot of wine, this was true, but sometimes that was the point at which a man, or a woman, might show their true colours, reveal what they could be capable of.

What could she do? What should she do?

As she got ready for bed a short while later, it was Dorset that was on Lara's mind. The house, the garden . . . how it all must be settled. And then she thought of Bea. Perhaps, she thought, there was a way after all.

CHAPTER 15

Lara

Dorset, September 1946

Lara was cycling uphill against the wind, coming home from work, her black handbag in the front basket, the silk scarf knotted under her chin keeping her hair more or less in place, her utility suit jacket fastened as far up as it would go. Around her, the trees and undergrowth knew that it was autumn; the crinkly oak leaves were starting to rust around the edges, the grasses were soft, damp and flailing in the breeze. Clusters of red hawthorn berries and black sloes were beginning to ripen, though the blackberries were already past their best. The scent of autumn – musty and fruity – was in the air.

She was on the outskirts of the village, almost home, when Lara saw a familiar figure walking along the verge towards her. Alice! She braked sharply and put her foot down to steady herself.

'Hello, Alice.' They had been close once, but hadn't seen each other for quite a while. Lara tried to remember when it had been. Her mother's funeral perhaps? Time had been blurred for so very long.

'Hello, Lara.' Alice was cool. She swapped her handbag to her other arm. She looked rather dolled-up with her immaculate make-up and not a hair out of place, wearing a pencil skirt and bolero jacket that accentuated her slim figure, a frilled blouse with a square neckline and cream peep-toe shoes. In comparison, in her work-day suit and plain white blouse, Lara felt a complete frump.

'How are you, Alice?' Lara recalled how they had linked arms and talked about school, about boys, about what they would do next weekend if they got the chance to go out, maybe into Bridport together. But now . . .

'I'm well enough.' Alice shrugged.

'I didn't realise you were still around,' Lara said. Since the end of the war, so many people seemed to have moved away. 'I'm sorry we lost touch.'

'Me too.' Alice seemed to soften slightly. Her red lips parted in that way Lara remembered when she was on to a juicy piece of gossip. 'I heard you got married. It was a bit of a surprise, I must say.' She shot her a rather arch look.

Lara felt a surge of shame. Charles hadn't wanted a big ceremony and neither had she, not really. And how could they anyway, with rationing still in place?

'We'll keep it small,' he had told her. 'You, me and a witness each. That's all we need. You don't want a church wedding, do you?'

'I suppose not.' Lara wasn't religious, though she'd attended Sunday school as a child and gone to Sunday services with her parents and then just with her mother. It had been one of those reassuring traditions that you kept up; it was part of being in the community. But the thought of walking down the aisle (and who would give her away?) to Charles with half the village watching filled Lara with a faint horror.

His witness was his sister Marjorie looking very prim and proper in her neat hat and gloves with her flat sturdy shoes, thick ankles and pursed lips. Lara's witness was her next-door neighbour Elizabeth, who had been so kind to her mother and to Lara in recent years. Lara would have liked to invite a few friends, but at the same time, she realised she'd let a lot of her friends go, not just Alice. While she'd been caring for her mother, she'd had neither the time nor the energy for socialising.

'Hardly anyone came to the wedding,' Lara told Alice now.

'Why's that?' She wasn't letting Lara off the hook. 'I'd have a bit of a do at least, if it were me.' Alice might be less friendly, but she was as candid as ever.

'It was what we wanted,' Lara told her. This wasn't exactly true; it had been what Charles wanted. For Lara, it had hardly seemed real. Perhaps marrying Charles had been such an act of desperation or gratitude (she hadn't yet decided which) that she hadn't wanted anyone from her old life to witness it. But Lara didn't say any of this. She wasn't close enough to Alice, not any more, to confide further.

'Well, like I say, it was a surprise.' Alice raised a pencilled eyebrow. 'I mean, Charles Fripp, he's a nice enough man, of course, but—'

'He was very good to me,' Lara cut in. 'After Father died. When Ma was poorly. When we were struggling . . .'

A look of pity crept onto Alice's face. She glanced around but the road and verges were empty of people. 'David never made it then?' she whispered. 'I'm so sorry.'

'He didn't, no.' Lara realised that she was gripping the handlebars with so much force that her knuckles were white.

'I assumed so.' Alice shook her blonde head and Lara noted that her hair didn't move at all. 'We lost a lot of our lads,' she said sadly.

'We did.' Lara tried to relax her arms, her shoulders. She tried to remember the last time she'd had this sort of conversation, this kind of normal chat with anyone. Before she was married, she supposed it would have been. Even before that, it had become a rare thing. She passed the occasional word or two with Elizabeth and her daughter Hester, but it was mostly about the garden and Lara tended not to linger; Charles didn't like her to dawdle. At work there was little chance for social chit-chat. It would be different if she was in a typing pool, but in the Savings Bank, she tended to work with either one of the partners or alone.

Alice was eyeing her appraisingly and Lara wondered what she saw.

'I always thought you'd get married first,' she told Lara. 'Of the two of us, I mean.'

'Hmm.' Marriage . . . It had not been what she'd expected at all.

'I'm seeing a lad, though,' Alice informed her. 'Johnny Miller. I met him at work.'

Lara remembered that Alice worked in a typing pool at an office in Dorchester. 'That's nice.' She smiled.

'Maybe we could get together, the four of us,' Alice suggested. 'Go to the pictures or something?'

Lara was gratified. It meant Alice had, at least partially, forgiven her – for not keeping in better touch, for not inviting her to their wedding. But when she tried to imagine a get-together with Charles and Alice's young man Johnny, she failed miserably. 'Yes, why don't we?' she said brightly. She knew why, but it was impossible to explain.

'Or you and I could meet up for tea one day?' Alice's eyes were shining.

'You're happy,' Lara said. 'I'm glad.' And she reached over to squeeze Alice's shoulder.

Alice took hold of her hand, quickly, before Lara could get the distance back, the distance she seemed to need these days, with everybody. She didn't really know why; it was something that had happened, almost without her realising it.

'Are you happy, Lara?' Alice asked.

For a moment, Lara met her clear-eyed gaze, the uncomplicated contemplation of her old friend. Lara missed her. She missed their friendship. She missed giggles and confidences. She missed fun.

'Yes,' she said, a little too loudly. She glanced down at her engagement ring and wedding ring sitting on the third finger of her left hand. The engagement ring was a smooth pearl surrounded by a ring of small diamonds. She wouldn't have chosen a pearl. Didn't a pearl represent tears and sadness to come? 'Yes, I'm very happy,' she reiterated as if she could convince herself.

'Good.' Alice finally released her hand. 'Pretty,' she said, nodding at Lara's ringed finger. 'How about next Saturday then?'

'Next Saturday?' Lara's mind went blank.

'The pictures? Fish and chips after?'

'Oh.' Her thoughts spun. 'I'll have to ask Charles,' she said. 'But I can let you know.'

Alice nodded. 'All right. Drop me a note. I'm still at Mum and Dad's. Same place.'

'I will.'

'I'd better get my skates on.' She grinned. 'See you then.'

'See you.' Lara watched for a moment as Alice sauntered off down the road. She thought of all the things she might have told her – how much she still missed her parents, how much she missed David, how lost she had somehow become. There was a lot she could have told Alice about how her life now was. But she hadn't said a word of it.

Lara checked behind her and set off for home, though oddly it didn't seem so much like home these days. The garden – well, that was different. Joe still helped in the garden, though Lara knew he didn't much like being ordered around by Charles and she guessed he only stayed for Lara's sake. But in the house . . . Shortly after their marriage, Charles had brought in a housekeeper, a woman called Mrs Peacock who cleaned and sometimes cooked for them and who came in most mornings. Lara had tried to be friendly – she knew Charles had done it to help her, out of kindness because she was always tired from work – but Mrs P. wasn't the friendly kind. She rattled around the house with her duster, her rubber gloves, her wax polish. She simpered at Charles whilst although she was polite and deferential towards Lara, she always seemed to be watching her with a critical eye.

Still, it was the price she'd had to pay, Lara reminded herself as she gathered speed once more and the autumn breeze stung her cheeks with the first chill of the changing seasons. Marriage was a compromise and this way she'd kept her promise to her mother and she hadn't had to sell the house. With Joe's help, she spent most of her days off restoring the garden to its former Arts and Crafts glory and by next summer, she hoped the restoration (if not the ongoing gardening work) would be complete.

But she should have invited Alice to her wedding; she had once been her closest friend. Lara remembered the cold little ceremony with a shudder and the small celebratory tea they'd had afterwards, at home, the cake baked by Lara herself and served with some of their own fresh raspberries. Lara had smiled and said the right things, but even on that day, her wedding day, she felt that somewhere inside, something important, some flame perhaps, had been extinguished. What had she done?

On their wedding night, Charles had been gentle when he came to her in bed. Lara wasn't scared of what would happen – she and David had made love in the woods several times that summer before he went away, and she had no regrets about that; she was glad that he had been the first – but she was nervous. Since their engagement, she and Charles had kissed, but not in the same way she and David used to kiss, and that was all they had done. In her true heart of hearts, she still belonged to David. What would it be like, she wondered, making love with another man?

'Don't look so anxious, darling,' said Charles as he climbed into bed. He was wearing green and grey striped pyjamas and for a second, Lara couldn't help but compare the way he looked with the way David had looked in the woods; David's urgency as he had kissed her, his hands pulling at her blouse; the way he ripped off his shirt and stood before her, tanned and lean, his hazel eyes burning with passion.

Lara pushed the disloyal thought away. It was her wedding night. This was her choice. This was her life now.

'I know this is your first time. But I won't hurt you, I promise.'

Lara had tensed. What should she say? She couldn't blame

him for making the assumption. But this was hardly the time to put him right. Only, if she said nothing, would he realise at once that she wasn't the virgin he imagined her to be?

He switched off the light and Lara waited in the darkness. Whatever she did, she mustn't reveal any experience or he would know. She felt a hot blush of shame – for not being a virgin, for not telling him; she should at least have done that. Not that she had any experience, not really. With David it had all happened so swiftly, so naturally; she had just been utterly carried away in the moment.

Charles kissed her on the lips, he nuzzled into her neck a bit and touched her breasts. Lara waited to feel something. He muttered her name, he went to hitch up her nightdress, she helped him and . . . Well, she wasn't sure what happened next. He seemed to be about to go further and then he stopped.

'Charles?' she said.

'Touch me,' he muttered. 'Just touch me, Lara.'

Lara steeled herself to reach out to him. But he wasn't remotely ready, she could tell that much. And then he pulled away. 'Never mind,' he growled.

'Charles?' Was it her fault? 'Sorry,' she whispered. Though she wasn't sure exactly what she was supposed to have done.

'Don't worry,' he said. 'This happens all the time to men. We'll wait till the morning.'

So they had, and it had been much the same story, and it had been much the same since then too, although Charles no longer attempted it as frequently. Sometimes he managed an erection, but he rarely sustained it, and although he didn't blame her in so many words, his disappointment always showed on his face before he turned away. Lara knew that she had somehow failed him. He never wanted to discuss it.

Perhaps it had happened because Lara didn't love him enough?

Charles opened the door as she wheeled the bicycle up the front path. 'You're late,' he said.

'Sorry.' She pulled open the shed door with one hand, balancing her bicycle with the other. Inside the cobwebby interior, she paused and breathed deeply for a moment.

Then she pulled back her shoulders and made her way into the house.

'What happened?' Charles was standing in the kitchen now. He seemed casual, but she felt that he was watching her closely.

'I bumped into Alice.'

'Alice?'

Lara was sure she'd told him about Alice. 'Alice Pearce. She's an old friend of mine. I haven't seen her for ages. It made me realise that—'

'Ah, yes.' He frowned. 'I know the Pearces.'

Lara shrugged off her jacket and hung it on the hook by the door. Seeing Alice had made her feel braver. She decided to ignore his tone. 'She wants us to meet up,' she said. 'With her and her boyfriend, Johnny.'

'Oh, my lord.' He laughed.

'What, Charles?'

'I don't think so,' he said. 'She's not really our kind of person, do you think, Lara, not any more.'

Over the last six months Lara had often wondered why Charles had pursued her so doggedly. It wasn't love, she realised that now. It wasn't his fault, but she didn't believe that Charles had it in him – true passion. So, what was the reason? She was a lot younger than him, yes, that could be a factor. She was middling attractive, at least people had given her compliments

140

in the past, but hardly a beauty. Her fair hair was too frizzy and flyaway, her eyes too grey rather than blue, and her mouth too wide. She didn't have a sparkling personality or a great intellect – though a woman possessing either of these two attributes would probably scare Charles half to death. She didn't credit herself with selflessness or with charisma. What, then?

Was it the house? The status endowed by it? Charles had known she had no money, but did Lara have something he valued more? A certain class maybe? It wasn't something Lara had ever given much thought to, but now that she had done, like a worm, it had wriggled into her head. *Not really our kind of person* . . . That said a lot.

She felt a spark of defiance. 'Alice was always my kind of person. She was my closest friend.' She opened the fridge. Inside, on the middle shelf, squatted a large cottage pie. 'Thank you, Mrs P.,' she muttered.

'You don't sound very grateful, Lara.' Charles's voice was cold.

'Sorry.' She sighed. She was grateful she didn't have to cook, but . . . She supposed it was the sense of no longer being able to make the decisions. Life was easier, but harder too.

'In fact, you seem different today.' He caught at her arm and turned her to face him. 'I don't think this meeting with your old friend Alice has done you any good at all, hmm?'

'It was nice seeing her.' There was something in his manner that made Lara squirm. Seeing Alice had made her feel more normal somehow. But he was right, they couldn't possibly meet up as a foursome – it would never work, though not for the reasons he'd given. And she could hardly invite Alice to the house and subject her to Charles's scrutiny. He was bound to find a long list of things about her that he objected to.

'And I've been thinking . . .' Charles continued as if she hadn't spoken.

She waited.

'That now we're married – you shouldn't be going out to work at all.'

Lara blinked at him. Not go to work? But what would she do all day? Who would she speak to? Who would she ever see? 'But how can we afford for me not to work?' was what she actually said. Where did Charles's money come from anyway – for Mrs Peacock, for the household bills, all of which, including the outstanding amounts, he had paid without comment? How exactly did Charles make his money? When she'd tried to ask, he'd just said, 'Business,' and given her a look that warned her not to ask too many questions. He didn't work away like he used to. He shut himself up in the study to do paperwork, but he never told her exactly what he was doing. She thought of all those black market treats he had obtained during the war. Where had they come from?

'We can afford it, Lara,' he said. 'Trust me.'

'But—'

'You don't have to worry about it.' He sounded exasperated now. He was speaking slowly and emphatically, making her feel about eight years old. He had both his hands on her shoulders and his gaze was locked on to hers. It felt heavy, as if he was squashing her under his fist somehow. 'That's the point. Don't you see? I don't want you to have to worry about anything.' He pulled her in close.

It should feel good, shouldn't it? Ever since her parents' death she had longed to be looked after. But . . . Lara's face felt suffocated against his jacket, which smelt of aniseed and tobacco, though he didn't smoke. *Was* this how it felt not to have to worry about anything? She definitely didn't want to be an eight-year-old girl again.

'I like working,' she said at last in a small voice. Everything about her felt small and diminished right now.

'You like working!' He said this as a joke, as if she'd said something hugely amusing.

'Yes,' she said. 'I do.' It was the independence she'd always wanted, the thing she could do for herself. It meant that she was achieving something for the house and garden; fulfilling her parents' legacy. It gave her some sense of self-worth. Her employers could be stuffy and demanding, complaining if she couldn't keep up with their dictation. But it was something and she didn't want to let it go. She could cycle to work and let her home life drift away down the road behind her quite happily; she could spend the day thinking of other things. It was keeping her sane, she realised with a jump of pure terror. 'I want to carry on working,' she said stubbornly. She knew that many women were happy in their role as housewife, but Lara was young and part of a new generation. It would be different if they had children. But how could she have a baby, when—?

'And I want you to stop,' he said smoothly. 'I'm your husband, Lara. And I want you to stop.'

CHAPTER 16

Rose

Italy, April 2018

Cesare Basso . . .

Rose lay there in the dark. His name filled her head until she was afraid it might burst. Beside her, Federico was snoring lightly, but it wasn't this keeping Rose awake. She was beginning to wonder if she would ever sleep soundly again.

Outside, she could hear the birds celebrating the new dawn. *Would that she felt the same* . . . Perhaps she should get up too – there was little point in just lying here awake, going over everything in her mind. But she didn't want to disturb Federico – not yet – so she stayed put.

Cesare Basso.

It was a name she'd never forget. She'd never forget the boy either and she'd recognised him almost immediately yesterday when she looked out of the window of the *trullo*. He'd always ridden a scooter – but then, so had nearly all the boys. But his swagger when he got off . . . despite everything, that had hardly changed.

Thank goodness Federico hadn't been around at least, and her mother clearly hadn't recognised him. Cesare had never come to the house back then, for obvious reasons. He wasn't the kind of boy you'd take to meet your parents . . . But had she managed to get rid of him? And more importantly, would he come back? She couldn't say for sure.

The moment she recognised him, Rose had left the *trullo* and rushed around past the little white chapel to the back of the house and through to the front door where Cesare Basso was waiting. She paused for a second to catch her breath. She had always known she wasn't free of him. She'd heard he was in prison, convicted on a string of charges of burglary and assault, but she hadn't known how long his sentence was, and in any case, offenders were often let out early for good behaviour or whatever. The fact was that Rose was still haunted by Cesare Basso whether he was in prison or whether a free man. It had only been a matter of time.

She swung open the door. At least she'd had a few vital seconds in which to prepare.

'Rose.' He was smiling. He'd always been an attractive man – that way of walking, those dark confident eyes, the easy smile. And besides, people always said you never forgot your first love; that your feelings for your first lover were imprinted on your soul. It wasn't quite like that for Rose. There was no preparation which would have made her ready to see this man.

'Cesare.' He was older, of course. There were new lines around his mouth and eyes. His skin was paler too – a consequence, she supposed, of years of incarceration. And he was thinner. He'd always been lean and well-muscled, but now he appeared almost gaunt. Still, she'd read the news story when he was convicted; he'd deserved a harsh sentence. He hadn't murdered anyone – that wasn't Cesare's style – but he was capable of violence, she knew that for a fact.

'It has been a while.' His hands had been in his pockets but now he took them out and ran his fingers through his hair in a familiar gesture. His hair was still thick and dark, though now threaded with grey.

Rose knew that she too had changed. She'd grown older, acquired deep frown lines, got aches and pains when she knelt for too long and she had the odd white hair. Sometimes, the girl she had once been seemed so distant that she could be an entirely different person. Rose often wished that she was.

'It has,' she agreed. *But not long enough.* 'What do you want, Cesare?' she asked, since he obviously wanted something.

He grinned. It took her back, that grin. Rose held on more tightly to the front door while the years skipped away.

'Do I have to want something?' he asked. 'Can I not simply call round to ask an old friend how she is doing?'

An old friend . . . 'Not really,' said Rose. She wasn't in the mood to play games. And Federico could appear from the olive grove where he was working at any moment.

Cesare shrugged. '*Allora . . .* So, you married him in the end then, Rose?' Rhetorical question. Cesare knew who this land, this house belonged to.

She remembered what she'd thought when she first met Daniela Basso's older brother. He was a bit rough, a bit wild. But he was compelling. Utterly compelling.

Rose and Federico had always been close – having grown up together they knew each other pretty well. But Federico had made Rose feel stifled. It wasn't his fault. It was just that

146

Federico Romano stood for everything her parents held dear, everything they wanted and expected her to do. He stood for duty, loyalty, tradition – values that to the teenage Rose seemed unutterably tedious. Rose glanced for a moment past Cesare, to the olive grove beyond her mother's Italian garden. That olive grove represented everything about Federico that she'd wanted to reject. Family, tradition, care and resilience.

Cesare Basso, though – he was a rebel. And like his sister Daniela who intimidated a lot of the girls at school but who had singled out Rose for friendship in a manner that had been intensely flattering at the time, Cesare Basso had stood for something different. Cesare represented freedom; he was part of an adult world that Rose wanted to be part of too – a world that rejected laws and conventions. At sixteen, she was bored with her family and school, fed up with being a good girl. So, when Cesare Basso came into her life, she was more than ready for him.

There had been a birthday party. Rose's mother never raised an objection to her going out, so long as she would be safe, and since Federico was going too, no one blinked an eye. It was at a schoolfriend's place and Daniela had brought her brother with her. Later, Rose suspected he'd just given his sister a lift there and then hung around, having nothing better to do that night.

'Let's spice things up a bit,' he'd said. Less than half an hour in and Cesare had upped the volume of the music – the parents of the girl whose party it was had gone out for a few hours to give them some space, so there was no one around to object. Cesare produced a bottle of vodka from his jacket pocket. His dark eyes gleamed and Rose had been pulled to him like a magnet.

Daniela had laughed as she introduced them – she must have

known what her brother was like. They had drunk the vodka and they had danced. Rose was vaguely aware of Federico hanging around nearby but she ignored him. It wasn't as if they were together or anything, he was just a friend, more like a brother as far as Rose was concerned.

'D'you want to have some fun?' Cesare had whispered in her ear.

Rose felt a hot shiver run through her. 'You bet,' she'd whispered back.

When Federico tried to take her home an hour later, Cesare laughed at him and told him to get lost.

'Rose?' Federico stood tall.

And what had Rose done? Nothing, that's what. She just tossed her head and carried on dancing. As far as she was concerned, she'd grown away from Federico Romano. Cesare Basso in his leather jacket and scruffy jeans was so much more appealing. In fact, he was irresistible.

'I did marry him, yes, of course,' Rose replied now. She wouldn't ask Cesare if he was married. First, she didn't want to prolong the conversation and second, she didn't care.

'Surprising.' He rocked back on his heels. 'I had you down as being a bit less . . .' – he paused – '. . . conventional.'

Rose felt herself flush. Damn him. He'd always been able to press the right buttons and he could still get to her, even now. 'I was very young, Cesare,' she reminded him. Sixteen, in fact. Not too young, though, to fall in love.

'Yes, you were.' His laughter was as deep and rich as it had always been. He hadn't had the life sucked out of him in prison then, she found herself thinking. 'And drop dead gorgeous,' he added.

'It was a long time ago,' she snapped. What she hated more

than anything was that she was standing here talking to this man, wishing that she'd put some mascara on this morning and spent more time doing her hair. *Mamma mia . . .* What was wrong with her to think that way?

He cocked his head. 'But you still have it, Rose,' he said. 'That certain something.'

Oh, for goodness' sake. Rose refused to feel flattered. At her age it was something that didn't happen too often. But she didn't want to hear this. It was dangerous, as she knew to her cost, to accept flattery from this man.

'I do not want Federico to see you here,' she said flatly. 'So, tell me the reason for this visit and then perhaps you will be on your way.'

He laughed again at this and she couldn't blame him – she sounded pompous and ridiculous.

'You have done well for yourself.' He narrowed his eyes.

'We work hard.' They had saved, yes, to help Bea get established, but they could hardly be described as wealthy.

'You have a lot.' He made a gesture which encompassed the house, the olive grove and the *trulli*, which he would of course have noted as having been restored and converted to holiday lets.

Rose folded her arms. Should she simply shut the door in his face? She didn't dare.

'The Romanos have always had a lot,' he said darkly. 'And you are one of them now, Rose.'

Rose remembered that old family feud. When her parents had found out she was seeing Cesare Basso and that Daniela Basso was her best friend at school, they'd gone ballistic, especially Papà. Rose had never seen him so angry. *Do you know who he is, Rose? Do you know about the Bassos and the Romanos?*

149

She hadn't, not really. But Papà soon put her right. How, though, was it any of their business? she'd demanded.

'I owe everything to the Romanos.' Papà's face was tight with emotion. 'Everything, Rose.'

But I don't, the teenage Rose had thought. *I don't.*

She had been so callous, arrogant and thoughtless; she could see that now, of course.

'Why are you here, Cesare?' Rose asked again. The sooner she got to the bottom of this, the sooner he might leave. And would he continue to haunt her? Oh yes, she thought. That would never go away.

'It is not easy coming out of prison, Rose,' he said, 'Making a new start. Everyone knowing who you are, what you have done.'

'Perhaps then you should make a new start somewhere else,' she suggested. 'Move away. Go to a place where no one knows what you have done.'

He eyed her appraisingly. 'Good to see you have not lost your spirit, Rose,' he said. 'It always suited you.'

Rose glared at him.

'But the fact is, there are people here who can help me, yes?'

'Oh?' She stiffened.

'Family.' He shrugged.

'*Sì?*' She thought of Daniela. She never saw her any more, of course – that friendship had come to an end a long time ago when Rose came to her senses and broke up with Cesare Basso. But Rose knew Dani still lived in Puglia, that she was married and had kids. The thought of Daniela never bothered her, though – Dani didn't know the half of it.

'And old friends.' He nodded. '*Sì*. Old friends like you.'

'I am not your friend.' She glanced up the driveway. Any

moment and Federico might appear. What would he do? She didn't want to imagine. And more to the point, what might Cesare do – or say? She liked the thought of that even less.

'Ah, so he does not know. I thought as much.' Cesare tapped his nose.

'Know what?' Her fists clenched.

He didn't bother to reply. They both knew what he was talking about only too well.

'Ignorance – it is bliss,' Cesare remarked.

Rose couldn't think of how Federico would react if he knew the truth. Over the years, she'd thought of it many times. Federico would forgive her many things – he already had. But this? She doubted he'd forgive her for this. 'And your point is?'

'I thought you might want to help that old friend,' he said. 'With his new start, I mean.'

'Help how?' Surely even Cesare would not come to her for money?

He sighed. 'Anything you are willing to give an old friend would be a true kindness, Rose. In prison a man misses many things.' There was a wicked gleam in his eyes that she chose to ignore.

'And then you will leave me alone?'

He looked hurt. 'Rose. You underestimate me.'

She doubted that. 'Wait there.'

She ran back into the house to fetch her purse. 'Here.' She thrust some notes at him. 'This is all I have.'

'*Grazie mille.* Thank you, Rose.' He touched an imaginary cap. 'Very kind. But I was thinking perhaps about work?'

'Work? In the olive grove, do you mean? For Federico?'

'Why not?'

Rose shook her head. 'Impossible.' She could give him a host of reasons why not. 'Do not come back, Cesare,' she warned him. 'This is my life now.'

He took a step closer. Rose could smell the scent of him, still familiar after all this time, of leather and sweat. It used to be appealing, in a macho sort of way. But not now. Now, it sickened her to the core. He leant towards her and she could feel his breath on her temple.

'You like it, do you? This life you have?' He made a move to touch her face and she stepped back abruptly.

'Yes,' she said. 'I do.'

Rose shut the door and leant heavily against it, willing him to go away. Her breathing was shallow and her legs felt weak. *After all this time . . .* Which showed, did it not, that you could never relax and imagine that something was over.

Now, Rose got out of bed quietly so as not to wake Federico. She would make coffee, she decided. Had she said enough? Would Cesare now leave her alone or would he play with her, like a cat with a mouse, enjoying her suffering?

Downstairs, she filled the percolator with water and ground coffee. For now, she must go on as before; she must live with it. She gripped on to the counter. She must do her best to pretend that all was well. Seeing Cesare Basso had brought it all back for Rose. But her family . . . they must never know.

CHAPTER 17

Lara

Dorset, April 1947

The winter months had passed slowly. It had been an exceptionally cold February and there had been power cuts because of fuel shortages; the coal that you did buy was likely to be half full of slate and stone and when the snowdrifts thawed earlier this month, there was wholescale flooding. And the rationing went on. It was all so bleak, so thankless. They weren't being bombed, but the country was still suffering, still living in the dark shadow of war.

However, the red and white tulips and cheery daffodils now blooming in the spring garden, the clusters of pale narcissi lining the rustic stone, the creamy climbing magnolia with its thick glossy leaves all seemed to be trying to give Lara a message of optimism. She rested for a moment on the wooden bench. That, at least, had been her mother's intention when she first designed this springtime garden. She had, after all, christened it the Garden of Hope.

Perhaps where there was growth, there would also always be hope. But Lara was struggling to feel it. Since she'd given up work, since she'd all but stopped leaving the house, she could feel herself drawing even more in on herself. She was retreating into a brittle shell, becoming smaller and smaller, diminishing, until some days she wondered how much was left. This garden was still her sanctuary; she spent most of her time here. She didn't much like being in the house, where Charles would usually be working in the study; though the door was kept firmly shut, she could hear his voice, sometimes imperious, other times jovial and whatever mood he was in, it set her on edge. In the mornings Mrs Peacock would be inside too – bustling around cleaning or cooking, practically shooing Lara outside what she clearly considered to be her domain.

And so, outside Lara came, even in the frosty winter months, wrapping herself up against the cold, continuing to work in the garden where there were always jobs to be done. Before the first frosts arrived, she concentrated on the dead-heading and pruning, adding cloches to her winter salad crop to protect it from the weather and pests, and taking the more tender plants into the greenhouse.

After the frosts, she did some digging too – it helped her keep warm and the frosts had broken up the soil structure so she could add a nourishing mulch which Joe had prepared some months before. She divided some of the spring bulbs and the huge clumps of rhubarb and she even planted some garlic. Once the fruit trees had become dormant, she pruned them, taking care to remove dead, diseased and damaged wood.

When it turned really chilly, she worked in the greenhouse which fortunately had its own heating system. She even took the portable wireless in there and listened to *Housewives' Choice*

154

and the *Morning Story*, which helped take her mind off the bleakness of this cold winter, the situation she now found herself in. What should she do? What could she do?

This morning, Lara had checked her apple and pear store as she did regularly, carefully removing any damaged fruit, which she left in the kitchen for Mrs Peacock to stew or make into a pie. And then she moved on to sowing her broad beans and leeks. There weren't as many to feed now the war was over, but old habits died hard. And now, here she was, looking for hope. Because she feared that this walled garden, her precious sanctuary, was in danger of becoming her prison and this thought filled her with dread.

She moved through to the kitchen garden where she'd done her early planting this morning. Her mother had christened it the Nurturing Garden and it had certainly done the job. But as she passed the greenhouse, Lara could see that the Virginia creeper had inched its roots so far into the wall that the mortar was crumbling and the bricks loosening.

'You may be beautiful in the autumn,' Lara told the Virginia creeper sternly, and this was very true, the crimson leaves were a sight to behold, 'but who gave you permission to destroy this wall?' Lara wasn't sure how long it was that she'd been talking to the plants, but it was comforting. It made her feel less alone.

But then she heard a low chuckle from the other side of the wall.

'Certainly not me,' said a disembodied voice. 'But Virginia creepers will always go their own way.'

'They will.' Lara recognised the voice as belonging to her young neighbour Hester. 'But this one needs to hold back a little.' Her mother wouldn't have been at all pleased at the thought of the wall falling down. Lara tugged at the offending tendrils, some of the roots tore away from the brickwork, a bit more, and . . . *Oh, dear.* She'd made matters worse, she realised. She'd now completely dislodged a couple of bricks.

Lara poked at them experimentally and they fell to the ground – on the other side of the wall unfortunately. 'Sorry about that,' she said. 'I hope you weren't in the firing line.'

'No, it's fine.' Hester's face appeared on the other side of the small hole at waist-height that Lara had unwittingly created. 'Do you want them back?' She picked up both bricks and passed them carefully through the narrow window between them.

'Thanks.' Lara put them on the ground. She'd have to mix up a mortar to try and replace them. She had no idea what this entailed, but she could find out.

'How are you?' Hester was still peering at her. She must be fifteen or sixteen by now, Lara realised, a sweet girl, with dark hair and eyes that were – like her mother Elizabeth's eyes – almost black. 'I haven't seen you around for ages.'

Lara sighed. 'I haven't been *out* for ages,' she confessed. 'Apart from here in the garden, that is.' And she wasn't even entirely sure how that state of affairs had come to be.

After their argument about Lara giving up work – because it had soon turned into an argument when Lara told Charles that she wouldn't do it – Charles had stomped around the house in a terrible mood for days. He accused Lara of being ungrateful, he informed her that she was failing to do her wifely duty, and he took to addressing her – when he addressed her at all – in polite tones which chilled her to the bone. Finally, when all else apparently failed and Lara continued to cycle to work every day, muttering, 'It's my decision. I need to work,' under her breath all the way to the office, he accused her of consorting with another man.

'What?' She couldn't believe it. Apart from anything else, when would she have the time?

Charles snorted. 'Why else would you insist on disobeying me?' He was getting very red in the face. 'Why else would you try to attract attention in the way you do? Why else would you dress up, deck yourself out, put on your lipstick and your perfume and leave the house all day, every day, when you know I want you to be here at home with me?'

Dress up? Deck herself out? Lara had looked down at her utility suit which she'd been wearing all through the war and which had certainly seen better days, at her plain white blouse and flat shoes. Yes, she always wore a splash of eau de cologne when she went out, and yes, she always wore lipstick – didn't every woman? – but that didn't mean she was trying to attract attention, nor did it mean she was seeing another man.

'Don't be ridiculous, Charles,' she said.

'What did you call me?' He looked angry now – very angry. He took a step closer.

Lara was suddenly frightened of him, this man, her husband, who had once been so kind. 'I mean that what you're saying is ridic . . .' She tried to backtrack. 'Because I don't dress up, I just have to look smart for the office, you know that.'

'You *said* that I was ridiculous.' His eyes narrowed. He leant towards her. He had his hands in his pockets and she saw his fists clench.

'Please try and stay calm, Charles,' she begged. She was frightened he might collapse; his heart was weak after all.

'Don't tell me to stay calm, Lara,' he snapped.

'But—'

'And don't cross me. Don't even argue with me. I'm fed up

157

with it.' He took another pace towards her. 'I may seem ridiculous to you,' he hissed, 'but I'm still your husband.'

'You're not ridiculous,' she whispered. 'I only meant . . . I'm sorry.'

He reached out and tipped up her chin so that he was staring right into her eyes. It wasn't a gentle touch and his expression showed not a hint of affection or warmth. 'The fact is that you don't behave as a wife should, Lara,' he told her. 'You are a huge disappointment to me.'

She swallowed with some difficulty.

'You don't obey me. You don't even try to please me . . .'

Lara thought of those awful nights in the bedroom. 'I . . .' She faltered. It was true, she supposed. She shouldn't have married him. She clearly wasn't the marrying kind. She wasn't lovable. She wasn't even pretty enough to properly arouse him in bed.

'You don't look after the house,' he continued. 'You don't look after me. You don't even look after your bloody garden.'

Lara flinched. She had never heard him speak like this before. She wouldn't have imagined him capable of it. She had driven him to it, she must have done. Only . . .

'Because, my darling wife, you are never bloody here.' His eyes were bulging now, his grip had tightened and his fingers were pinching her throat. He raised his other hand and for an awful second, she thought that he would strike her. But he let it drop. He relinquished his hold on her and turned away.

They couldn't continue like this. Something had to give. Lara put her hand on her throat where he had held her. She knew what she must do. 'I'll give up work, Charles,' she told him. 'If it's what you want, if we can afford it, then I'll stop.'

'Yes, you will.' He turned to face her. He eyed her

appraisingly. 'I never thought it would be like this, Lara,' he said coldly.

'I'm sorry.' She hung her head. But neither, she thought, had she.

'Why not?' Hester asked now. 'Why don't you go out? Are you ill? Mum thought you might be. She's been worried. She called round a few times in the early days. But Mr Fripp and that housekeeper of yours . . .'

'Mrs Peacock,' Lara supplied. It was a stupid name. But it rather suited her. She strutted around the house as if she owned it.

'Yes, well, they always tell her you don't want to talk to anyone.'

'I see.' Lara hadn't known that, though she wasn't surprised. 'Please apologise to your mother for me, will you, Hester? I had no idea she had called in.' On impulse, she eased away another brick. There was enough of a gap now for a proper face-to-face conversation.

Hester looked very solemn. 'You mean, they don't tell you?' she whispered.

'Exactly.' Lara turned around to check she wasn't being observed, but no one could see her from the house. In the garden, she could always be safe, always alone.

'Are they keeping you prisoner?' Hester's dark eyes were wider than ever. 'Do you need help?'

'Not really.' She made it sound so melodramatic. Lara wondered how she could possibly explain. It wasn't simple and it didn't make sense, even to her. 'I used to work. I used to have friends, but . . .' She thought back to what had happened after she'd done what Charles wanted and given in her notice at the

159

Savings Bank. They were very understanding; they probably all assumed she was pregnant.

At first, bearing Charles's criticisms in mind, she had tried to increase her wifely duties. She'd gone shopping and she'd told Mrs P. that she would be taking over the cooking from now on. But then Charles had told her she was being silly – that there was no point in having a housekeeper if they didn't let her cook for them and that Mrs Peacock's hearty casseroles and crusty pies were too delicious for them not to take advantage of her skills. Charles liked his food, and the food he liked best were the puddings and pies that probably weren't good for him, given his heart problems. As for what Lara herself dished up – he always seemed to find something to criticise.

Lara then offered to go to the shops to buy whatever might be needed for dinner, because at least this was a chance to have a short normalising conversation about the weather with the butcher or Mrs Stone from the post office, but Mrs P. insisted that she had everything under control. Which was, Lara thought, rather the problem in the first place. Mrs P. had the house under her control too, Charles intended to continue looking after the bills and finances and Lara couldn't avoid coming to the conclusion that, as a wife, she was redundant. Joe had already left, fed up with Charles's carping no doubt, and so there was only one thing for Lara to focus on – her mother's Arts and Crafts garden. Charles had no objection to this; Lara supposed that gardening was considered a suitably wifely hobby; the garden was a feminine domain.

She told Hester a bit of the story, but not every detail. It made her feel ashamed – not just of marrying Charles in the first place when she certainly hadn't loved him, but of allowing herself to get into this situation, allowing herself to be so belittled and unvalued, of somehow becoming this small diminished person who felt unworthy and desperate and who couldn't see a way out.

Hester was sympathetic, although Lara guessed she was too young to properly understand. Perhaps she wondered why Lara didn't simply walk out of the front door? Lara had done that in the early days; she'd walked around the village and returned to such a barrage of questions that she hesitated before she contemplated it again. And on the second time . . . Was it her imagination or were people staring at her in a way they'd never stared at her before? Were they reluctant to talk to her? Were they giving her looks of sympathy? Lara tried to hold her head up high but she ended up scuttling back home. She'd never had a huge amount of self-confidence and now, apparently, she had less still. She tried to talk to Charles about it, but he just shrugged and told her that it was her imagination. He said that a lot these days. 'I don't see what the problem is, Lara,' he said. 'You have a lovely home. You really don't need to go out at all.'

'But we can meet now,' Hester said. 'Here at the wall.'

'Yes.' Lara smiled. She felt tears welling up inside. 'Thank you.'

'Mum says your garden is incredible.' Hester was peering past her, craning her neck to see. 'I wish I could see it for myself.'

'I wish that too, Hester.' But Lara couldn't even contemplate how she could manage this – with Hester no doubt deemed unsuitable and Charles and Mrs P. watching her every move. It was true, she thought. Hester had been right. Without even being aware of it, Lara had become a prisoner in her own home.

'Mum said there are seven little gardens all separate from each other, all different.' There was a note of wonder in Hester's voice.

'Yes. You're interested in gardening then?' Lara was surprised.

'Oh, yes. Mum's a herbalist, you see. She knows everything there is to know about plants – their healing qualities, what to put where, and she's taught me everything.' Hester looked proud.

'That's marvellous.' Lara'd had no idea. She realised that she'd only really spoken with Elizabeth when her mother was ill and dying. 'Perhaps that's how our mothers got friendly in the first place.' Though this wall was too high for them to have held conversations over like normal neighbours.

Lara told Hester more about the seven gardens and what they represented, from the Romantic Garden to the Garden of Hope with the spring bulbs, to the Nurturing Garden where they were now, to the Thinking Garden with its white blooms and cool pond, the Rose Garden bursting with scented blooms and finally to the Wild Garden where they still kept a few hens, their Rhode Island Reds. 'The idea is that the more formal areas should be closer to the house, and then the planting becomes more natural and wilder towards the boundaries, blending with the landscape beyond,' she explained. 'The Arts and Crafts idea, that is.'

'But that's six.' Hester frowned.

'Ah, yes. I think the seventh is the orchard,' Lara told her. 'We have Victoria plums, warrior apples for cooking and russets for eating, figs and even pears. But it's part of this Nurturing Garden really. Mother said the seven gardens were the seven levels of spiritual elevation, but I'm not sure what she meant by that, to tell you the truth. A sort of journey through life maybe?' Though she probably got the idea from the Arts and Crafts garden designer Gertrude Jekyll – her mother used to study Gertrude Jekyll's book for hours at a time, Lara recalled. Gertrude Jekyll was a great advocate of harmony in garden and architecture, and she also – according to Lara's mother anyway – encouraged the rediscovery of nature and 'ordinary' cottage-garden plants like hostas, lavender and old-fashioned roses. And they certainly had plenty of them . . .

'I'll ask Mum,' Hester said. 'Will you be here tomorrow? After school – say, four thirty?'

'Yes, I will.' Where else would she be? Lara wondered.

'Good. We'll talk more then.'

Lara watched her dart away and as she did so, she felt a small flame flicker inside her. It was the act of speaking with someone who seemed to want to talk to her, she realised; someone who didn't look at her as though she was losing her marbles, or even with contempt. It was hope after all – the hope of finding a friend.

CHAPTER 18

Bea

Italy, May 2018

Tonight, it was Bea's turn for a sociable evening with Matteo's parents. She had been invited for dinner at their apartment in Polignano on the one day of the week that the restaurant was closed and she wasn't much looking forward to it.

For a start, there was the tricky question of what to wear. This evening was important to Matteo, she knew, and she didn't want to let him down. Bea had already worn the more stylish items in her wardrobe – there weren't many; she'd never had so much use for them before – and would have to resort to the simple but well-cut black dress she had worn on their first date. She smiled as she slipped it over her head. It was elegant, she knew he liked her in it and it had led to their first kiss, so that was all good. Perhaps he would think she'd chosen it as a sign to him that this was an equally special evening; it was the kind of gesture he'd appreciate. She pulled a rueful face. In truth, she'd been so busy with work that she hadn't had time to go clothes shopping as she'd intended. It was a situation she must rectify – and fast. She didn't want Matteo to think of her as some sort of country bumpkin. He liked taking her to fancy places so she should at least try to look glamorous . . .

Different earrings, though, she decided, and the lavender pendant he'd given her – which she now wore most of the time. During the day it nestled under her shirt between her breasts, close to her heart; in the evening it was more on show. Bea loved it – it was delicate and beautiful and she was thankful that Matteo hadn't selected something with more bling. That showed, didn't it, that deep down he knew who Bea was?

On her way out to the car she looked for her grandmother, who she found sitting in her favourite seat by the front window.

'I'm off now, Nonna.' She bent to kiss her lined cheek.

'You smell divine, darling.' Her grandmother closed her eyes for a moment.

'Good.' Bea hadn't forgotten the perfume. She gave a little twirl. 'Will I do?'

Nonna chuckled. '*Certo*, you will do. You have scrubbed up beautifully as always, my love.'

Bea noticed her expression and knew that her grandmother was thinking about what Matteo had said when he came to dinner – about her not making an effort with her appearance. There was nothing wrong with Nonna's memory, that was for sure. 'I want to make a good impression.' She tried not to sound defensive.

'And so you will.' Nonna's countenance was inscrutable now. 'But you know Matteo's parents already, do you not? You have worked for them, after all.'

Bea gently stroked the fuzzy cloud of her grandmother's soft white hair. 'Yes, of course – but in a different capacity, Nonna,' she said. When she was gardening, she could wear what she liked. As Matteo's girlfriend . . . that was very different.

The truth was that Matteo's words that evening had hurt. She knew he hadn't meant to sound critical – in fact, he had apologised many times later that night, blamed the amount he'd had to drink and even voiced a fear that perhaps he didn't mean enough to Bea for her to try harder. She'd told him it wasn't that at all; she'd simply run out of time. And she was surprised that it seemed to matter. Was she being unrealistic to expect Matteo not to care about such things? To see her inner self rather than worrying about what was on the out-side? Perhaps. And he was right. She should have ensured she got back earlier. She must remember that now, she had other responsibilities. She was Matteo's girlfriend. He mattered. She must think not only of herself and her gardens, but of his feelings too.

'Of course. *Allora*. Don't be so worried you forget to have a good time, my love. And report back on the food, if you please. Your mother and I are keen to know if Signore Leone's food is as delicious as his reputation suggests.'

Bea laughed. 'I will.'

When she arrived at the stone steps that led up to the terrace at Polignano, Matteo came down to meet her. He must have been looking out.

'Beatrice, my darling.' He held her at arm's length. 'You look amazing. *Bellissima*.'

'*Grazie*.' Bea sensed that he was nervous and so was she. As she'd indicated to her grandmother earlier, being an employee of the Leones had made her feel uncomfortable about her abrupt change of status to Matteo's girlfriend.

He seemed to sense her unease. 'I want them to love you,' he said fiercely. 'And they will.'

Bea couldn't help smiling. He was very determined. 'Love doesn't always come so fast,' she murmured.

'It did for me.' He put an arm around her shoulders and squeezed her tight.

'And me.' She laughed. But did he expect her to somehow *make* them love her? Bea thought of the way Matteo was with her family. He made it all seem so easy. They did love him, she was sure, except perhaps Nonna who hadn't quite made her mind up yet. *Wise and wary* . . . Bea thought of those old stories about the girl and the garden in Dorset, England. Was that why? Was Nonna trying to teach her something, even back then?

'Come on.' Matteo pulled her up the steps with him.

'*Va bene.* I am coming.' Bea barely had time to admire the look of the restaurant terrace by night, now that the plants were filling out and the terrace strung with tiny fairy lights, other night lamps picking out the focal points of the more structural pieces. It looked good, though, she knew it looked good.

'*Andiamo.* Let us do it. Into the lair we must go. But they are not dragons, honestly, my love. And I have a feeling that they adore you already.'

The dinner was, however, a little awkward. They sat on high-backed white leather chairs at a glass-topped table laid with silver cutlery, an array of condiments and tasteful cream linen napkins rolled in silver rings placed neatly on each gleaming white side plate. The dining room was formally arranged, not conducive to relaxation – or so Bea was finding – and very different from her own family's country kitchen.

Bea looked around her as Signora Leone brought out an impressive array of *antipasti*. The entire room was painted white from floor to ceiling, the effect broken only by two colourful abstracts on the walls and a glass chandelier, while the stone floor was naturally of limestone. The overall effect was very tasteful, when viewed from her designer's eye, but also rather cold, she thought. As for the signora herself – she was polite and friendly, but Bea sensed Matteo's mother was still sizing her up. How did she score? she wondered. She was glad she was driving and therefore not drinking; she needed all her wits about her this evening.

She tried to remember each course so that she could report back. Surprisingly, though, Matteo's father was not cooking.

'It is my day off,' he told Bea. 'And you know, Matteo's mother was an excellent cook when I first met her, as she still is today.'

The signora brushed away the praise, but it was true. The aubergines, peppers and zucchini were charred to exactly the right degree and yet still had the perfect bite, and the bowl of fava bean purée had been paired wonderfully with *cicorie*, bitter green wild chicory, one of the most popular vegetables in Puglia. The dark *orecchiette* made with black durum wheat was served with a fresh tomato sauce and *caciocavallo* cheese and the pasta was *al dente*. Everything was delicious – though perhaps not quite up to the high standard of her own mother's cooking, Bea thought loyally. Maybe her mother put more love into the food.

'You never wanted to take the position of chef yourself then, signora?' Bea hoped she wasn't touching any raw nerve.

'Oh, no.' The signora laughed. 'I do not have the temperament, as Matteo will tell you.'

Bea looked across at Matteo enquiringly.

He gave a little shrug. 'My mother, she prefers the management side of things,' he said.

'What he means is that I am bossy.' The signora swept the plates away with a practised hand. 'But in fact, I am a perfectionist.'

'Which is a good quality for a chef to possess, no?' Matteo's father drawled from his seat at the head of the table.

Bea hadn't talked to him very much, before now. Matteo had told her that he liked ordering people around, and that this was what had put Matteo off working under his father in *la cucina*, but to Bea, the signore didn't seem too intimidating and after all, in the kitchen someone had to be in charge.

'It depends on the extent of the perfection,' the signora replied with a toss of her head. 'One has to know when to stop, especially when there are diners waiting.'

Signore Leone rolled his eyes at Bea. 'Perfect is perfect,' he said. 'But it is true that very little would stop my wonderful wife striving for perfection.'

And although they all laughed at this, Bea wondered just how perfect Matteo's mamma expected his girlfriend to be.

'What about you, Beatrice?' the signora asked as they began tucking into the main course – a complex array of seafood that would certainly make its mark, Bea found herself thinking, on the pristine linen napkins.

'Me?' She stifled the feeling of dismay. She was about to be interrogated, she knew.

'You are a talented garden designer.' With an elegantly manicured red fingernail, the signora sliced into the shell of a langoustine.

Bea flinched. '*Grazie.*'

169

'*Prego.* But do you intend to do that all your life?'

'Mamma.' Matteo cut in. 'How can Beatrice possibly know what she is going to do for the rest of her life?'

'Oh, but I do know.' Bea took a sip of her sparkling water. She must stay calm. But Matteo's mother had spoken as if her business was not important, and this rankled. 'I cannot imagine myself ever giving it up. I love it so much, you see.'

There was a small silence. Had she made some sort of gaffe? Bea didn't much care if she had. What were they expecting? She was only telling the truth. And she couldn't see any point in building up a business if you planned to give it up any time soon.

Matteo, however, changed the subject with his usual ease and the awkward moment passed.

After the rest of the meal, which included a pastry dessert, fresh fruit and *burrata* cheese, with a deliciously gooey, creamy inside that oozed onto her plate when Bea cut into it, Bea helped Signora Leone take the plates and cutlery into the kitchen.

'You probably know this already, my dear.' The signora put a hand on Bea's arm. 'But I shall tell you anyway.'

'*Sì?*' Bea wasn't sure where to put the plates. Every surface was covered with the remains of the food preparation.

'My son – he is very headstrong.'

'Well . . .' Bea wouldn't have put it quite like that, but she thought she knew what the signora meant. Matteo certainly had a forceful personality, but Bea loved that. It was what made being with him so exciting.

'Sometimes,' the signora confided, 'he needs to be held back, made to be more cautious.'

Bea was surprised. 'I would not hold him back,' she said

170

quickly. She wasn't sure if this was the response Matteo's mother was hoping for, but it was, at any rate, how she felt.

'And the restaurant . . .' The signora shot her a sharp look. 'It means a lot to us all.'

'But of course.'

'It is a family business, you see.'

Bea flinched at the steeliness in the signora's eyes. 'Yes, signora,' she said. 'I understand.'

But Bea didn't know exactly what Signora Leone was trying to tell her. Had she failed the test – if it even was one? She wouldn't hold Matteo back, it was true. And she appreciated how much the restaurant meant to the family – hadn't she grown up in the shadow of a family business herself? But nevertheless, this relationship was moving very fast, a bit like the roundabout in a children's playground when the older children were pushing it and someone smaller and younger was clinging on for dear life. Did she want to get off? No. Because although she wasn't sure where it was going, and although she was both terrified and exhilarated at the same time, this ride was giving her more of a thrill than she'd ever known.

After Bea had been assured that no further help was required to clear up, after she'd thanked Matteo's parents profusely and said her goodbyes, he accompanied her down the steps and back to her car, parked just outside the Ponte Vecchio.

'I wish you could stay, *cara*,' he said as they made their way down the narrow streets.

'Me too. But I have an early start in the morning, remember?' Bea giggled as she remembered the *trullo* episode and how Matteo had sneaked out trying not to touch anything, so as not to upset Bea's mother, and then tried to get to Bea's room silently, so as not to upset her father. They'd made love almost silently too, which in a way had made it even more urgent, even more electrifying than usual. And Bea had the foresight to set the alarm on her phone for the morning, so that Matteo could return to the *trullo* and make an unobtrusive escape before anyone else got up.

'And was it so bad?' He slung an arm around her shoulders as they crossed the piazza. It was quite late by now but the bars and restaurants in the square were still buzzing with the sounds of chatting and laughter over that final glass of wine or *digestivo*.

'No, of course not,' Bea reassured him. 'It was a lovely evening.' Because what else could she possibly say?

He squeezed her shoulder. 'Did I not tell you it would be?'

'*Sì.*' She laughed and wound her arm around his waist as they walked on out of the *centro storico* and towards her car.

'Thank you, my love.' When they got to the car, Matteo pulled her close.

'What for?' She nestled closer into his arms.

'For being beautiful. For being you. For answering all Mamma's questions.'

They both laughed and then the laughter changed and they were kissing; long sweet kisses that Bea could drown in. She caught her breath and managed to disentangle herself from his arms. There were very few people around at this moment, but even so . . .

'I must go,' she said. 'Your mother's probably timing our goodbye.'

And although Matteo laughed again at this, it wasn't quite as convincing as before. While he poked fun at his mother, Bea concluded, she had better be careful not to do too much of it herself.

On the way back home, Bea had more time to think about

the evening. It had been a glimpse into another world, a world that she sensed she could be part of. But what had Signora Leone meant when she'd talked about holding Matteo back? As if Bea had any chance of doing that . . . And what compromises would Bea have to make if she were to become part of this world which the Leones inhabited? Could she do that and still be true to herself? She was not entirely sure.

CHAPTER 19

Lara

Dorset, April 1947

The next day, Lara was pottering in the kitchen garden, giving the earth a gentle hoe between the rows of spring salad, when she heard a noise on the other side of the wall. Hester? She made her way over.

'Lara? Psst!' Sure enough, her young neighbour's face was visible through the makeshift window in the wall. Lara couldn't help but smile. Hester looked excited. Lara guessed that in some way she was enjoying this adventure.

'Yes, I'm here.' She moved closer, pleased that Hester hadn't forgotten their assignation. It made her feel more substantial, more real.

'I've found out some stuff about your seventh garden from Mum,' Hester told her.

'Really?' Lara was curious. 'About the seven levels of spirituality, do you mean?'

'Mmm. It seems that seven is an awfully significant number in all sorts of ways.'

Lara considered. 'The seven days of creation?'

'Yes.' Hester nodded eagerly. 'The seven wonders of the world. There are seven oceans and seven continents. And Mum says it's important in folklore too – you know, the seventh son of a seventh son and all that.'

'I see.' Lara frowned. 'But how does that relate to the garden?'

'I'm not sure.' Hester leant closer. 'But Mum said the seventh garden is hard to find. And that when you've found it, well, it might not be immediately clear what to do with it.'

'Hard to find?' Did that mean the seventh garden wasn't the orchard at all? And how could you not know what to do with a garden? It was so intriguing. How could a seventh garden possibly exist without Lara being aware of it? She knew the entire garden so well – she had grown up with it and these days she spent most of her time here. Lara pondered. All the gardens except the Wild Garden led off from the main path which began with an avenue of hollyhocks, continued with iris, lupins, agapanthus and achillea and ended in a dense yew hedge. From the Rose Garden, the Wild Garden could be accessed via a small yew tunnel.

At the far end of the Wild Garden was the stout wooden gate which led to the woodland beyond. When Lara was a child, she'd learnt how to open it and slip out into the woods and so her mother had a lock fitted – at first to keep her daughter safely inside and then to keep intruders out. The key had always been there, on the inside, rusty and difficult to turn.

When Lara first met David, when their relationship became so intense, so passionate, she had arranged to meet him, on several occasions that summertime, in the woods beyond the gate.

175

It was perfect. She would run soundlessly barefoot down the winding stairs in her nightdress and robe, put on her shoes at the French doors and scoot down the mossy steps from the veranda, and along the central pathway past the hollyhocks to the Rose Garden. Feeling almost drunk on the heady perfume, she would duck through the yew tunnel to the Wild Garden. She'd skip through the poppies, daisies and cornflowers waving in the night breeze and she would open the gate with the rusty key.

On the other side, David would be waiting. He would take her in his arms and kiss her with a longing that told her everything she needed to know. He would lay a blanket on the woodland ground under the spread of the nearby horse chestnut tree and they would make love under the moon and the stars, the scent of the woodland sinking deep into her.

'I can't believe you're mine,' David would whisper, and Lara knew that he was thinking of the gap he perceived between them — him a farm labourer on a tenanted farm earning less than two pounds a week and having to do extra contract mowing during the hay-making season just to make ends meet; Lara living in what must seem like such a grand house. Little did he know how hard times really were.

'I am yours,' she would assure him. 'Forever yours.'

Lara knew that she shouldn't take the risk, though they tried to be careful. But she couldn't help herself. She couldn't control the waves of desire that swept over her at his touch and, besides, she didn't want to control them when soon he would be gone.

Later, all too aware that David's day would begin before six in the morning, Lara would slip back through the gate, turn the key and return to her room, with her parents still sleeping soundly and no one any the wiser. She was seventeen and they were intoxicating times. Times that now, she could hardly bear to recall.

But some months ago, when Lara had gone down to the end of the garden one day, soon after she'd left the Savings Bank, just wanting to take a walk in the woods that reminded her so much of David, the gate had been locked and the key nowhere to be found. She'd asked Mrs Peacock – their housekeeper seemed to know everything that was going on, after all – and when she'd looked blank and said, 'What gate would that be, Mrs Fripp?' Lara had asked Charles.

'I have no idea where the key is, Lara,' he'd said. 'But why do you need it?'

'I wanted to walk in the woods,' she told him, though saying the words out loud sounded childish even to her own ears.

Charles gave a little laugh that confirmed this. 'It's not safe to walk alone in the woods,' he said. 'So perhaps it's no bad thing that the key has gone.'

And that was the end of that.

But it was a doorway, Lara thought; an opening, a route to the outside world. And it seemed another way out that was now closed to her.

'Mum said that your mother believed the spiritual elevations were all about a quest for a simple life,' Hester said. 'A return to innocence. Being at one with nature, you know?'

'That makes sense.' It was an Arts and Crafts ideal after all. But it was ironic. Lara spent much of her time being at one with nature and yet her life was far from simple.

'And she's sure that if you think about the seventh garden a bit more, then you'll find it.' Hester leant still closer to the gap in the wall. 'Oh, she also mentioned woodland and water. I think that's a clue.'

'Thank you, Hester.' Lara stood upright. If there was a different seventh garden, a hidden garden, perhaps some sort of secret garden, then she needed to find it.

'But she also said you should be careful,' Hester warned. 'Everything might not be what it seems.'

Hmm. What did Elizabeth mean by that? And why hadn't Lara's mother ever mentioned a hidden garden?

'Will you tell me tomorrow – what you find?' Hester asked her.

'I will.' Lara smiled at her enthusiasm. 'And please, thank your mother too.'

'Oh, yes.' Hester's face clouded. 'She would like to come down to speak to you herself, but . . .'

'She's not well?' Lara felt awful. Elizabeth had been so kind when her mother was sick and yet Lara had been so full of her own concerns that she had barely asked after her.

'She hasn't been herself for a few weeks,' Hester admitted. 'She hasn't had much energy. She broke her ankle a while back and she hasn't really got going again since.'

'Has she seen a doctor?' Lara remembered Elizabeth as being full of energy, so something must be amiss.

'Yes, but he doesn't know what's wrong and Mum, she doesn't have much faith in doctors, you know, so . . .'

'You're treating her with herbs?' Lara guessed. She remembered that Hester had said Elizabeth was a herbalist.

'Yes.' Hester gave a little shrug. 'It's our way.'

Lara was thoughtful as she walked out of the Nurturing Garden and down the central avenue. Most of the bedding plants weren't in flower yet, but she could see them all in her mind's eye: the hollyhocks, irises and lupins. Lara ducked through the archway into the Rose Garden. Some of the early roses were flowering, though, their sweet scent filling the air. That was the thing about a garden, she thought. In every season, there was so much ahead, so much to look forward to.

She took the pathway through the yew tunnel to the Wild Garden where the hens were scratching about in the stone and gravel. Lara came here every day to feed them and to collect the precious eggs. She must give some to Hester, she thought, ask her if there was anything Lara could do to help.

Lara stood still for a moment, aware of the rustling and clucking of the hens. She scanned the area of ground, up to the locked gate and the ribbed vines of the old lilac wisteria.

Woodland, Hester had said. But the woodland was on the other side. Still . . . It was almost as if something was missing. On the left-hand side of the Wild Garden the unruly bank of grasses and tall bamboo was so high that the side wall was no longer visible beyond, and in fact, Lara had never seen it. This started her thinking . . . She'd left the grasses – she tended to leave everything in the Wild Garden; that was the idea, her mother had always said, to leave it to grow as nature intended, because nature was not and should not be subject to human control. The Wild Garden, so close to the boundary of the natural woodland beyond, should remain a haven for insects and wildlife. And for the hens, of course.

But the grass bank must go back an awfully long way . . . Because this part of the garden surely wasn't quite wide enough? She put her head to one side and considered the dimensions. She hadn't seen it before. But something wasn't right. She went up to the feathery grass and bamboo and cautiously moved some aside. Nothing. It was thick as a forest. She did the same all the way along the bank and then she saw something. A piece of stone paving. Her breath caught. Some sort of stone pathway had definitely been laid here among the tall, whispering grasses. If only they could really speak. If only they could point her in the right direction. But perhaps she'd found it anyway . . .

She pushed the grasses aside and stepped onto the stone paving. Every time she moved forwards, the rustling grass and thick curtain of bamboo closed up behind her as if letting her through but keeping their secret. After a few yards, the pathway opened out into a small square surrounded by the grasses on the side from which Lara had emerged, the yew hedge to the left fronted by a few tired hydrangea bushes, and in front of her and to the right-hand side, the garden wall.

This garden, if it could even be called such, was unkempt, but different from the Wild Garden. It was more sheltered by the woodland and the wall – only a little fractured sunlight filtered through the trees. A small stream trickled off and under the wall into the wood beyond and she spotted the grey-green leaves of some foxgloves. There was another tall plant she couldn't identify, at least until it flowered – a bush with pale green pointy leaves that she suspected to be some kind of nightshade and the distinctive spike of an early purple orchid. By the stream was a plant with leaves a bit like parsley . . . and in the shade by the wall were lily of the valley, some still in bud, a few tiny bell-like flowers already open and giving off a honeyed green scent that was like the essence of spring itself. But Lara had never liked lily of the valley – their fragrance was too cloying, especially here where the air itself smelt dank and mysterious.

The clucking of the hens was muffled by the grasses that

separated the gardens. Even the hens hadn't found this place . . . 'A secret garden,' Lara whispered. So she had found the seventh garden at last. Hard to find, it certainly was. But Hester had said something else — that it wouldn't be immediately clear what to do with it. And that everything might not be what it seemed. Which was very confusing . . .

Lara walked slowly around, breathing in the atmosphere. Undeniably, this tiny garden provided privacy. When Lara was here, no one would know where she was, no one would be able to find her. She spun slowly around and hugged it to herself, that thrill of discovery. A secret garden. A place where she could always be safe.

CHAPTER 20

Rose

Italy, May 2018

Rose, Federico and Lara were having coffee with Bruno and Sabrina Romano in their house on the other side of the olive grove, the house in which Federico had grown up. Federico still worked closely with his cousin Bruno. Although Federico was an only child – Eleanora and Augustine had been sadly unable to have more – the Romano family remained huge, at least in Rose's eyes. Augustine Romano was one of six siblings and Eleanora one of four; hence Federico had numerous aunts, uncles and cousins. Almost too many to keep track of, Rose thought with a pang of all too familiar regret.

As usual, the two men were discussing olives. They'd begun with current weather conditions, moved on to the ailments of individual trees and were now deep into the subject of soil and nutrients. Sabrina on the other hand was toying with the idea of introducing tourist tours of the olive grove and olive oil production process. Somebody she knew was already giving talks and tours in Martina Franca on this very subject and another *masseria* in Ostuni had begun doing the same. It would bring in a good bit of extra income, Sabrina informed them.

'Do tourists really want so much detail about how the olives are grown?' Rose mused. Those guests she'd had staying in the *trulli* liked to peek inside the chapel and admire the faded fresco on the wall, the simple cross, the old flagstones. They liked to look at the olive trees, take pictures and certainly eat the olives and taste the oil with freshly baked bread as they sipped their first glass of chilled white wine of the evening, but she wasn't sure their interest went much further. She drank the final dregs of her coffee and sighed. She should get back. There was supper to prepare.

'*Sì*. Apparently so. These people, they want to know everything about our region,' Sabrina said proudly.

'Hmm.' Rose remained sceptical. How long would it be, she wondered, before the novelty waned and they moved on?

'Who would do the tours?' Rose's mother asked, casting a concerned glance Rose's way. Well now, she needn't be concerned about that. Sabrina had already broached the subject once or twice before, since Rose spoke fluent English and was therefore the obvious candidate. Rose's parents were both English, after all, and Rose was already in the tourism business – at least to some degree.

'You know that I have already told Sabrina I do not have the time,' she told her mother. She put down her coffee cup.

'What about Bruno?' Rose's mother asked doubtfully.

Sabrina burst out laughing. 'Him? Do you think he would have the patience? No, no. And he cannot speak English for another thing.'

'Who says I cannot speak English?' Bruno turned to them, visibly bristling.

Sabrina ignored him. 'Marcelo might do it.' She named one of her sons. 'He speaks English and even a little German, you know.'

Rose's mobile pinged with an incoming text. '*Mi scusi.* Excuse me.' She pulled it from her pocket. She was so jumpy these days.

It was an unknown number. *I think we should meet. How about it? C*

Mio Dio. Rose felt sick. She'd dreaded that she hadn't heard the end of this. But what more did he want from her?

'Rose?' Her mother didn't miss a thing. '*Va bene?* Are you all right, darling?'

'Oh, yes, I am fine, Mamma.' She forced out the words. 'But we must be getting back home, you know.' She turned to Sabrina. 'Sorry, Sabrina, but we should be going. You know there is supper to cook and the laundry – it will not sort itself.'

Sabrina waved away her apology. 'I know. I know. Please do not worry. There is always some chore waiting for us, no?' She got to her feet. 'Now, please take some of these little cakes I made. I will put them in a container. I want Bea to try them.' She rattled on.

She was so kind, thought Rose. They were all so kind. *And now this . . .*

How had Cesare Basso got her number? Through a mutual friend perhaps? She couldn't think of anyone she was still in touch with, though. Rose thought back to that awful visit the other day. She'd left Cesare on the doorstep for a few moments when she ran to fetch her purse. And her mobile . . . She frowned. Could it have been on the hallstand? She often left it there for the best signal. But could he have found her number from her phone in such a short space of time? Was it possible? Rose shuddered. Anything, she realised, was possible.

Another text pinged in. Rose was almost afraid to look at it. She glanced at her mother who was gazing at her with an expression of such acumen in her blue eyes that Rose almost wondered if she knew.

'You're popular, darling.' Her mother smiled.

She couldn't know . . . Rose opened the message. *I could come to your place again?*

Jesus, no. Was that a threat? It certainly sounded like one. Rose panicked. 'Sabrina, could I use the bathroom before we go?'

'Of course, Rose, go ahead.'

Rose half ran into the downstairs cloakroom. Once there, she texted back hurriedly, terrified he might be on his way round here already. *It is impossible for us to meet, Cesare, you must see that. Please leave me alone.*

She waited. Stared into the mirror above the washbasin. She looked the same as always – but her eyes were scared, and no wonder.

Ping. *What are you scared of, Rose?* The text came back immediately.

Rose groaned. It was almost as though he could read her mind. *Nothing*, she wrote. *No one.* If only that were true. Even replying to his texts felt so deceitful, so wrong. What could she say to him to make him leave her be? He knew she was scared and no doubt he was enjoying it – the power he still held over her. Rose was trapped.

'Rose?' Federico was outside the bathroom door. '*Va bene?* Are you okay, my love?'

'Fine,' she called back breezily. But how much worse would it be if Federico knew the truth? 'I will just be a moment.'

185

Yeah, right, the text came back.

Of course he didn't believe her. Cesare was not that stupid.

Another text. *See you around, Rose.*

Rose exhaled slowly. Ran the taps. Washed her hands as if she could wash the thought of Cesare Basso away.

Back home, Rose was about to dish up the supper when Bea came rushing into the kitchen as if on fire.

'Mamma!' she called. Her daughter's face was white and she looked very upset.

'*Cara,* what has happened? Is it a client? Matteo? What?' Rose went to her daughter and put her hands on her shoulders. Bea was trembling. Rose pulled her into her arms. 'There, there, it is all right, my darling.' And then a thought took hold. Surely Bea couldn't have found out – about Cesare Basso, about what her mother had done? Rose felt a pulse of fear.

'It is Matteo's father.' Bea drew back, wide-eyed.

'Sit down.' Rose pulled up a chair. She felt a jolt of guilty relief. But what was she thinking? How low had she sunk? 'What is it?' she asked. 'Is he ill?'

'He had a heart attack, Mamma. Oh, it was terrible. They were all so upset. Matteo was crying . . .' She tailed off.

'But Signore Leone? Is he alive? Is he in hospital?' Rose took a glass and filled it with some water for Bea – she looked as if she was about to faint.

'*Sì.*' Bea took the glass and gulped greedily. 'He is in hospital. It was serious, though, Mamma,' she said. 'It happened in the restaurant kitchen at lunchtime apparently – he got angry with the sous chef and it was hot and then he collapsed and Matteo . . .' Her voice broke.

'Matteo was with him?' Rose could imagine how upsetting that must have been for the boy.

'Yes. He tried to revive him. He called the ambulance and went with him to the hospital. The signora wasn't at home. Matteo called me from the hospital a couple of hours later.'

'The poor family.' Rose's heart went out to them, her own troubles forgotten, at least for the moment. 'But how is he now?'

'He has been in surgery this afternoon,' Bea said. She was clearly exhausted. 'It was touch and go.'

'And you were there with Matteo – at the hospital, I mean?' Bea would have had to be strong for Matteo and the rest of the family. Plus, she'd clearly taken on some of Matteo's emotions. Perhaps, too, she was thinking of her own father and how easily, how suddenly a parent could be taken from you.

'Yes, I was. I wanted to leave when the signora arrived. I mean, I am not part of the family, am I?' She straightened her shoulders. 'But Matteo, he begged me to stay a bit longer.'

Rose nodded. 'Do you know how the signore is now?' she asked cautiously.

'They think he will recover,' said Bea. 'Thank God.'

'That is good.' Rose sat down on the arm of the chair and stroked her daughter's hair. It had been a long time, she realised, since she had done that. 'Then you must not worry, my darling,' she said softly. 'He will get better. The heart attack – it was a warning sign and he must pay heed.'

Bea looked up at her. 'That's what the doctor said. He said that Signore Leone must listen to that warning and make changes to his lifestyle. He must slow down.'

'Absolutely right,' said Rose. But what would that mean to the head chef of a busy restaurant? she wondered. It would be very much easier said than done.

CHAPTER 21

Lara

Dorset, May 1947

It had been raining all morning, so instead of returning to the secret garden as she'd intended to do first thing, on impulse, Lara decided to sort out the kitchen cupboards – they were chock-a-block; there were things in there that probably hadn't been used since her grandmother's day. She'd clear everything out, clean the cupboards and only replace what they still used. *Out with the old*, she thought. It would be an act of cleansing. It might make her feel better.

The ancient three-tier steamer was at the back of the pan cupboard; her mother had only really used it for Christmas puddings, so whenever it appeared, there would always be an air of excitement in the kitchen, not to mention the sweet fragrance of dried fruit and breadcrumbs. Mother would make one pudding for Christmas Day, one for New Year's and one for Easter Sunday. Lara smiled as she touched the thin and rather battered grey aluminium. Should she keep it?

Would there ever be a family here for Christmas – a real family? She squeezed her eyes tightly shut. The image of David appeared, because this was what she had always imagined: Lara, David and a family of their own. How stupid she was. But sometimes it was so hard to be positive. The pudding basins had been family-sized, covered with a square of white muslin and tied with string, and although there had only been the three of them to tuck in to the puddings, as a family unit they had felt complete. But Lara didn't feel part of a family, not any more, and there seemed little chance that this would change.

'Mrs Fripp. Oh, my goodness gracious.' Mrs Peacock stood in the doorway; her hands (still in her yellow rubber gloves, Lara couldn't help noticing) planted on ample hips. 'What in heaven's name are you doing?'

Lara realised that she'd left all the pans and bowls she'd unearthed from the cupboard littered over the kitchen floor. She leant back on her knees. As usual, she was wearing blouse and slacks – she didn't bother much with dresses these days. 'Some spring cleaning,' she replied. 'Half this stuff never gets used.' Surely someone in the village would need it more than they did?

'That's all very well, but we can't have this mess.' Mrs P. bent down and started picking up the saucepans. 'Let me.'

'No, it's fine.' Lara tried to wave her away but Mrs P. was a force to be reckoned with. In her confusion, Lara dropped a saucepan lid and it clattered loudly on the floor.

'Butterfingers.' Mrs Peacock winced. 'And it is not fine, Mrs Fripp, if you don't mind me saying, especially not when I've just this morning cleaned the kitchen floor.' She clicked her tongue.

'Oh, I'm sorry, but I've been remembering how my mother used to . . .' Lara's voice trailed. Did she really want to confide?

'It's not good for you to brood.' Mrs P. lowered her voice and seemed to soften slightly. 'You should be resting.'

'Why should I be resting?' Lara frowned. She wasn't ill.

Mrs P. was looking flustered now. She glanced around as if to check that no one was listening. But who would be? Charles had disappeared off somewhere looking furtive. The two of them were alone. 'What I mean is that you should be out in the fresh air,' she amended. 'Not worrying over pots and pans or anything of that sort. That's my job.'

'I wasn't worrying.' Nevertheless, Lara got to her feet. She supposed she could do it later when Mrs Peacock had gone home, but the pleasure had gone out of it now and the moment had passed. She wasn't even sure she wanted the memories – they were too upsetting, despite the fact that she craved them.

Lara wandered out into the garden where at least no one was continually telling her what to do. The plants looked fresh and green after the rain. She made her way down the central pathway, breathing in the sap and the earthy scents, dipping past the roses and through to the Wild Garden. She approached the tall grasses with caution, took a deep breath, reached out and swept them aside. Her sleeve was damp and droplets of water clung to the fabric of her trousers, but Lara didn't care. She could even feel it on her face – the wetness from the morning's rain and the rough graze of the grasses against her cheek.

During the night, lying awake in the dark, Lara had wondered if she'd imagined the entire thing. Tomorrow, would the secret garden still be there? But now, she stepped forwards, let the tall grass and bamboo close up behind her like a stage curtain – and there it was, the light dimmer than ever today, the little stream trickling out into the woodland beyond the wall, the earth damp, the hydrangeas still covered in droplets of rain, their serrated leaves shivering in the soft breeze. It felt other-worldly. Lara looked around her – at the plants growing in the dappled shade by the water, the brick wall covered in mossy lichen. She lingered for several minutes, breathing in the atmosphere. It felt as if the garden was trying to tell her something. But what, she had no idea.

Later, back in the Nurturing Garden, she was weeding the vegetable patch when she heard Hester's familiar, 'Psst, Lara,' from the other side of the wall.

'Did you find it?' Hester wasn't wasting any time. 'Did you find the secret garden?'

'I did.'

'And did you recognise the plants?' Hester's black eyes gleamed through the makeshift window.

'Some of them, yes.'

'Mum has a few similar varieties,' Hester said. 'Down the bottom, by the stream. She uses them in her work.'

'Really?' Lara's interest quickened. 'Perhaps I could talk to her about it one day – when she's feeling better, I mean? Do you think that she . . . ?'

'She would, yes.' Hester smiled. 'But I can tell you about them.'

'Can you?' Lara returned her smile. Hester was a rather unusual girl. And it seemed that she wanted to keep Lara to herself.

'Oh, yes. Mum's taught me everything she knows about plants and herbalism, I told you. And I could teach you too. I'd like to.'

'All right. Thank you.' Lara realised how much she missed

companionship. She had thought that Charles would be a companion, but he wasn't, not really. They had polite conversations over dinner, but she was always worried about saying the wrong thing and besides, Charles didn't think women should be interested in politics or current affairs. Not that Lara was particularly, but she read books and listened to the wireless and she'd always tried to be well-informed. But Charles didn't seem to have the time or inclination for conversation and he could never wait to get back to his papers in the study. Lara was lonely, lonelier than she had ever been. Being alone would never have been as lonely as this marriage, she thought.

Added to this, Charles had taken to saying that Lara should sign over half the house, so that it was in joint names.

'Why?' she'd asked him when he brought the subject up again last night. 'What difference does it make?' They were married. If anything happened to Lara, then the house would belong to Charles anyway. She gave a little shiver. *Someone walking over her grave . . .* And until then, well, they both lived here, didn't they?

'Because I'm your husband, Lara.' This was one of his stock replies.

'But—'

'And so, what's mine is yours and what's yours is mine.'

Lara couldn't say so, but now that he had revealed so much more of his true character, she hated the idea of Charles legally owning any part of this house which had once known and witnessed such love, so many happy family times. It seemed like the worst kind of betrayal. So, she decided to fight for it.

She sat up straighter and took a deep breath. 'I simply don't understand the need, Charles,' she said.

He sighed. 'Sometimes, my dear,' he said, 'I think you go out of your way to make things more difficult. You are exceedingly stubborn. I even think that you want me . . .' He hesitated.

'Yes?' Though she wasn't sure she wanted to hear.

'Want me to feel less of a man.'

He got up and left the room. Lara was stunned. Was this something to do with what happened in the bedroom? *Want him to feel less of a man?* That was absurd. How could that be? She considered. *Was* she simply being stubborn? Did it really matter whose name was on the deeds? She wasn't sure she understood exactly what she would be signing away and there was no one she could ask.

'Never marry someone you don't love, Hester,' she said now, on impulse.

'Oh.' Hester looked down at the ground and then back up at her again. 'Do you mean that you don't love Mr Fripp then? Not at all?'

'I didn't marry for love, no,' Lara told her. 'And it was the biggest mistake I ever made.'

'Oh, Lara.' Hester put a hand to her mouth.

'What is it, Hester?' She reached through the wall and touched her shoulder. She seemed so upset. 'What's the matter?'

Hester gulped. 'It's something I heard in the village yesterday. I was in the post office and a woman came in, and afterwards, someone said . . .' She sniffed.

'Said what?'

'I didn't want to tell you, but now, after what you've told me, well, crumbs, Lara, you have the right to know, after all.'

The right to know . . . ? 'Hester?' Lara tried to remain calm but she was on tenterhooks. 'I can't find out anything for myself – not any more.' She had told Hester that she wasn't a prisoner – but what else could she call herself? She was a prisoner, even though it was a situation partly of her own making. Because would Charles or Mrs Peacock forcibly prevent her from leaving the house by the front door? Surely not? But there were other ways of stopping someone from leaving; other more subtle, insidious ways.

Lara thought of what Mrs Peacock had said earlier about her needing to rest. Did Mrs P. imagine that there was something wrong with her? And if so, who would have told her such a thing? She remembered the looks some people had shot her way when she'd ventured to the village – pitying looks, furtive too – and she thought she knew the answer. 'If you know anything, if you've heard anything that concerns me, if we are, or could ever be friends, please tell me.'

Hester hung her head. 'I want us to be friends.'

'Me too. And so?'

'They said the woman who had just left the post office was Mr Fripp's fancy woman.'

'Fancy woman?' Lara stared at her. She wasn't sure what she'd been expecting, but it wasn't that.

'Yes.' Hester bit her lip. 'I'm sorry. But I thought you should know.'

'Who was she?' Lara's voice was a whisper. It should hurt, shouldn't it? But although it was awful, it hardly seemed to touch her.

'I don't know,' Hester admitted. 'I've never seen her before.'

Lara patted her hand. 'It's all right,' she said.

'But aren't you angry? Aren't you upset?'

Lara thought of how it was in the bedroom. Charles demanded intimacy less frequently now and this must be the reason why. 'No, I'm not upset.' This was true. 'I'm not even angry, Hester.' She felt numb somehow. She still wasn't sure why Charles had pursued her – was it her youth, her class and background? Or did he imagine that Lara had much more money than she really had?

She knew one thing – she would not be signing any part of the house over to him; every instinct was telling her no. Besides, she'd made a promise to her mother and she was determined to do all she could to honour it. She doubted that Charles would do the same. She didn't trust him; she knew that now. It was a dreadful thing to say, to realise and to come to terms with. But come to terms with it she would have to. They were married, for better or for worse.

'What then?' Hester asked her.

'I just bitterly regret that I ever married him,' Lara told her. 'That's all.' And it was more than enough.

'So, what will you do? Will you leave him?' Hester leant closer, her expression a mixture of horror and excitement.

'Where would I go?' Lara was asking this question of herself too. This was her home. There was nowhere left, she thought, nowhere for her to escape to . . .

CHAPTER 22

Bea

Italy, May 2018

'How is your father?' Bea leant up on one elbow to ask the question.

She had been surprised when Matteo said he wanted to take her to Costa Merlata for the afternoon. 'I will pack a hamper,' he said. 'We will have a picnic – a very special picnic because I know a very special place.'

Bea chuckled. Of course he did. And naturally, she was tempted . . . 'I'd like to,' she told him. 'But . . .' Surely, he would prefer to keep things quiet and low key, stay with his family, help out at the restaurant, which must be struggling with its head chef out of action? And besides, it was a weekday and Bea had to work. She was halfway through some planting in a garden in Fasano and she needed to get the more delicate plants bedded in that very afternoon. 'I have to work.'

'Really, Beatrice?' His eyes had grown cold. 'After everything that has happened? You cannot spare me one afternoon?'

Put like that, Bea backtracked immediately. 'Of course I can,' she soothed. 'Do not worry. It is no problem.' Because *certo*, she would offer Matteo all the support she could at this difficult time.

'He is better, yes, *grazie*,' Matteo said now. 'He has been resting and he will recover fully, for sure.'

'That's great.' They were lying on a blanket on a narrow beach of fine golden sand – which was deserted, apart from the two of them.

The tiny cove was in a natural park. They'd driven past Ostuni through meadows of olive groves, parked the car and taken a sandy walkway which wound around the bays, rocky ledges and juniper trees of the serrated coastline, with the blue ocean always beckoning. The pathway seemed to go on forever and Bea kept wanting to stop at first one idyllic spot and then another, but Matteo insisted they carry on walking – it would be worth it, he said, to get away from other walkers and beach-goers. It was still only the end of May and early in the season, but certainly warm enough today to swim and sunbathe.

And he was right – it was worth it. Bea tried not to dwell on the garden in Fasano that she was so immersed in right now. A small statue of Jupiter stood on the middle terrace of that garden, above a lemon pergola. As god of the sky and the weather, he held a bolt of lightning with which to destroy his enemies – very dramatic. But she'd been wondering quite what to do with him, whether to plant around him so that he blended in, or leave him more space to stand out as a focal point. For now, though, Jupiter could wait.

Bea let out a sigh of satisfaction. They had finally settled in a private spot between two rocky outcrops, sheltered by pines and junipers. Beyond the narrow inlet lay deep, dark sea caves and the vastness of the Adriatic Sea. She gave a little shiver. *So far from civilisation*, she found herself thinking. The sky was the dense blue of early summer and the water shone like sapphire. It was a taste of paradise.

'Papà, he wants to get back into the kitchen,' said Matteo.

'So soon?' Bea was surprised. 'Is that a good idea?'

'Naturally not.' Matteo reached towards the picnic hamper he had carried all the way from the car and began unloading neatly packed little containers of various delicacies onto the blanket. 'But my father . . . it is hard to stop him, you know.'

'I suppose it must be tough for him.' Bea took the paper plates Matteo handed to her and looked around appreciatively at the spread of food.

'Cooking, it is his life,' Matteo agreed.

'And your mother?' Bea asked. He had pushed his sunglasses onto his head; in the bright sunlight his dark blue eyes seemed to have flecks of silver dancing within them. 'How does she feel about it?' Wasn't the signora the decision-maker? But at the hospital, Bea had noticed how she had leant on Matteo for support. It had been good to see. Feeling in the way, Bea had tried to leave. The signora couldn't have wanted her son's girlfriend hanging around – what help could she possibly be? But Matteo had been insistent she stay.

He glanced across at her now, as if gauging her reaction. 'My mother, she has decided that they should retire.' He made a gesture towards the food and began to dish out the zucchini and carrot salad.

'Oh, I see.' Bea guessed that the signore wouldn't relish full retirement – it would be a dramatic change. And for the signora too. But Matteo had already mentioned that the consultant had advised a change of lifestyle and told them they must heed the warning. So, she supposed she shouldn't be surprised. 'Give up the restaurant, you mean?'

'Not exactly.' He frowned. 'Ristorante Leone is our family business, remember.'

'Yes, I know.' Bea tried to read him. Normally he was so ebullient. By now he would usually have run with her into the waves that were curling seductively only metres away, kissed her with intensity as they surfaced together from the ocean, slipped down the straps of her black bikini as they lay on the golden sand . . . But today he was quiet and inscrutable. Because of what had happened to his father, no doubt. It had hit Matteo hard.

He passed her a piece of focaccia with mozzarella and a few tiny tomatoes.

'*Grazie.*' She watched him as he ate. He was definitely on edge. 'Would *you* take over the Ristorante Leone?' she asked. Because hadn't that always been the plan?

He gave a modest little shrug. 'It is possible, *non*? You do not think I could do it?'

'I did not say that.' Bea bit into the delicious focaccia. The olive oil was so good — as good as their own, she would say. Matteo seemed rather on the defensive, which proved he was nervous at the prospect. But she had no idea, she realised, of his true potential or capabilities as far as the restaurant business was concerned. Matteo was a fun companion, a dynamic per-sonality, a skilful and passionate lover. But did he have what it took to manage a high-end establishment like Ristorante Leone? She simply didn't know. 'I am sure you could do it,' she added loyally. Because, why not? 'But you are not a chef like your father, are you?'

Matteo clicked his fingers. 'It is simple to hire a chef,' he said. He popped a tomato into his mouth and Bea followed suit. It was sweet, tangy and delicious.

'A good chef?' A golden and green dragonfly was hovering nearby and she watched it land delicately on the juniper that was hanging over the rocky ledge before flitting away.

'We have plenty of good chefs here in Puglia, Beatrice.' Matteo was focused on slicing *caciocavallo* cheese for them both. 'Many of them would be delighted to have the opportunity to work at Ristorante Leone, I am certain.'

Bea supposed he was right. The place had an excellent reputation, an unrivalled location and Polignano was an undisputed hub of tourism so there was plenty of eager clientele. 'And you would continue to work front of house?' She took a forkful of the fresh minty salad. She could see now why Matteo had brought her here. The sun was warm on her skin and the rhythmic sound of the ocean was relaxing her to the core. She looked past the jagged cliffs, into the distance, to the thick navy line that was the horizon. It was a chance for him to get away from home and mull over the changes that were happening in his life. Bea felt honoured that he had chosen her to be his sounding board.

'At first, yes.' He bit into some fennel *taralli* with a crunch. 'I would take over the management duties from Mamma. That is a full-time job in itself.'

'I can imagine.' Bea took a swig from her bottle of fizzy water. He would be very busy. She wondered just when she would manage to see him.

'And until they move . . . my parents, they will act in an advisory capacity,' he added.

'They are moving?' Again, she was surprised. Quite aside

from the restaurant, the Leones seemed to belong in the village of Polignano. If they left, they would really be abdicating and leaving all responsibility to Matteo. No wonder then that he was not quite his usual self. And then there was his father's health. He must be worried sick. Bea reached out and put a hand over his.

'They have always wanted to move to Salento,' he said. 'They have decided that now is the right time.'

'Goodness . . .' She gazed out over the ocean. The sun was streaking the waves with gold, and the water glittered invitingly as it crept up the sand. *So many changes . . .*

Matteo sat up straighter. 'And so, Beatrice, I have something to ask you.' He seemed very serious. He leant over and began rummaging in the picnic hamper.

More food? Bea couldn't eat another crumb. 'I am not going to be one of your waitresses if that is what you are thinking.' She laughed.

But Matteo did not laugh with her.

'What, Matteo?'

He gripped on to something in the hamper and half turned to face her. 'I know we have not been together very long . . .'

Bea stared at him as the realisation came. *Surely not . . . ?*

'And so, you may think it is much too short a time.'

'Matteo . . .' She didn't want to hear this, she realised. Not now. Not yet. He was right. It was much too short a time.

'But the fact is, Beatrice, I fell in love with you the first moment I saw you in that garden in Ostuni.' And from the hamper Matteo produced a bottle of champagne, glistening with condensation in its ice wrapper.

Bea couldn't help but smile. Champagne too – the gesture was typical Matteo. 'The first moment?' she teased. She supposed she'd fallen for him pretty quickly too. It had been such a bizarre initial conversation when he'd come to find her in the lower echelons of the garden. She'd known immediately that she wanted to see him again.

'The first moment.' Matteo began unwrapping the foil. He glanced across at her. 'And now, because of this, because of what has happened to my father. Because my life is changing . . .' He twisted the wire. 'I am asking you to marry me, Beatrice.' He began to ease the cork loose. 'And so. Will you accept? Will you do me the honour of becoming my wife?'

Bea was incredibly flattered. It was so sweet, so old-fashioned and charming. And characteristic of Matteo, to bring her here to a deserted beach with a delicious picnic in order to pop the question in style. But . . . 'It is so quick, Matteo,' she whispered.

He put the bottle of champagne to one side and took her hand. 'But when you are in love . . .' He let the words trail.

'Yes, I know what you are saying.' Bea closed her eyes. Around her she could feel the rush of the ocean, sense the swell and hear the draw and the hiss as the waves curled inexorably into the shore. She could smell the salt in the air, the chalkiness of the limestone cliff, the gritty dryness of the sand crackling with tiny shards of shell. It was a perfect location, and of course, that was why Matteo had chosen it.

'And you and I, we are in love, *non*?' His voice was soft, caressing her senses.

'Yes.' Yes, of course. She didn't doubt that. But once again, she found herself thinking of that childhood roundabout. It was still spinning very fast.

'Then why not be together?' He brought her hand to his lips and kissed it tenderly. He took off his sunglasses and fixed her with an intense gaze. 'Properly together,' he said. 'All the time.'

All the time . . . That seemed like a lot. But he was so gorgeous, so persuasive. Bea was tempted to just shout it. *Yes!* Because how wonderful it would be – to have a husband like Matteo, to be wined and dined and taken on amazing days out. To swim in the ocean on glorious summer days like this one, to make love all night with all the time in the world.

Matteo gave the bottle a little shake and popped the cork. He reached into the hamper for tiny glasses.

And drinking champagne, thought Bea. She'd never known anything like this. She'd never been treated like this. It was all such utter bliss.

Matteo was pouring the champagne. He assumed she'd say 'yes', she knew. He was behaving as if she already had.

He passed her a glass and she took it. 'To us,' he said.

'To . . .' Bea stopped. That wasn't what marriage was really about, though, was it? And besides, if Matteo was taking over the restaurant, there would be neither the time nor the opportunity for all those things. She was, she realised, living out some sort of romantic fantasy.

'Beatrice?' He eyed her quizzically.

'I do not know, Matteo,' she said.

He drew away very slightly. 'You do not know?'

Bea registered the disbelief on his face. He'd been so sure of her. And why wouldn't he be? She hated to disappoint him, but . . . 'Marriage is a big commitment,' she said.

'You think I am not aware of that?' He was irritated, she knew.

'So, why the rush? Why can we not go on as we are for a bit longer?' And yet even as she said this, Bea realised it was too late. How could they? His proposal had already changed their relationship – how could it not? Accepting him would change it further. As would refusal. Nothing would be the same.

She looked around her. Further to the south was the ruined tower of Pozzelle where they had planned to walk after lunch. Instinctively, she knew they would not walk there now. Already she could see a few distant clouds scudding their way. They would never recapture this perfect moment in this perfect place again. It was like a stage set, she thought, almost not real.

Matteo let out a deep sigh. 'I thought you understood, *cara*.'

'Understood?' Bea sipped at her wine.

'Running the restaurant is a full-time job for two, my love,' he said.

And she could see now his vulnerability – his fear of taking this on alone.

'It is our family restaurant, remember. Ristorante Leone – it is our name. My wife would be a part of it. You would be a part of it. And I am asking you to marry me now, so soon, because the time has come for me to take over. I have no choice.'

'But—'

'And because I love you,' he added before she could continue. 'I would have proposed to you anyway, just perhaps not today.' He smiled ruefully.

'But, Matteo . . .' Bea blinked at him. She'd had little idea that this was how things were.

'Yes, *cara*?'

'I have my own career,' she reminded him. How could he not understand that? She had told him right from the start how much her business meant to her.

'Yes, I know,' he said. 'And that is important, of course. But in the end . . .' He paused. 'It is just gardening, *non*? And I cannot run the restaurant alone.'

Just gardening? Bea hardly knew what to say. Gardening was her life. The pleasure of designing and planning a garden, the anticipation of the creation, the foundations and the evolution, watching the garden grow . . . 'I love my gardens.' This was all she could articulate for now. But suddenly the champagne tasted bitter, the clouds were getting closer, the tide was coming in and they would have to move.

'I know you do.' His tone was conciliatory. 'And I am sorry – I did not mean it quite like that.'

But he did. And she supposed that to most people gardening might not seem very important. But to Bea, it was.

'Although you know we do have a garden in Polignano.' He was teasing now. 'The beautiful terrace garden you created.' He kissed her shoulder. 'You are so clever. I am very proud of you.'

Was she being selfish? Matteo's family restaurant was long-established and hugely successful. How could Beatrice Romano's Gardens possibly compete? The business was still in its early stages. And it was just Bea who worked and derived an income from it – at least for now. But all the same . . .

'Think about it, my love,' he said. '*Per favore*. Please think about it. I know it's a big decision. But you mean so much to me and it is you I want by my side.'

Bea stared out at the waves, leaving their foamy footprints in the sand, pulling more grains back with them into the sea. The sand was shifting. All the time, the landscape was changing in front of their eyes. '*Grazie*, Matteo,' she said.

But Bea could sense her career dream drifting inexorably away from her. And so, she had to ask herself: how much did she want it? How much did she want Matteo? And why did love mean having to give anything up at all?

CHAPTER 23

Lara

Dorset, May 1947

'That's me done for the day.' Mrs Peacock gave a small sigh of satisfaction.

Lara watched as the housekeeper put her duster and rubber gloves back under the sink. The chemical smell of disinfectant in the kitchen battled with the fragrance of wax wood polish emanating from the hall. 'Thank you, Mrs P.,' Lara said.

The woman nodded, looked doubtfully towards the door of the study as if she couldn't leave without Charles's say-so. But he *had* made it clear that he didn't want to be disturbed. 'I'll be off then.'

'See you tomorrow.' Lara didn't want to sound too eager, but she wanted her to be gone.

As soon as the back door closed behind the housekeeper, Lara moved to the front hall window to observe her departure down the tree-lined drive. She watched her reach the lane. The coast was clear. Charles was still closeted in the study, which left Lara as free as she'd ever be to prove a point – to herself, if no one else.

She slipped on her spring coat, which was hanging on the hall stand by the front door, took her pale green silk scarf from the pocket, shook it out and tied it under her chin, watching herself in the hall mirror which was gleaming even more than usual after Mrs P.'s morning ministrations. Lara had chosen to wear a dress this morning – nothing fancy; she didn't want to attract attention. Then again, she had very little that was fancy, and why would she need new clothes?

She paused, regarding herself in the mirror, this woman preparing to go out. Did she look confident? Did she look like a normal housewife about to walk down to the shops to call into the post office or purchase some meat from the butcher perhaps?

You can do this, Lara, she told herself. *You're not a prisoner . . .* And this would prove it. Just down to the post office and back – that was all she had to do. It was nothing really. She might even bump into someone she knew – Alice perhaps, though Lara was aware that her old friend would be at work at this time. *Work . . .* Lara felt a pang of longing for those old days – for the freedom of riding her bicycle, the wind at her back as she flew down the hill, off to the Savings Bank, with only herself to answer to.

With a final glance back at the study, she opened the front door as softly, as quietly as she possibly could. It obliged without a creak, just the merest whoosh of air, hardly more than an exhalation. It was no good going out the back way – she'd have to pass the window of the study and Charles was bound to spot her. This way, though . . .

Lara couldn't believe how fast her heart was beating. Was

this what she had come to? Frightened to leave her own house in broad daylight? She straightened her back, held her head high. Opened the door a little wider so that the spring sunlight stole in.

Behind her, she heard the study door open. Lara froze.

'Lara?' Charles sounded almost amused – the worst thing, she thought.

'Yes, Charles?' She swung around, attempting an air of non-chalance, as if this was quite the most normal turn of events.

He leant on the door frame, assessing. 'Where are you going?'

She eyed him warily. 'Down to the shops.'

Charles glanced at his watch. 'But it's nearly lunchtime.'

'I'll be back in less than twenty minutes.' The words came out in a rush. Lara drew the door open wider. She would not be put off. She would not back down. She had to do this.

'But why do you need to go out at all?' he enquired mildly.

Lara swung the door fully open. The sunlight hit her full in the face and she blinked. 'I want a breath of fresh air,' she said.

He laughed. 'Don't be daft. Haven't you been in the garden all morning?'

Damn. She'd walked right into that one.

Charles took a step towards her. He put his hands on the door. An image filled Lara's head – of her and Charles both tugging at the door, her to open it, he to close it. She looked at the crimson and blue stained-glass door panel and imagined it broken, in pieces at their feet.

Lara stepped outside, before he could take her decision away. 'I'm just nipping down to the post office,' she said.

His eyes narrowed. 'I have stamps, if that's what you need.'

'No, I'm not going for stamps.' Lara took a step down and

onto the drive. She glanced ahead. She had never before noticed how very long it was.

'You don't have your handbag.'

'I don't need my handbag.' Another step. *See how easy it is,* Lara thought. *You can walk away – anytime you like, you can leave by the front door.*

'Good idea!' Charles's tone changed.

This worried her. She hesitated and turned around. He was taking his coat from the hook. 'Sorry? What?'

'I'll come with you,' he said. 'It'll be just the ticket. Exactly as you said – a breath of fresh air after being stuck inside all morning.'

Lara stared at him. She hadn't foreseen this scenario. She had imagined Charles dragging her back inside, pictured his cold anger, even seen him locking the door and pocketing the key. But she hadn't envisaged this breezy good humour.

'Yes,' he said. 'I shall accompany you. Why not? It will be a pleasure.'

What could she say? Why not indeed? She could hardly object to going for a stroll with her own husband. 'Very well,' she said. 'That will be . . . nice.'

It took Charles only a few minutes to put on his shoes, hat and coat. He offered his arm to Lara and together they walked without speaking down the driveway lined with lime trees and onto the lane, heading down the hill towards the post office. Lara was agonisingly aware of the way she had to scurry to keep up with his pace, the scratchy graze of his gabardine coat sleeve against her wrist, the smell of him that was an uneasy mix of hair cream, oil and tobacco.

Charles seemed relaxed, though. He nodded, smiled and touched his hat to various passers-by. He even said 'good morning' to one or two of them. Meanwhile, Lara was a bag of nerves. Supposing they ran into this woman with whom Charles was apparently entangled? Would he acknowledge her? Would they laugh at Lara behind her back? Probably. She imagined they were doing that already.

Lara managed to smile – just – when Charles greeted people, but she hardly knew who she was smiling at. She could be wrong, but she fancied they were giving her those strange looks again – as if they were surprised to see her up and about. And all the time, Charles held her hand gripped inside his arm, as if to warn her not to attempt any escape. It was excruciating.

At the post office, Charles looked expectantly at Lara, but of course, she had no errand in mind and besides, she hadn't even brought her purse.

'Time to go home?' he suggested pleasantly.

'Yes,' she said. All of a sudden there was nothing that she wanted more than to be in her garden again – alone.

Later that night, Lara couldn't sleep. She crept out of bed – Charles was snoring heavily and taking up most of it – put on her bathrobe and went downstairs for a glass of water. By the study door, she lingered. This house had been very different back when her parents were alive. Now, the study was Charles's domain; back then, all the doors were kept open and she could hear Father's cheery banter from here or from his art studio upstairs, anywhere in the house. There were no secrets – or so it had seemed.

And yet . . . Lara thought of the secret garden – there had been a secret after all.

She glanced up the winding staircase but all was quiet – except, that was, for the nasal rise and fall of Charles's

snoring – and so she opened the study door, very cautiously, with a dangerous but rather thrilling sense of unease. It was still her house; why shouldn't she enter any room whenever she pleased?

She went over to the desk and looked for a moment out of the window into the dark night. There was barely a sliver of a crescent moon to illuminate the driveway, the shrubs and the trees. Lara thought of Hester's mother Elizabeth who, according to Hester, was very knowledgeable about the cycles of the moon. Hester had also talked to Lara about herbalism and healing. Lara was glad to have someone to talk to, but she wasn't sure it was enough. And no plant could heal Lara's diminishing sense of self. After what had happened today when she tried to leave the house, she was more scared and apprehensive than ever. Something had to change, she knew. But she didn't have the first clue how to make it happen.

She switched on the lamp and turned to look at the desk. Charles was very neat. All his paperwork was arranged in well-ordered piles, his fountain pen had been placed at the top in a straight line parallel to the blotter and all the desk drawers were closed.

Lara opened one at random, mainly to see if it was locked. It wasn't, but there was nothing interesting inside, just a box of paperclips and elastic bands, a few pencils, an eraser, a pencil sharpener, that sort of thing.

She tried another. This contained some cardboard wallets. She opened the first. Bank statements . . . Curious, she flipped through, glancing out of the open door and up the stairs as she did so. From her vantage point in the study, she would hear if Charles were to stop snoring and if he should get up to look

for her, she would see him on the stairs before he could know precisely what she was doing.

What *was* she doing? What was she looking for? Why was she even in this room? She looked down at the bank statements she was holding. What was strange was that the account – their joint bank account – seemed to be in the red. How on earth could that be? She peered closer. Charles hadn't said there was a problem; the opposite, in fact – he had been so insistent that she stopped work, so sure that there was nothing to worry about financially. Lara frowned. Clearly, then, he had not been telling the truth.

Lara tried the top drawer. It was locked. She replaced the wallet, quickly checked the other drawers, which revealed nothing of interest, and turned her attention back to this one. What was in it? Something that he didn't want anyone to see – even more than he didn't want anyone to see their bank statements? This was hard to believe.

The key would be somewhere not too obvious and Charles would want to access it immediately from the vicinity of the desk, she decided. Not in a drawer, though; he would be more careful than that. She ran her fingers under the desk top. Nothing. She looked at the chair; this would be where he would be sitting when he opened it. So, with another quick glance up the stairs, she sat on the leather cushioned seat as he would, ran her fingers inside the ledge of the mahogany frame. And there it was – a tiny key tucked out of sight but within reach, just as she'd guessed.

Lara felt a small lift of pride. *Not so stupid then. Not so hopeless . . .* She slotted the key in the lock and turned it. The drawer opened easily. Inside were some sheets of white paper. She picked them up and stared. One single name had been

written over and over. She swallowed hard. Her name. *Lara G. Fripp.* Written with a flourish and a loop, like a signature. Like her signature, in fact.

She sat down again in the chair, all the breath knocked out of her. Charles had been practising her signature. She stared at the pages, spread them out over the desk. What did it mean? The writing seemed to dance in front of her eyes, mocking her.

A sound from upstairs suggested Charles might be stirring. Lara swiftly bundled together the sheets of paper, replaced them in the drawer, shut and locked it, and tucked the key back under the mahogany frame. He mustn't know that she had found him out.

Lara checked that everything was as he had left it, switched off the lamp and crossed the room, closing the door as silently as she could behind her. She glanced up the stairway – nothing, though she could no longer hear his snores. She darted into the kitchen as if for safety and ran the tap. She felt that she could hardly breathe. Charles was practising her signature. But for what? She remembered how much he had wanted the house to be signed over into joint names. Was that why then? For the house? It must be; Lara owned little else.

She slipped silently out of the kitchen and through into the sitting room, to her favourite thinking spot – the window seat by the French doors looking out over the veranda. She was in trouble. She knew that she was in trouble. But there was no one to turn to and Lara had no clue what to do.

CHAPTER 24

Lara

Italy, May 2018

It was a Saturday morning. Rose was busy in the *trulli* and Lara was just summoning the energy to go out onto the terrace for a while, where she could gaze contentedly at her Italian garden and think, when Bea appeared at her side.

'*Va bene*, darling?' Lara asked softly. Bea was hovering. It was clear that there was something on her granddaughter's mind.

'I wondered if you would like to go out for a drive, Nonna?' asked Bea.

'What a wonderful idea.' Lara gave a little clap of the hands. 'I would love that.' She glanced at Bea. 'Not working today, then, my dear?'

'Not today.'

'And Matteo?'

'Busy in the restaurant.'

Was it Lara's imagination, or had she answered just a little too quickly? 'Then that would be delightful,' she said.

Bea smiled. 'Where do you fancy, Nonna?'

That was easy. 'A drive through the Valle d'Itria would be perfect,' said Lara. She loved seeing the olive groves and the historic gardens, the vineyards and the *trulli* dotting the landscape.

'Okay. Anything you need to bring with you?'

'Oh, just my bag and sunglasses, and perhaps my wrap.'

It didn't take them long to get organised. They left a note for Rose on the kitchen table in case they didn't see her on the way out and made their way to the car, a slow progression because Lara had to lean heavily on her granddaughter's arm and take a breather after every half a dozen steps. It was so frustrating. When she thought how fit she used to be, so active. But with old age must come acceptance, she supposed.

As they drove down the narrow road lined with dry-stone walls, Lara saw Bea's shoulders gradually relax and drop. She was holding in a lot of tension.

'You wanted to get out too, my dear?' she guessed.

Bea glanced across at her. '*Sì*. I wanted to talk to you, Nonna,' she said.

'Ah.' Which was a coincidence, since Lara wanted to talk to Bea too. She'd come to a conclusion these past few days. She could no longer avoid the fact that something must be done about Dorset. And as far as she could tell, her granddaughter was the one person who could help her do it.

Bea would understand Lara's precious Arts and Crafts garden; she would know instinctively what it needed. Lara could trust her. Her granddaughter could save the garden, thus enabling Lara to fulfil the promise she'd made to her mother before she died. It wasn't the best timing – Bea was only just getting on her feet as far as her gardening business was concerned and Lara hated to take her away from it, but

Lara could pay her like any other client, provide the air fare too and even if Bea only spent a month over there, it might be long enough to find a gardener, to sort things out with the place, to put the house on the market, she reluctantly supposed. And it would be rather wonderful for Bea to see the house and garden in which Lara had grown up. The memories weren't all bad, far from it. There had been good times when her parents were alive, before the war, when the house and garden and the people living in them had positively basked in a sense of happiness and well-being.

But for now, neither spoke. Lara loved being driven through this landscape of red-brown earth and olive groves – she always had. There was such an air of peace to the countryside and the silence between them was the comfortable silence of two people who understood each other well. Lara let out a breath of satisfaction and glanced across at Bea. However . . . there was also the question of Matteo.

Lara remembered how hard it was to be away from the man you loved – even for a day or two – when he was always on your mind. And Bea must love Matteo; Lara had seen it in her eyes. But it might do her granddaughter good to have a longer project to get her teeth into. And yes, it might be expedient for her to have some space, to get away from Matteo for a while. It was all moving very quickly and Matteo could be – as Bea herself had said – an overwhelming personality. Lara thought of David as she still so often did. If the love between Bea and Matteo was worth anything, it would surely survive a short parting.

'Allora. And what did you want to talk about, my dear?' Lara asked Bea at last. They were approaching Locorotondo which was situated on a hilltop on the Murge Plateau; as they

216

drove, they had a superb view of its shimmering white domes and the rooftops of the old town set against the blue skyline.

Bea glanced from left to right as if they might be overheard by the olive trees on the roadside. 'I will tell you when we stop,' she said. 'It is hard to talk about anything at home, is it not? There is always someone listening.'

Lara knew what she meant. Once, when she'd first come to Italy, it had been even more hectic in the *masseria*, with the Romano clan always around. Coming from Dorset and the life she'd been leading there, it had seemed to Lara like a different world. It truly was a different world, she thought grimly. 'And your mother's been a bit on edge,' she remarked.

'You have noticed that too, Nonna?' Bea cast a brief worried glance her way.

'*Certo.*' What else did she have to do these days but think and observe?

'But do you know why?' Bea slowed as they approached the crossroads.

'No.' *As if Rose would tell her anything . . .*

Lara was glad, though, that she could still be a confidante to Bea, ancient though she was. They had always been close; she supposed that sometimes it was easier when there was a generation removed. She closed her eyes for a moment. She remembered how worried she used to be about Rose, when, as a teenager, she'd got in with that bad crowd. How her daughter changed. Rose no longer had the slightest interest in her school work or the farm, she was rude to her parents and other members of the family who'd done so much for her, she started drinking and smoking and even sneaked out of her bedroom at night to meet up with God knows who.

Only Lara *had* known who.

She opened her eyes again and let the tranquillity of the landscape soothe her. 'Shall we stop in the town for a drink?' she suggested.

'Yes,' Bea agreed. 'Good idea, Nonna.'

Bene. Then they would talk and sort out the problem, whatever it might be.

Lara settled further into the seat and allowed her thoughts to drift back to Rose. She knew who had been taking their daughter away from them back then; it was Cesare Basso and his sister Daniela, who, given that old family feud, had probably found it hilarious that they were corrupting a girl so closely associated with the Romano family, pulling her into their clutches. Lara had always tried to bring Rose up with a strong sense of right and wrong, but she'd tried to be a liberal parent too; she wanted to give Rose the freedom that Lara herself had lost as a young woman. Rose, though, had seemed to turn even this against her. It had been such a difficult time. Eleanora Romano used to reassure Lara that Rose would snap out of it one day and all would be well. But when? Lara had worried that they might be losing her forever.

Bea overtook a little *Ape* trundling down the lane. Things moved more slowly, Lara thought, here in the Valle d'Itria. Eleanora had been right, however: something – Lara had no idea what – had happened and Rose had come back to them. Federico meanwhile had stayed steadfast. He had always been there for Rose and the day Rose told them that she and Federico were to marry had been one of the happiest days of Lara's life.

They drove through the village, which was clean and well-kept, a maze of white alleyways, crumbling facades and baroque archways, and Bea parked near the Villa Comunale, the public garden where the market was held on Friday mornings. It was only a few minutes' walk under the mature pine trees to a pleasant café just inside the *centro storico*, but Lara wasn't relishing the prospect of having to get out of the car again. When had this small action become so hard to achieve? *Allora.* She knew that Bea wouldn't start talking until she also stopped driving.

'So, what is it, my dear?' Lara asked her, once they were seated outside the café at a table with a red and gold tablecloth under a cream umbrella and the waitress had taken their order. 'What is it that's troubling you?'

Bea was fiddling with the menu as if desperate to do something with her hands. Was it that awful?

'It is Matteo,' she said.

'Ah.' Lara wasn't surprised. She let her gaze drift towards the pink geraniums and red and white dipladenia planted in shiny ceramic pots on the terraces and pretty balconies opposite. 'Matteo, *sì*,' she repeated.

'But it is nothing bad,' Bea said quickly. 'It is the opposite really.'

'Go on, darling.' Lara was intrigued.

Bea took a deep breath. 'He proposed to me on the beach yesterday.'

'Proposed?' On the beach? Now, Lara *was* surprised. Things were moving even faster than she'd imagined. 'That's very—'

'Quick, I know.'

'And why does it have to be so quick, my love?' Lara asked her gently. 'Or does Matteo want a long engagement?'

'I do not know.' Bea bit her thumbnail and Lara winced. 'At least, I know why he wants to get married, and I think he wants it to be as soon as possible.'

Lara raised an eyebrow. 'Indeed? And what is that reason — can you tell me?'

Another deep breath. 'It is the restaurant,' she began. And it all came out.

By the time Bea had finished explaining, Lara was feeling quite cross. What a cheek, she thought, to expect Bea to give up her own career to support his. Now that was something you wouldn't expect to hear nowadays. Except that selfishness still existed, of course, and not everyone was adept at empathy.

She opened her mouth to speak, but held back as the waitress arrived with their drinks.

'What do you think, Nonna?' Bea asked when she'd gone back inside.

That was easy. 'I think it's very selfish of him,' Lara said. 'But it's what you think that matters, my dear.'

Bea drank her juice thirstily. 'It is a long-standing family business,' she reminded Lara. 'And Matteo must be under a lot of pressure from his parents.'

'Yes, I'm sure.' But that was his concern. No reason to put that same pressure on Bea. Lara couldn't see why her granddaughter had to be dragged into it too. Couldn't the Leones simply employ a business partner if that was what Matteo required?

Bea meanwhile was looking dreamily into the distance.

'He's swept you off your feet,' Lara remarked.

Bea turned to her. 'I think that I love him, Nonna.'

'Yes.' Though that was neither here nor there. Or was it? And why did Bea only 'think' that she loved him?

Lara looked across to the corner of the piazza, where a tall vine was growing from the wall up to an old balcony and beyond as if trying to find the sky. 'But do you love him enough to give up your business?' she asked. 'Do you love him enough to drop your own career plans for his?'

Bea hung her head. 'I do not know,' she admitted.

Hmm. This was a relief – Bea was at least considering her options. Lara patted her hand. 'You must give it plenty of thought,' she said. 'Because if you give up your dreams for Matteo Leone, you might end up hating him for it.'

Bea's eyes widened. 'Oh, Nonna, I would never hate him.'

She was so innocent. A lamb to the slaughter, thought Lara. She recalled what Matteo had said when they were all sitting around the family dinner table that evening – about Bea not taking the trouble to dress up for a special occasion. She thought about all the days off Bea had been taking – and how bad she seemed to feel about it. Matteo was a charming young fellow – but Lara recognised a controlling man when she met one. And she knew it would only lead to heartbreak for Bea. Her granddaughter had to be strong from the outset. She must hold her ground.

'Even so,' she said, 'it's a big decision. Would *you* ask Matteo to give up Ristorante Leone and come to work for you as an assistant gardener?'

Bea giggled. 'No, of course not, Nonna.'

Lara was glad to see she hadn't lost her sense of humour. '*Allora*. Well then, it's much the same thing, Bea,' she said.

'I suppose . . .'

'And why the big hurry? Why can Matteo's parents not stay around to help the transition for six months or even a year and then see whether Matteo still needs you as a business partner and how you feel about it all six months down the line?' Lara sipped her juice. *Geronimo*. An idea had come to her.

At first, it had seemed as if Matteo's marriage proposal

221

would make her own proposal to her granddaughter redundant, but now, she saw that it could still work – and be of benefit to Bea at the same time.

'I agree, Nonna,' Bea admitted. 'It is too soon for all sorts of reasons. I've only just got the business going. I want to see if I can build it up. And I do not want to work in a restaurant.' She pulled a gloomy face. 'I want to be working outside. In a garden.'

Lara chuckled. 'Then you've answered your own question.'

'But, Matteo . . .' Bea put her head in her hands. It wasn't easy, Lara knew that. Matteo was a very persuasive young man.

'Darling, no one should ask the person they love to give up their dream.' Was it not as simple as that?

'Oh, Nonna.' Bea sighed. 'I know that you are right. But it is so hard to explain to him.'

'Bea.' Lara took her hands. 'If you will allow me to change the subject for a moment, I have something to tell you too. Something to ask you, in fact.'

Bea's expression changed. She leant closer. 'What, Nonna?'

Lara paused as the soft buzz of conversation continued around them. She caught notes of several different languages; there were various nationalities here in the café today. 'It's to do with the garden I used to talk to you about,' Lara said. 'Do you remember those stories, my dear?'

'Yes, I do.' Bea's voice was eager. 'The garden in Dorset, you mean?'

'The walled garden, yes.' Lara could see her trying to recall the detail.

'The garden was the girl's sanctuary,' said Bea.

'Yes, it was.' Lara felt the sadness wash over her. 'But she needed to escape.' She chose her words carefully. 'She always loved the garden, but she had to get away, you see.'

'But, why, Nonna? Why did she need to get away?'

Lara shook her head. There was so much more to tell her, but not all at once, she decided. One step at a time. 'I wondered if you might go there for me?'

'To England? To Dorset?'

Lara nodded. 'There are some things that need to be done, Bea,' she said. 'Especially in the garden.'

'The garden?' Bea was staring at her, not understanding, but getting there.

'It's a project,' she said. 'I would pay you for your services just like any other client would do. It would mean being away for a few weeks at least – maybe more.' She hesitated. 'It's something that must be undertaken before I die.'

'No, Nonna.' Bea had tears in her eyes. She clutched at Lara's hand. 'Please do not talk like that.'

'But I must.' Lara was firm. 'I'm old, my dear, and no one lives forever.'

'I do not want to talk about it.' Bea sounded mutinous. Her lower lip was jutting out just like it had done when she was a child of two.

'I need to be at peace,' Lara said. 'I need to know that this matter is being dealt with. And going away from here for a few weeks – it will give you the opportunity to consider what Matteo is asking of you.'

'A chance to get away for a while . . .' Bea said thoughtfully.

'Do your other commitments allow it?' Lara asked. Because the business must come first.

'Sì. Yes, I think so.'

'You need time, my darling,' Lara said gently. She didn't want to tell her granddaughter how to run her life. But equally, she didn't want Bea to give up her own pathway without proper consideration. She didn't want Bea to become something she was not, because she knew her granddaughter would regret it. It was so important to give these decisions due reflection, as Lara knew to her own cost. Lara was old, but the dangers were still familiar to her. 'Perhaps you need this time.'

Bea bit her lip. 'Matteo, he will not like it.' But her eyes were shining.

Lara knew that she was thinking about the garden. About their family history, which was Bea's legacy, along with the Arts and Crafts walled garden. 'But what about you, Bea?' she asked. 'Would *you* like it? Would you do this thing – for me?'

CHAPTER 25

Rose

Italy, May 2018

'England?' Federico spluttered.

'England?' Rose echoed, more softly.

'To sort out the house and garden in Dorset,' Bea said. 'For Nonna.' And she cast an affectionate glance towards her grandmother.

They were sitting around the old wooden kitchen table, the usual venue for family discussions. Bea had cleared away the plates and Rose had poured them all a small *digestivo* – she'd had the feeling there was something on her daughter's mind. Bea had been restless throughout the meal and Rose had intercepted a couple of meaningful glances between her mother and her daughter – thick as thieves those two were.

'What needs to be sorted out exactly?' Rose asked. Her mother rarely talked about the house in Dorset where she'd grown up. Rose used to ask questions – because it was strange, surely, that her mother still owned the place and simply rented it out over the years to various tenants? But her mother had always shaken her head, a pained expression in her eyes, and changed the subject as soon as she could. Rose didn't want to upset her and, in any case, what difference did it make to her life if there was a house in Dorset that belonged to the family? She and Fedi certainly had no time spare to visit it. 'Are you selling the place, Mamma, is that it?'

'Perhaps.' She didn't look happy at the prospect, though.

'But why now?' Rose turned to her daughter. 'And why Bea?' Bea, after all, had her gardening business to run. She couldn't just hare off to England on some whim of her grandmother's.

Rose's mother rested her hands on the ancient wooden tabletop. Her hands were old too – lined and worn and even trembling a little, Rose could see.

'It is time,' her mother said.

'Time?' Federico sounded cross. 'We do not need the money, Lara, if that is what you are thinking.'

Rose doubted that was what her mother was thinking. She was becoming more fragile every day. Perhaps Rose should have asked her more about Dorset before now.

But, 'Why Bea?' she asked again. She loved the connection between these two, her mother and her daughter, but sometimes she wondered exactly where she, Rose, had gone wrong. She loved them both, but she'd never been able to confide in either of them, not really. Something always made her hold back. And that something . . . Was it Cesare Basso? Was it Rose's shame at what she had done? She repressed a shiver.

See you around, he had written. Not if Rose had anything to do with it. The pulse of fear seemed to be there every day now – in her temples, deep in her belly. But she didn't know how she could rid herself of it, how she could possibly be free.

'I need to get away for a bit,' Bea replied.

'From home?' growled Federico.

Bea glanced again at her grandmother. She gave the slightest of nods in response.

Bea sighed. 'I didn't really want to say . . .' she began.

'But now you will, yes?' Federico drummed his fingers on the table. He had always worried about Bea. If they'd had another . . . Rose stifled this thought. Then perhaps it would have been different.

Bea gave a little gulp. Rose reached out, put a comforting hand on hers. 'It is all right, darling,' she said softly, hoping that it was.

Bea gave her a grateful look.

She should reach out to her daughter more often, Rose found herself thinking. She should talk to her more, instead of allowing herself to be swallowed up by domestic tasks, by anxiety, by her own demons.

'Matteo has asked me to marry him,' Bea said at last.

'Well!' Federico picked up his glass and chinked it against Bea's. 'Congratulations are in order then. Why did you not say?'

'Because I have not said yes.' Bea spoke quickly. 'Not yet.'

Rose was beginning to understand. When she first met Matteo, she'd been charmed by him, it was true. He seemed everything she could want for Bea. But as time went on . . . In truth, recently, Bea had not always looked like a young girl in love. Sometimes she had looked harassed, like a girl who didn't know which way to turn. 'You need to think about it,' said Rose.

'Yes, Mamma.' Another grateful look.

'And so, she will go to England for a month or so to do exactly that,' Rose's mother said.

Federico spread his hands. 'What is there to think about, huh?'

Rose tapped him briskly on the wrist. 'It is a big decision, Fedi,' she said. '*Certo*, she must consider. This is the rest of Bea's life we are talking about.'

He stared at her. 'But I thought you liked him.'

'I do.'

'I thought you approved of the family?'

'I do.' Was she really so shallow? Rose wondered. Apparently so.

'Then . . . ?' Federico downed his *digestivo*. 'Women!' he said. 'Who is to understand them?'

'Papà,' Bea began.

'Do you love him?' he demanded.

'Yes, but—'

'Then what is the problem?' Federico shook his head in despair.

'He wants me to help him run the restaurant.'

There was a silence as they all absorbed this. Rose and Federico had fully supported Bea's decision to study horticulture and they had given her some money to launch her business. Rose might not know everything about her daughter, but she did know that Bea loved her gardens.

'He is expecting you to give up your gardening?' she asked.

'*Sì*.' Now it was Bea's turn to down her *digestivo*. 'So, now you see why I need to think about it.'

Rose did indeed and she could ascertain from his expression that her husband did too. It was an awful lot to ask of someone. And in her view, a terrible waste of Bea's talents.

Federico snorted. 'But why do you need to go to *England* to think?' He made it sound as though England was on another planet. 'Why not think here in Puglia?'

'Matteo is here in Puglia,' Lara pointed out. 'Bea needs to get away.'

'I see.' Rose did. Her mother was helping Bea and Bea was helping her grandmother. That was what families did.

'But how can you go to England on your own?' At this point, though, even Federico sounded as if he'd given up the argument. He tore a hand through his hair and looked pleadingly at Rose.

'I will be fine, Papà,' said Bea. 'I want to go. And of course, I need to go – for Nonna.'

CHAPTER 26

Lara

Dorset, June 1947

Now that the longer evenings were here, it was both a pleasure and a relief for Lara to spend even more time in the garden, tending to the planting, gathering the vegetables and the fruit, sometimes simply watching the setting sun as another day slipped away from her. Was the garden her prison or her sanctuary? Lara wheeled the barrow towards the compost heap behind the greenhouse. She wasn't always sure. Things seemed to have become so blurred. And yet how could she think of the walled garden as anything other than the place she could escape to?

Along the main avenue, the hollyhocks grew high, their first flowers blooming from the most delicate of lemon through to a dark burgundy that was almost black. They were a grand gesture of a flower, waving in the breeze; a proper welcome to the garden. At the entrance to the Nurturing Garden, the thick spiky clumps of dark blue agapanthus would flower soon and further down the path the vibrant achillea – yellow and grainy as the brightest pollen – complemented the elegant irises and lupins in the opposite bed. Lara paused to straighten her aching back. She couldn't look after the garden as well without Joe's help, but she was doing her best and she hoped that her mother would be proud – of the garden at least.

She bent again to trundle the barrow through the archway. Hester was teaching her about herbalism, and when she was able, Elizabeth too had walked down to join in the conversation.

There were plants already growing in the garden which, according to Elizabeth and Hester, had healing qualities. Lara believed it too. Camomile, sage and borage made a delicious and calming tea; jasmine and rose had a sweet and soothing fragrance; and mint and rosemary seemed to give Lara energy when she was feeling tired. Hester made teas and potions for her mother too, and Lara felt that Elizabeth was definitely getting stronger.

Hester had confided in Lara during their afternoon talks through the wall and Lara worried for both mother and daughter. Like so many others, Hester's grandparents had died during the First World War, and it was when she was working for a well-to-do family living just outside Bridport that Elizabeth had an affair with the eldest son and became pregnant with Hester. The family had paid her off and given Elizabeth and Hester lifetime use of the cottage next door, but there was no contact between Hester and her father and if anything happened to Elizabeth, Hester would be completely alone. Lara knew exactly how that felt.

She paused for a moment to breathe in the scents of the garden. Lavender was uplifting too. Lara's mother had always made small bags of dried lavender to put in the clothes drawers, but Hester had taught her that lavender was also good for fear. 'It can help with headaches, insomnia and depression too.' And

Hester had met Lara's gaze in the candid way she had. It must then, Lara thought grimly, be her ideal flower.

When she had first found out that Charles was practising copying her signature, Lara had been at a loss as to what to do. Should she confront him? A few months before, maybe she would have done. But now, there was a chill to his pale eyes that frightened her. She knew how furious he would be that she'd trespassed into his territory. And she couldn't face that. Whatever control he was exerting over her – and she had come to accept this as an indisputable fact – it had become all-encompassing. It was waking her in the night, making her sweat and hyper-ventilate, so that she had to splash cold water onto her face and run down to her window seat by the French doors to escape the bulk of him snoring in the bed beside her, to get away from the sound of his nasal breathing, even the smell of him. Everything about this man had become repugnant to her.

Should she then try to leave? Even the very thought made her heart beat faster. Part of Lara wanted nothing more than this – to break free, to run from this life that she had never wanted. But then she would think about the promise she had made to her mother. How could she? How could she walk away from this house and garden and leave him here to cast his dark shadow over everything? And besides, where would she go?

Beneath all this, too, was the other, deeper question – who had she become? Where was Lara – the practical and inde-pendent girl who had cared for her mother when she was sick, who had looked after the house and helped restore the Arts and Crafts garden? Where was the girl who had taken dictation so efficiently and typed so speedily at the Savings Bank? Where was the girl who had fallen in love with David Curtis from his grandparents' farm in Lodestock?

232

Sometimes, when she was working in the garden or talking with Hester, Lara would laugh at something Hester said and catch a tantalising glimmer of that girl – and then she was gone.

'What's wrong, Lara?' Hester had asked her one day soon after Lara had ventured into the study. 'You look so sad.'

How *did* she look exactly? Lara tended to avoid the mirror these days.

'It's Charles,' she said. Why should she keep his secret? Besides, confiding in Hester seemed important. If it weren't for Hester, Lara thought she'd go mad.

'What about him?'

'He's been writing my name. Writing it over and over. In my handwriting.'

'Your name?'

The best thing about Hester, Lara thought, was that even when Lara knew she sounded a bit bonkers, Hester didn't remark on it.

'It's the house.' Lara glanced back towards it, to the slope of the low, asymmetrical roof and small-paned windows so pleasing to the eye. 'I think he's trying to take it away from me.'

'Can he do that?' Hester's black eyes were wide.

'I don't know.'

Hester seemed to come to a decision. 'I'll ask Mum. She'll know. Or she'll know how to find out.'

Elizabeth must be one of the few women in the village who hadn't fallen under Charles's spell. Lara had seen it for herself on the few occasions when they had gone into the village together. Everyone liked Charles. He had a way about him and he had been so helpful to the community during the wartime years. People probably felt sorry for him too because of his angina, a condition that he had felt necessary to mention to

Lara and her mother at the start of their acquaintance, so no doubt everyone in the village knew about it too. Charles was a very convincing man and his sister Marjorie was active in the WI apparently – which must count for something too. Most people were far more likely to believe his version of events than Lara's; according to Hester, he'd already let it be widely known that Lara was suffering from her nerves, and who knew what else he'd said besides? That would make them feel sorrier for him than ever. Did they know about his mistress? If so, they probably thought he deserved to have her, some small compensation for what he was going through.

'Don't worry,' Hester told Lara. 'You can trust us.' She put her hand through the wall and Lara squeezed it. Human contact. It was so essential to one's well-being and yet she'd never fully realised that before. Hester kept her in touch with the real world – literally.

'How does he do it?' Lara mused out loud. And yet, hadn't Charles duped her too? What a fool she had been. No wonder he laughed at her; Lara had made it all so ridiculously easy.

'He flatters people,' Hester said. 'It works every time.'

Lara glanced at her, surprised at the wisdom from one so young. 'Yes,' she said. 'You're right.'

'Although that could be his weakness too,' Hester added.

Lara put her head on one side and contemplated this. It sounded almost as though Hester was making a plan.

'And he tells them he's protecting you,' Hester continued.

'From what?'

'I'm not sure, exactly.' Hester frowned. 'From the outside world?'

'Hmm.' Everyone in the village was under the impression that Lara had suffered some sort of mental breakdown. Had she? Was she going through it still? Lara wasn't sure she knew the answer to this question.

'People also believe what he says because you aren't there to say any different,' Hester pointed out.

She was her own worst enemy.

In the event, Elizabeth hadn't been able to find out much – at least not yet, which was hardly surprising since she was still far from being in the best of health herself. Lara thought about it a lot – that signature, those bank statements. But she hadn't dared to go into the study again to take another look. Perhaps she was scared of what she might find . . .

But something had to change. Lara owed it to herself. She had to take action.

Nevertheless, as they moved further into summer, the situation remained the same. Lara could feel the shift, though, in the garden, in herself. In the Rose Garden now, she did a bit of dead-heading with her secateurs and sniffed the honeyed scent of her mother's old-fashioned tea roses. She touched the white silken petals with her fingertip. They were so soft – until you came into contact with a thorn.

She walked through the grasses on a now familiar pathway to the secret garden. As always, the atmosphere was dank, the light dim. The hydrangeas were blooming a dusky and papery pink and the foxgloves were deceptively pretty with their speckled purple blooms. Hester had already taught her a lot about how these plants could be used medicinally. It had been a revelation – the white wild water hemlock had seemed so unassuming and as for the sweet-smelling lily of the valley . . .

All these plants grew well in the shady secret garden with its narrow trickling stream and high humidity. But all of them held their mysteries too. Had Lara's mother had any idea? She doubted it.

As Lara re-emerged through the grasses into the Wild Garden, she stopped and drew back into the concealing bamboo and grass curtain. She could see something blue through the gaps in the wooden panels of the gate. Someone was standing on the other side.

She waited for a moment. It was late in the afternoon and the light had that yellow shade to it that she loved, that tinged the yellow and white garden flowers with a hint of green. Everything seemed peaceful. But . . .

It was all right, she thought. There was nothing to worry about. People often walked in the woods, after all.

She heard a low whistle. It was a whistle she'd heard before.

Lara couldn't move. Someone was taunting her. How could they – after all she had gone through? Charles? But no, it couldn't be Charles. She took a step forward. Then another. She summoned up all the courage she thought she'd lost.

'Who's there?' Her voice shook slightly and she fought to control it.

'Lara?'

Her heart seemed to turn over. She stepped closer to the gate, gripped on to the latch. But as always, it was securely locked. 'David?' she breathed.

'Yes, it's me.' He sounded so normal. She couldn't believe that after all this time he could come here, just turn up like this and sound so normal. 'Lara. Can you open this gate? Can we talk?'

As if he had been away weeks or months instead of long years. 'David?' she said again, afraid to be certain, in case he was snatched away once more.

'Yes, Lara. I'm sorry. I wrote to you. I'm—'

'You're alive,' she whispered. And he had written to her? When had he written to her? She realised that she was clinging to the gate. 'I can't open it,' she said. 'It's locked.'

'Don't you have the key?' He sounded breathless now. But what had happened to him? So many questions were bursting into her mind, Lara felt giddy.

'No, I don't.'

'I see.'

Did he? How could he see? Where had he even come from? And why . . . ? But there were too many questions, far too many questions, and she needed to see his face, needed to see for herself that it was true, that he was true and not just some mad fiction from a damaged mind.

She could hear his breathing. She put her eye to the gap in the wooden panels. She could see his face. He looked so much older. But it was David. It really was David.

'But, how . . . ?' The words wouldn't come.

'Lara. I need to talk to you properly.' His tone was urgent. 'I'm worried about you. Can you leave the house and come round to the woods?'

'No. I can't do that.' How could she even begin to explain?

'Can I climb the wall and come over to you?'

Lara shuddered. 'No. It's too risky.' She couldn't think. Supposing Charles looked out of the bedroom window and saw him?

She glanced around. The vines of the wisteria were thick and ribbed. Enough to hold her weight? She looked for the courage she had felt a few moments ago and she found it, still close to the surface. 'Stay there,' she said. 'I'm coming to you.'

CHAPTER 27

Bea

Dorset, June 2018

Bea had been staring out of the window for the best part of two hours as the train took her from the airport – slowly, slowly into the heart of the countryside of south-west England. She was fascinated by it all: terraced houses with squares of lawn and washing hanging on the line; fields with dappled brown cows and sheep grazing; farm buildings, barns, red tractors. The grass was so green . . . She couldn't get over that. The grass here hardly looked real.

Last night, she'd stayed at a hotel at Gatwick, scarcely able to believe that she was here, in England, about to see Nonna's Dorset garden with her own eyes. Bea had travelled abroad before, of course, not so much as a child, because her parents were always busy with the *masseria*, but later, to Spain and France with various friends. But this was different. This was personal. She was here on a job that was so much more than a job – about to see for herself the place where Nonna had grown up. And she was here alone.

At first, Bea had been hesitant about agreeing to the trip. She'd already upset Matteo by her less than enthusiastic response to his proposal. But it was clear Matteo wasn't only talking about marriage – he was talking about a complete change of lifestyle that worried Bea for so many reasons. Obviously, she had to give it a lot of thought. It wasn't a decision to be taken lightly. But how would it help to disappear to England for a month?

Nonetheless, the more Nonna told her – about the Dorset Arts and Crafts garden, which would not have been properly tended for many years, according to Nonna; about Lime Tree House in which Nonna had grown up with her family – the more intrigued she grew. Bea knew that her grandmother hadn't told her everything. There were huge gaps. And there were those old stories. Bea desperately wanted to know the whole truth of what had happened there. The house and garden were Bea's legacy, her grandmother told her, so why wouldn't she want to find out more about the secrets they held? She had to go there in order to find some answers. She needed to see for herself what Nonna had left behind.

Bea watched the landscape flit past. It was a distraction from the sadness she couldn't help but feel. Neat hedgerows, dry-stone walls, high banks of bracken and wildflowers – noticeably some time behind the Italian varieties, but just as pretty. She noted a church spire and a row of little thatched cottages. She was glad that Dorset was so rural – she wouldn't have felt at home in a big town or a city – and already she liked the fresh look of it, the sense of peace it seemed to hold.

Bea had other questions too. If the house belonged to Nonna, then why hadn't her grandmother simply put it up for sale when she left England? And since she hadn't done that – why had she never gone back there? Was there nothing or no one her grandmother might want to see here in Dorset? No friends? No family? That seemed very sad.

'There will be much that needs sorting out, my dear,' her grandmother had told her. 'You will need to do some work in the garden, of course.' She lifted her hand and then slowly let it drop to her side as if the movement was simply too much for her.

She was so frail, thought Bea. It broke her heart. 'What about the house?' she asked.

'I suppose that it might need clearing. There will be . . . furniture and things.'

Didn't she even know what was there? She seemed awfully vague. But then again, it had been a long time.

'And then I suppose we'll have to put it up for sale.' Nonna sighed. 'It would be wonderful if the place could be taken over by someone who would restore the house and garden to their former glory.' Her expression was wistful now. 'I always hoped the garden would go on and on.'

Bea patted her hand. She wished that her grandmother could have visited with her. She wished that Nonna had asked her to go years ago. But Bea's mother had told her that Nonna had hardly spoken of it; it was only now that she seemed to have been spurred into action. 'You loved the garden,' Bea said.

Her grandmother nodded. Her blue eyes were bright. 'It was my mother's pride and joy,' she said. 'She wanted it to last forever. And I made a promise to her. At first, I took care of it for her, loved it for her . . .'

'And then?' Bea prompted.

'Everything changed,' she whispered. Her eyes grew misty, her voice failed; she seemed too emotional to go on.

This then was Nonna's story. And so, Bea would have to go there – it was part of her family history. Bea was half-British after all. Nonna was bound to the place by a promise, and that promise had just been passed on to Bea. It was a commitment she felt compelled to make, for Nonna's sake as well as her own. And Bea sensed that her mother also understood. Before Bea left, she had seemed softer somehow, more approachable. 'Take care, my darling,' she had told Bea. And she had held her with such warmth, such love . . . Bea would miss her family, she knew.

The train pulled in to another platform and Bea watched as a couple enjoyed a lingering kiss, before she jumped on the train and he waved her off, blowing kisses as the train departed. Bea sighed. It hadn't been like that for Bea and Matteo. She had left without even a goodbye.

Telling Matteo about her plans had not been easy.

'You are doing what?' First, he had looked so confused that her heart went out to him. 'You are going where?' But already, he was starting to sound annoyed.

'I have promised to do this project for Nonna,' Bea explained.

'But why?' he asked. 'Why now?'

'She is very old.' Bea hated to think of it, but she knew her grandmother didn't have long to live. How much time *did* she have? A few months? A few years? Bea liked to think that Nonna would reach the grand age of one hundred; she couldn't bear to think of her grandmother no longer being around, no longer a part of her life, a sounding board for Bea whenever she needed to make a difficult decision or talk something through. But she had to be realistic. Bea could lose her at any time and so all time with her was precious. If her grandmother needed Bea to do this thing – and clearly, she did – then Bea would do it. No question.

'So?'

Bea didn't like the look in his eye. She knew already that Matteo liked to get what he wanted. But now she wondered if he lacked the compassion she would always look for in a man. He seemed thoughtful where his mother was concerned, and he'd certainly been upset when his father's life had hung in the balance, but what about other people, not so directly connected to him? What about Bea's family?

'Nonna needs me to do it before she dies,' she told him bluntly. 'She does not have much time left, Matteo.'

He gave a little nod of acknowledgement – something, at least, she thought.

'But right now?'

They were sitting on the restaurant terrace – just a brief chat before Matteo started helping prepare for the evening dinner service – and the fragrance of the herbs Bea had planted hung in the air. Matteo was already stressed; she could see it in the tension around his mouth and she felt bad about adding to that. She put her hand on his arm. 'I am sorry,' she said. 'I know it is a bad time.'

'The worst.' He didn't respond to her touch and she could hardly blame him. They were sitting close together and yet they felt so far apart.

'But I do need a bit of space. I need to think about things.' She willed him to understand. How could she say it without it sounding like rejection?

'You just do not get it, Beatrice.' He pulled away. He wouldn't even look at her now.

Bea sighed. She did get it. She had tried explaining to him – that it was all too quick, that surely she didn't have to step in as his partner immediately, that she had little interest in the restaurant business, that she loved her gardens. But Matteo didn't seem to see any of that. It was one-way traffic. All he could see was what he wanted.

Bea looked around at the terrace garden she had designed and created such a short time ago. It was still in the early stages of its growth, of course. But already, much was in bloom – the erigeron daisies, the echinacea and the purple flowers of the rosemary. If she married Matteo, she would be here every day to witness that growth, to see it evolve into the garden she had dreamt up for Signora Leone.

But there were so many other gardens . . . The peace and tranquillity she found in her gardens, the quiet joy of working within the world of nature was something that Bea needed in her life. Would Matteo ever respect and understand that? It seemed not.

He turned to her. His blue eyes were as intense as ever but there was a coldness there too that she hated. 'What if I told you I would not let you go to England?' His tone was belligerent now.

Bea moved fractionally away. Unless he was joking – and he didn't appear to be – that was definitely going too far. 'Then I would tell you that it is my life, Matteo,' she said. 'And not your decision to make for me.'

He nodded gloomily. 'I do not think you want a husband, Beatrice,' he said. 'I do not think you are a team player.'

Perhaps he was right. Perhaps Matteo needed someone very different from Bea – someone who would love to host dinner parties, chat to guests at the restaurant, float around looking elegant and being charming. That wasn't Bea – and it never would be. She took a breath. 'I would understand if this has made you change your mind, Matteo,' she said. 'About us, I mean.'

He glared at her. 'And if I changed my mind – would that make it easy for you?'

'Oh, Matteo.' Nothing would make this easy. Bea was tired

and they weren't getting anywhere. She supposed that he had his agenda and she had hers. Who was being the selfish one? Could they meet in the middle? Or was it just wrong? The wrong time? The wrong relationship? The wrong man?

'Go to England then.' He glanced at his watch and jumped immediately to his feet. 'Go to England.' He swept his hand through his thick dark hair as if to add more emphasis to his words. 'But do not expect me to be around when you come back, that is all.'

Now, Bea held back the tears that were threatening. She couldn't cry on a train on her first day in Dorset. In the past two weeks since that conversation with Matteo, she'd shed enough tears already.

Bea hadn't told her family how Matteo had reacted to the news that she was going away for a while. She didn't want them to think badly of him and she didn't want Nonna to have second thoughts about asking Bea to go. In fact, Bea hadn't seen Matteo since that afternoon on the restaurant terrace. She'd texted a few times, tried to explain, but it hadn't gone well, although neither of them had acknowledged that it might be over between them. She supposed, then, that it wasn't . . . But his pride had been hurt and that meant a lot to a man like Matteo. As for Bea, she knew she'd made the right decision – for now. This time away, this space was exactly what she needed.

Bea gazed out of the window at trees, fields and villages as the train passed by. She spotted horse chestnut, apple trees, elderflower and blackthorn. It was a bright early summer's day and the sky was a clear and silvery blue. But as she'd stood on the railway platform earlier, the chilly breeze had made Bea shiver. This was England, she reminded herself.

The truth was that being here on this train, coming to Dorset, felt right in a way that the restaurant in Polignano did not. This was something she had to do for herself, for Nonna, for her family, which was, in its way, just as important as what Matteo had to do for his family back in Puglia. Bea might only be gone for a month – she hadn't bought a return ticket; she'd wait until she'd taken stock of what needed to be done. And in a month, she'd know, wouldn't she, which pathway she should take?

Nonna seemed to think so. 'Things have a way of working out for the best, my dear,' she'd said when Bea was leaving. 'One step at a time. Everything will become clear.'

Bea hoped that this would be the case. Although if things became clear and she realised that she did want to marry Matteo, would he still be there for her? *Allora* . . . She supposed that if Matteo couldn't wait a month or two, then he wasn't the right man for her after all.

With a jolt, Bea heard the guard announce that they were approaching Crewkerne, a station in Somerset, but nonetheless the place where she needed to get off. She jumped to her feet and pulled her case from where she'd stuffed it in the luggage hold almost three hours ago.

The station was quiet. From the platform, she followed a few other travellers through a gap in the fence to the car park on the other side; clearly, they didn't bother with ticket barriers here. Fortunately, though, there were a few taxis parked by the station entrance and she got in the first one and told the driver where she would like to go.

He didn't try to start a conversation, which suited Bea. She didn't want to answer anyone's questions. She was content to sit back and gaze at the rural landscape they were driving through, so different from Puglia but very beautiful. The roads were narrow and winding and bordered with hedgerows; on the other side she glimpsed rolling hills and fields of sheep and various agricultural crops including the acid yellow of rapeseed.

She noted the point at which they crossed into Dorset. *At last*, she thought. They passed through a couple of small villages and then finally the taxi driver indicated right and they swept between a pair of battered wrought-iron gates onto a tree-lined driveway.

This must be it . . . There were Lime trees, of course. Lime trees, with their heart-shaped leaves symbolising love and liberty, Bea seemed to recall from her studies – which was interesting, to say the least. She leant forwards in her seat, eager for a first glance of the house. *And here it was* . . . A large and low-roofed, gabled building made of stone. Not grand exactly, but elegant and adorable. Though as they drove closer, even to Bea's inexperienced eye, she could see that Lime Tree House was in need of some loving care – the stone was crumbling, the window timber was worn and bare and some slates were missing from the roof. Nevertheless, it was so much more than she'd been expecting.

The taxi drew to a halt and Bea paid the driver. He got her case out of the boot, said goodbye and, with a final curious glance her way, off he drove. Bea turned to look at the house once again. Her grandmother had told her that she'd written to some neighbours who had been keeping an eye on the place for her. In fact, it had been tenanted for years, managed by a company in a small market town nearby, but empty for the past few years and now in need of modernisation. The front door key, Nonna had told her, would be under the large azalea pot.

Bea wheeled her case up to the steps leading to the front door. There were several pots outside, the terracotta cracked and worn, the plants looking the worse for wear. The azalea was still alive, but straggly, and the soil was dry as desert sand with probably about as much nourishment. Her first job, Bea decided, would be to get watering.

She eased the pot up and found the key. *Phew.* That was a relief. She went up the crumbling stone steps to the front door which was a work of art in itself, made of gorgeous but rather weathered panelled wood and boasting a beautiful crimson and blue stained-glass door panel. Bea inserted the key into the lock. It was stiff and it creaked as she turned it, but the lock was moving . . .

Suddenly, the door opened from the other side with such force that Bea half fell into the house.

The person who had opened the door – she registered young, male, paint-splattered overalls – put a hand under her arm to halt her forward momentum.

'Oh, my God. Sorry,' he said.

'It is okay, I am fine.' She stared at him. He had a mane of unruly blond hair and his clear green eyes showed confusion. But who was he? Nonna hadn't said anything about the house being occupied at the moment. Was he a squatter? He looked unkempt enough. So, what was she supposed to do now?

'Who on earth are you?' The man – he wasn't a boy; he was probably older than Bea, in fact – was eyeing her with suspicion. His gaze fell on her suitcase, still on the front step, and he frowned. 'What do you want?'

Some welcome . . . Bea straightened her shoulders. Her arrival might have been undignified so far, but she knew her rights. Her grandmother had never let her down. 'My name is Beatrice Romano and I believe this house to be the property of my grandmother,' she said clearly and in her best English accent. 'And who, may I ask, are you?'

CHAPTER 28

Lara

Dorset, June 1947

How difficult could it be? Lara took hold of two of the thickest vines, one in each hand. She pulled hard to test their strength, found her first foothold on a lower vine, then her second a little higher. Fortunately, as usual, she was wearing her thin summer slacks rather than a dress, though the relief she felt about this was followed immediately by concern. David was on the other side of this wall and what in heaven's name did she look like? Lately, Lara had stopped caring.

She heaved herself up and located her next handhold. Up again she went. She was now balancing precariously several feet from the ground. 'Oh, my giddy aunt,' she whispered.

'Lara? Are you all right?' From the other side of the wall, David sounded concerned. His voice spurred her on.

'Yes,' she called. How ridiculous she must look, attempting to scale an old brick wall by way of an ancient wisteria. Suppose someone saw her? Charles, for instance. Her breath caught.

She took another step up, testing first, because if she fell from here, she'd be badly bruised at the very least. Then another. The ribs of the wisteria vine held. She exhaled. The branches were wide apart. It was easy to tell which were the safest and strongest vines. Fortunately, this wisteria was so old that it was sufficiently embedded in both the ground and the wall for its roots to have inched out narrow footholds in the brick.

'Lara?'

'Yes, I'm fine,' she called back. She wouldn't look down, not now. Her hands were scrabbling, reaching for the top of the wall, which was rough to the touch, scraping the skin of her palms. And then with a final heave, she could look over, she could see him.

'Oh, my Lord. Lara, be careful.' His eyes were wide, his arms too as he took a step forward. He was ready to catch her, she knew.

'Hello, David.' She felt shy suddenly, and very exposed. She couldn't help noticing the differences that the years had made. He was more of a man, less of a boy. And he was thinner. There were fine lines around his mouth and eyes and his dark hair was a little longer, more unkempt. But he was David and he was here. Where had he been? And why now . . . ?

He laughed. 'There you are!'

'Here I am.' Rapunzel in reverse, she thought. Something like that anyway.

Filled with an adrenalin she hadn't known she could summon, Lara somehow swung herself up, and swivelled her legs over so that she was sitting on the top of the wall looking down on him. He was wearing working trousers and a shirt with the sleeves rolled up. He looked for all the world as if he'd just got off a tractor in a field somewhere.

'Jump,' he said. 'I'll catch you.' And he opened his arms wider still.

It wasn't hard to trust him again. Lara took a breath, pushed herself off and made the leap.

Ouff. He caught her just as he'd promised. 'I've got you.' He held on for a few extra moments, probably just so that she could regain her balance.

Lara felt his breath warm on her neck. And she was certain that she could hear his heart beating through the thin cotton shirt he wore. *David,* she thought.

He steadied her and let go. Took a step back as though suddenly conscious of this new distanced relationship between them. *What had happened to him?* His gaze slid away from her and she wondered immediately – was he with someone else now? Was he married perhaps? Or was it her situation and the time that had passed that was keeping him at arm's length?

'Rather an undignified arrival.' She brushed the brick dust and flaking bits of vine from her blouse and slacks to stop herself from staring at him. His arms were browner than before, though they had the same sinewy strength. His face was browner too and more weathered. His hazel eyes were the same as ever. Would he kiss her? It didn't seem so.

'You look beautiful,' he said.

'David . . .'

And then she was in his arms again, properly in his arms this time, and he was holding her tight, her face against his warm chest, and she felt safe as she hadn't felt safe for years. *Oh, David,* she thought. He still didn't kiss her, though. And why hadn't he come to the front door? He must know that she was married. He must know about Charles.

Lara didn't want to step out of his embrace, but at last, she did.

There was so much she needed to know. She brushed herself down again; at least it was something to do with her hands.

'Shall we walk?' she suggested.

He nodded, and side by side they made their way along the grassy path between the beech trees. It wasn't a well-trodden path, thank goodness, and so hopefully there was little chance of bumping into someone she knew.

'I was worried about you,' he said, when they had only been walking for a moment. 'I talked to a couple of people in the village. They said . . .' – he hesitated – '. . . that you weren't well.'

'David.' She turned to him. 'For God's sake. Where have you been?'

'Ah.' He took her arm and pressed her to keep moving, as if he too was worried about seeing someone.

What if Charles had already found out she was gone? Her heart seemed to flutter beneath her ribcage and she rested her other palm on her chest for a moment as if she could still it. They came to the little stream. He took a big stride right over and held her hand to guide her over the stepping stone. His touch was so warm, so sure.

'I suppose I should start by telling you something about the war,' he said softly as they walked on under the canopy of the translucent beech leaves. 'Not about the fighting and the bloodshed – you don't need to know all the grisly details. But, oh Lara, it was such a bad time – and a time that went on for longer than people know.'

Lara nodded. She and those who had been here in England, those who had never seen any of the actual fighting, could only imagine. 'You must have seen a good deal of suffering,' she ventured. Because much as she wanted to bombard him with more personal questions, she recognised the need to allow David to tell his story in the way he wanted to tell it. She would find it all out soon enough – why he hadn't come home, what he had done since the war ended, where he had spent his time.

'The fact is . . .' His footsteps faltered. 'Oh, Lara. It was ghastly, I can hardly bring myself to tell you.'

'Tell me what?' Lara braced herself. She realised that his fists were clenched.

'I saw my pal Colin die in the field right beside me.' His voice broke.

'Oh, David.' Lara stopped walking. 'I'm so sorry.' It was her turn now to open her arms; to stop, to hold his dear head as close as she dared, to stroke his hair, to soothe.

At last, he looked up. His eyes were red. He seemed so lost, so broken. Lara could see how much damage those events he had witnessed, the loss of his comrade in arms had done to him.

'I didn't shout quickly enough,' he whispered. 'To warn him.'

Lara shook her head decisively. She gripped his upper arms. 'It wasn't your fault,' she said. 'It could so easily have been you.'

'For months I wished it was,' he admitted. He took her arm in his and they continued walking at a slow pace. The linking of their arms felt so peaceful, so good, that Lara hardly dared breathe for fear of breaking the spell. It was a warm afternoon and the beech trees were providing a welcome dappled shade. The woods were so tranquil. It felt to Lara that she and David were entirely alone and she sensed that it was easier for him to tell his story while he kept moving; perhaps it helped keep those raw emotions at bay.

'But you survived,' she prompted him as they continued down the path. It was just wide enough to walk side by side.

They were so close; she had never dreamt they could do this again; she had grown used to the thought that she'd lost him.

'I was taken prisoner in southern Italy,' he told her.

Lara let out a little gasp.

'That's where we were when it happened. I was put in a POW camp. It was a while before I managed to get out of there.'

She could feel the tension in his arm now. They came to a slight incline and as the woodland opened out at the top, Lara saw some foxgloves growing in a glade to one side. They made her think of the speckled purple blooms in the secret garden: beautiful, wild and mysterious.

'But how did you get out?' She wanted to know everything, but she was wary of asking too many questions. All these memories must be difficult for him. Was that why he hadn't come home? Because he wasn't well enough? She didn't want to think about that.

'I escaped with a couple of other men,' he told her. 'We got separated but I was lucky enough to fall into the hands of the Romanos.'

'The Romanos?' They sounded like a rather frightening gang of some kind, but David's voice had softened when he mentioned their name, so she hoped she was wrong about that.

They walked on, the trees becoming thicker around them, the lime-green leaves providing a woodland roof under which Lara felt that they were truly alone.

'They're simple agricultural workers,' he said. 'They have an olive farm – twenty hectares in all. And they are very kind.'

'They looked after you?' Lara guessed it would have been dangerous for them to do so. She knew something of Italy's war, but she would certainly have made it her business to find out much more, if she had known that David had been there. He had made no mention of it in the last letter she'd received, but that letter had been written an awfully long time ago.

He nodded. 'Like many other Italians, they were anti-fascist – supportive of the Allies.'

Lara frowned as they walked on. 'When . . . ?' She needed to piece together the timings.

'The Allies occupied Italy in 1943 after Mussolini's surrender,' David supplied.

Yes, of course. They came to a fork in the track and he looked at her, head on one side. She gestured towards the thinner and winding path on the right. She knew these woods so well from her childhood. The narrow grassy path would take them on a loop away from the direction of the village and eventually back to their starting point. He led the way, in single file now.

'And what did you do then?' she asked his departing back. But already she thought she knew the answer.

'I stayed with the family,' David said. 'I was in a bad state, Lara.' He turned around to look at her and she thought she could see it etched in the new lines on his face – the pain and suffering he had endured, the guilt too at surviving when his comrade and friend Colin had died before his very eyes.

'Did it bring you some peace?' she asked tentatively. She hoped he didn't think her question too foolish. But she needed to know. She couldn't bear to think of him so broken.

'It was peaceful, yes.' He turned around and continued walking between the tall, slender beech trees. 'The rural landscape, you know.' Once again, he turned back towards her and his hazel eyes lit up. 'I wish you could see it, Lara. Italy is so beautiful.'

Yes, and here I was waiting for you . . . Lara didn't say it, though. She looked up through the shiny leaves of the trees to the afternoon blue of the sky, which seemed to be turning almost to gold. She must wait and hear him out, because she was sure there was a lot more to come.

'It was a simple life,' he continued, walking on once again. 'And a hard one. There was very little food to go round during the occupation. Many people were starving.' He paused to hold a wayward branch away from the path so that Lara could safely pass by. 'Sad to say, the Allies didn't always make sure the Italian families got their share. And they didn't always,' he hesitated, 'treat them well.'

'But you helped them?' Lara guessed. She could tell that there was a lot that David was omitting from this story. Was he protecting her – or protecting himself perhaps? She didn't mind which it was. The war was over. Now, the time to move on was well overdue.

'It was the least I could do.' David tore his fingers through his dark hair and looked through the surrounding woodland as if the beech and hazel trees might provide him with some answers. 'It was a terrible time, Lara. Plenty of Allied soldiers were being accused of taking advantage of their privileged position by keeping supplies to themselves – and with good reason. As for the Italians – many of them were forced to turn to crime and prostitution simply in order to survive.'

Lara recognised his passion. He had become involved with these people; she could see that. The qualities of courage and fairness that she had always admired in him had come to the fore. David had always been a man with integrity. 'They stood by you too.' She could picture it all. David, grateful for their loyalty; the family full of gratitude for all he did for them.

They must have formed a close bond. And who else was in that family? she wondered. Some dusky Italian girl who might have fallen in love with David and he with her? And who could blame him? Not Lara. They had been strange times – and she had married Charles, had she not?

Charles . . . An involuntary shudder ran through her. *If Charles knew where she was and with whom . . .*

'Yes,' he said. 'I have so much to thank them for. My life. My sanity, even. Everything.'

Everything. That was a lot indeed. Lara let her hand trail against the smooth grey bark of a beech tree that stood next to the path. 'And what about me?' she couldn't help asking. Because surely, she must have featured somewhere in all this? 'Did you ever think about me?'

'Oh, God, Lara.' Abruptly, he stopped walking. He turned. He took her face between his hands and stared into her eyes. He didn't kiss her, though. Still, he didn't kiss her. 'I thought about you constantly,' he muttered. 'I thought about you and I thought about our love. Sometimes – in the dark days – it was all that kept me going.'

Lara stared back at him. It was what she had longed to hear. And yet . . . 'You didn't write to me,' she said. 'You didn't even let me know that you were alive.'

'No.' His hands dropped to his sides. 'Not then.' He turned back and continued walking along the path, distanced from her once again.

The breeze whispered some unknown message softly through the leaves. *Pass it on. Pass it on.* Lara wished she knew what she should say to him.

'I should have done, I know. It was unfair of me. I was a total brute.'

'No.' She almost laughed. David could never be that.

'I started letters,' he said. 'I started dozens of letters.'

Lara waited. *Dozens of letters* . . . If only she had received dozens of letters.

'But each time, I couldn't go on.' His voice broke once again and her heart went out to him.

'Why not, David?' Lara's voice was low. She had wanted to hear from him so badly. When she thought of all those sleepless nights. *Missing in action* . . . *Missing, presumed dead* . . . She had been desperate to know that he was alive. *If I had known that* . . . What would she have done? If David hadn't come back to her, would she still have married Charles?

He stopped in his tracks. 'There just seemed too much to say.' He spoke so quietly that Lara could barely hear the words.

'I see.' She didn't see – not entirely – but she was trying to.

The path was wider again now. David took her arm as he had done before and they walked on. It seemed so natural. Lara recalled the way it had felt when she'd walked with Charles into the village that spring day and she felt sick with regret – of what she had lost, of what she could no longer claim as her own.

'It's hard to understand, I know,' he said gently, 'but I wanted to try and explain to you, Lara.'

Here it is then, she thought. This is where he would tell her that he had fallen in love with someone else. Not that she had anything to offer him now, but having seen him for just this small part of this afternoon, she knew that her life would be even bleaker now without him.

CHAPTER 29

Bea

Dorset, June 2018

'Your grandmother?' He seemed perplexed.

So, who exactly was this man in the painting overalls – and more to the point, what was he doing in Nonna's house?

Behind him, Bea took in the sight of an elegant – though somewhat dilapidated – hallway and a wide winding staircase that managed to look both sad and grand at the same time. *Goodness*. This house was quite something. It must, she realised, be worth quite a lot of money – even in this state of disrepair. Which made it even stranger; why had Nonna just left it here – tenanted for many years by all accounts, but not cared for?

'Are you decorating Lime Tree House?' she asked him. Was that it? 'Did the neighbour call you in?'

His mouth twitched into a smile. 'You're Italian.'

Damn, and she'd believed her English accent to be so good . . . 'Half-Italian,' she corrected.

'Lara's granddaughter,' he said.

Hmm. She scrutinised him once again. 'You are not a painter and decorator,' she said.

He laughed. 'No, I'm not.' He looked around them at the tatty but spacious hallway. The ceiling was more sepia than white, the wallpaper was peeling and the plasterwork crumbly. 'Though the place could do with one, I agree.'

She couldn't resist a smile. 'Then . . . ?'

He stuck out a paint-stained hand. 'The neighbour,' he said. 'I've heard quite a bit about Lara over the years.'

'Oh.' Bea had gathered from her grandmother that the neighbour was an old lady called Hester. Nevertheless, she took his hand which was warm, his firm grip somewhat reassuring. What might he have heard about her grandmother? she wondered. 'So, you are . . . ?' Really, it was difficult to find out anything concrete here in Dorset.

'Lewis Tarrant,' he supplied.

Clear as mud. She raised an enquiring eyebrow.

'Hester's grandson.'

'I see.' It had not been a good start, she felt. She'd also noticed that the paint stains on his hands and overalls comprised a medley of colours. So, either he was painting a wall the colours of a rainbow, or . . . 'And you are an artist, yes?'

'Sort of.'

Bea nodded, though she had no idea what 'sort of' might mean in this context. She wanted to ask what he was doing in the house too, but obviously that would be rude. Equally obviously, he'd had no idea she was on her way.

'My grandmother wrote to Hester,' she told him. 'Perhaps she did not receive the letter?' To Bea, it was a little strange that people still even sent letters rather than emails, but Nonna had said that of course Hester wouldn't have anything as newfangled as email and they had communicated perfectly well by letter up till now.

'Ah,' he said. 'I don't know. That is . . .' He pushed the unruly mane of blond hair from his face.

Good cheekbones, she thought. He wasn't conventionally attractive; his face was too angular and he had a slightly haunted look about him. But his eyes were lovely – clear, green and honest-looking (if eyes could be honest-looking and Bea was sure that they could) – and his mouth was wide and . . .

'My grandmother has Alzheimer's,' he said.

Oh, dear. 'I am so sorry to hear that.' Was Nonna aware of this? Bea doubted it – she certainly would have mentioned such a thing.

'I look after her affairs these days,' Lewis Tarrant went on. 'She's in her late eighties, as you probably know.'

Bea shook her head. She realised that she knew very little. Nonna had not been very forthcoming and Bea had assumed her grandmother wanted Bea to find out everything for herself. 'It must be hard for you.' How fortunate they were that Nonna still had all her faculties intact.

'At times, very,' he agreed. 'I'm her carer, which means that at least she can stay in her own house. But she likes having some independence, so it's possible that a letter could have arrived and . . .' He shrugged. 'She might not have mentioned it.'

That made sense. He wouldn't be able to watch her every minute of the day. But at least he was looking after her; at least Hester hadn't had to go into a nursing home.

'She gets confused,' he continued. 'She forgets things. You know?'

'Yes.' At least, she could try to imagine. Bea saw the emotion in his eyes and her heart went out to him.

He slapped himself on the temple. 'But what am I doing? I

260

haven't even offered you tea.' His frown was deep and sudden. 'Do you want to come next door for a cuppa? Or I could nip out and get you some supplies? There's nothing here, you see.'

Bea hadn't really thought of that. She'd been so eager to get to the house. 'Some supplies would be great.' Much as she appreciated his offer of hospitality, what she really wanted to do was take her first look around the house and garden – alone.

'Sure.' He pulled a pad and pencil from a cavernous pocket in the overalls. 'Tell me what I can get you. It's a small village store but it sells essentials.'

'Just something for tonight, please,' she said. 'If you're sure you don't mind?' It was very kind of him. She decided that she liked Lewis Tarrant. He was just the sort of person anyone would want as a neighbour. And since she was likely to be here for at least a month, in a country she'd never visited before, she was grateful for that.

'Nope.' He shook his head and grinned. 'It's the least I can do after the way I introduced you to the house.'

'Well then, coffee and milk. Maybe some fresh or tinned tomatoes and pasta, a few vegetables. I can go shopping tomorrow.' She would get properly organised then. Make a list, devise a plan, work out all the things that needed to be done.

'No problem.' He shot her a searching look. He must be wondering what she was doing here if Hester hadn't told him.

'Thank you,' she said.

'You must be tired from the journey,' he observed.

'A little.' But not so tired that she couldn't wait to take a look around. 'Can I settle up with you when you get back?'

'Of course.' He patted his pockets again and this time produced a battered black leather wallet. 'I'll be half an hour or so.' He cocked his head towards the doors leading off from the hallway – all but one closed, all panelled and all holding who knew what secrets from the past. 'Give you a chance to take a quick look around.'

He wasn't wrong. But which should come first – the house or the garden? No contest, she thought. A quick glance at the downstairs and then the garden it would be.

Lewis paused in the doorway and looked back at her. 'You're probably wondering what I was doing here?'

Now that he'd mentioned it . . . 'I was actually.' She waited.

'You were right the first time,' he said. 'I was doing a bit of painting. Or drawing, at least. Not in the house, but of the house, if you get my drift.'

She didn't. 'Of the house?'

'It's a stunning piece of architecture,' he said. 'All sorts of original Arts and Crafts features. You'll see.' He put her suitcase in the hall, gave her a cheery wave and shut the front door behind him.

Bea turned slowly around. She exhaled and then properly breathed in her surroundings for the first time. The air was musty but the house smelt of wood – sweet and mellow. She touched the panelling of the nearest door with her fingertips, opened it and peeked into the kitchen. She was immediately struck by the simplicity of the style and the materials. Bea had googled 'Arts and Crafts' and understood that the movement had advocated the use of local stone, slates and wood, thus valuing the skills of the traditional craftsman. The Arts and Crafts movement had emerged from deep moral and social concerns following the effects of the Industrial Revolution, she'd read, and it represented a rebellion against High Victorian tastes. Bea didn't know much about that – but Nonna had said this was a beautiful house and it certainly was. Even so, she hadn't expected anything like this.

Bea pondered the mystery once again. If Nonna had loved Lime Tree House so much, why had she never been back? And if she'd left the house for good all those years ago, why had she never sold it – if only so that she could use the money to buy something in Italy or even to put into the farm? Bea knew that her grandparents had started their life in Puglia living in what was little more than an agricultural shack. Which seemed crazy, when they owned a house in England like this one. And had left it just sitting here.

Back in the hallway, Bea opened a door that led to a bright and airy sitting room. To her surprise, the room was fully furnished, the large sofa and two armchairs covered in a faded fabric that must once have been very elegant. The flowery wallpaper was faded too and peeling at the edges and the wooden flooring was a bit battered, but the intimacy of the room was immediately apparent. Bea noticed the little cushioned window seat – that would have been a favourite spot of her grandmother's, she guessed.

The large inglenook fireplace and exposed beams gave Bea a good flavour of how stunning the room had once been. Perhaps this was what Lewis had been drawing? There were rather a lot of cobwebs, though. She pulled a face. Thankfully, Nonna had been generous with the money she had given her to sort things out. The place could do with a thorough spring clean. After that, it might be clearer what other work needed to be done.

Bea flung open the French doors and walked out onto the veranda.

She caught her breath – it was obvious that the garden was beautiful. The yellow and cream honeysuckle and dark purple clematis was rampaging over the pergola and she could see an avenue of hollyhocks not yet in flower and a charming little garden space to her right with what looked like a stone sundial lying amongst a mass of undergrowth. The beds were so overgrown and tangled with weeds that it was impossible to discern their shape, but she could make out a lavender parterre and some gangly herbs. Someone – presumably her grandmother – had created a romantic and sensory little area here, right in front of the house.

Bea wandered down the steps which were cloaked in thick moss and made her way along the central path in order to access the little garden. There was a pond behind the lavender which hadn't been visible before, thick with algae and bordered with tall grasses. Everything was choked with weeds; it was a wonder any of the more delicate plants had survived. She breathed in the scent of the lavender, rosemary and thyme and looked around her. It was a pleasingly private garden. On the far side was a brick wall; as Nonna had told her, this was a walled garden divided into separate sections, or rooms according to the Arts and Crafts concept.

Exciting . . . What did each garden represent? She had no idea – yet. Back in the central avenue, she explored the garden on the other side – clearly, a spring garden with some sculptural euphorbia and the bleached remains of bluebells, primroses, tulips and daffodils scattered amongst the tall grass. Under the flowering cherry tree, a wooden bench was falling apart, the blossoms scattered all around. Once again, weeds and grasses had grown up all around the spring flowers, but someone had tended this garden until fairly recently, because the plants and the spirit of the garden had certainly survived.

She returned to the central avenue and soon discovered an old allotment to her left, a glasshouse with cracked panes of glass and nothing still living inside, and various fruit trees and brambles growing alongside the wall. She wandered through the mini orchard beyond; all the trees were in desperate need of pruning. A rambling Virginia creeper had dug its roots into the mortar; there were bricks missing here and there and the wall was in danger of falling apart. Bea touched it and felt the dust crumble between her fingers.

Through a small gap in the thick and unruly yew hedge on the other side of the avenue, she found a rose garden, sadly overgrown, with another section beyond that, which had gone completely wild. On the other side of this was the far wall topped with barbed wire, with woodland beyond.

It was overgrown, yes. It was in need of love and attention. But despite the neglect, it was a whimsical and delightful garden and Bea couldn't wait to get her hands on it. She started walking back to the house.

'Hi!' Lewis was waving to her from the veranda. 'What do you think?'

'It is glorious.'

'A lot of work to be done, though.' He put his head to one side. 'I hope you're into gardening.'

'It is my job.' Bea looked past him towards the small-paned windows and red roof tiles. It really was such a pretty house. How could Nonna have allowed it to be so neglected? She remembered the stories about the girl who had needed to escape from the walled garden. But if that girl was Nonna, then what had happened here? She thought of the barbed wire and repressed a small shiver.

'Ah.' He was still watching her appraisingly. 'Is that why you're here then?'

'Yes, it is.' At least in part . . . Bea walked back towards the house. She shielded her eyes from the sun which was lighting up the blond of Lewis's hair and catching the glorious stained glass in the panel above the French doors. She must clean it, she thought. In fact, she must clean everything. It was a daunting task. 'I need to sort out the house too,' she told him. But where to start?

'Can I help?'

'With the gardening?' Surely that was taking neighbourliness to another level?

'Why not?' He shrugged. 'At least I can do some of the heavier stuff.'

'That would be great,' Bea said. She supposed that he couldn't work and had to stay close to home because of having to care for his grandmother. Or did he earn money from selling paintings? 'If you have the time? Though I'd pay you, of course.'

'No need,' he said. 'I do a bit of this and that to keep the wolf from the door. Sell a bit of art, do a few odd jobs, that sort of thing. But you should talk to my grandmother – about the garden, I mean. She always kept an eye on it and I'm pretty sure she used some of the rent to keep it maintained. But that was some time ago now.'

'I would love to talk to her.' It was possible that Hester wouldn't remember very much, but any snippets of information could be useful.

'Tomorrow? Come for lunch?' He glanced at his watch. 'I should be getting back now to check on her. Your stuff's in the kitchen by the way.'

'Oh, thanks, let me get my purse.' Bea started up the steps to the veranda but he shook his head.

'Tomorrow will be fine. Shall we say twelve thirty?'

'I will look forward to it,' said Bea. Hester had lived in the house next door to Nonna all those years ago. What might she remember about the girl who needed to escape from the garden? Bea couldn't wait to find out more.

CHAPTER 30

Lara

Dorset, June 1947

'You see, because of what's happened to me,' David said, 'because of everything I felt, everything I went through, I've become a different man.'

A different man. Lara could almost put her finger on it now, the change that she had perceived in David from the very first moment. There was a quietness in him, but it was more than that. He had lost something, she realised. He was emotionally and mentally scarred by it all. This, she thought, must be what war had done to so many men – and to those they loved.

'A lesser man,' he added. A lone shaft of sunlight darted through the trees and for a moment it lit up his face. Lara saw the weariness and the pain, but she also saw the man she had never stopped loving.

'No.' She took his hand and squeezed hard.

'It's true, I'm afraid, Lara,' he said. Gently, he took his hand away and Lara felt bereft. 'I'm not always well, you see. I have bad nights, even what the doctor calls panic attacks where I feel I can't breathe.' He struck his chest as if in anger. 'I've tried to overcome it. But I can't help remembering, I can't help seeing it, seeing him, just as he was that day.'

'And you thought I wouldn't understand?' she asked him gently. All she wanted to do was hold him in her arms, but she sensed that they'd moved past that moment now.

They walked on more slowly. Perhaps David thought that he would never be healed. Or perhaps he had found someone else to look after him.

'It wasn't that,' he assured her. 'You're so good. I knew you would care for me if I asked you to. But I didn't want you to have to. I didn't want to appeal to your sense of duty.' His mouth twisted. 'I didn't want you to have to martyr yourself, Lara.'

'Oh, David . . .' Her steps faltered.

'I wasn't sure I could go back to my old life.' She could see that he was struggling now. But he was still walking and he was still talking. 'That was part of it. It's hard to explain. I couldn't even bring myself to write to my grandparents at first – although I kind of guessed that they had gone. I was in a bad way, Lara.'

'David—'

'I've changed, you see.' He spoke more harshly now.

'I know.' Of course she knew. But what David wasn't aware of was that she had changed too. She too was scarred, half broken. She looked across the woodland. The gorse was more prominent in this part of the wood, the yellow flowers so bright they almost hurt her eyes. And the woodland floor was covered in dog's mercury, a plant she'd learnt about from Hester, a poisonous coloniser of ancient woodland which threatened some of the more delicate species, such as the violets and the orchids.

While they had been walking, the sun had dipped lower in the sky. She dared a glance across at him. What more did he have to say? Clearly, it was too late for them for so many reasons, not least the fact that she was married now. And yet still she wanted to know it all. 'And when the war ended?' she asked him.

'I wasn't sure whether I was strong enough to come back,' he told her, with his usual honesty. 'And I knew I should set you free. Allow you to find someone undamaged, more suitable, richer.' His laugh was a hollow one.

And look who she had turned to . . . A man who was none of those things. A man who she had thought she could rely on, even if she didn't love him. *And to think she had imagined a love might grow* . . . She shook her head. What a fool she had been.

'I didn't want to burden you, Lara,' he said, 'with the man I've become.'

'Perhaps, David,' she said rather more crisply, 'you should have let me be the judge of that?'

He smiled. 'Perhaps.'

But she couldn't be angry with him, not now. She stepped onto a small branch and felt the brittleness of it as it snapped under her weight. David had taken it upon himself to make that decision and now they both had to live with the consequences. 'It was the worst thing – not knowing what had happened to you,' she blurted. 'Missing presumed dead, they said.'

'I'm sorry.'

Lara sighed. But she squeezed his hand again – to let him know that she understood, that she forgave him. 'And no one knew you were alive?'

He shook his head. 'I wasn't known to the authorities, you see. Effectively, the Romanos helped me disappear.'

'You ran away,' she whispered. Because that was what he had done. David had hurt her. David had destroyed her life. And yet if he hadn't come back, she would never have known.

'You're right.' He met her gaze. 'It was easier in so many ways to stay with them,' he said. 'I admit that. I worked on the olive farm – there was plenty to do. The family treated me as one of their own. They wanted me to stay.'

Lara thought about this. The only sounds in the wood were the occasional birdsong, a rustle from the undergrowth from a squirrel or a vole perhaps, and the soft brush of the breeze through the beech trees. They hadn't seen another soul. David had not yet mentioned any dusky Italian girl. Was that to spare her feelings? Perhaps. But if only he had finished one of those letters he tried to write, she was sure she could have persuaded him to come home. Then she remembered what he'd said earlier. 'But when did you write to me, David?' She felt breathless suddenly, at this chance they had missed.

'Eventually I realised that it wasn't fair on you,' he said. 'I'd let you go and yet I hadn't even told you that I'd set you free.'

Exactly. They were still walking arm in arm through the woodland, for all the world like two old friends or lovers . . . The touch of his arm, his hand, was comforting and Lara felt a twinge of guilt. They had done nothing wrong. *And yet if Charles could see her now . . .*

'I kept thinking about you. What if you were still waiting for me? I felt so guilty and I felt so sad and then, well, I spoke to Eleanora about it.'

Ah. This was it then. Lara braced herself. 'Eleanora?'

'Eleanora Romano, Augustine's wife. They were the couple who took me in.'

Lara exhaled the breath she hadn't realised she'd been holding. 'And what did she say?'

As the path narrowed once more, David let go of her arm. Was it her imagination or did he seem reluctant to do so? Once again, Lara felt bereft. He gestured for her to go first this time.

'She told me that no matter how hard it might be, I owed it to you to at least write and explain what had happened to me,' he continued from behind her. 'She might write back to you,' Eleanora told me. 'She might still be waiting. Unless you try, how will you ever know?'

'She sounds very wise.' Lara turned to face him for a moment, still feeling slightly jealous, even though Eleanora was clearly not the rival she had dreaded.

'She is,' David said. 'And so, I wrote to you in August last year,' he said. 'It was unforgiveable not to have done it sooner. But . . .' His voice trailed.

Why had she never received this letter, a letter that could have been the most important of her life? 'I never got it,' Lara told him bleakly. She and Charles had married in August — whether before or after David's letter, she couldn't say. It made no difference. David had waited just a few months too long.

'I suppose that post sometimes goes astray.'

'I suppose it does.' But Lara was wondering . . .

'When you didn't reply,' he continued. 'I guessed that you must have found a new life for yourself.'

Lara remained silent at this. She plunged on through the woodland. The trees were closer together again now, the path barely discernible. But Lara knew where she was going.

'And I didn't blame you.' He was still close behind her.

Lara stopped. 'Then why did you come home?' She turned to face him. 'Why did you come home now? When it's too late?' The tears were close to the surface and she blinked them back. Tears wouldn't help her now.

'It was the memory of us.' He took her hand. 'It itched away at me and I knew I wouldn't rest until I'd seen you, checked that you were all right, until I'd tried to explain face to face.'

'Oh, David.' She shook her head. It was good to hear that, to know that she had still been in his thoughts, but in some ways, it made the loss more bitter still.

'I saved up the money for the fare,' he said. 'It took a while. And here I am.'

'And here you are.' She smiled, turned around and they walked on for a few moments in silence. Lara knew that she must tell him her story in return, but like David with his letters, she couldn't quite see how to begin. She was beginning to realise just how hard it must have been for him. It was, she reflected, too easy sometimes to judge.

As the path widened once more, now that they were on the last section of the loop that would lead them back to the house – or at least to the garden – and once more they were able to walk side by side, Lara began to speak. She told him only the bare bones of the story. About her mother's illness and subsequent death, how alone she had felt, how she'd promised to look after the house and garden. And then . . . 'I waited,' she said. 'I waited for a long time.'

'I know you did.'

She told him how Charles had been there, always offering to help, wanting to marry her, keen to give her the security she needed. And all the time she was talking, David said hardly a word.

272

'I came to the house,' he said when she'd finished. 'I asked to see you.'

'Oh.' Lara hadn't been expecting that.

'Your husband answered the door.' Lara noted the small flicker of distaste. 'He told me that you weren't well enough to see anyone.'

'I never knew,' she said. She wasn't surprised, though, that Charles hadn't told her. He had always known about David, of course.

'I decided that if I wasn't going to be let in the house, then I would try to get to you from the garden. I couldn't imagine you not going in the garden.'

'Thank you,' she whispered. And she did feel grateful – that he had cared enough to do that, even after all this time.

He took her arm once again and she felt that surge of longing. They turned left towards the walled garden, walking past a hedgerow of pale pink dog roses which seemed to Lara to symbolise civilisation, in contrast to the isolated path they had been walking through the dense woodland.

'How could I go back to Italy without seeing you? Without making sure that you were well and happy?'

Happy . . . That was an emotion Lara hadn't felt for such a long time . . . And then she realised what else he had said. He was going back to Italy. David hadn't come home for good. Italy was his home now.

David leant closer. His breath was warm. 'Is he kind to you, Lara?' he asked.

She shook her head. 'It's not that.'

'He doesn't hurt you?'

'No.' At least, not in any obvious way.

273

'I was worried,' David told her. 'I asked around, tried to find out a bit more.'

Lara laughed without humour. 'I suppose they all told you I'd gone bonkers?' she asked.

David drew her closer. 'You don't seem bonkers to me,' he whispered. 'Although what they told me made me more worried still.'

Lara pulled away. It was too much. All this was just too much to believe, to cope with. If only she had waited for longer . . . And now, what was she to do? 'They're right, though,' she said. 'I don't go out. I'm frightened to.'

'Tell me what's wrong, Lara.' He sounded very serious. Once again, their pace had slowed. She should get back, Lara knew that. The longer she was out with David, the closer they got to home, the riskier it became. But there was still so much to say. And she didn't want to leave him.

He was asking a big question. Where should she start? 'I don't have a life,' she said. 'Not any more.'

He frowned. 'In what way?'

'I used to work at the Savings Bank,' she told him. 'I was a shorthand typist there.'

'But not now?'

'Charles insisted I give it up.' Put like that, it sounded as if Charles had done her a favour.

'He has money then?'

'I don't know.' She thought of the bank statement she had seen in the study. 'I don't know anything.' There was so much more she could say – about the house, the signatures, the awful silences . . . What would David say to all that? And she felt a rush as she realised that she could tell him, that at last she might have someone on her side, who she could turn to for advice – while he was here anyway, which might not be very long. And what else could she turn to him for? She couldn't think about that, not yet.

'But, Lara,' he began.

'Charles doesn't like me going out.' She chose her words carefully. 'Which is fine. Mostly, I stay in the garden. But people talk, naturally.'

'But you see your friends?' His voice was gentle.

'I don't have any friends.' She held her head up. 'Not any more. At least . . .' She gave a little smile. 'There's Hester next door.' And she told him about the window in the wall.

David's gaze was troubled. Lara wanted to smooth out his frown with her fingertip. But how could she? When all was said and done, she might be here walking in the woods with David, but she was still a married woman.

'You make it sound as if you're a prisoner,' David said.

She didn't reply.

'Lara?'

'Yes?'

'Is that how you feel? As if you're a prisoner?'

He knew about prisons, of course, he had been through so much. 'I must get back,' she said again. They'd been gone an hour at least and now they had walked round the loop and were almost back at the house.

'Of course you must.' David stopped walking. His eyes were so kind. 'By the front door?' he asked.

She shook her head. 'I'll climb back over the wall.'

'Lara . . .'

She took his hand and she kissed it. She didn't trust herself to speak.

At the wall, he gave her a long look and it was Lara who

eventually looked away. How was it possible? How was any-thing possible?

'Are you sure about this?' he asked.

She nodded.

He gave her a bunk up and she found a couple of footholds in the worn brick to get her up to the top of the wall again.

'Will you be all right?' he asked her.

Was he asking about the climb or was he asking about Charles or even the future? 'Yes.' She swung her legs around and scrabbled for her first hold in the wisteria on the other side of the wall.

'Can we meet again?' He hadn't even kissed her, but his eyes were saying so much.

'Yes.' She didn't hesitate.

'Tomorrow?'

'Yes. Same time.'

He watched her. 'Will you be able to find an easier way to . . .' His words tailed off.

'I'll get better with practice.' And for the first time in weeks, Lara smiled.

CHAPTER 31

Rose

Italy, June 2018

Rose was at the colourful market on the outskirts of Ostuni, but she had no heart for the usual banter, the requisite examination of the gleaming fruit, the swollen vegetables, the fragrant meats and cheeses. Instead, she was thinking of Bea so far away in England, of her mother who seemed to become more fragile each day and of Federico, who trusted her so implicitly and always had.

'*Va bene, cara?*' he had asked her this morning. 'Are you okay? You do not seem quite yourself lately.'

Rose picked up a jar of fresh almonds in brine. *If only she could be someone else . . .* Of course, Federico had no idea about what she was feeling. He had no idea of the dread that over the years had faded but which had never quite gone away. But Rose knew. She knew what a sham she really was.

Rose pulled out her purse, about to pay for the almonds, when she heard a voice she recognised. She spun around. Please God, she was mistaken.

'Another vine, yes, *per favore*. But last week – the tomatoes, they were cheaper, *no?*'

Rose could see her quite clearly beyond the aromatic bunches of oregano and the vibrant red chillies. Once, they had been close friends – but *certo*, it had never been a friendship based on love and trust. Her friendship with Daniela Basso had been more about intimidation and flattery. Why Daniela had singled her out, Rose had no idea; her family weren't wealthy, she was a bit of a rebel but not obviously so. In fact, she'd been quite shy, not one of those girls who had all the confidence in the world at their fingertips. And so, when Daniela had strolled over to her outside the school gates that day and asked her casually if she wanted to walk with her to the local café, Rose had looked behind her to see if she was talking to someone else.

Daniela had laughed. 'You, you idiot.' But she had taken her arm – almost possessively – so Rose hadn't minded. In fact, she'd felt a warmth spread through her; the warmth of belonging. She forgot that she'd always been a bit scared of Daniela with her brash manner, her way of answering back to the teachers, the hoicking up of her school skirt to attract all the wolf whistles from the boys. All of a sudden, Rose felt special.

At first, she'd been too self-conscious to contribute much to the conversation. She'd listened, though, and she'd told Daniela exactly what she wanted to hear. It was easy, she realised. Yes, the teachers were stupid; yes, the other girls were boring; yes, maths was the hardest subject, but actually Rose didn't find it too difficult, so yes, Daniela could copy her homework anytime. It had felt almost an honour.

And then she'd realised that this was her strength, this was what she could offer. Rose was brighter than Daniela by far and so she could give her not only homework to copy, but also some witty repartee. She could think of things to say about the other girls and the teachers that made Daniela laugh. Rose preferred to follow rather than lead and yet she wasn't scared to rebel – something in her wanted it. And she was pretty – not like most of the girls, though. She was pretty in a different, blonde-haired and blue-eyed way. Daniela liked that too – and so did Cesare, in time.

Daniela had bartered; got the price down to what she was willing to pay and now she was holding up her hand to the woman on the market stall. '*Basta*, that is enough, *grazie.*'

'Why do I bother to trade at all, when all you do is steal my money?' the woman grumbled, adding the rosy flushed tomatoes to a pile of produce that included papery white-skinned onions, a fat lemon, a large dewy lettuce and a bundle of rocket.

And then, as if suddenly aware of the scrutiny, Daniela whipped around (she had always been quick, Rose remembered; too quick) and saw her.

'Hey, hey, Rose! It is Rose, *sì*?' She put the things in a large shopping bag, gave the stallholder some money and proceeded to push her way through the people milling around the fruit and vegetables, making her way to Rose's side. Rose couldn't move. Just like in the old days, she was stuck fast.

'Daniela,' she said. '*Ciao.*'

There were three main reasons why they had lost touch. The first was Cesare and what Rose had done. The second was that at much the same time, Daniela's family had moved her to another school. The third was that it had not been a deep or lasting friendship in the first place. Daniela and Cesare Basso had always belonged to a different world and Rose had believed only for a short time that she wanted or could be part of it.

'So, it is really you, huh?'

Rose laughed awkwardly. 'It really is,' she said. She shifted her shopping bag onto her other arm, conscious how drab and unexciting she must look. A shapeless skirt, an old blouse, a nondescript jacket; her only stab at style was a silk floral scarf tied jauntily at the neck. She hadn't bothered to change her shoes and she needed a haircut and a bit of colour. She was wearing make-up – but the bare minimum – and it had been a busy morning so her mascara was probably smudged and her lipstick had doubtless worn off as usual.

Daniela had not changed so very much. She'd put on a little weight and there were dark shadows under her eyes. Her hair, which had always been raven-black and lustrous, was now streaked with grey and there were more lines etched around her mouth and eyes. But she still wore her signature scarlet lipstick and she remained instantly recognisable.

'How are you?' Daniela looked Rose up and down as brazenly as ever. 'Still at the *masseria*? Still married to Federico Romano?' She shook her head as if at a loss as to why that would be.

'*Sì.*' Rose wouldn't rise to it. She stood a little straighter. 'And you?'

Daniela let out a low cackle. She picked up a jar of pickled *lupini*, yellow beans, examined it briefly and replaced it on the stall. '*Merda!* I got rid of the first shithead,' she said. 'He left me with three kids and no money. But *sì*, I am all right. I found myself a decent man. And my kids – they look after me now.'

'Good, good.' Rose was wondering how quickly she could make her escape. The last thing she wanted was for Daniela to mention her brother. Neither did she want Daniela to mention their meeting to Cesare. She didn't want him to have any reminders. But how could she stop her?

'Have you seen Cesare?' Was she a mind reader? Daniela's dark eyes were sharp as ever. Rose wondered how much she knew.

'He called by.' It was pointless to lie about it. *Just be casual, Rose*, she told herself. That was how you got away with things.

Daniela nodded. 'It is good that he is out at last,' she said. 'Prison, it is a bad place. And he always had a thing for you.'

Rose shook her head. 'Not for years,' she said.

'Hmm, well, between you and me . . .' Daniela leant forwards and Rose couldn't stop herself from doing the same.

Old habits . . . Daniela didn't smell as good as she used to – in fact, she smelt of stale perfume with a faint whiff of BO. Nevertheless, it seemed Daniela could still make Rose feel special.

'He never lost that feeling,' she said. 'He is my brother.' She struck her chest. 'I know him.'

Rose's mind flipped back to that party – the night she first met Cesare. She'd never had a proper boyfriend – unless you counted Federico, who had often tried to hold her hand and drop sweet kisses her way, that had seemed almost brotherly at the time.

And then Cesare . . . Holding her close to him as they danced, his warm skin pressing on her skin, the scent of him drilling into her senses; his hands on her shoulders, around her waist, exploring lower . . . His lips nuzzled into her neck; he whispered into her ear that she was beautiful, so beautiful, and the hot rush of those whispered words had streaked through her, filling her with desire. *Desire.* She had never fully understood that word before, but back then it was all she could feel. Cesare Basso's mouth was on hers, warm and demanding, and that desire was overwhelming her, filling her, taking her under.

They made love for the first time that evening in the room where everyone had left their coats. He'd pulled her in there, laughingly pushed a table behind the door – to stop them from being disturbed, he said. Rose was scared. She'd never even been touched, but now his hands were on her breasts, his fingers were playing their magical patterns and she was on fire. As he undid the button at the waist of her jeans, she gasped, instinctively put a hand out to stop him. She'd always been a good girl. She didn't want to go all the way.

'It's okay, Rose,' he murmured in her ear. 'I'll look after you. I know what to do.' And then he was slipping down her jeans and his fingers were inside her and she couldn't even think about stopping him any more.

Rose shuddered. 'I am married,' she reminded Daniela. 'And I am happy.' The hand holding her purse was so tightly clenched that she'd lost all feeling. She relaxed her stiff fingers. *Crazy times*, she thought. The sex with Cesare had been exciting but rough. He'd never considered her pleasure, and neither, come to think of it, had she. Afterwards, she always half hated herself. Afterwards, she always told herself no more. She was getting in too deep. But he had that easy, elusive confidence that was so attractive in a man. And she couldn't stop herself wanting him.

'Oh, well, good for you.' Daniela's voice had that slight jeer to it.

'I do not want him to come round to my place.' Because perhaps Daniela might have some influence? She might pass the right message on.

Daniela picked up another jar of beans and examined the contents. Once again, she put it back on the stall and Rose took the opportunity of moving a couple of steps away. But Daniela moved with her. She shrugged. 'You know Cesare does what Cesare wants,' she said. 'That is the attraction, *no*?'

'*Arrivederci*, Daniela,' Rose said firmly. Engaging with the Basso way of thinking was where she'd gone wrong before. And she didn't want to consider the word 'attraction' in connection with Cesare. She winced. Never again.

'*Ciao*, Rose.' Once again, Daniela let out a low laugh. 'Shall I tell Cesare I bumped into you?'

'Probably best not.'

Rose hurried away. She didn't think that Daniela was about to suggest swapping phone numbers or meeting up, but even so, she didn't want to risk it. She bought the rest of her food shopping in a blur, unable to focus on the task in hand. What a fool she had been to imagine she could ever escape the Bassos and the shame of what she had done . . .

Back home, Rose checked on her mother who was sitting with her eyes closed in her usual place in the shady section of the terrace.

'Mamma? *Va bene?*' She spoke softly, not wanting to wake her if she was asleep. These days there seemed less of a distinction between sleep and wakefulness for her mother. Rose was concerned for her. She put a hand to her mother's brow.

'Ah.' Her mother seemed to relax under her fingertips. 'That feels good, my darling.'

There was much to do in the house and lunch wouldn't prepare itself. But Rose found herself lingering, enjoying the intimacy. Who knew how much time they had left, she and her mother?

'Have you heard from Bea this morning, Mamma?' she asked gently. Bea had messaged to say she'd arrived safely and Rose hoped that everything was going well. Already, she missed her.

'*Sì*. A short message,' her mother confirmed. 'She is looking forward to starting work on the garden. Bea will bring it back to its former glory.' She smiled sweetly.

'I often wondered, Mamma,' said Rose. 'Why did you not sell the house before you moved here?'

For a moment, Rose thought that her mother wouldn't answer at all. Then she sighed. 'It was a difficult time,' she said at last. 'Your father and I . . .' Her voice drifted. It seemed she lacked the energy to go on.

'Never mind,' Rose said, after a minute or two had passed. It wasn't fair to press her. 'As long as Bea is helping you deal with it, that is the main thing.'

Her mother gave her a grateful smile. 'Thank you, my dear.'

At any rate, thought Rose, it was one less worry for her to concern herself with. '*Allora*. I must get lunch prepared.' She could see Federico approaching already and as usual he would be hungry.

He came into the kitchen just as she was putting the pasta into boiling water.

'*Ciao, Bella.*' He caught her around the waist.

'Hey, mind the hot water.' Rose laughed, but she was still on edge from seeing Daniela at the market.

'The water, it will wait.' Federico kissed her neck, in the precise place that made her crumple up and beg for mercy.

She pushed him away. 'But the sauce, it will burn.'

'Oh ho.' But at least he gave up and went over to the sink to wash his hands.

Rose softened. 'Have you had a good morning?' She tweaked the pasta in the water so that it was separated and stirred the tomato sauce in the other pan. They could have it with some fresh parmesan she'd purchased at the market.

'Not bad.' He turned around to face her. 'And you?'

'Okay.' She shrugged. 'You know.' Though how could he know? About Daniela? About her anxieties?

He came to stand behind her once more and she leant back slightly, to rest against him. It was comforting. Federico had always been comforting. She hated to think of how she had hurt him all those years ago – she could never quite forgive herself for that, although she knew that he had let it go a long time past. And she didn't want to hurt him again. She really did not want to hurt him again. With Federico, Rose had discovered the true meaning of making love. It could be exciting, even now – though more often it was comfortable and pleasurable. Best of all, it was tender and it was always, always infused with love. A tear crept from her eye. Quickly, she lifted her arm to wipe it away on her sleeve.

But he saw it.

'Rose.' He turned her so that she was facing him. 'Tell me,' he demanded.

She stared at him.

'Tell me the truth,' he said.

'The truth?' If only she could.

'Is it too much for you? This place? The *trulli*? Looking after your mother?' His shoulders slumped. 'Because if it is, we will do something about that, you and I. We will give up the *trulli*, the tourists. Pah.' He clicked his fingers. 'What do they matter? We can manage without them. You and I, Rose. We are a team.'

'No,' she said. 'It is all fine, my love.' He was right, they were a team and she was determined to keep it so.

He frowned. 'But you seem on edge. You look tired. Should you see the doctor perhaps?' He pulled her closer. 'Rose, I could not bear it if something happened to you.'

She did not deserve him. Rose closed her eyes and cherished the moment. Crushed against his chest, she could smell the bitterness of the olives, the earthy scent that clung to his shirt, his skin. 'Don't worry, *caro*,' she said. 'I am okay. Just a little tired and emotional, that is all.'

'I miss her too,' he whispered.

Rose nodded. 'Yes,' she said. And when Bea returned, she would give her daughter more time. She would take more time to be with all her family, because it was important.

'But does all this bore you?' Federico had gone off on another tangent. He drew her away from his chest and looked into her eyes. His gaze was a dark pool that she longed to dive into.

'Bore me?'

He flung out an arm in an expansive gesture. 'The *masseria*, the family, the *trulli* business.'

'No.'

'Do you want to do something different?' He pushed his dark hair from his face. 'Did you always want to do something different?'

'No.' And this time she had to laugh.

'But you are so clever.' He let go of her and paced over to the window looking out towards the olive grove that was his life. 'You were always so clever. You could have done anything. But you chose me.'

It was Rose's turn to come up behind him and clasp him around the waist. He was still a fit and fine figure of a man, though his waist had thickened since their first days together and his skin was weathered by the sun, by the outdoor work he loved. 'I never wanted to do anything else,' she whispered. And this was true. She'd never particularly craved a career of her own as Bea had. She was perfectly satisfied with Federico and her life on the farm.

'Really? This is true?' And this time he tilted her chin and kissed her gently on the lips.

'It is true,' she agreed.

'Oh, Rose . . .'

'And it is also true that the sauce will burn.' She slipped out of his arms and returned to the stove where the sauce was already catching around the edges and the pasta would be *al dente*.

But there were other truths, she reminded herself as she scooped the pasta onto plates. She could not forget those. And it was those other truths that haunted her.

CHAPTER 32

Lara

Italy, June 2018

The screen started buzzing again and this time Lara managed to swipe across with her fingertip in the way her granddaughter had shown her. Something happened. There was a flicker of colour. Then Bea's face appeared on the screen.

'*Ciao*, Nonna.' She was smiling – that was good.

'Hello, my darling.' Lara's breath caught. Bea was in England, in Dorset. Lara wasn't sure she was ready for the onslaught of emotion. 'Can you hear me?'

'*Sì*, I can hear you.' Bea laughed. 'How are you, Nonna?'

'*Molto bene, grazie.* Very well.' There was no need to tell her how tired she was feeling today. In any case, Lara was tired most days, but at least she was still alive, hey? 'And you? How was your journey? Are you really there in Dorset?' It had been such a long time and there were so many questions – she would have to ask at least three at a time.

'Yes, I am here at the house.'

The house . . . The screen changed. All of a sudden, instead of Bea's face, Lara saw the window seat with its floral cushions where she used to sit – faded but still recognisable – and a glimpse of the veranda outside. *Oh, my goodness.* She put a hand to her throat. This was too much. She wasn't prepared. 'Oh, Bea,' she said.

'The house needs a lot of work, Nonna.'

This wasn't a surprise. Hester had told her as much and that had been a few years ago. But it had been hard to know what to do, living so far away.

They seemed to be moving now, through the sitting room and out of the French doors. Bea's footsteps on the stone paving . . . It was just as if Lara was there with her. She could even hear the breeze. How clever her granddaughter had been to insist Lara bought a phone and to install this ingenious way of making contact. Lara had certainly had her doubts at first, but this method of communication was wonderful – and apparently free of charge too. The world had moved on indeed.

'And what of the garden?' Lara asked. Because that was where they were going. Her heartbeat quickened.

'Nothing that a bit of clearing and weeding won't sort out,' Bea said in a brisk tone. 'Though the beds are rather out of control.'

Control. The irony was not lost on Lara. 'They were always full to bursting.'

'Do not worry, Nonna,' her granddaughter soothed. 'I know that abundance is part of the Arts and Crafts concept. That will certainly not change.'

'Oh, yes.' *To escape from the rigidity of carefully controlled Victorian bedding schemes* . . . Lara was relieved that Bea sounded so positive about the task ahead, that she understood. She saw that they were on the veranda now. *Oh my* . . . She held her breath. And there was the Romantic Garden, the stone sundial, the bench where her mother used to sit. 'Can you do it, darling?' she whispered.

'You bet.' Bea sounded cheerful too. 'Did you do all this planting yourself, Nonna?'

The screen changed back to her granddaughter's face and Lara felt a little calmer. 'We had a gardener once,' she told Bea. 'Joe, his name was.' She had been so sad to lose him. 'Mother did a lot too, before . . .' Before she was ill. Before she died. The house had seen happiness but it had seen sadness too.

'It's an incredible design.' Bea's eyes shone with excitement. 'I've looked up the Arts and Crafts ideas and I can see how the garden is made up of six rooms.'

'Seven,' said Lara. The seven levels of spiritual elevation. Wasn't that what Mother had said? But Bea would have to find the seventh garden for herself just as Lara had done. If, that is, it was meant to be.

'Seven?' Lara saw her granddaughter frown. 'So this one . . . ?'

There was another sweep of the picture. 'Oh . . .' Lara spotted the erigeron daisies she'd planted – who would have ever thought they would cover the wall in a beautiful drift like that? – and the buddleia. 'The Romantic Garden.' She sighed.

'Are you okay, Nonna?' Her granddaughter's concerned face appeared back on the screen.

'Yes.' It was hard, though, seeing it all again. Lara had spent so long in that garden. So many hours and so many summers – and winters too. She had loved it and at times she had almost loathed it; for it had been both her prison and her sanctuary. She had worked on it, for her mother's sake, and it had saved her life. Since leaving, she had thought of it so often, dreamt of it even, imagined how it was growing and what it would become. But she had never been able to go back.

'I understand about the sequence of outdoor rooms.' Bea sounded thoughtful.

Seven distinct rooms to dream in . . .

'Each leading to another.'

Bea was walking now, Lara could tell. She would be moving into the next garden.

'I am at the pond.'

The screen changed. The poor pond was a blur of green plant matter; Lara could hardly see the water. 'That's the Thinking Garden,' she told Bea. 'The plants are mostly white and reflective.' She looked out towards her Italian garden. She had always intended it to be an echo of the walled garden in Dorset. After all, if she couldn't be there, then she could at least try to emulate the spirit of it here.

'Ah, how lovely. They are not all out yet, but I see.'

'And beyond that is the Rose Garden.' Lara waited for Bea to walk through. 'Are they in bloom?' she asked wistfully.

'Oh, yes. I love this one, Nonna.' An orange rose blossomed onto the screen.

Lara gasped. It was the Lady of Shalott, named after the Tennyson poem. The bloom was shaped like a chalice with salmon-pink outer petals and golden-yellow undersides. How many times had she run past this very rose on her way to the solace she was seeking in the outside world? 'Beautiful,' she murmured. She could almost smell its old-fashioned sweet scent of honey, spiced apple and tea.

'Gorgeous,' agreed Bea. 'And through here . . .' The screen changed to undergrowth, long grass and brambles as her grand-daughter moved on.

291

'The Wild Garden,' murmured Lara.

'It certainly is.'

She was right. It had clearly been left to go its own way and the strongest weeds had won through. 'The planting was intended to become more natural towards the boundaries, blending with the landscape outside,' Lara said doubtfully.

'Hmm. Though this is not just blending, Nonna, it is more a case of total annihilation,' said Bea.

'I can see that the garden's overgrown.' Lara peered at the moving images as Bea walked on. 'But it's not as bad as I was expecting.'

Back came Bea. 'Well, apparently, Hester used some of the money from the rent for garden maintenance,' she said. 'When she was in charge of things, I suppose.'

'Yes, she did,' said Lara. 'And have you seen Hester, darling? How is she?'

There was a tiny pause. Lara didn't like the sound of it.

'I am seeing her at lunchtime,' Bea said. 'Lewis was in the house when I arrived yesterday – he was the one who told me about the garden maintenance.'

'Lewis?' Lara tried to think where she'd heard the name. It did sound vaguely familiar.

'Hester's grandson.'

'Ah.' That must be it. 'What was he doing in the house?'

'I think he was drawing something.'

Lara frowned. Whatever was she talking about? 'Is he living next door?' she asked. Hester hadn't always lived there. Lara had kept in contact with her old neighbour by letter and she was aware that when she married, Hester had moved out, but later when her marriage fell apart, she'd moved back in to look after her mother in Elizabeth's old age.

'Yes, he is.' Bea's voice softened. 'Nonna, I am sorry to tell you this, but apparently Hester has Alzheimer's. She is quite poorly and Lewis is living there as her carer.'

'Oh . . .' Poor Hester. Lara's memory of the young girl Hester had once been flashed back into her head, as clear as the picture on the screen of the phone. Dark hair. Dark eyes. A sharp and enquiring mind. *If not for Hester . . .* 'That explains it,' she said softly.

'Explains what, Nonna?'

'Her last few letters have been a bit . . .' – she hesitated – '. . . confused.' It was cruel. Hester had always had such a clarity about her. She was an organiser, a planner.

'You two were close friends then, Nonna?' Bea was probing. Lara understood why, but there were things she couldn't tell her about that time, things she still couldn't bring herself to think about.

'Yes, we were.' And that was all she would say. Once again, Lara sighed. She was feeling very tired again. 'When you see her, my darling . . .'

'Yes, Nonna?'

'Please give her my love. Please thank her.'

'I will.'

'It doesn't matter if she doesn't understand. *Non importa.* It doesn't matter if she can't remember. Please tell her anyway.'

'Yes, Nonna.'

Lara closed her eyes for a moment to bring herself back to the present. 'And Matteo?' she asked. 'Has he been in touch?'

'I have heard nothing.'

Bea's tone was crisp now. Was crisp a good thing? Probably. 'Then that gives you a chance to think about the situation without any pressure, darling,' she said.

'To tell you the truth, Nonna,' said Bea, 'there has been so much happening here that I have not had much of a chance to think about Matteo.'

Lara raised an eyebrow. *Indeed?*

'You did not tell me that Lime Tree House was so . . . grand.'

Ah.

'Or that the garden was so . . . big.'

'Is it too much?' Perhaps she shouldn't have asked it of her. It had been Lara's legacy and she should have sorted it out for herself. 'Because if so, you must come back home, you know. I'll think of another solution.'

Bea was shaking her head. 'It is not too much,' she said. 'Just a surprise.'

'You must get in whatever you need,' Lara told her. 'I have more money I can send you.' Over the years the payments from tenants had crept into her bank account. Predictably, it was Hester who had suggested she rent out the house. They both knew she wouldn't be coming back. 'It'll stop it going to rack and ruin,' Hester had pointed out. 'I can keep an eye on the place and use some of the money for maintenance. Then I can send you the rest.'

'Minus your management cut,' Lara had insisted.

It had worked out pretty well. Lara had told her she didn't want to know anything – she didn't need a reason for those memories to come flooding in – and Hester had taken charge. Some years ago, she had written to suggest she handed things over to a management company because it was all getting a bit too much, and this she had done. But then there came a point when the place needed more than the occasional bit of maintenance and there was no one to oversee the project; no one to care. For some years there had been no tenants and no maintenance and that's when Lara knew she had to face facts. Lime Tree House was never going to go away, but she couldn't allow it to simply fall down, derelict and unloved. And as for the garden . . . She had made a promise, after all.

'But what should I do, Nonna?' Bea's voice was gentle. 'Do you want me to get the house done up and put on the market? Should I sell the furniture? Have the house cleared? Because everything's still here, you know? It is like a house lost in time. And the garden . . .' She tailed off.

'The garden needs your love, Bea,' Lara told her. This much she did know. 'If you can focus on that for the moment, then we'll think about the house later.' One thing at a time. Of course they would have to sell it, but Lara wasn't sure she would even see that moment. For now, the garden was Bea's project and they would see where it took her.

'That's fine by me.'

And Lara could hear it in her voice – the anticipation of the job ahead, the challenge. *Good* . . .

'Thank you, darling,' she said. 'Let's talk again soon.'

'Tomorrow,' said Bea. 'I will report back on Hester. And . . .' she hesitated. 'Will you tell me more about the garden, Nonna? What your mother planned? The significance of the different outdoor rooms?'

'Perhaps,' Lara said. 'But most of it I rather think you will enjoy finding out for yourself.'

CHAPTER 33

Bea

Dorset, June 2018

Bea went round next door at the appointed time and found herself gladdened by Lewis's friendly smile when he opened the front door. Yesterday, she'd been happy to explore the house and garden alone, and this morning, after talking to her grandmother on WhatsApp, she'd already got stuck into the clearing of what Nonna had called the Romantic Garden. But despite her anticipation of the rather daunting task ahead, it was nice not to feel completely alone.

'How's it going?' he asked cheerily. 'Come on through.' Today, he had exchanged the paint-stained overalls for faded blue jeans, a black T-shirt worn with Converse trainers and a rather fetching apron patterned with pink flamingos.

'Great, thanks.' Bea followed him inside. 'Nice apron,' she said.

He laughed. 'I'd love to tell you it's my grandmother's but actually she bought it for me last Christmas.'

Bea laughed with him. She liked the fact that he was confident enough not to care.

'I can't wait to hear your first impressions of Lime Tree House.' Lewis led her through a narrow hallway decorated with family photos on the walls. Bea spotted a mother and daughter, both with the same raven hair and dark eyes, and another of two boys standing in front of a caravan. She guessed that one of the boys was Lewis. And the mother and daughter could be Elizabeth and Hester, perhaps? More than anything, Bea couldn't wait to meet Hester.

'It is bigger than I was expecting,' she said. Unlike this cottage which was small and cosy though also detached.

'Uh-huh.'

'And rather grand.' Bea had wandered through the rooms one by one, drawn to the rich wooden panelling and floors, the bespoke hand-carved furniture, the charming natural motifs of animals and flowers on the wallpapers. From the first floor, some stairs had led up to a glorious attic room, almost entirely bare of furniture apart from a large table and an easel – clearly this had been her great-grandfather's art studio. The whole house seemed to want to tell her a story, though for the moment, she had no clue as to what that story might be.

Her first decision had been where to sleep. Fortunately, she had found clean sheets in the airing cupboard and she had chosen a small room at the back that overlooked the garden. She guessed that it might have been her grandmother's bedroom when she was a girl and she immediately imagined her there, looking out over the clematis and honeysuckle cloaking the pergola. When Bea had opened the window, the honeyed scent seemed to lull her into relaxation and a peaceful sleep. In contrast, the largest bedroom at the front had made her feel uncomfortable somehow, as if she would be sleeping on her great-grandparents' graves.

297

'The whole place is made from local materials,' Lewis told her. 'From the slate on the roof to the hand-hammered pewter in the fireplace.'

Arts and Crafts, thought Bea. She followed him out of the back door onto a little patio where a wooden table was set for lunch, with plates, cutlery and glasses on a checked tablecloth, and three wooden chairs arranged around it. In front of the patio was a garden, much smaller than next door and laid mainly to lawn with a deep flower bed on either side.

'My great-grandmother Elizabeth used to grow a lot of plants.' Lewis sounded apologetic. 'But when her health began to fail, she had most of the garden turfed, apart from that little circular herb garden over there.' He pointed. 'Much to my grandmother's horror.'

Bea laughed. 'I can imagine.' That would be any horticulturalist's nightmare. But the little herb garden was sweet. She would look at it properly later, she decided, but the arrangement of it reminded her of an old-fashioned *hortus simplicium*, a Garden of Simples, as the first botanical gardens were called, where medicinal plants were laid out in small beds so that different species could be identified and experimented with – a plan that was both scientific and decorative.

Bea looked up as a slight and white-haired figure emerged from the far side of the house. She smiled at them both and put her head to one side. 'Hello.'

She had a sweet childlike manner about her. Bea returned her smile. 'Hello.'

'This is Grandma Hester,' said Lewis. 'Grandma, this is Lara's granddaughter, Bea, come to stay next door for a bit.'

'Lara,' said Hester. Her dark eyes were vague and it was impossible to tell how much she remembered; how much she knew.

'I made a quiche,' Lewis said. 'I'll just go and—'

'Lovely.'

Bea waited for him to go back into the house and for Hester to sit down beside her. 'It is lovely to meet you,' she said. 'My grandmother – Lara – has told me so much about you.' Which wasn't remotely true – in fact, Nonna had been sparing with the information, but never mind, Bea would simply have to find out for herself.

'Lara,' Hester repeated, and this time her voice had a sing-song quality to it, as if she was trying the name out for size.

'Do you remember her?'

Hester shot Bea a quick and anxious glance. Perhaps it worried her when people asked her if she could remember things? *Perhaps it wasn't the best way in . . .*

'She had a beautiful garden,' Bea said. 'The garden next door, I mean.'

Hester began to hum, softly, gathering pace and volume.

Lewis came out looking slightly harassed. 'Quiche,' he said. He put the plate down on the table and rested a hand on his grandmother's arm. 'Okay, Grandma?' His voice was so soft and tender that Bea almost felt she should look away.

Gradually, the humming quietened.

'Sometimes she gets a bit agitated,' Lewis explained. 'Every day is different. We can't predict. Sometimes I feel I can leave her for a couple of hours, sometimes not.'

'I see.' Lewis must have made considerable sacrifices in order to be Hester's carer, Bea realised. Thanks to him, Hester was able to enjoy her house and garden and at least a little independence.

Lewis went away again but soon reappeared with a bowl of salad and a bottle of sparkling elderflower water.

'Do you have any siblings, Lewis?' Bea was wondering if there was anyone who could ever help him out.

'One younger brother who lives in Spain.' He sighed. 'We're not close.'

The two boys in front of the caravan in the photo, maybe? 'And your parents?' Bea accepted a slice of the asparagus quiche.

'They're both in Australia.' He served his grandmother with a slice of quiche and green salad.

'Australia?' *Hmm.* His family were very spread out to say the least.

He shrugged. 'My dad, Grandma Hester's son, was the original hipster,' he said. 'Isn't that right, Grandma?'

Hester didn't reply, but she seemed happier now that Lewis was with them. She nibbled her quiche slowly, nodding and smiling at Lewis at the same time. She seemed to adore him and small wonder.

'Yeah, he travelled so much it's a miracle he managed to stay in one place for long enough to have me and Josh.'

'Really?' Bea glanced across at Hester. How bad was she? Bea wondered. How much did she understand? Was she even aware that they were talking about her son?

Lewis seemed to read Bea's mind. 'We're talking about Robbie,' he told Hester gently. And then to Bea: 'Dad went off travelling when he was eighteen and never really came back – at least not for very long.'

'But you came back,' Bea pointed out. 'Were you born in Australia?' She could see him there with his sun-bleached blond hair and faded blue jeans.

He shook his head. 'Mum was an Australian living in London when Dad met her. I was born here and sometime later we all went to Australia.'

'That must have been difficult for you, Hester.' Bea wanted to draw her into the conversation, although she seemed perfectly content in her own world. 'You must have missed Robbie and your grandsons.'

No response. Alzheimer's was a cruel disease, thought Bea. By taking away people's memory, it took away their identity too. Hester seemed to still relate to Lewis, but how could they interact in any meaningful way when she now lacked the context that made him her much-loved grandson? It was heartbreaking.

'I was there for a few years before they split up and Mum came back again,' Lewis continued. 'Then later, when I was around twenty-one, she announced she was going back there to live.'

'But you did not want to join her?' Bea indicated the quiche. 'This is delicious by the way.'

'Thanks.' Lewis cut another slice and offered it to her. Bea accepted it gratefully. She had built up quite an appetite in the garden this morning.

'I had my own life by then.' Lewis gave another little shrug. 'I still keep in touch with Mum and we see each other once every year or two, but Dad . . .' He gave a sideways glance at Hester. 'We don't even know where he is any more.'

'Oh, I am sorry.' And impulsively, Bea laid a hand on Hester's. Because even if she was no longer aware of it at this moment in time, she must have felt great sadness at losing touch with her son. Lewis, too, at losing his father.

'Thank you,' he said. 'I hardly knew him. It's not so bad for me. But . . .' He didn't need to say more.

Hester looked straight at Bea. Her gaze was unflinching. Bea was sure now that the other photo she'd noticed in the hallway was of Hester and her mother Elizabeth back when

Bea's grandmother was growing up next door. 'Lara worked very hard in her garden,' Hester said. 'Do you know her?'

Bea nodded. 'She is my grandmother,' she told her again. 'Were you good friends?'

'Oh, yes.' Hester beamed. 'She found me through a crack in the wall.'

'Really?' Bea thought of the old and crumbling brick wall that separated the two gardens. That wasn't so far-fetched after all. 'My grandmother Lara told me that there were seven separate gardens next door. Is that right, Hester?'

'Yes.' Hester was vehement. 'Seven gardens. Mother talked about the seven gardens. And I told Lara.' She sounded wistful and Lewis leant over to squeeze her hand.

He was so good with her, thought Bea. 'But I can only find six,' she told them both.

'That's strange.' Lewis collected up their plates. 'Can I get you some coffee, Bea? Grandma?'

But before Bea could reply, Hester had leant forwards, confidingly. 'The seventh garden is a secret garden.' She sat back triumphantly.

'A secret garden?' Bea thought of her grandmother's Italian garden. Nonna had always maintained that a garden should have some sense of mystery, a surprise or two, both light and shade. And Nonna had a secret garden there too. So . . . 'Where is it then?' She frowned, trying to imagine.

But if Hester knew, she wasn't saying. She just sat with an enigmatic smile on her face.

'Coffee would be lovely,' Bea told Lewis. She sensed that there was more Hester wanted to say.

Sure enough, when he'd gone back inside, Hester turned to her. 'There were a lot of secrets,' she said knowingly.

302

'Were there?' Bea had guessed as much. But how could she find out the nature of these secrets? 'Secrets between you and Lara?' she asked.

Hester put a finger to her lips. 'But you know, we mustn't speak of them, Lara,' she said. 'Shh now.'

'Why not?' Bea whispered back to her.

Hester looked around from left to right. 'Someone might get into trouble,' she hissed.

Really? But who? 'Why—?' Bea started to speak again but Hester shushed her.

'Don't tell anyone,' she urged. 'It's best if we say nothing, you know.'

She seemed quite agitated now, so Bea soothed her as Lewis had done by gently patting her arm. 'Okay,' she said. 'Do not worry. We will not say a word.' Which seemed to satisfy her.

Lewis returned, Hester went back inside the house to have a rest, and the two of them stayed on the patio for half an hour or so, drinking coffee and chatting desultorily.

'So shall I come round tomorrow morning and help in the garden?' Lewis asked.

'If Hester doesn't need you?' Bea didn't want to take him away from his more important duties.

'I like to give her some space,' he said. 'I don't want her to think I'm watching over her the whole time.'

Bea held her face up to the sun. Earlier on, it had been dodging in and out of cloud cover but now it was quite warm and pleasant and she found herself reluctant to leave. 'You are not worried, though – that she might leave the house and wander off somewhere?'

He considered this. 'She never really wants to go out any

303

more,' he said. 'It's as if she's scared to. Which is awful, obviously, but at least makes things a bit safer.'

Bea couldn't help thinking of her grandmother once again and her stories about the girl who needed to escape from the garden. Somehow, she must find a way to ask Hester about this. And what had Hester meant about secrets? Did she know something? Or was she simply getting confused?

'Okay then.' Bea got to her feet. 'That would be great.'

He waggled an eyebrow. 'And maybe we can find the secret garden.'

'Maybe.' She grinned. 'Ah, well, better get back to it.'

Lewis let her out and Bea walked back next door. She changed into her old gardening clothes, went through to the veranda and looked out over the Romantic Garden. Already, it looked tidier; already she had revealed some plants, struggling and weak, desperately trying to find a way through the weeds and brambles. There were buddleia and verbena which would come into bloom later in the summer and lilac and catmint already in flower. Plus the lavender and a whole host of straggling herbs.

She walked down the mossy steps. It would be good to work with Lewis tomorrow for a few hours, she thought, and perhaps she'd cook supper as a thank you and as a chance to talk some more with Hester about the old days.

Before she put on her gardening gloves, Bea checked her phone. There was nothing from Matteo. She couldn't blame him. She felt guilty – not only about leaving, but about not giving him a proper answer to his proposal. And yet Matteo, the restaurant, his proposal of marriage – it all seemed so far away now. She felt so immersed in this walled garden that was her grandmother's legacy, in this new and blossoming time here in Dorset, that she was almost unable to think of anything else.

CHAPTER 34

Lara

Dorset, July 1947

Lara waited until Charles left the house – mid-afternoon was the time he visited his mistress in the village; she had come to recognise the signs.

How deceitful he had made her; how desperate . . .

She would be working in the Romantic Garden if the weather was fine – and oh, the weather had been glorious these past ten days as if conspiring with her in this madness. A little pruning or weeding perhaps, humming to herself and waiting. Only Lara knew how her heart was hammering in her chest. Because at any moment, Charles would come and stand at the French doors looking out towards the garden. And when he saw her here, quietly working, seemingly absorbed in her task, he would nod to himself, satisfied, turn abruptly from the window and be gone.

Lara would wait – five minutes, maybe ten, though every second seemed like an eternity wasted. And then she would

drop her fork or her pruning shears, fly past the lavender parterre, down the pathway, through the scented Rose Garden to
the Wild Garden, past the cornflowers and poppies waving in
the breeze as if to echo the freedom she craved, the freedom
that she could glimpse at last in front of her.

It was a freedom that lay on the other side of the old brick
wall.

She would whistle, soft and low, and back it would come,
David's familiar whistle that she had first heard at the agricultural fair where they had met all those years ago.

This afternoon was no different. Charles came to the doors.
Lara waited. Lara ran. And now, here she was, climbing the
wisteria vines with sure footing and a relative ease, that had
come, as she'd promised David, with practice.

After that first meeting with David in the woods on the
other side of the wall, when she'd returned to the garden
breathless and trembling, Lara had taken some time to compose
herself before venturing inside the house. That evening, eating
dinner with Charles, trying to make polite conversation, she
had felt like someone else entirely. These two women could
hardly be the same person: the wife she was now and the lover
she had once been. And at the same time, she felt utterly carried
away by the events of the afternoon, by the fact that not only
was David alive, not only had he come to find her, but she was
planning to meet him again tomorrow . . .

It was almost too much, and from time to time she cast a
discreet glance towards Charles, looking down again quickly
at her plate, the food hardly touched, worrying that he could
see the difference in her, that he might discern what she was
feeling.

The second time she and David met, the following afternoon,

was the first time Lara had made the effort to observe Charles's movements. She realised then that he was a creature of habit, that he depended on her disinterest. She had made it so easy for him.

As soon as she made the leap over the wall, the moment that she was once again in David's arms as he caught her, Lara knew that this meeting would be different. This wasn't an old lover coming back from the war to find his girlfriend married to another man. This was an illicit assignation.

He didn't kiss her straightaway, though she could see the kiss in his eyes, just waiting to happen. Instead, they walked, he asked her more about her life and her marriage and it was impossible to hold back the truth; Lara found herself confessing to him how unhappy she really was. She didn't tell him about what happened in the bedroom with Charles, she was far too ashamed and embarrassed to do that, but she told him about the bank statements and the copies of her signature that she'd found in Charles's desk drawer.

David's brow darkened and his eyes were grave. He stopped walking. 'You can't stay there with him.' He sounded so confident of this that Lara almost believed it herself.

'But—'

'It's intolerable.' He let go of her arm, tore his hands through his dark hair as if in pain. 'You must leave.'

'But, Mother . . .' Her voice trailed. 'I promised her.' Lara alone knew how much the house and garden had meant to her mother. How could she leave them under the control of a man like Charles? It was unthinkable.

He took her hands. 'Do you think she would want you to live like this, Lara?'

Miserably, she shook her head.

'She would be desolate. Knowing what you were going through.'

'But what else can I do?' This was what she'd needed to hear; Lara knew that now.

'Come away with me.' He held her face in his hands.

So, he still cared for her. At least enough to want to help her now. She looked into his hazel eyes, felt the glow, held it inside for a brief, comforting moment. 'Away?'

'To Italy,' he whispered.

Lara shivered. It was so much. More than she had expected.

'Don't you want to?' he asked her gently. 'Don't you want to get away from him?'

Lara thought of her marriage vows. *For better, for worse.* She did want to get away; she longed to get away. But could it really be that simple? She hesitated.

'I know I don't deserve you.' His shoulders dropped.

'That's not true.' She pushed back at him, angry now. 'David, you know I never stopped loving you.' She had told him as much yesterday. 'But I feel . . .' – she hesitated again – '. . . different from the way I was, when you and I . . .' So much had happened, to Lara as well as to David. She knew he would understand because he had said as much himself. 'I feel broken,' she admitted.

Look at her – at what she had become. She couldn't even go out of the house. She hardly spoke to a soul. She had lost such a big part of herself. How could she leave the house and garden she loved and go to Italy? Even with David, whose smile still made her heart sing, who still somehow was able to give her a small sliver of hope. The very thought made her pulse quicken, made her flush hotly with panic.

David was smoothing her hair from her brow and that

helped to calm her. 'I'm here, Lara,' he said. And then she lifted her face and his lips were on hers and they were kissing as if they'd never been apart all these long years, as if she weren't married and as if he was the same David she had first fallen in love with.

His hands were on her shoulders, he was drawing her closer, she could feel the heat of him, feel his desire. And she felt it too. All the passion that had been sucked out of her during those dreadful and cold night-time encounters with Charles throughout the empty shell of the marriage she was trapped in.

'David.'

They pulled at each other's clothes, more urgently now. She undid the buttons of his shirt, quickly, quickly, needing to feel skin on skin. He caught his breath, took her hand and drew her away from the path, deeper into the woodland where the purple-spired foxgloves bloomed. And as they made love, fear and passion were so tightly woven together that they seemed to be the exact same emotion. Lara felt herself become David's once again; and he was hers. She knew that they were bound together, come what may.

In the days since then, they had met almost every afternoon at the same time. Their meetings took on a dreamlike quality for Lara; they consumed every day. All morning, she felt the quickening of excitement in her belly at the thought of seeing him; all evening she relived the pleasure of it.

They walked together arm in arm through the woods, talking about their lives and the time they had spent apart. So many regrets, so many broken dreams . . . And then they made their way down to the secret place where the foxgloves rose in clumps of speckled purples and where the wood was at its quietest and most lonely. David took the blanket from his knapsack and laid it on the ground and they would make love under the blue summer sky, the dappled sunlight warming their naked bodies.

Today, when they were wrapped in each other's arms, she heard a rustling on the forest floor nearby. 'Wait.' She put her fingers to her lips and they both looked around, fearful of discovery.

'Some woodland animal,' he said. 'There's no one here.'

And he was right. This part of the wood was deserted. They were safe. Safe and in each other's arms.

Afterwards, David propped himself up on one arm and looked down at her. 'Your hair is like gold dust, Lara,' he said.

She smiled.

David splayed her hair out like a fan around her head. 'Or a halo,' he teased.

She shot him a glance. 'Hardly,' she laughed. What Charles himself was probably doing right at this moment, what had become hard to endure in her life . . . even these things couldn't excuse what she was doing now.

But David's gaze had drifted away from her; he seemed lost in thought.

'David.' She pulled him back to her. 'What is it?'

He sighed, gently stroked her cheek. 'You know, I must be getting back home,' he said.

'Home?' Lara had been terrified of this. Their time together had seemed to hold such an illusory and romantic quality that reality had remained at the edges, and she for one had been happy to keep it there. But now, she sat up. Part of her had known he would have to go, but some other part of her had hoped – that he would stay here, that he would somehow belong to her life forever. Which was impossible, she knew.

'I need to work,' he said. 'They'll be missing me on the farm. I promised them I'd be back for the summer.'

Lara reached for her dress. 'Then you must go,' she said. Why should he linger – just to make love with a woman who was married to another man, a woman who was frightened to leave that man and go to Italy with David? Even David hadn't mentioned it lately. Perhaps she wasn't the only one keeping reality at bay.

'Come with me.' He clasped her hand.

Lara felt the small leap of hope. Could she? Could she really do it? Could she, after everything that had happened, find the strength? The panic ran through her body as fast and hot as liquid fire. It was as if suddenly, she couldn't see. 'I don't know if I can,' she said. She wanted to – of course she did. But the house, the garden, the promise to her mother . . . It was the enormity of it, she supposed.

He drew her closer. 'I'll help you.'

The panic grew. Lara pulled away and got to her feet. Her legs were so shaky that she was sure they couldn't hold her weight. 'I must go,' she said. She could barely breathe, barely function. All she could think of was Charles. She had been such a time away – every afternoon they'd stayed out longer, taken more risks. How long could it possibly be before . . . ? Her breath caught.

'All right.' David's eyes were sad. 'I understand.'

They ran back to the wall. He cupped his hands for her first foothold.

Once again, Lara hesitated. 'Will you be here tomorrow, David?' she asked him.

He sighed. It was as if he couldn't look at her.

What could she do? Lara placed her foot in his hands and

311

felt him push her up. She balanced herself with a hand on his shoulder.

'Careful now,' he whispered.

'Tomorrow?' she asked him again.

'Tomorrow,' he said. 'Tomorrow will be the last time.'

Oh, God help her . . . Lara ran back through the garden, only slowing when she knew she could be seen from the house. How could she survive this without David? She stilled her breathing; she smoothed her hair, shaking out a few leaves; she straightened her dress.

Charles was standing by the French windows. She couldn't see his expression. Slowly, summoning every ounce of self-control she possessed, Lara walked towards him.

CHAPTER 35

Bea

Dorset, June 2018

The following morning, Bea was working in the Spring Garden. The bulbs had finished flowering, so she snipped off the dead heads so that the plants would put their energy into producing a good bulb next spring, rather than seeds. There was no need to tie up the foliage, better to leave it to go yellow. And she wouldn't take the bulbs out of the ground; instead, she just cleared the soil around them of weeds and grasses to give them some breathing space. Later, she'd prepare a high potassium mulch to give back some nourishment; she'd carry on watering the ground too – at least until next month when the bulbs would become dormant. *Next month*, she thought. Would she even be here next month?

Bea paused to glance over the rest of this section of the garden. It was looking a bit sad now that spring was offi-cially over, although the euphorbia still stood proud. If only someone – her grandmother perhaps – had made a plan of the entire garden, she thought. If she knew where all the plants should be, she was more likely to be able to find them.

She loaded more weeds into the barrow. Nonna – or Nonna's mother perhaps – had called this section the Garden of Hope, which was nice. Spring was traditionally a time of new beginnings, of promise. It was the time to change direction, find a new pathway if things weren't going right. *Hmm.*

Bea glanced up at the low rafters and gables of Lime Tree House. Nonna had told her that she'd made a promise to her mother Florence that she would care for the garden, and so Bea was here to help fulfil that promise. But there seemed more to it than that. Who had sat on the bench under the flowering cherry tree some long-ago springtime? And what had Nonna needed to escape from?

When her wheelbarrow was full, Bea trundled it back into what Nonna had called the Nurturing Garden. It was a good name for it; the kitchen garden, orchard and old glasshouse would have provided nourishment for the family – and probably others too – during wartime; Bea had heard the stories of digging for victory from Nonna and the discarded bamboo canes, probably used for runner beans but now split and half rotted over time, told their own story.

In the centre of the plot, Lewis was digging, turning over the soil, forking it through and discarding old plant growth and weeds. Bea watched him for a moment. This morning, he was wearing long shorts and a faded red T-shirt which was already damp with sweat. As he paused in his digging, he caught his breath. He wiped the perspiration from his brow with the back of his arm, half turned and saw her watching him.

Bea trundled the barrow towards the compost. 'Another load cleared,' she said cheerily. So far, Lewis had been the perfect gardening companion – strong, capable and helpful, but not talking incessantly and crucially, not intruding on her space.

'The old greenhouse could do with a bit of TLC,' Lewis said thoughtfully, looking over at it.

He wasn't wrong. Several of the long, narrow, rectangular panes of glass were broken or missing and the wooden frame had rotted almost right through in places. But it must have once been very fine. The stone – a local stone, so Lewis had told her – rose a metre or so from the base, and the glasshouse structure was dictated by a shallow-pitched roof, which echoed the house perfectly. But it was unusual. 'It could be a specialist job,' she said.

'So, you'll keep it?' He was eyeing her curiously.

She met his gaze. 'I think so.' The glasshouse seemed integral to the garden to Bea. It might be costly to fix, but Nonna had assured her that funds were not as limited as she'd first thought.

'Because you want to preserve the Arts and Crafts elements of the garden?' he said. 'Or . . . ?'

Bea didn't answer at first. How could she explain that already this garden was reaching out to her, drawing her in, just as she imagined her grandmother had been drawn in before her. Already, Bea was enchanted by the garden. But for her grandmother, this garden might have been lost forever. Bea knew that she must save it.

'I'm not sure what I'm going to do with it yet,' she said at last. 'It depends on my grandmother and what she decides.' Though she had the feeling that it might also depend on Bea herself.

'Wait.' Lewis leant heavily on the fork handle. 'So, you're saying you might not sell this house after all? What will you do with it then? Rent it out again? Because you'll be going back to Italy when you've finished here, right?'

315

'Yes, of course.' Where else would she go? Bea pushed the thought of Matteo away. But she couldn't imagine renting out the house either. 'I suppose we'll have to sell it in the end.' She sighed. Lewis was right – she lived in a different country, so it was crazy to be feeling so attached to it, and in such a short space of time as well. But her grandmother had loved it too. Bea was sure of that. So, why did Nonna ever leave?

The breeze rustled through the fruit trees in the little orchard, but other than that, there was no answer.

'And have you thought about where it might be?' Lewis was still watching her in that disconcerting way.

'What?' Bea was confused. She tipped the contents of the barrow into the compost. There might be some good stuff at the bottom of that, she thought.

'The secret garden. Don't tell me you haven't been thinking about it.'

Bea glanced back at him. Thanks to the effort he'd been putting into the job, Lewis's T-shirt was clinging to his chest in a way that she found most unsettling. Bea looked away. What was the matter with her? So, he was an attractive bloke; there were plenty of those around and she was spoken for – sort of. Although, since Matteo was still maintaining a stony silence, she had no idea whether he considered them still together or not.

'A bit.' After yesterday's lunch, Bea had walked through the garden and concluded that the entire garden was accounted for. There was nowhere it could be. 'Though perhaps Hester got it wrong,' she said gently.

He shrugged. 'Perhaps. But what's at the end?'

'I'll show you if you like.' Proudly – it was her family's garden, after all – Bea led the way down the central avenue to the Rose Garden.

'Wow.' Lewis was suitably impressed by the roses, now at their best. 'What a great space.' He inhaled deeply.

'I know.' Bea, too, drank in the mingled fragrances of sweet apricot, honey, lemon and musk.

'And what's through there?' He pointed to what had once been the yew archway but now was little more than a bedraggled hole in the hedge.

'The Wild Garden.' She chuckled. 'And prepare yourself, because it really is. Wild, I mean.' They walked over and climbed through the gap. The grass was thigh-high, but on the plus side, an abundance of bees and butterflies were buzzing and fluttering around, clearly appreciating the natural meadowland it had become. There was a lot of cow parsley and campion, plenty of daisies and poppies, but perhaps a few too many dandelions, nettles and docks. Nettles were good for caterpillars and butterflies but in Bea's experience, they did have a way of taking over. Even a wild garden should be managed.

'Your ancestors were quite ahead of their time.' Lewis gestured towards the dense sea of grasses and brambles scattered with wildflowers and nettles. 'Lots of people are doing rewilding these days, aren't they? Trying to reclaim natural habitats for birds and insects.'

'Right on both counts.' Bea closed her eyes in order to fully appreciate the wild nature vibe. She could hear the insects humming and birdsong too. The grassy scent of wild meadows was intoxicating. She loved it.

When she opened her eyes again, Lewis was watching her. 'What?' she asked.

'I was wondering about the other side,' he said.

'Other side?' There was no other side. The end of the Wild Garden was the end of the garden itself, as marked by the high brick wall topped with barbed wire and covered with a dripping purple wisteria. 'The other side is the woodland.' She pointed to the trees. 'I haven't been around the back yet, but this is definitely the boundary.' As her grandmother had said, the Wild Garden led to the woodland.

Lewis squinted. 'But what about over there? Our side is rectangular. Your side has a gap – this wild section doesn't stretch across the entire width of the garden, does it?'

Bea frowned. She'd never had much of a sense of direction and she knew her spatial awareness wasn't the best . . . but he was right. The entire garden was a long rectangle and the little orchard on the other side only went as far as the yew hedge. As he'd said, the Wild Garden wasn't as wide as the full width of the garden. So . . . 'I see what you mean.'

Tentatively, she made her way over to the even taller grasses on the far side. Bea loved planting grasses in the gardens she designed – they created such a tactile environment with their movement and flow. And here . . . There was a thick swathe of tall bamboo and she recognised the stately, feathered *Stipa gigantea*, one of her favourite sculptural grasses. There could be birds nesting in this long grass, even reptiles or small mammals; clearly it hadn't been looked at by a gardener for years.

Lewis was close behind her.

'But there's no way through,' she said. 'It must be just more grass right up to the far side.'

'Yeah, maybe.' He swept back some of the grass, peered down at the ground, swept back some more, looked down again.

'What are you looking for?'

'Signs of a way in,' he said. 'An old path perhaps.'

An old path? A way in? Bea felt a surge of excitement. She joined him in the task of sweeping back the long grasses. And now she thought she could see something different, a place where the ground was flatter, as if once trodden down. Like he'd said, a sign.

She swept back some more of the *Stipa* grass and it rustled in reply. 'Lewis?' Bea had no idea why she felt nervous, but she did. Perhaps it was because she sensed she was about to make an important discovery.

'Have you found something?' He peered with her, their two heads so close together that she could smell the scent of him – paints, turpentine, earth and sweat. Very different from Matteo, she found herself thinking. She gave a little jump away as if stung.

But Lewis didn't appear to notice. His green eyes were shining. 'Here,' he said. 'You've found it. This is definitely a path.'

Bea felt a cold shiver run through her. They shared a look – conspiratorial and strangely intimate.

And then Lewis grabbed Bea by the hand and pulled her forwards. 'This is it, Bea. The way to the secret garden. Come on!'

CHAPTER 36

Lara

Dorset, July 1947

'Where have you been, Lara?' As she walked into the room, Charles stood perfectly still.

She was uncomfortably aware of his scrutiny. There was a glitter in his eyes that unnerved her. 'Oh, just in the garden.' She waved her hand in the direction from which she'd come. 'Such a glorious afternoon . . .' Her voice tailed off. *Did he know?* But how could he know?

'A nice day for walking.' Charles shut the door behind her.

Immediately, Lara felt trapped. She took a step towards the door that led to the hallway. Sometimes, every room in this house seemed too small for the two of them. *A nice day for walking?* How was it that such an innocuous phrase could sound so menacing?

'Walking?' She tried to stifle the sense of unease. A guilty conscience, that was her trouble.

'Around the woods perhaps?' He was still watching her closely.

She focused on the subtext. Like everything that was just under the surface with Charles, it seemed dangerous. 'The woods?'

'Really, Lara.' He clicked his tongue. 'You seem incapable of any conversation other than repeating what I've just said. Don't you have anything remotely original to say?'

She didn't. Her mind was a blank. Lara decided to remain silent – it seemed safer. She had no clue what he expected of her or what he might know, but the sense of unease was definitely growing.

Charles took a step closer and frowned. 'Goodness me, my dear, your dress looks rather grubby.'

Lara looked down. Sure enough, there was a grass stain, another earthy brown mark, and was that a—?

'And torn.' His voice was clipped, angry. He took a breath. 'Whatever can you have been doing?'

'Weeding,' she said. 'It must have got caught on some brambles at the end of the garden.' Or on the brick wall as she launched herself over.

'Hmm,' he said. 'That would explain it.' He regarded her coolly. 'However, I think you should get changed in time for dinner, don't you?'

'Oh. Well . . .' Lara was flustered. Charles had never shown the slightest interest in what she was wearing, at least not since the early days. She doubted he even noticed. She drifted around the house, a pale shadow of what she had once been; he went his own way.

He laughed mirthlessly. 'So go upstairs and make yourself decent, Lara.'

Decent . . . Lara didn't need telling twice. She couldn't wait to leave the room. She slipped past him and out of the door but even as she had one foot on the stairs, she realised that he was following her.

She turned. 'Charles?'

'On you go.' He waved her forwards, looking irritated now.

Lara obeyed, trying not to hurry, trying to keep calm, even as her breath snagged in her throat. She glanced at the stairs that led up to her father's old art studio. *How she missed him. How she missed them both . . .*

Charles followed her into the bedroom. He shut the door.

She turned to face him, waiting.

'Marjorie popped in earlier.' Charles stuck his hands in his pockets. To anyone else, he might seem to be making friendly conversation. He wasn't, though. He was standing in front of the closed door. There was no way out.

Lara took a step back towards the window. She cleared her throat with a little cough. 'How is she?' Because if only she could keep things normal . . . Not that she had much to do with his sister; she rarely visited. Lara presumed that Charles sometimes saw her when he was in the village. When he wasn't with his mistress, that was. What a horrible, deceitful, pointless life they were both living. She shuddered.

'She's very well.' His gaze slid down Lara's body.

Lara fidgeted. He was behaving so strangely. But how could he know anything? It wasn't possible.

'But as a matter of fact, her visit wasn't entirely pleasant.'

'Oh?' She waited, but he didn't elaborate. If she could, she would retreat even closer to the window, but her lower back was already pressing against the sill. 'I'm sorry to hear that.'

Charles took a step closer, seemingly casual. He was gazing out of the window behind her. 'She had her dog with her.' He

322

screwed up his nose. 'Smelly thing. I can't understand what she sees in it.'

Lara took a shallow breath. 'Company?' she suggested.

'Sorry?' He glanced back at her as if he'd forgotten she was in the room.

'Perhaps she's lonely,' Lara suggested. It seemed important to engage with him, to play for time.

'Ah, yes.' He nodded. 'We're not all fortunate enough to have a loving spouse waiting for us at home, are we?'

Lara tried to keep her expression neutral. She was pretty sure he didn't require a response to that.

'Anyway . . .' Charles scratched his chin thoughtfully.

He was playing with her, Lara realised. He had something up his sleeve and he was teasing her, like a cat playing with a mouse before going in for the kill, enjoying watching it squirm. 'Yes?'

'She'd been for a walk with the pooch.' Another step closer. 'In the woods.' He was watching her closely again now.

Lara tensed. In the woods? Was that it then? But she must stay calm, she realised. Marjorie might think that she'd seen her, but she might not know for sure. She swallowed. 'That's nice.'

'Oh, very nice, I'm sure.' He stepped forwards again. He was right in front of her now, almost touching. He reached out and tipped up her chin – not gently. 'But while she was out, she had rather a nasty shock, I'm afraid. And that wasn't nice at all.'

'A shock?' She was back to repeating what he'd said, but what else was she supposed to say? If only she could think of a way out of this conversation, she'd take it.

'Yes.' He put a hand on her throat, his fingers pressing into her Adam's apple. Lara wondered if he could feel her trembling.

'She saw this couple. A man and a woman. Cavorting, would you believe? Half-naked in the woods. Thoroughly disgusting behaviour.'

Lara couldn't speak. For one thing he was pressing so hard on her throat that she could barely breathe; for another, she was plain terrified. He stared at her, his pale eyes so cold, and she stared back, forcing herself not to panic. And yet panic was there in every part of her, the adrenalin coursing around her body.

Both of his hands were on her throat now. This was it then, Lara thought. He was going to kill her. He knew about David and he was going to kill her, right here in their bedroom, scene of so much humiliation and shame. Marjorie had seen them together. Perhaps the rustle she'd heard had been Marjorie, or her dog chasing rabbits, both of them finding much more than they'd bargained for deep in the heartland of the woods. 'Charles, you're hurting me,' she managed to croak.

'It can't be my lovely Lara, I told her.' Charles's voice had a sing-song rhythm to it now. He loosened his hold slightly and began to stroke her neck, her throat, his fingers reaching and pressing under the collar of her dress. 'She's in the garden. I'll call her. You're mistaken. You'll see.'

Lara continued to stare at him, half hypnotised.

'So, I called you,' he told her. 'But you weren't there, were you?' He pressed harder, his fingertips digging into her flesh. 'You were in the woods, weren't you? With some man.'

'I . . .' But she couldn't deny it. It had happened and she'd been seen.

'Weren't you?' He was shouting now, all semblance of calm gone from his expression. With one swift, rough movement, he ripped open the thin fabric of the bodice of her dress.

324

Lara gasped. Instinctively, she crossed her hands in front of her breasts. 'Yes,' she said.

'Whore.' He slapped her.

It was so fast, she hardly registered it until he drew his hand away. For a few seconds, she felt nothing, her face numb, and then came the sharp pain in her cheek, in her eye.

'You go to the village.' Lara held her head high. Her face was flaming but from somewhere, the courage came.

'What?' He glared at her, the pupils of his eyes black pin-pricks.

'You go to see your woman in the village,' she said. 'I know about her. Everyone knows.' Her eyes filled. The pain, the humiliation, the shame of what she had become.

But it stopped Charles in his tracks – at least for the moment. 'Ah,' he said. His eyes narrowed. 'So, you think that gives you permission to behave like a cheap whore, is that it?'

Lara flinched. She shook her head. Her love with David had seemed like something beautiful, not cheap at all. She had run into his arms not thinking, not caring about any consequences. It was as if he had never gone away, as if Lara had never married. All her unhappiness, all the mad desperate thoughts that seemed to fill her head every waking hour had disappeared when she was with David. He was her escape, her rescuer. But this wasn't so, she realised. She had done wrong just as Charles had. She was a married woman. And David couldn't help her now.

He stepped back, looking her up and down as she stood there in her torn dress trembling from head to toe, as if she was worthless, just a piece of dirt in the gutter. 'And who could blame me?' he muttered. 'Who could blame me for looking for something more welcoming than a lump of ice in my bed?'

Lara closed her eyes as if she could block his voice, his words from her mind. She didn't care what he called her, nor what he thought of her. She just wanted this to be over.

But his attention snapped back. 'Tell me his name, Lara.'

She shook her head wearily. 'What does it matter?'

Then just when she thought the worst was over, his hands were there, back around her throat, squeezing, squeezing. 'Of course it fucking matters,' he growled. 'It's him, isn't it? That farm boy of yours who had the bare-faced cheek to turn up here looking for you.'

'Yes,' she spluttered. 'David.' Of course it was David. But in that second, she felt as if she'd betrayed him.

'I'll kill him.' His voice was low. 'Writing his bloody letters. Sniffing around here after you. And I'll kill you too if you try and see him again, you treacherous bitch.'

He tightened his hold. He squeezed harder.

The world went hazy and then the world went black. She was dimly aware, but not there in the room, not really. Another slap – across her mouth this time. Her legs flailing beneath her. Torn clothing. A rip. A scratch. A fall, as if she'd been thrown like a rag doll. A weight on top of her, squashing, squeezing, suffocating. Breath. Rancid breath. A thick and heavy hand over her face. Panting. Muttering. A male smell. A different kind of pain that streaked up inside her. And then silence. Blessed silence.

CHAPTER 37

Bea

Dorset, June 2018

That evening, Bea was making pasta with a simple ragu sauce
and a salad. She'd invited Lewis and Hester to share it with her.

'I owe you,' she'd told Lewis when he finally left the garden
to go back next door to spend some time with his grandmother.
He'd checked on her several times that morning too – Bea was
impressed by his level of care.

'For the quiche?' There was a gleam of humour in his eye.

'For helping me find the secret garden.' She wasn't sure she
would have found it alone. 'And the quiche.'

They had pushed back the tall bamboo, edged through in
single file, carefully following the narrow trail. After a few
yards, the pathway had opened out into a little woodland glade.
This, then, was the seventh garden . . .

Fascinated, Bea had looked around. She would never have
known it was here. The garden was sheltered by the woodland
and the brick wall, thick with moss and lichen, and only a few

rays of sparse sunlight flickered through the trees. There was a small stream, and she was able to identify various woodland plants – foxgloves not yet in flower, nightshade and lily of the valley, among others. In front of the yew hedge to the left were a few bedraggled hydrangea bushes.

Lewis walked over to the stream. 'This runs through to our side,' he said. 'My grandmother spends a lot of time down there, just looking into the water.' He shook his head. 'I never quite know what she sees.'

Bea went over to join him in the dappled shade. 'The sound of water can be very therapeutic,' she said. But she was thinking about Hester and Elizabeth's interest in herbalism. There were some plants that loved this kind of habitat.

'Why would your ancestors have had a secret garden in the first place, do you think?' Lewis turned to face her.

'That is for me to find out.' She smiled. 'But to be honest, it is probably just a bit of garden design fun, you know, like building a folly. It does not have to have a clear purpose.'

'It does have a mysterious feel to it,' Lewis conceded.

'You are right. Almost other-worldly.' Bea bent down to examine the plants at her feet. There was a water hemlock, some pretty and delicate larkspur and some bracken and ferns, which clearly loved the dampness and humidity. Something was niggling at her, but she couldn't pinpoint what it was. If anything, the secret garden seemed to pose more questions than answers.

'They both loved their gardens, our grandmothers, didn't they?' said Lewis. 'They had a lot in common. No wonder they got on so well.'

Bea considered. 'Do you think your grandmother remembers everything she once knew about plants and herbalism?'

Bea didn't count herself an expert on the use of herbs in medicine, although the subject had been touched on in her course on horticulture.

'I wouldn't be surprised. She seems to remember the distant past much better than what happened yesterday.'

Bea had heard this was often the case. 'I should talk to her again.' She sensed that there was a lot more she could learn from Hester.

Lewis eyed her curiously. 'What exactly are you hoping to find here? In the garden, I mean? In Dorset?'

He was perceptive. Bea glanced away, focusing on the softly rippling stream, which was far safer. 'I am not sure.'

'But there is something, isn't there?'

She realised he wasn't going to give up until she told him more. And why shouldn't she confide in him? He was a good listener and there was something honest in his open, green-eyed gaze that made her instinctively trust him. 'Yes, you are right. I came here for my grandmother. She promised her mother she would look after the garden and I suppose she felt she had failed her by going to Italy and leaving everything behind.'

'A bit of a strange thing to do, you think?'

'Yes, I do.'

'So, you came here to do what she asked but also to look for some reasons why?'

'Exactly.'

He put his head to one side. A shaft of unexpected sunlight fell onto his blond hair like liquid honey. 'Wouldn't it have been simpler to just ask her?'

She laughed. 'You do not know my grandmother. She is incredible in all sorts of ways, but when she decides not to say anything, she will not budge.'

'Determined then?' Lewis bent down and put his hand in the stream.

Bea watched the water trickling through his fingers. Artistic hands, she thought. Long, slender fingers, lean arms . . . 'Yes,' she said. And determined wasn't the half of it.

'So, either it's something she doesn't want to think about, or it's something she wants you to find out for yourself,' he said.

He should have been a detective. Or a psychologist . . . 'Hmm.' She wouldn't commit on that.

'But I'm not sure that you'll get any more answers from Grandma Hester.' He splashed some water from his hands onto his neck to cool down.

It was surprisingly warm in this shady garden. It felt as if they were alone in the world. Bea moved a few steps away from him. They should go back. She should get on. 'I know,' she said. 'I am not really expecting to. But she has already led us to the secret garden. It was lost and now it is found. So who knows what else we could discover?'

Now, Bea left the sauce to simmer and went upstairs to change. She already felt at home here – perhaps because this was where her beloved grandmother had grown up. Bea was half-British after all. And she no longer felt daunted by the garden either. It was a challenge, yes, but one she knew she was up to, especially with Lewis's help.

She let her thoughts drift back to this morning. She'd enjoyed working with him, and discovering the secret garden with him by her side had been a bit special too. Bea had been expecting to come here and feel isolated. It didn't worry her; she was happy in her own company and being solitary didn't

330

freak her out in the least. But . . . Rather surprisingly, she felt that she'd found a friend.

It was a warm evening and so Bea chose a simple shift dress, teaming it with a chunky copper necklace and thonged leather sandals. As she brushed her dark hair, she caught a glimpse of something in the mirror that surprised her. Anticipation. Was she hoping to find out some more answers from Hester as she'd mentioned to Lewis earlier on? Or was it Lewis himself she was looking forward to seeing? He had such an easy way about him, he was gentle and good to talk to. *But* . . . She frowned.

Why was she even thinking about Lewis – a man she hardly knew? Why wasn't she thinking about Matteo and his proposal? It had only been a few short weeks ago after all. If she loved Matteo, if he was the man she wanted to spend the rest of her life with, then shouldn't she be thinking of nothing else? Shouldn't she be missing him with every fibre of her being?

And what about Matteo? If he loved her as he'd said he did, then why wasn't he responding to any of her messages? Surely that could only mean that he'd given up on her, that as he'd threatened, he wasn't willing to wait for her to return? Bea wasn't sure yet how she felt about this. People said that absence made the heart grow fonder, but for her it seemed that once she was out of Matteo's orbit, the feelings she had for him were fading.

It was confusing. Could she imagine spending the rest of her life with him? Bea grimaced. Not if it meant she had to give up her gardens. And did she miss him? She wasn't sure that she did – at least not in that all-consuming way she'd expected to. She certainly didn't miss the pressure he'd put her under and she didn't miss the way he managed to get her to do things she wasn't comfortable with, like taking the afternoon off when she'd been looking forward to getting some plants bedded in. How sad was that? Shouldn't she appreciate it more – having an exciting boyfriend who was spontaneous and fun, who wanted to whisk her away from boring old work whenever he felt like it?

Bea turned away from the mirror and made her way downstairs to check the sauce. Only work wasn't boring. And whenever *he* felt like it was exactly the point. Matteo had swept her off her feet. But Bea quite liked standing on solid ground – of the earthy variety. And Matteo wanted to do what Matteo wanted to do. Bea's desires – at least as far as her gardening was concerned – came a very poor second.

Even so . . . Bea paused as she descended the elegant but dilapidated staircase that her grandparents and great-grandparents must have descended so many times before her. Matteo had been able to chase away her doubts, he'd always made her feel special, and he'd shown his vulnerable side too when his father had been taken ill. And he'd offered to share his life with her. Bea had thrown it back in his face – as good as.

In the kitchen, she peered at her ragu, which was bubbling nicely, a delicious aroma of tomato and caramelised garlic wafting into the air. Bea repressed a sigh. And now she'd travelled to another country leaving Matteo alone and facing a position of great responsibility – taking over his parents' restaurant, no less – saying she needed to think things through. No wonder he wasn't answering any of her texts.

Bea put a pan of water on to boil for the pasta. She checked her phone. Nothing. She didn't know whether she was as good as engaged to Matteo or if it was all over between them. And how was she supposed to find out, when he wouldn't even acknowledge her messages?

Later, the three of them were seated around the table Bea had set up in the sitting room by the French windows leading out onto the veranda, Lewis and Bea drinking a velvety red wine Lewis had brought round tonight. It was a Primitivo from Bea's own region of Puglia, which reminded her of home. *A nice touch . . .* She felt relaxed and happy. Tired from her work in the garden, but in a good way, because she knew they'd achieved a lot. Her ragu had gone down well with Lewis and Hester and she'd enjoyed chatting to them both about her family, their family, Dorset and Italy. At times, Hester was quiet, apparently content to listen to their conversation, and at other times, she surprised Bea by joining in enthusiastically – sometimes sounding very rational; other times not quite so much.

'If we were in Italy now, we'd be sitting outside,' Bea said. Even so, despite the fact that the evening temperature had dropped, she'd left the veranda door open so that they could breathe in the night air, perfumed by the honeysuckle. She was glad to be here, she realised. In fact, she was loving it.

'And yet you wonder why Lara left Dorset and went to live in Italy,' Lewis teased.

A good point . . .

'Lara was unhappy,' Hester said. 'Very unhappy.' She shook her head sadly.

Bea sat up straighter. 'Was she, Hester?' she whispered. 'But why?' After all, Nonna had enjoyed a happy childhood by her own account and she had her beloved garden.

'How could she be happy?' Hester asked. 'With him?' Her voice dripped distaste and scorn.

Bea and Lewis shared a quick glance of surprise.

'Him?' Bea asked weakly. 'Who do you mean?' Her mind was racing, her previous mood of relaxation quite gone.

But Hester's attention had wandered. 'I'm tired,' she told Lewis.

'Okay, Grandma.' He got to his feet, clearly reluctant to end the evening and Bea realised that she felt the same. 'We should head off,' he said.

But his eyes were telling Bea something else. *Another mystery*, he seemed to be saying. *Could this be the answer that you're looking for?*

'Okay,' Bea said. 'No problem.'

She refused Lewis's offer of helping to clear up. Hester was looking a bit agitated so it was better for him to get his grandmother home. Bea just hoped she hadn't upset her by encouraging her to think about the past.

Lewis kissed her lightly on one cheek. 'Thanks for supper.'

'You're very welcome.' She smiled. 'Thanks for your help today.' There was a lot, she felt, to thank him for.

His gaze lingered on her face. 'Shall I come over again tomorrow for an hour or two?'

Bea felt a rush of pleasure. She supposed that right now she simply didn't want to be alone. 'That would be great,' she said. 'If you have the time.' She hesitated. 'And the energy.'

Jokingly, he flexed his right bicep and laughed. 'I'll do my best.'

Bea said goodbye to Hester and stood at the front door watching as they walked down the drive arm in arm. Halfway down, Lewis turned and waved. 'Sleep tight,' he called.

'Sleep tight,' she murmured as she closed the door.

Bea wasn't sure why she did it, but instead of going back to the sitting room to clear up, she opened the door to the study and stood there for a moment on the threshold. She didn't like the atmosphere of this room – she was sure that it had never been her grandmother's space; it felt cold and unwelcoming and very different from the cosy sitting room with its warm colours from nature and the light flooding in through the French windows, the pull outside into the walled garden.

Sleep tight . . .

But sleep proved elusive as Bea tossed and turned in bed that night. There was so much to think about. Was Hester right? Had her grandmother been unhappy? This fitted in with Bea's theory about the girl who needed to escape from the garden and her grandmother being one and the same. But why would she have been so unhappy? Had she been badly treated? And if so, by whom? Presumably, this mysterious 'he' that Hester had referred to. Her husband – Bea's grandfather? Nonna's father? They both sounded unlikely candidates. *Or . . . ?*

But she couldn't think of any other possibilities, and as dawn was about to break, she eventually fell into a deep sleep full of dreams about secret gardens and ogres from fairy tales. If she was going to find out the answers, Bea knew that she would just have to keep looking.

CHAPTER 38

Rose

Italy, June 2018

Rose and Federico had driven into Martina Franca. Federico had some business there and at her husband's request, Rose had gone along – partly to provide the moral support he said he needed but mostly to stop him from losing his temper with the local businessman concerned, who seemed to know how to press all of Federico's buttons simultaneously. Rose was tempted to simply let her husband get on with it and suffer the consequences, because she'd told him often enough not to rise to it, but she felt the need to get away from the *masseria* for a couple of hours herself. She was restless; she knew that something was wrong in her life right now, but she wasn't at all sure what to do about it.

They parked in the square near Porta Stracciata as the signore lived in the depths of the *centro storico*, which was a tantalising mix of golden baroque, rococo and Greek white architecture with more than its fair share of grand *palazzi* and churches.

It was impossible to negotiate the narrow streets in there, let alone park the car, as Federico grumbled. They walked under the white stone arch, past the butcher's shop, beside the ornate stone doorways in Largo San Pietro and under the twisty curlicue wrought-iron balconies so low they almost touched the ground. Rose could smell the fragrances of cooking emanating from Martina Franca kitchens: onion being sliced, garlic crushed, pasta sauces bubbling away on unseen stoves. Federico was still talking, Rose only half listening to him. She had other things on her mind.

There was an old church on their left, Chiesa San Pietro; Rose and Federico had gone to a wedding there once. Rose smiled at the memory of the young girl – one of Federico's cousins, her freshness and beauty, her excitement at the prospect of the life ahead of her . . . Rose hoped that Sofia's life had indeed turned out to be as happy as she had expected, that she hadn't been ground down by work, by arguments, by secrets.

They passed the stylish ochre house with the green shutters that Rose had always admired and entered the square, Piazza Maria Immacolata, actually more of a semicircle with its curved baroque buildings and *portici* archways. As always, she was struck by the elegance of this piazza. Martina Franca was a town largely overlooked by tourists but, in fact, its buildings were very fine; this square in particular with its graceful arched colonnade and delicate filigree balconies was stunning. And the elaborate facade of the cathedral peeked gloriously through the gap in the buildings promising further resplendence to come.

Federico was still talking. 'It is all very well you saying that, Rose.'

Rose glanced at him in surprise. She didn't remember saying a word.

'But I have to make him see sense, you know. If he would only listen, if he would only see things from someone else's point of view for a change, then—'

'Sì, sì, I know,' she soothed. She must keep her mind on what mattered. She was here to support her husband. He did not ask for much, after all. And the meeting really shouldn't be a problem – if Federico would only remain calm. 'I agree with what you say,' she assured him. 'But think of your blood pressure, caro. If he will not agree—'

'That is the point, though, Rose.' He'd interrupted her, but Rose had stopped mid-sentence anyway.

On the other side of the square, lounging against one of the arches of the colonnade, was a familiar figure. Cool as you like, casually smoking a cigarette, dressed in his usual dirty blue jeans, black leather jacket and scuffed boots. Cesare Basso.

Dio santo . . . Rose didn't say this; she kept her curse silent. But what in God's name was Cesare Basso doing here in the quiet town of Martina Franca on this of all days? She glanced across at him and then quickly away. Had he seen them? It would be only seconds before he did because they were heading his way. Pray God that Federico didn't look over to the other side of the square. Would he recognise him? Probably. Plenty of people annoyed Federico, but only one made his blood boil.

She must stop that happening. Who knew where it might lead? Rose took Federico's arm and half turned in the other direction, pointing to something in a shop window – anything to prevent him from looking over.

'What is it, Rose?' He was impatient with her. He wasn't in the mood for window-shopping, she knew that.

It was a newsagent's. Rose babbled something about a lotto

ticket; she hardly knew what she was saying. Her senses were on red alert. If Cesare came over, what would she say? And more to the point, what would Cesare say? Would he betray her? She felt a cold shiver run through her. Was her secret about to come out? *No, per favore, no . . .* And what would Federico do? Rose couldn't bear it; she really could not.

'Oh, not now, Rose.' Federico patted her hand in a conciliatory manner and walked on. He was on a mission; lotto tickets could wait.

Cesare was still there. For God's sake, what had she ever seen in the man? Unfortunately, she knew damn well. But was this a coincidence? Or had he *known* they were coming to Martina Franca today?

'Ah.' Rose paused again, gazing in apparent rapture at the baby photos framed in the window of the next shop. 'Just look, darling.'

'What now?' Federico frowned.

Rose moved to the other side of him, hoping to block his view of the far side of the piazza. 'Do you think that Bea . . .?' she murmured, squeezing his arm.

'It is a bit early for that, *non*? Especially when she is not even in the country.' He looked more than a little irritated now, which suited Rose as he began to walk more quickly and they were almost past Cesare.

But not quite. Rose risked another glance across the narrow street as she hurried to match her husband's pace. Cesare was looking right over. He smirked and lifted his hand in a wave as they drew level. Rose ignored him.

As they passed Cesare (and thank goodness the square was so wide) Federico was talking once again about the forthcoming meeting and what he was planning to say to the signore.

Thankfully, he was therefore too distracted to be looking around him.

Rose's glance flicked back to Cesare once again, though she was careful not to turn her head. She glared at him the briefest of warnings, but he only smirked all the more. *See you around,* he had told her in that last text message. Now, it seemed more like a threat than ever.

Rose gritted her teeth. A few more steps and he'd be behind them. She'd be safe. And then they would turn the corner and be out of sight. She glanced at Federico. His eyes were focused straight ahead and he was still talking.

Rose risked a final sideways glance just as Cesare dropped his cigarette butt on the ground. He stepped on it, grinding it under his boot. Rose felt a jolt of sympathy for the cigarette as Cesare slunk back into the shadows. Was that supposed to mean something? She wasn't sure. But one thing she did know – he wasn't finished with her yet. Cesare Basso continued to haunt her.

As they sat in the back room of the shop with the businessman from Martina Franca, Rose couldn't stop her mind from wandering away from the conversation and onto remembering how it had been all those years ago with her and the Bassos, when she had been so under the influence of both Cesare and Daniela.

At first, she'd pretended to herself that Cesare wasn't a bad person. So what if he wasn't always on the right side of the law? So what if he took chances and hung around with a rough crowd? Wasn't that what made him so exhilarating? Cesare laughed at conventions. He was different and proud of it. He scorned those – like Federico – who worked hard, who respected their parents, who always did the right thing.

Rose had been sure back then that Cesare would never do anything that was *so* bad. It was simply that he was his own man and he followed his own rules. That assurance, that devil-may-care attitude only made him more attractive in Rose's eyes. No one was going to tell Cesare Basso what to do. He would take what he wanted to take from this world – but he wouldn't hurt anyone. Rose had been convinced of that.

Blind infatuation, she thought now. That was exactly what it had been. She didn't see what he was, because she didn't want to see. And by the time her eyes were opened . . . It was too late. By then, she was much too scared to break away. At least, until she herself was involved. *Until* . . .

CHAPTER 39

Lara

Dorset, July 1947

Lara awoke with no awareness of how much time had passed. She was in bed, she knew that much, and someone was speaking to her, quietly and with a note of compassion that seemed all wrong.

'Mrs Fripp? Mrs Fripp? I've made you some tea.'

Lara tried to speak but it hurt. She put a finger to her lips. They were swollen. And her eye – it was hard to open, so that must be swollen too. And she was sore; all over sore, inside and out, it seemed. But she could see and she could breathe. She was alive. And Mrs Peacock of all people was there at her bedside.

'Thank you,' she managed to croak. Her throat was parched. She struggled to sit up. Where was Charles? A bolt of fear made her start to shake again. She glanced around the room. He wasn't here. Thank God.

'There now.' Mrs Peacock's eyes held an expression Lara hadn't seen there before. Kindness, she thought. 'You must stay in bed for now. You must rest.' With a final glance at Lara, she turned and left the room, as if afraid to say too much.

Lara squinted towards the window. The curtains were still half drawn, but the morning light was filtering through the nets. She had slept all night then – she must have. She was even wearing her nightdress and yet she had no recollection of the evening or night that had passed. Who had put the nightdress on her? Charles? She shuddered. Her last memory was hazy. She didn't want to let it in.

She sipped at the tea which was sugary and stung her sore lip, but tasted good nevertheless. She moved her limbs cautiously. Nothing was broken, though bruises were beginning to flower on her upper arms and probably on her throat from the feel of it.

With some difficulty, she crawled out of bed and to her dressing table, where she sat on the padded stool and peered into the mirror. Gently, she touched her face, examining the damage. One side of her face was swollen, one eye red and still half closed. Her lips were swollen too and a cut on her lower lip had bled and formed a scab. Her hair was tangled, there were blue-black bruises on her throat. *My God.* He had practically strangled her . . . She touched the bruises gingerly, wincing at the pain.

Lara stared at her reflection. Charles knew about David. He would stop her from seeing him again. She was a prisoner, and one who could be physically assaulted now and at any time in the future if she didn't do as he dictated. This was her life. Everyone in the village – except Hester and hopefully Elizabeth too – thought she had lost her sanity. She was alone. And she was tired, so tired. She closed her eyes.

After a few minutes she opened them again. She still looked

the same, beaten and exhausted, but there was a new note of steel in her expression and she recognised that. She had to get out. She must break her promise to her mother because David was right – she would not want Lara to go through this awful nightmare, not in any circumstances. She must be spinning in her grave. *Get out, Lara. Get out.* She could almost hear her mother's voice. But how?

David was coming to meet her for the last time today. How could she blame him for deciding to return to Italy? If she had been braver, they could have made plans, they might have found a way forward. But now, if she didn't turn up, he would assume it was over, that she'd decided not to torture herself by seeing him one last time. He would go back to Italy and she would never see him again. Lara couldn't bear that. She had lost him once before and she had found him. She had never stopped loving him. And now . . .

Lara got up from the stool and began to get dressed. It was painful and it was slow, but she needed to do this. She needed to take action now, while Charles thought she was unable to. Later, she might not get the chance.

She forced herself to go downstairs, slowly, hand on the banister all the way. At some point, she would have to face Charles, she would have to behave as if everything was normal. She couldn't challenge him – she didn't have the strength and it would no doubt result in another beating that might be even worse than the one she'd already endured. But first, she had to think.

She could hear them talking – Charles and Mrs Peacock – in the study and so she slipped quietly into the kitchen where she might listen unseen. His voice was low and she couldn't make out the words but he certainly didn't sound remorseful.

Mrs Peacock's voice was firm, even stern perhaps. What was she telling him? What would she do?

The study door opened. Lara shrank back into the shadows.

'I'll say no more.' That was Mrs P. 'It isn't my business. Your marriage is your own affair and I'm not one to gossip. But as I told you, Mr Fripp, I'll not stand by and watch this. I shan't be coming again.'

Not coming again? Suddenly, and rather surprisingly it had to be said, Lara felt as if she were losing an ally. Mrs Peacock's voice didn't sound at all like it usually did when she was addressing Charles. She had always been deferential, always respectful; not cold and disapproving as she sounded now.

Lara's legs felt weak. She clutched on to the kitchen worktop for support.

'You must do as you see fit.' That was Charles. As detached and clipped as ever.

The study door closed. Lara breathed out. And then Mrs Peacock was standing in the kitchen doorway looking right at her. The housekeeper shook her head and put her finger to her lips. She closed the kitchen door noiselessly behind her.

Lara stared at her. 'Mrs Peacock? I—'

'You should be in bed resting, Mrs Fripp.' It seemed as if the woman could hardly bring herself to look at her. Mrs Peacock took her coat which was hanging over a kitchen chair and put it on. She was shaking her head and her lips were pulled into a thin line of censure. She frowned, jammed her hat onto her head.

'You're going?' They were all deserting her – even those who had never seemed to be on her side.

Mrs Peacock gave a little nod of understanding. There was pity in her eyes. 'Goodbye,' she said softly. She made her way over to the back door, opened it and was gone.

Lara's eyes filled. But there was no time for crying, no time to feel sorry for herself. She had to do something and she had to do it now. She opened the kitchen door as silently as she could. The study door was still closed. Could she risk it? It seemed to be now or never.

She pulled on her shoes and a wrap and slipped soundlessly through to the sitting room and out of the French doors. Down the steps from the veranda she ran, half stumbling, through the garden, panting for breath, ducking under the arch that led to the Nurturing Garden. She checked behind her. Nothing. No one. Charles couldn't see her from the study. He would assume she was still upstairs languishing in her bed, but she didn't know how long she had. For now, at least, she wasn't locked in.

There was only one person who could help her. At the window in the wall, she bent low. 'Hester!' she called. 'Hester!'

For a while she thought she wouldn't come. It was a Saturday and she should be home, but perhaps she was running some errand for her mother? Lara should have thought this through more carefully. She should have written something down so that she could at least leave a message. 'Hester!' she called again, more loudly now. 'Hester!'

Footsteps. *Ah* . . . Lara sank gratefully onto the ground, exhausted.

'Lara?' Hester's concerned young face appeared at the wall. She gasped when she saw her. 'Oh, Lara. What's happened? Tell me.'

Where should she start? 'You must get a message to David,' she began. Because this was the most urgent thing. 'He'll be here at the end of the garden in the woods at three thirty. I won't be able to get there. I . . .' She faltered, her mind going off at tangents. 'Otherwise, he'll leave. He'll go back to Italy and I need to tell him . . . Mrs Peacock has left too. It's Charles—'

'Slow down,' urged Hester. 'Is it Charles who's done this to you?'

Lara nodded.

'And Mrs Peacock is your housekeeper? She's left, you say?'

'Yes, Hester. And I have to leave too.' And it all came out, the whole story, as Lara struggled to explain.

For a young girl, presumably inexperienced in the ways of the world, Hester seemed to grasp the nub of the situation very quickly. 'Leave it to me,' she said. 'I'll tell David. Don't worry. Go back to the house. Stay safe.'

'But . . .'

'I'll come to you,' Hester said. 'Trust me. I'll find a way.'

'Thank you.' Lara grasped her hands and squeezed. The tears filled her eyes once again. Hester was a true friend.

Lara didn't go back into the house straightaway. She didn't want to go back at all. She sat in the Romantic Garden in sight of the house so that he could see she was there. And when he called her in and locked the door behind her, she went in like a lamb. He didn't mention anything that had occurred the evening before. He stayed quiet and calm.

'Go to your room now and rest, Lara.' His voice was gentle.

Meekly, she obeyed. But inside, she was raging. Inside, she couldn't stop thinking, couldn't stop planning. How she could do it, how she could get away from him, how soon she could be gone.

CHAPTER 40

Bea

Dorset, June 2018

'What was it that drew you to Dorset?' Bea asked Lewis. 'Apart from your grandmother, I mean?' She passed him a mug of tea. They were standing in the Nurturing Garden. He'd been working hard here this morning and it was starting to look much more respectable.

Lewis had gone to the garden centre first thing and come back with a few bags of compost, among other things requested by Bea. She'd been tempted to accompany him, but didn't want to be distracted by any plants that might be on offer. Plenty of time for that when she was a bit further into the project. And in any case, she'd promised herself to spend a few hours this morning tackling the Thinking Garden, which had been sadly neglected for far too long.

On his return, Lewis had spent an hour forking compost into the kitchen garden, which would, she knew, be grateful for the much-needed nutrition.

'Thanks.' He took the mug, wiped his brow with the back of his hand. It was a warm and rather muggy day and the sun had yet to make an appearance. 'You could say I fell in love.'

'Ah.' Bea hadn't meant to get so personal. She liked Lewis – in fact, she liked him a lot – but right now, something was also warning her to keep a safe distance. 'Sorry, I didn't mean to pry.'

'Hmm.' He looked beyond her, beyond the confines of the walled garden it seemed, and the look in his green eyes was unfathomable. 'Well, that's another story probably best kept for another day.' He turned his attention back to her. 'But what I really fell in love with here in Dorset was the landscape.'

'The landscape . . .' She wondered what the other story might be. 'I see.' Since she'd arrived, Bea had spent most of her time in this garden, but she wasn't blind to the lure of the green hills of Dorset. She'd seen something of the countryside from the train on her way here, and she'd discovered that the village itself, which she'd walked to several times now, was charming with its thatched cottages with roses and wisteria clambering up whitewashed walls. She loved the individual little front gardens lined with wrought-iron railings or dry-stone walls, the pretty golden-stoned church with the deep mullioned stained-glass windows and the quirky low-beamed pub which she'd briefly explored one lunchtime a week or so ago.

Lewis was eying her thoughtfully. 'I suppose you haven't had the chance to see much of it,' he said.

'Not yet,' she admitted. Without a car she was somewhat limited. She'd thought about hiring one, but how long would she be here for? As yet, she had no idea. Italy seemed a long way away at this moment, but she could fly back anytime. She would hire a car for a day or two when she needed to, she'd decided, in order to pick up plants or take garden waste to the tip, but not for the entire length of her stay – it would be far too expensive, and she was determined to spend her grandmother's money wisely.

'I could take you out somewhere at the weekend.' Lewis gave a little shrug as if the offer meant nothing significant at all. 'I normally take Grandma Hester out anyway, and she'd be glad to have some different company.'

'Thanks. I'd like that.' And Lewis? Would he be glad to have some different company? She guessed so. Hester was lovely, but it must be very hard caring for a beloved family member when they had become so different from the person they'd once been. Anyhow. Bea gave herself a little shake. She wouldn't read anything into it. Lewis was simply being friendly, that was all.

'There's a lot to see.' His eyes lit up with enthusiasm. 'The road from Bridport down to Weymouth is stunning – there's the Fleet and some lovely villages, Portesham and Abbotsbury, there's a swannery and some interesting architecture there. Or we could go the other way to Charmouth and Lyme Regis. The beaches are great for fossil hunting and Lyme is known as the Pearl of Dorset, so . . .' His voice trailed.

'It all sounds wonderful.' And it did. Bea would love to explore properly, as if she were here on holiday, instead of tasked with restoring an Arts and Crafts walled garden. Not that she wasn't emotionally invested in doing that too. But what a shame that she had so much gardening to do that she wouldn't be able to do more than skim the surface of this lovely place.

He seemed to notice her expression and gave a rueful grin. 'We can see some of it at least,' he promised.

'Thanks.' Bea wished there was some way she could repay him for his kindness. She suspected that Hester and Lewis were not wealthy, but equally, she knew he'd be far too proud to accept any payment for the help he was giving her. For Lewis, it was a question of friendship – the friendship of their grand-mothers, that was, and perhaps theirs too.

'It'll be fun.' He grinned. 'I can bore anyone to death on the subject of Dorset.'

Bea thought of the paint-stained overalls he'd been wearing when they first met. 'And do you paint the Dorset landscapes you love?' She was curious about his painting. How much of his work did he manage to sell? And just how good was he?

'I do.' He laughed and brushed back his mane of blond hair. 'Grandma says I'm a dreamer. She says I like to imagine I'm one of the Impressionists, you know, painting in the outside air, *en plein air*, seizing the moment, getting my inspirations from the landscape, land, air and sea, all that stuff.' He waved an imaginary paintbrush in the air to illustrate.

Bea laughed with him. 'How exciting.' It was nice that he was a dreamer. And she liked the fact that he was inspired by nature, just as she was when it came to her garden design. She hesitated. *If you didn't ask* . . . 'Would you show me?'

'Show you?' He took a sip of tea, his gaze holding hers over the rim of the mug.

'Your work.' Once again, Bea felt flustered. She looked away, gazing down at the soil Lewis had just been digging. 'I'd love to see some of your paintings,' she said. 'If you don't mind, that is.'

He put his head to one side in that thoughtful way he had and then seemed to come to a decision. 'Course not.' He rolled down his shirt sleeves. 'There's no time like the present. I need to nip back to check on Grandma. So, I could show you now if you like?'

'Oh, okay, great.' Bea took his empty mug from him. 'I'll be two minutes.'

She returned to the house via the Thinking Garden. As Nonna had told her, the plants here were white and reflective. This morning, she'd been clearing the soil around the lace-cap hydrangeas and white agapanthus which would be flowering soon. Already in bloom were a white hebe, white lilies and geraniums in circular beds, and the effect was stunning with the backdrop of the green foliage. There was still plenty more to do, though, and she hadn't even got started yet on the pond. But already Bea loved this area of the walled garden. It told her something about her great-grandmother for a start – that Florence had cared about the world, about life; that she was a thinker as well as a creator. This part of the garden was a perfect space for reflection, and Bea was determined to bring it back to what she was sure was Florence's original vision.

Half an hour later they were in Lewis's studio. They had spoken to Hester, Lewis had made tea and all was well. 'I'm afraid it's a bit cramped in here,' Lewis said. 'It's not really a studio at all, just a spare bedroom, but it makes a good enough workroom, I reckon.'

'Wow.' Bea was immediately bowled over – not by the room, which was indeed pretty cramped, but by the vibrant colour of the canvases which seemed to fill every square centimetre of this small space, stacked as they were just about everywhere, on the floor, against and all over the walls.

'Yeah, I know, there's a lot of them.' Lewis laughed.

'It's the colours.' Bea made her way into the room and stood in front of a particularly striking picture on the far wall. It was a beach scene. The cliffs were serrated dark ginger topped with a vibrant dewy green and the sea was bright turquoise deepening into navy. The beach itself was made up of tiny orange and brown stones, moving into grit, into grains of sand, seemingly shifting with the tide. 'They're spectacular.'

'Well, thanks.' Lewis was fidgeting with embarrassment. He clearly wasn't used to taking compliments. Did he even know how good these paintings were?

She remembered what he'd said about doing odd jobs and DIY to make a bit of cash. 'You shouldn't be spending so many hours digging in other people's gardens,' she told him. 'You should be spending all your time painting.' He was a talented artist. The beach scene was realistic and yet the fluidity of the painting, the refusal to stick to conventional boundaries, made it almost abstract. She remembered what he'd said about seizing the moment. The curl of the waves, the movement of the spray, the wind that she sensed had been blowing when he painted it, created shapes in the picture that were the shapes of the sea. Bea was no expert, but this was the sort of painting she could gaze at for hours, she felt, and see something different every time she looked at it.

'It's nice of you to say so.'

He *definitely* didn't want compliments . . . 'I mean it,' she said. 'I'm not just being polite.'

He frowned. 'But with a landscape like this one, it's hard to do it justice.'

'I can imagine.' Though he had done it justice, at least in Bea's opinion. She pointed to a stack of canvases on the floor. 'May I look at these?'

He gave a little shrug and a nod as if he really couldn't care less, but she saw him lean forward to catch her expression as she began to flip through the pictures stacked against the wall. He cared what people thought, she realised, and he seemed to have little self-belief. But with paintings like these, why on earth would that be?

'They're great.' Bea smiled as she came across a picture of an interior. 'Is this Nonna's house?' It featured two chairs placed around a fireplace which looked very much like the one next door.

'It is.' Lewis peered over her shoulder. 'I shouldn't have intruded, but that's a beautiful fireplace.'

'It is fine,' Bea assured him. As far as she was concerned, he could paint the entire house if he wanted to.

Many of the pictures were seascapes, but others were of old hill forts and farmland, of rivers and valleys and chapels and trees on hills. If this was the landscape of Dorset, then Bea could fully understand the lure of the place. 'Do you exhibit?' she asked him. Because if not, he should do.

'I do the Dorset art trail,' he said. 'But exhibit? Not really.'

'The art trail?' It sounded interesting.

'It's something we do once a year. Artists and makers living in the area group together and open their houses and studios for people to come in and take a look at their work.'

'What a great idea.' Bea looked around the room. She couldn't imagine people coming in here to view anything, though. Even with just Bea and Lewis and all these paintings, it felt crowded. 'But Lewis, isn't it difficult to work in this tiny space?'

'Yes.' He went over to the window and looked out. 'But it's free and it means I can keep an eye on Grandma Hester at the same time.'

'Of course.' Bea realised she had been insensitive. And then she had a sudden thought. She looked across at him. He seemed fragile somehow in here, more vulnerable than he had ever seemed before in the garden or when they had shared lunch or dinner in each other's houses. Creative people were like that, though, she reminded herself. She knew how much a creative needed their own space, their me-time. Lewis didn't have much of either right now. But she could help. It would be a way of paying him back for all his kindness. 'You could use the studio next door,' she said. 'At least, while . . .' While what? While she was in residence? Because what would happen to the house and garden when she left? As yet, Bea had no idea.

'Oh, really, it's lovely of you to suggest it, but I couldn't.'

But Bea thought she spotted a glimmer of excitement in his green eyes. Which would make sense – because the attic studio next door, her great-grandfather's studio in fact, was a glorious room; big and full of light from the windows in the roof. 'No one uses it any more,' she reminded him. Lewis must have seen the room. After all, he had been looking after the house in a manner of speaking for the past few years since he'd lived next door. 'It's empty, and that's a terrible waste when it's such a beautiful room.'

'It is a beautiful room,' he agreed wistfully.

'Maybe Hester might be happy to come over for a few hours every day,' Bea suggested. 'She could spend some time in the house or garden. She'd be most welcome. Or if not, it would be easy for you to pop back and check that she was okay, don't you think?'

She could see him weighing it up. On the one hand, she could tell that he didn't want to be beholden, but on the other hand, that attic space was a huge temptation. Bea understood that Lewis liked to paint in the open air, but she assumed that quite a bit of the painting process would still normally be undertaken in a studio, and it seemed that there were plenty of days in England when the weather wasn't conducive to painting *en plein air*.

'It's very kind of you,' he began.

'Nonsense.' Why was he being so formal all of a sudden? She turned to face him. He was closer than she'd realised, but he sort of had to be in this room. 'It's nothing. And it is very kind of *you* to come over and help in the garden, to look after the house, everything you've done.'

He eyed her steadily. 'If you're sure?'

She gazed back at him. 'I am sure.'

And then something strange happened. Bea almost felt that she was saying something quite different. Something that had nothing at all to do with the attic studio next door.

Lewis took a half-step closer. Bea found that she couldn't move at all.

'And how about you?' he said.

'Me?' In fact, she found she could hardly breathe.

'You never say very much about your life in Italy.'

He was perceptive. Their gazes continued to lock together. Bea found it impossible to look away. 'It is difficult,' she said at last, though with no idea to what she was referring. Her life, her job, her family, Matteo . . .

'Do you have a boyfriend?' His voice was soft, so soft. She almost had to lean forwards to hear the words.

'Sort of,' she said. 'Yes. But actually, no.' Bea had still had no response to her messages and Matteo hadn't taken any of her calls. She'd heard nothing from him now for almost three weeks. It was beginning to make her angry. Matteo felt hurt,

356

she understood that, but refusing to even talk about it . . . It was childish and petty. Refusal to communicate was no basis for a long-term relationship.

Lewis gave a gentle laugh and the tension eased between them. 'Let me guess,' he said. 'It's complicated?'

'Yes,' she said. 'You?'

'There was someone.' He moved away from her now, back to the window, and Bea let out a breath of relief, of regret.

'What happened?' she whispered.

He turned to face her. 'It's a long story.' And now his expression had changed and she knew the moment was gone.

That same story, she realised, the story about falling in love. But he'd already refused to tell it once and now would be no different. Sure enough, he made his way to the door. Bea straightened up and followed him out of the room. *Lewis*, she found herself thinking. She so wanted to hear it. But clearly, it was a story for another time.

CHAPTER 41

Lara

Dorset, July 1947

Hester had told Lara to trust her, but it wasn't easy. As the minutes and the hours crept by all she could think of was David – waiting for her in the woods, making his plans to return to Italy alone. Would Hester find him in time? Would he still want Lara to come with him? Could she even do it? And how? There were too many questions unanswered.

She was exhausted, though, and so she slept fitfully and it was almost five p.m. when she heard the rap of the front door knocker. *David?* This was her first thought. She must get down there and warn him. Charles was dangerous. She had married a monster and she had no idea what he was capable of, nor what he would do next.

Lara quickly began to make her way downstairs, but to her surprise, the front door had already been opened by Charles and she could hear only Charles's voice and a female voice responding. It was Hester, she realised. But Hester was talking in a way that Lara had never heard her talk before.

'It was my mother who spoke to her in the village today.' Hester's voice was soft and confiding. 'She said you might be needing some help. And as we live next door . . .' She let her voice trail.

Ingenious, Lara thought. So that was why she had been so interested in the fact that Mrs Peacock had left them. Clever, clever Hester and Elizabeth.

'I see.' Charles had his back to Lara; she couldn't tell how he was reacting. Was it too soon? Would he be prepared for anyone to see Lara and thereby witness what had been done to her?

'We understand,' Hester went on smoothly, 'how hard it must be for a man like yourself with important business matters to attend to, to have the bother of dealing with domestic trivialities.' She lowered her voice. 'You've done your bit for our village these past years, Mr Fripp. We're so grateful.'

Lara held her breath. Every word sounded well-chosen. But was Hester being a bit too grateful? Surely she was going too far? Charles wasn't stupid.

'How sweet of you to say so.' Lara could tell by his tone that he was flattered. She realised that Hester's little speech was pitch-perfect. She was young and she was pretty. And hadn't she mentioned to Lara a long time ago that flattery was the sure-fire weapon to use with a man like Charles? She was a clever girl indeed.

'My mother is a very good cook,' Hester murmured in that new and soft little voice of hers. 'Homemade soup. Pies. She can't get out much. But I'm here to help. I can come every day from three forty-five in the afternoon for an hour or two.'

How could Charles resist? Hester's offer must seem like a dream come true. How else would he be able to safely leave Lara in order to visit his mistress in the village? And if he procured a good cook and a pretty face into the bargain . . . But Lara despised him all the more for being so easily manipulated.

'Come in. Come in. Let me take your coat. We can't discuss this on the doorstep.' He laughed that hearty laugh of his that had so easily convinced Lara of his good humour back in the past.

In came Hester, eyes downcast, looking uncharacteristically demure.

'Thank you, Mr Fripp.' She looked up to Charles with a wistful little smile and seemed to suddenly notice Lara standing on the stair. Lara must still look a fright but Hester hardly batted an eyelid. 'Oh, Mrs Fripp,' she said. 'Good afternoon.'

'Good afternoon.' Lara bowed her head.

'This way.' Charles opened the door to the study. 'We must discuss terms. Over tea perhaps?' He raised an eyebrow at Lara.

'Oh, I'll make it, Mr Fripp.' Hester's expression was earnest now. 'May as well start as I mean to go on.'

'Very well.' Charles rubbed his hands together as if congratulating himself that a replacement for Mrs Peacock had appeared so quickly, so miraculously at his door. How important he must be. Perhaps he imagined that the entire female population of the village was poised to take up the revered role that Mrs P. had squandered so recklessly.

Hester moved towards the kitchen and as Charles turned to go back into his study, she looked over her shoulder and shot Lara the broadest of winks.

Lara started down the stairs. She must talk to Hester. There was so much she needed to know — had she seen David? What was he going to do?

But Hester stopped her with the slightest shake of her dark head. And Lara understood. She must be careful now — more careful than she had been before. She must trust Hester and let her lead the way.

The following morning, Charles suggested that Lara might take a walk in the garden.

'I'm still allowed to go into the garden then?' Lara knew she sounded sulky. She felt sulky. She felt angry too. She hated this pretended gentility of his, this fake tenderness. She'd almost rather he ranted and raved and said what he really thought. Almost, but not quite.

'Of course you are, my dear.' He looked offended. 'But come back to the house every twenty minutes so that I can make sure you're all right.'

Or make sure she hadn't run away, she thought. He hadn't mentioned any of it — what she had done, what she had accused him of doing, his violence towards her. And that, she found herself thinking, made him more dangerous still. He had moved into another bedroom, though she was sure he would come back at any moment he felt like it. What did he intend to do with her? Keep her a prisoner for the rest of her life?

She went straight down the path to the Rose Garden and slipped through to the Wild Garden beyond. Only then did she release the breath she was holding. Only then, did she let herself relax, let herself remember . . .

But then she gasped in horror. Someone — Charles? — had cut down the ancient and beautiful vines of the wisteria and piled them in a heap in the centre of the Wild Garden among the daisies, the poppies, the vivid blue cornflowers. Could the plant survive such desecration? And the wall . . . Someone — Charles again, she supposed — had put a length of barbed wire

361

on the top of it. So. She sighed. There was no escaping now – not over the wall, at any rate.

Hester returned to the house at three forty-five p.m. and it wasn't long before Charles took the opportunity to go out. No doubt Hester had been instructed to keep a close eye on Lara while Charles was gone. Lara was glad to see the back of him even for an hour or two. She hadn't had the opportunity of talking alone with Hester yesterday but now was their chance.

The moment Charles was out of sight they flew into each other's arms and embraced as if their lives depended on it.

'Oh, Hester.' Lara held her tight for a moment. They had clasped hands through their little window in the garden wall, but never hugged, she realised. She hadn't even noticed how slight Hester was, how much smaller than Lara. 'Did you see David?'

Hester drew back. 'I did.' Her dark eyes gleamed with excitement. 'I told him everything.'

Lara took her hands. 'What did he say?'

'What do you think? He was furious. He was beside himself.' Hester's eyes were wide. 'It was all I could do to stop him from racing round here, beating down the door.'

'Thank goodness you stopped him.' Lara knew that wasn't the way.

Hester nodded. 'He's making the preparations now,' she said.

'Preparations?'

'For leaving, Lara.' Hester squeezed her shoulder. 'It's what you want, isn't it? You want to go to Italy with him, don't you?'

'Oh, yes,' Lara breathed. She'd hardly dared hope. 'But how can I?'

'You don't have a passport, I suppose?'

Miserably, Lara shook her head.

'Don't worry,' Hester said. 'We have a plan for that.'

'But what about Charles?'

'Leave me to deal with Charles.' Hester shot her a knowing look and all of a sudden, she appeared much older than her years. 'We have that part of it under control.'

Lara didn't doubt it. This was one very capable young woman. But even so, Hester must take care. Charles was a manipulator himself. He was an experienced man of the world and he had so many contacts, so many friends. 'We?' Did she mean David?

'Mum and me.'

Ah. That explained a lot. Because surely Hester couldn't have thought of all this alone? She caught her arm. 'Don't make the mistake of underestimating him, Hester,' she warned. 'Be careful.'

'I won't underestimate him,' Hester assured her. 'But you are the one who must be careful, dear Lara. At least for the next week or so. Until we are ready.'

'Yes.' Lara knew that only too well. 'And David?' she asked quickly. 'Can I see him? When do you think we'll be able to leave? And how? What should I do until then?' The thoughts and questions were bubbling quickly to the surface and she was asking herself as much as she was asking Hester, she realised. As for leaving, the sooner the better, as far as Lara was concerned. She didn't know how long she could go on like this, how long she could pretend, when all she wanted to do was run.

Hester gave her another swift hug. 'You must stay calm,' she urged. 'Do what he says and make sure that you look penitent.'

Lara screwed up her face. She wasn't sure that she was such a good actor as her young neighbour.

'It won't be for long,' Hester said. 'I'll be here every day and I'll keep you posted.'

'You'll be in touch with David?' Lara asked.

'I certainly will.'

Lara was reassured by her confidence. With David, Elizabeth and Hester on her side, maybe she could do it after all. 'And . . .' Lara hesitated. 'Has David written to me at all?' How she longed to see his face, hear his voice. Even a note on a piece of paper would be so precious, something she could hold close to her heart.

Hester wagged a finger. 'Too risky,' she said. 'And you shouldn't write to him either.'

'But—'

'Supposing Charles found a note you had written, or that he had written to you?' Hester cut in. 'Imagine what he might do to you next time?' She shuddered. 'We mustn't risk it, Lara. It's not safe.'

She was right, of course. 'Perhaps I'd be better staying somewhere in the village.' Lara tried to think who she could stay with. She'd let most of her old acquaintances go – or had been persuaded to, by Charles. There was Alice. She hadn't spoken to her since their meeting in the lane that time, but if Lara explained what had happened, what Charles had done to her . . . But then again, some people might think that after the way Lara had behaved, he had every right to knock her around. She was his wife, his property – as good as.

'The village is too supportive of Charles Fripp.' Hester – or Elizabeth – had already considered this option, Lara could tell. 'And staying next door with us is too close, too chancy.'

Lara could see that. She must be brave. She held her head

high. 'I can stay here,' she said. 'I can do it. For as long as I need to.'

'It won't be too long.' Hester reassured her again. 'David's doing all he can. We all are.'

David . . . 'I should pack a bag.' Lara was thinking out loud.

'Not until the last minute.' Hester and her mother seemed to have thought of everything. Hester glanced around the kitchen. 'I'd better clear up a bit in here,' she said.

'I'll give you a hand.' They shared a swift, complicit glance.

Hester paused as she examined Lara's face. 'We must sort something out for the bruises,' she said. 'I never asked you how you're feeling?'

Cautiously, Lara put her fingertips to her cut lip, her eye. 'Bruised. A little sore.' Violated, in fact. She knew that Charles hadn't only hit her. She knew that he'd raped her too; she had felt that pain deep inside her where it still hurt the most. Yes, they were married. But now she understood that for Charles, love and marriage weren't about companionship or care, nor about passion. Marriage and love were about control and brutality for him – violence was the way in which men like Charles became aroused. She shuddered. And she was married to him. It sickened her to the core.

'We must pick some daisies.' Hester frowned. 'I will make you a salve.'

Lara smiled. She was so kind. 'That would be wonderful. And there are plenty in the garden.'

'And in ours.' They shared a quick smile. It wouldn't be good, thought Lara, for Charles to return home to find Lara and Hester picking daisies together.

'Of course,' she said. It seemed that Hester was so much more quick-thinking than she. But since yesterday, she'd felt in such emotional turmoil. Whatever she thought about – whether it was David, or Charles, or the fact that she might be able to escape to Italy with the man she loved – would make her legs shake and tears fill her eyes. It seemed that she was even more broken than she had known.

'Crushed daisy flowers were once used where they grew on the battlefields to staunch a wound.' Hester nodded wisely. 'And with good reason. They have antiseptic properties.' She lowered her eyes. 'The tea can also be a remedy for deep internal bruising,' she whispered.

'Thank you, Hester.' This girl was knowledgeable beyond her years, thanks to her mother, no doubt. Lara hadn't forgotten Elizabeth's kindness when Lara's mother was sick. She couldn't have wished for better neighbours. And they were true life savers now.

They worked silently together for a few minutes, Lara cleaning the surfaces, Hester sweeping the floor.

'You know, Charles will never forgive me for leaving him,' Lara said. 'He will be looking for revenge.'

Hester stilled. 'I know. But you'll be far away.'

Lara ran the cloth under the tap and squeezed it out. 'He'll probably try and follow us.' She leant for a moment on the counter for support.

'Yes, we've thought of that.' Hester continued to sweep.

'You and your mother, you mean?'

'Yes.' Hester put the broom to one side and went to fetch the dustpan. As she passed the table, she gently brushed her hand over the flowers Lara had gathered this morning from the garden.

She had picked blue and purple larkspur which was so pretty with its multitude of blooms on long stalks and airy foliage, and lily of the valley – both from the secret garden.

Hester seemed to be deep in thought. She took one of the flowers out of the vase and sniffed. 'Larkspur is so vivid,' she said. 'So graceful. But . . .' She came back to the moment; replaced the stem in the vase. Lara noted her enigmatic expression.

'And what should we do about it? Might he not guess what's happened and that you must have helped me? I wouldn't want you or your mother to be put in any danger.'

'We'll think of something.' Hester seemed very sure. She bent to sweep up the small pile of dust on the floor.

But the thought of Charles following them, of finding out who had helped them, and of Hester and Elizabeth being in danger too, made Lara break out in a cold sweat. 'I can never thank you enough, Hester,' she said. 'For everything you've done.'

'Thank me when you're free.' Hester's smile was grim as she got to her feet. 'That's all I ask. Just thank me when you're free.'

CHAPTER 42

Rose

Italy, June 2018

'Rose! Rose, where are you?'

Rose was in *la cucina*, slicing onions. She heard her husband's voice and her hand holding the sharp vegetable knife froze in mid-air. She looked down at the shiny blade, wet with onion juice, a shred of onion skin hanging like a spider's web.

This morning she had gone to the market in Ostuni. There were several things Federico had asked her to get and she needed to buy food supplies too. But her mind wasn't on the task at all. Instead, she was thinking of Bea in England, working on her mother's old house. She'd spoken to her earlier and Bea had sounded happy and content. Whatever doubts she and Federico had harboured about her daughter's trip, it seemed that they had been wrong and Rose's mother — as usual — had been right. It was doing her good; Bea would have a chance to think things through and she would be back soon enough.

And then she thought of Cesare Basso. Like some grim

spectre of the past, that man was haunting her every waking hour. When she was at home, she could no longer feel at peace because he had invaded her house once and he could certainly do so again. When she went out it was even worse. He had been in Martina Franca; he could be anywhere. And when she saw his face — that knowing smirk — all she could think was of what she had done and how Federico must never know. It seemed the past that Rose had always tried to escape from had caught up with her at last.

Instead of going to the market, Rose had ducked into the small church just down the road from the Piazza della Libertà. The thought of the busy market had been daunting; what she actually needed was a few minutes of quiet contemplation. The stone steps were worn from thousands upon thousands of feet and there were diamonds carved on the ancient wooden door. Inside, she walked past the old confession box and sat in the front on a simple wooden pew. The church was cool and quiet; there was a purity here, an innocence that Rose longed for. In front of her, the golden candlesticks and white church candles pointed to heaven; the image of the dead Christ lay in the casket below. Above her, the golden dome loomed high and the windows all around it let in shafts of sunlight that lit up the ochre and blood-red marble.

Afterwards, she had stood on the other side of the road, looking down at the olive groves and the distant sea. She heard the dull clang of the church bell. The olive trees soothed her senses although she didn't feel for them quite as strongly as Federico did. How could she? For him, they were a life force quite literally, a family tradition that was more like a bloodline; a need, a desire, a way of living. But still, Rose too loved the wise old trees, twisty and gnarled with time as they were, hazy with leaves, sunshine and olive dust. Their green gold . . .

The thought that Federico might find out what she had done . . . It had made her grip the railings tight as she tried to control the dull pain of anxiety in her chest which seemed to have become a constant companion of late. How could Federico forgive her? Family had always been the most important thing in her husband's life. And if he didn't forgive her, what then? Would they live together still or would they separate? Would Federico want a divorce perhaps? How awful would that be for their darling Bea? Rose felt the tears threatening to come, but she blinked them quickly away. Somehow, she must maintain control, even while she felt it slipping from her.

'Rose.' Federico was in the kitchen now. 'You have been to Ostuni, yes? Where are the things I asked you to get?'

'Oh.' Rose wiped the web of onion skin from the knife with her fingertip. She could lose everything. *Everything* . . . 'Yes, I went. But I could not do it, Fedi.' She pressed the knife back into the globe of onion, hard and crisp; again, again, again, so that the slices fell neatly onto the chopping board.

'You could not do it?' Federico frowned. 'What do you mean, you could not do it?'

'I do not know.' How could she explain? Rose sliced the knife down into the other half of the onion. Again and again. She felt the bitter tears spring into her eyes.

'Did you forget? Is that it?' His voice was quiet and steady.

'Yes,' she said, because this was easier than trying to explain.

'Look at me, Rose.'

She heard him sigh. She looked up, but her eyes were blurry from the onion tears. She blinked. 'Yes?'

'It was important, Rose,' he said.

'I am sorry.' Sorrier than he could know. She turned back

to the onion. She simply hadn't been able to face the market – not after having seen Daniela Basso there the last time. Smaller pieces now, she decided. That was more manageable. The chopping motion was familiar to her; she had been doing it all her life. Sliced thinly into rounds and then finely chopped, that was the way.

'Rose.' At the new tone in his voice, she stilled.

'What is wrong with you?' he asked. 'What is going on?'

'Nothing,' she said. And then, because she was so ashamed, because it was all suddenly so overwhelming, she felt an anger, coming in great gusts. 'But I have other things to do, Fedi,' she said. 'I cannot be around simply to run errands for you.'

'Errands for me?' His voice began to rise. A danger signal.

This was the sweet contradiction about Federico. He was kind and he was loyal – he would never hurt anyone knowingly. He was even easy-going – most of the time. But like most of his family he had a short fuse and a big temper which could explode without warning and which would thankfully die down equally fast. But when Federico was angry, everyone should beware. Rose had learnt to fight back, because that, she'd found, was the best way to manage it. But . . .

She forced herself to shrug carelessly. 'I am busy, you know,' she said.

There was a pause that scared her.

'This is hard to comprehend,' he said at last. 'It is surely a small thing to ask.' Rose swept the chopped onion to one side of the wooden board. She almost wished he would lose his temper. At least then she would know what to do. 'I said I was sorry.' She took a garlic bulb from the jar and thumped it with her fist.

Federico winced. 'Can you please stop?'

She swung around. 'And I am busy now, Federico.' She was also close to tears but hopefully he would be too angry to see.

'And I want to know what is going on,' he shouted. 'I am your husband. You are suddenly so different. Everything has changed. For the love of God, tell me!'

'Nothing.' But she couldn't look at him. 'Nothing is going on.'

'There is something,' he yelled. 'I know there is something.'

Now he was properly angry and this Rose could deal with much better than the hurt incomprehension. She had always half enjoyed the volatility of their relationship – the shouting and the tears, the letting it out and the comfort and new closeness that came right behind. And besides, Rose could yell just as loudly as he could. 'Why do you always question me?' she shouted.

He stared at her. 'I do not. You can—'

'You do.' The tears were coming now and they were real tears, not onion tears. 'You always cross-question me. I cannot do the smallest thing on my own, I—'

'But Rose, you can. I—'

'I cannot!' She tore off her apron. 'There you always are. Complaining. Nagging. Questioning. Accusing . . .' She was into her stride now. Only suddenly she noticed that he wasn't yelling back at her. Federico seemed to have forgotten the rules.

'I thought we were a team.'

Rose registered that his anger had gone. And she had hurt him, really hurt him. *Oh, Federico . . .*

He shrugged. 'Obviously, I was wrong.' And then he brushed his hand across his face.

Was he crying? Surely he could not be crying? Federico never cried. Rose caught her breath. She took a step towards him.

372

But already he had turned from her and was walking away.

Rose watched him go, her hand over her mouth. What had she done? *You were not wrong. We are a team.* But she couldn't say the words. She just watched him walk away, her fists bunched at her sides, her nails digging into her palms, not even feeling that pain.

CHAPTER 43

Bea

Dorset, July 2018

The following Sunday morning, Bea wandered downstairs and into the study. It felt like a man's room; the decor was austere and at odds with the rest of Lime Tree house with its warm floral-patterned wallpapers and fabrics. There were a few musty books in the bookcase but nothing interesting that caught her eye, and the furniture was dark to match the wooden panelling. But there might be some old family paperwork still in the desk . . .

She opened the top drawer – nothing. In fact, they were all empty. Someone must have cleared the house, she supposed, before it was rented out. One of her grandparents perhaps? Hester? But as Bea stood by the desk, she felt uncomfortable, as if a chill hand was resting on her shoulder, and she hurried out of the room to the warmth of the kitchen. It probably didn't matter; Bea was perfectly happy not to have to go in there again.

She made breakfast, her mind slipping back to when she'd gone to see Lewis's paintings. Nothing had happened between them in that little workroom next door, or since then, but nevertheless, Bea felt on the edge of it – leaning forward, leaning back, that temptation to jump right in. Which would no doubt be disastrous . . . Just as Lewis had guessed, it was complicated.

She glanced at her watch. Today, Lewis was taking her out to Lyme Regis as promised. Hester would be there too, but Bea knew the proximity might be dangerous, she could feel it in the flush of anticipation she'd had ever since she woke up this morning. *For goodness' sake, get a grip.*

She would phone Matteo, she decided. She couldn't put it off and it was early, so he might even answer for once. He had told her that when she returned to Italy, he wouldn't be there for her, but those words had been said at a moment when he was hurt and upset. True, he hadn't answered any of her messages since she'd been here in Dorset, but since they hadn't spoken, their relationship hadn't ended – not properly.

And so Bea had to do it now. She knew that for sure. She could see how wrong they were for one another. Matteo had always been generous and good company, always exciting to be with. Physically, there had been an amazing chemistry between them. But it wasn't enough. He hadn't always taken her wishes into consideration and often it had seemed that he wanted her to be someone quite different from what she really was. Even so, Bea had loved him – or thought that she'd loved him. But she was no longer convinced that it had been real. She'd been swept off her feet by the force of his personality. She'd hardly had time to consider what was happening between them. But she'd considered it now.

She had to get things straight between them. Matteo had

375

asked much too much of her. And here she was, emotionally at sea. Here she was, responding to another man . . .

Bea waited, unsurprised as her call went to voicemail. She decided to leave a message – it was the only way.

'Matteo,' she said. 'I wish you would return my calls.' *Because this should be done voice to voice if not face to face.* She hesitated. 'I know you're hurt. I know you're angry . . .' She took a breath. Although she didn't even know that much, not really. 'But I needed to get away and think.' She paused. That sounded weak, but she had explained herself at the time – at least as much as he'd allowed her to. 'And now that I've thought about it some more, I know I cannot do it. You have probably changed your mind anyway . . .' How could she know when he hadn't contacted her for so long? 'But I wanted everything to be clear between us.' She sighed. 'I cannot be the person you want, Matteo. I cannot give up my gardens and I cannot be your wife. *Mi dispiace.* I am sorry.'

She rang off. It was done. She'd broken the fragile thread that she'd imagined still joined them. It was pretty awful doing it by a voice message but what choice had he given her?

Later, Bea sat in the back of the car, so Hester could be in the front with Lewis. She was glad of the opportunity to think, while taking in the sights of the Dorset landscape that Lewis loved so much. Again, she was struck at how green it was. The fields, the trees, the hedgerows ran through shades from delicate lime to sage, to dark forest. It must be all that British rain . . . Bea was conscious of Lewis's proximity and relieved that she wasn't sitting right next to him. All the same, if she reached out, she'd be able to touch his blond hair, put her hand on his shoulder, feel the warmth. She shook the thought away, felt the heat rise up her body from nowhere. She couldn't believe what she was thinking, imagining. But she didn't seem able to stop.

In search of a distraction, she stared out of the window. They were driving through a small village; the narrow road was lined with the cutest houses she'd ever seen, thatched and constructed of blocks of honeyed sandstone. In front of her, Lewis half turned to Hester to make sure she was comfortable. He was a relaxed and confident driver. Bea shifted in her seat. Perhaps it was just friendship between them. Surely it must be? She took a few deep breaths and tried to relax. Then she caught him eyeing her quizzically in the rear-view mirror and she stared out of the window again.

But perhaps . . . She could go no further. She hadn't been expecting it. But something *had* happened in that little work-room of his next door. There was a spark between them – she hadn't imagined it. And it was at risk of becoming a flame. But with a man who lived in England? How was that ever going to work? She shook her head. She must stop these fantasies right now. It was impossible.

They parked near the harbour in Lyme Regis since Hester couldn't walk very far, and Lewis showed Bea the iconic grey curved wall that protected the Cobb, Lyme Regis's harbour. While Hester sat on a nearby bench watching the paddle-boarders, Lewis and Bea strolled along the Cobb to admire the panoramic view along the coast, Lewis pointing out Charmouth, Golden Cap and the ginger cliffs of West Bay.

Bea would visit all these places if she could, she decided. This was her grandmother's landscape, her grandfather's too and her great grandparents' before that. It was a strange feeling – that old legacy stretching out behind her. Bea lived in Italy, but half her roots were here in Dorset and always would be.

The three of them walked along the promenade, admiring the quirky houses that looked straight out to sea. Bea was utterly charmed. 'Have you painted these?' she asked Lewis, guessing what the answer would be.

He groaned. 'Many, many times.'

Bea laughed. If ever there was a town that deserved to be painted, it was Lyme Regis.

He showed her the quaint Marine Theatre and the old mill at the River Lym which still functioned in its original capacity, although the courtyard was now also home to a gallery, a small brewery, a café and other assorted independent units.

They sat outside the café and ordered coffee for Bea, and tea for Lewis and Hester.

'It's so pretty here.' Hester was beaming. 'And shall we go back into your garden when we get home?'

Bea laughed. 'Yes, if you like.' She knew how fond Hester had always been of the Arts and Crafts garden. Yesterday, Lewis had brought his grandmother over to Lime Tree House and Hester had seemed content to potter around in the garden while Bea dug, weeded and cleared. Hester continued speaking to Bea as if she were her grandmother. Bea had hoped for some more nuggets of information about her grandmother's life but so far, nothing had emerged. She knew that she'd just have to be patient. Lewis, meanwhile, got to work in the attic studio, and seeing his face a few hours later had been reward enough for Bea – she could tell that he loved working up there. And when she returned to Italy? When the house was sold? Bea pushed these thoughts from her mind.

After their drinks, Bea, Lewis and Hester wandered back through Langmoor and Lister Gardens, taking in the sculpture trail, the far-reaching views to the Cobb and coastline beyond, and of course, the planting in the garden itself. Then Hester watched Bea and Lewis play a hilarious and inept game of al fresco table tennis which ended with them both doubled up in laughter.

On the way home, Lewis took a small detour to show Bea the golden cliffs at West Bay that she'd admired in his painting.

'What do you think?' he asked.

'It's stunning.' Bea loved the sweep of the ginger beach, the soft green-grey of the ocean and the tall toffee-coloured grass-topped cliffs. She turned to him. 'West Dorset is as beautiful as you promised.'

'I'm glad you think so,' he said. 'Mission accomplished.'

Bea couldn't help but smile. She was glad that she'd seen a little more of the surrounding countryside and coast. She'd taken some pictures and she'd be sending them to Nonna just as soon as she got back. Nonna loved Italy, Bea knew. But Dorset was very special and this was where Nonna had grown up. Bea's grandmother had never been back, but still, she must miss it.

Later, back at the house, Lewis went up to the studio to work on one of his sketches, and Bea did a few jobs in the garden while Hester sat nearby. There was still so much to do and it seemed a shame to waste these long early summer evenings. Bea glanced across at Hester. She seemed so serene most of the time, but Bea couldn't help wondering what Hester was thinking, what she might be wanting to say.

'You know, Lara,' she called, as Bea was collecting a pile of weeds and nettles from the Romantic Garden. 'There's no shame in ending an unhappy marriage.'

Bea stood up straight and stared at her. Where had that popped up from? 'Unhappy marriage?' But her grandmother had been so happy with her grandfather, hadn't she? He had died when Bea was young, but she still remembered him, the warmth in his eyes, the undeniable tenderness that had existed between him and Nonna.

Hester nodded emphatically. 'I know you love to be in the garden,' she said.

'Well, yes, I do, but—'

'But no one should be a prisoner.'

'No, indeed.' Bea went over to Hester and took her hand. Something clicked into place in her head. 'And if they are kept a prisoner, then they need to escape,' she said.

'Oh, yes.' Hester's smile was conspiratorial. 'Over the wall,' she whispered. 'The roots of the wisteria are so very strong, you know, Lara.'

Over the wall . . .

They sat together for several minutes in the Romantic Garden, both deep in their own thoughts. Bea didn't want to press Hester to say more – she'd learnt already that doing this could upset her and that was the last thing Bea wanted. But she knew where she was heading, the first opportunity she got. To the wall at the far end of the garden where the wisteria grew. Had the wisteria once been even taller than it was now? Had the barbed wire been put there for a particular reason? Was it to keep intruders out, or could it possibly be to keep someone in? Had the girl in those old childhood stories climbed over this very wall when she needed to escape? Maybe Bea should get rid of that barbed wire and try climbing it for herself?

Bea thought about what she'd found out so far. Her grand-mother had indeed, or so it seemed, been kept prisoner in the very garden which had also been her sanctuary. But it was hardly the Dark Ages, even back then. Could it possibly be true that someone could keep a woman prisoner like that? Bea tried to work it out. She had been so sure that her grandparents were happily married and this Romantic Garden certainly seemed to echo that thought.

The Spring Garden seemed to represent hope, the Nurturing Garden did just as its name suggested, the Rose Garden was a feast for the senses, the white Thinking Garden the place for reflection. The Wild Garden represented the boundary where formal garden shifted into the landscape beyond. Oh, yes, the meaning of this Arts and Crafts garden was beginning to come clear, Bea thought. But what of the secret garden? Was it simply a design folly as she'd suggested to Lewis when they first discovered it? And if not, what did it represent, because she was certain it must mean something?

Bea patted Hester's hand and looked into the old woman's rheumy eyes. Why was Nonna kept prisoner here – if indeed she was? And who by? Bea wondered if she was ever going to find out the truth.

CHAPTER 44

Lara

Italy, July 2018

Lara's thoughts these days were bound up past with present; they were tangled, fragile and formless, mixed up and therefore hard to unravel; they could slip through her mind like gossamer to be felt briefly and then lost.

As she sat in the shade on the terrace, looking out onto her Italian garden, half dozing in the warmth of the afternoon, she thought of Bea in Dorset – of the updates her granddaughter sent that were both terrible and tantalising. It was hard to see the old garden untamed and neglected, and the sight of it brought back conflicting memories: of happy times in her childhood and when she and her mother had worked together growing vegetables and fruit to help with the war effort, and then later of her days alone in the garden which had become her sanctuary, her prison. But Lara loved to see how Bea was interpreting the garden; how her granddaughter was beginning to make it glow again.

Lara let her head sink back further into the cushion Rose had placed on the wicker chair. There was a man too – Hester's grandson. Bea mentioned him often, and there was a certain tone in her granddaughter's voice. Could it be that . . . ? Well, *allora*, it was too tempting to read things into perfectly ordinary situations. It would, though – if it were true – be an extraordinary coincidence.

When Lara first heard the sound, she had no idea what it was. It merged into the background like birdsong or the distant rumble of farm machinery. But after a while, it prodded at her consciousness and she stirred from her reverie, from the memories, from the hot and hazy afternoon and listened.

Someone was weeping. Lara was sure of it. But who? She looked around. A visitor to the *trulli* perhaps? She strained to hear more clearly. No. The sound was coming not from the direction of the *trulli* or the little chapel, or from the house, but from Lara's own garden. She frowned. There was only one person it could possibly be and that was her daughter. Come to think of it, Lara had not seen Rose for an hour or so and this was unusual. As a rule, at this time in the afternoon, she was bustling around preparing supper. It would be so unlike her. But . . .

'Rose?' she whispered.

Of course, there was no answer. But Lara recalled that of late, Rose had not been herself. She had always been troubled, her Rose, and yet it seemed there was no way Lara could put it right.

She shaded her eyes and looked deep into the garden, up to the row of cypresses which lined the avenue and separated her Italian garden from the olive grove. Where might Rose be? Sitting by the pond perhaps? Or beyond that, in the Mediterranean garden among the broom and the juniper? Only when had Rose ever sat, rested, or given any time to reflection? Her daughter was not reflecting, though; she was not resting or trying to find a peaceful place away from it all. She was weeping. What could be wrong? Lara tried to think. When Rose had put that bad business with the Bassos behind her (now, that had been a difficult time indeed), when Rose and Federico Romano had married and had Bea . . . Lara had hoped that was an end to it. But Rose's troubles had never entirely disappeared and Lara had remained at a loss to know how she could help her daughter carry this unidentified burden.

Perhaps now . . . ?

The sobbing continued and it tore at Lara's senses. She felt powerless. And yet . . . She had to get down there. Could she? Warily, she eyed the stone steps that led down from the terrace. Old and infirm she most definitely was. But they were only steps – and she had to do something.

Carefully, she eased herself upright. Leaning heavily on the arms, she got shakily to her feet. Now, where was her stick?

She located it and gingerly made her way across the terrace to the top step. The honeysuckle was still in bloom, cascading along the trellising, and it filled the air with its intoxicating fragrance. Lara took a moment to rest, gather her energy and breathe it in. She knew why Rose – for she was now certain it was Rose; she could recognise her daughter in the sobbing – had retreated into the depths of the garden. She didn't want to be seen or heard. Like a wounded animal, she had crept there to be alone.

Something was horribly wrong.

Lara took it very slowly, one hand on the railing, the other leaning on her stick. It had been a while since she'd tackled these steps leading down into her garden; the last time had been with Bea and then she'd had her granddaughter's arm to rely on. But since Bea's departure, Lara had, she knew, grown more frail. It wouldn't be long . . .

Halfway down, she paused to catch her breath once more before negotiating the remaining steps one by one; slowly, slowly.

She reached the bottom and again, stopped for a moment. *How exhausting it was to get anywhere . . .* But it would be easier now she was on the flat. The sobbing would lead her to Rose. But what if Rose did not want to be found? *Allora,* she must take that chance.

Cautiously, she made her way along the path between the rose beds, barely glancing at the flowers, hardly registering the scent she had always loved so much. Lara knew she must put everything she had into the effort of finding Rose. She followed the sobbing on towards the pond.

Lara's relationship with Rose had never been straight-forward. She was fully aware that as a result of her own experiences back in Dorset, she had taken a liberal approach where the parenting of her daughter was concerned. Rose would not have a strict upbringing, she had determined. Lara would encourage communication; she would listen and try to understand. If there were rules – and there must always be rules – they would be fair ones.

Therefore, she had never expected Rose to go so spectacu-larly off the rails, because why rebel when there was so little to be angry about? But also, perhaps Lara had been *too* easy-going, perhaps she had not given Rose enough boundaries, perhaps she had not protected her enough.

Parenthood. It was a complex task; so hard to get right.

And then, of course, everyone had to live with it. Once again, she paused to catch her breath. There was no sign of Rose near the pond where the water lilies floated so serenely, shimmering in the faintest of breezes. Lara pushed on.

But if Lara was so understanding, so liberal, so easy-going, then why hadn't Rose found it easier to confide in her? Why had she taken it upon herself to run away into the garden to weep as if her heart might break?

The sobbing was growing more desperate as Lara drew closer to the patch of natural scrubland that made up the Mediterranean garden. Lara's breath was shallow now in her chest. It was almost too much. But her daughter must be through here, in the small *giardino segreto*, the secret garden. Because where else would you go, if you did not want to be found?

She took another breath. One more step inside. 'Rose,' she said.

Rose looked up from where she sat on the small stone bench, eyes red-rimmed and sore, hair awry, face blotchy and tired. 'Mamma?' She blinked.

'Darling, whatever is the matter?' But just on the last word, Lara missed her footing and lurched to one side.

Rose sprang forwards to stop her from falling. 'Mamma, you should not be down here. You certainly should not have walked down on your own.'

Even now in her misery, thought Lara, she still managed to be reproving. *But no . . .* Lara corrected herself. Rose still managed to *care . . .*

'I heard you crying,' Lara said. She allowed herself to be seated on the bench, though it was a little too hard and uncomfortable for her liking. She caught her breath. Now, she thought.

'Rose,' she said sternly. She wanted to tell her that she had named her after the wild rose in the Arts and Crafts garden at Lime Tree House in Dorset. Suddenly there seemed to be so much she needed to tell her, so much her daughter needed to know.

'Yes, Mamma?'

'You must tell me what is the matter.'

Rose shook her head. 'It is no—'

'Do not tell me it is nothing.' Lara sounded fierce even to her own ears. 'It is something, clearly. I am your mother and you must tell me what it is.'

'I cannot.' But Rose sat down next to her and leant her head gently on Lara's shoulder. This was progress.

Lara stroked back her hair. 'Nothing you can say will shock me,' she said. All her thoughts seemed suddenly arrow-bright and true. 'I am always on your side. I am here for you whatever you say or do.'

Rose sniffed. 'If you knew . . .' Her voice was bunched up and plaintive.

Enough now. 'We all have secrets.' Lara thought of her own past. 'The most important thing is to let them go, learn from them, move on. Now, tell me.'

Her daughter took a deep and shuddering breath. 'It is Cesare Basso,' she said.

CHAPTER 45

Bea

Dorset, July 2018

Tempted though she was to ask her grandmother more about her past here in Dorset, something stopped Bea from doing so. She sent the pictures of Lyme Regis and West Bay to her grandmother, and she kept her in touch with progress, by sending photos of each section of the walled garden as she continued to work on them. They chatted too, but during these conversations, her grandmother was quieter than usual and Bea worried that her health was failing. She grew silent whenever Bea mentioned Lime Tree House, though she seemed eager to see what was happening in her beloved garden. Bea grew even more convinced that whatever had happened to her in the past, it had been painful for her grandmother and Nonna was still not ready to talk about it.

'How is she?' Bea asked her mother when she called.

'A little tired today, darling,' her mother would reply.

'And you?' Because her mother too sounded subdued and

Bea couldn't help but worry about what was happening at home in Italy.

'Absolutely fine,' her mother replied in that breezy way that told Bea nothing. Bea surmised that she would have to wait until she went home before finding out anything about what had been happening in her absence.

Lewis, meanwhile, was dividing his time between the attic studio, helping Bea in the garden and caring for his grandmother. He still refused to take any payment for his hard work, though, so Bea had taken to cooking supper for all three of them almost every night, by way of expressing her gratitude. It was also a selfish act, she had to admit. For someone who had always thought of herself as a solitary being, she was glad to have both Hester and Lewis around.

A few days after Hester's comment about Lara being in an unhappy marriage, when Hester was next door, resting after lunch, Bea related the conversation to Lewis. She had been brooding on it and he was so easy to talk to. Already, she felt as if she had known him for years.

'You didn't know your grandparents were unhappy?' Lewis was working on the greenhouse, carefully extracting the broken panes of glass. He'd given Bea the name of a local glazier who was coming round to give her a quote for replacement glazing, but Lewis wanted to get rid of all the broken glass before he did so.

'I am sure they were not unhappy.' That was the conundrum.

Bea was checking out the fruit trees. She'd given them a good water with some fertiliser, since they wouldn't have had any nourishment for years, and now she was thinning the fruit. It wasn't the right time of year to give them a proper prune, though they were in dire need, but with any luck, there would be a reasonable harvest. Bea paused in her work. *If she was still here at harvest time . . .* But surely, she wouldn't be? She had been here for over a month already, mind, and had made no plans to leave.

'Perhaps they just went through a bad patch.' Lewis eased out a lethal piece of glass. He was wearing thick gloves, but even so, Bea wished he'd waited for the glazier. She wasn't confident about her first aid skills, should there be a nasty accident.

'It is possible, I suppose.' Bea considered. 'Every relationship has its ups and downs.' She thought of Matteo. There had been no reply to the voicemail she'd left, or to her subsequent texts to check he'd received it. What was she waiting for – some sort of confirmation? Clearly, he didn't wish to communicate with her now that their relationship was over. And it had been over, she realised, ever since she hadn't accepted his proposal on Merlata beach.

Bea had expected to be more upset than she actually was. She still couldn't quite believe that she had been so mistaken about those feelings that had seemed so deep at the time. But she clearly *had* been mistaken, because she felt only a faint sense of regret. And relief. She didn't have to give up her gardens. Nonna had been right. She shouldn't have to do that for anyone. Because her gardens were part of her, part of who she was. And if any man didn't understand that, then that man was not for her.

'Ye . . . es.' Lewis raised his eyebrows.

'And no one can be happy all the time, of course. But . . .' She paused in her work. 'Hester seemed to be implying that my grandfather was cruel. That he kept my grandmother trapped here somehow.'

The eyebrows shot up again. 'It sounds a bit far-fetched.'

'And unlikely,' Bea added staunchly. 'He died when I was young, but I know he was a kind man.'

Carefully, Lewis placed a broken section of glass in the barrow. 'But, like I told you, Grandma's not the most reliable these days, sad to say. I don't think you should take what she says as the gospel truth.'

'Maybe not.' Bea snipped off a brown and withered part of the branch with her secateurs. 'But she sounded so sure, Lewis.' She turned to face him. 'I believed her.'

'Maybe it was some sort of misunderstanding.' Lewis stood back to survey his progress so far. 'But if you want to find out about the past and you can't ask your grandmother, then why don't we ask someone else who was around at the time?'

We? Bea knew why she was confiding in Lewis. It felt good to have someone to bounce ideas off, someone with whom to share your thoughts. And there was something vital about him, something energetic that really appealed to her. 'Any suggestions?' she said lightly. It was a long time ago and Nonna and Hester were very elderly themselves, especially Nonna. Who else would even be alive?

Lewis considered. 'There's an old biddy who still lives above the post office with her daughter,' he said. 'She used to run the place herself and I think her parents ran it before her.' He gave a little shrug. 'This is a small village, so she must have known the family, but I've got no idea how much she might remember.'

'It is worth a try.' Bea turned back to her clipping. Some people probably remembered ancient village history forever.

Lewis dusted off his gloves and withdrew them gingerly. 'All done,' he said.

'Thanks, Lewis.' Bea came over to see. 'It looks much better already.'

He glanced at his watch. 'I'll nip back home to check on Grandma and then we can walk down there if you like?'

'To the post office, you mean?' Bea was continually impressed by the speed in which Lewis seemed to get things done.

'Yep.' He was already halfway out of the Nurturing Garden.

Bea put her hands on her hips. 'Now?'

He turned around. He had that grin on his face that always made her want to smile right back at him. So, she did.

'You want to find out the truth, don't you?'

'Oh, yes,' she said. 'I definitely do.'

The younger woman at the post office – about to retire herself, she informed them – let them in and told them that not only did her mother like to receive visitors, but also that she had an excellent memory.

'She misses chatting to the customers,' she confided. 'And her mind is still razor-sharp, believe me.'

She made tea and soon all four of them were seated in a cosy back room. Dorothy Walker, a sweet old lady with snow-white hair and cornflower-blue eyes, had worked with her mother, Mrs Stone, in the post office, she told them; Dorothy was several years younger than Lara and yes, she remembered her well.

Bea felt a leap of excitement. 'Did you know her when she was a young woman?' she asked. 'When her parents were alive?'

'Not well,' the old lady admitted. 'But I remember her mother too, and I remember how hardworking they were, all the vegetables they grew in their garden during the war years and beyond, and my ma telling me how grateful we should be.'

'Nonna told me a bit about that,' said Bea. 'And we have been working on the garden.' She glanced across at Lewis. 'Trying to restore it to its former glory.'

'That's nice.' Dorothy nodded her approval. 'Lara was always ready with a wave and a greeting in the early days.' She smiled at the memory. 'Cycled everywhere, she did, up and down the hills, wind in her hair, free as a bird.'

Free as a bird . . . Bea liked the thought of that.

'But then her mother died.' Dorothy left a respectful pause. 'And Lara was left to manage everything alone. That big house, that garden . . .' She clicked her tongue.

Poor Nonna. Bea tried to imagine how that might have felt. Nonna had already lost her father and after that she was living in a world still ravaged by war with plenty of responsibilities and no one to turn to.

'Did she have someone? A sweetheart?' Lewis glanced across at Bea as he spoke.

'There was a lad who went off to war,' the old lady mused. 'I used to see them out walking sometimes, hand in hand, in a world of their own, they were.'

Bea caught her breath. 'And what happened to him?'

'Missing, presumed dead, I think it was.' Dorothy sighed. 'We lost so many, you see.'

'I am sure.'

They were all silent for a moment as they took this in. Bea wondered about Nonna's sweetheart who had been missing in action. Had her grandmother continued to mourn the loss? Was Bea wrong about the love she'd believed her grandparents to share? It was all very confusing.

'So, no one could blame Lara for getting married, first chance she got,' the old lady continued.

Bea sat up straighter. 'That is when she got married?'

'Oh, I think she waited until a year or so after the end of the war,' Dorothy quickly clarified. 'She wasn't that hasty. But when she knew her young man wasn't coming back . . .'

'And the man she married?' Lewis asked. 'Where did he spring from?'

'His sister had moved to the village some years earlier,' Dorothy said. 'He was very good – he helped people out during the war, he was a dab hand at getting hold of things, if you know what I mean.'

Bea thought she could guess. But was this her grandfather they were talking about?

'He was rather charming and very well-liked.' Dorothy was still speaking. 'But . . .'

Bea held her breath. *But?*

'After they married, well, we hardly saw Lara,' she said. 'People remarked on it. It was a strange thing. He let it be known that she wasn't strong.' She tapped her head. 'Up here, you know. He was very protective.'

Bea frowned. This was putting an altogether different slant on things. Only, Nonna had always seemed so strong mentally. Could she have had some sort of breakdown when she was young? Grief could certainly do that to a person.

'And when we did see her,' Dorothy continued, 'she didn't seem quite herself somehow.'

Bea was trying to unscramble all this information, trying to make it fit the grandmother she knew. Nonna had changed after she got married. But why? Because she was unhappy? Because she was grieving for that lost sweetheart? Because she had some sort of breakdown? Had her grandfather just been protecting her after all? 'What happened next?' she asked.

Dorothy gave her a dark look. 'There were rumours . . .' she said.

'Rumours?' This was exactly what Bea wanted to hear. Because there was no smoke without fire and rumours might lead her to the truth. 'About my grandmother, do you mean? What sort of rumours?' She leant forwards, searching Dorothy's face for clues.

But she shook her head. 'About him,' she said.

Bea and Lewis exchanged a look. 'Yes? What about him?' asked Bea.

Dorothy hesitated. 'I'm not sure if I should say.' Once again, she shook her head. 'I'm not sure if any of it was even true. But you know, people talked, and they often talked in the post office, and even if you weren't trying to listen, sometimes you couldn't help but hear.'

'Of course,' said Bea. 'We understand. But what was it that people were saying about him?'

'That he had another woman.' Dorothy pursed her lips. 'Here in the village.'

'I see.' That didn't sound at all like her grandfather either. Though Bea was aware that she was hardly in a position to say. And it might not even be true. Nevertheless, she added the possibility to the heap of information she was mentally compiling.

'And Lara?' asked Lewis.

'That's the strangest thing,' said Dorothy. 'One day, she just disappeared.'

'Disappeared?'

'Yes. Someone from the village saw her getting into a car. And then that was it.' She threw up her hands in a little gesture. 'No one ever saw her again. She was gone.'

Bea tried to compute this information. She leant forward,

about to ask more, but Dorothy had closed her eyes with a little frown. She was obviously getting tired from all the talking.

'Perhaps we should call it a day for now?' her daughter suggested gently. 'You could come back another time?'

'Of course.' Bea and Lewis both got to their feet.

'I'll give you my number,' the younger woman suggested. 'Just send me a message and we'll arrange something.'

Bea and Lewis thanked Dorothy for all her help and said goodbye.

'We found out a fair bit,' Lewis said as they walked back. 'Do you think she knows any more?'

'Possibly.' Bea would certainly like to talk to her again. But he was right, they'd found out enough to be going on with and now, Bea wanted a chance to think.

CHAPTER 46

Lara

Dorset, July 1947

During the next few days, the tension in the house seemed palpable. Did Charles notice? He didn't appear to. Perhaps he assumed the edgy atmosphere was due to what had occurred between Lara and himself on that awful evening. There was no longer any intimacy between them or any pretence of affection. But what was he planning to do with her? Lara didn't want to imagine, but she was conscious of the way she thought of herself in relation to Charles – as a rather tiresome possession, of limited use, to be kept on a tight leash at all times. She wasn't sure what he wanted from her. But there was no prospect that he would ever voluntarily set her free.

Lara and Hester (and Elizabeth and David too, she assumed) continued to make preparations for her escape. Hester turned up one day with a Brownie Box camera to take Lara's photograph. 'Mum has a friend in the village,' she explained. 'We can trust him. He'll develop it tonight and then tomorrow we'll fill in the passport application form.'

She had it all worked out. She was by Lara's side each step of the way and Lara continued to be astounded at how capable she was. She touched up Lara's face with make-up for the photograph, so that the remaining marks of Charles's violence wouldn't be seen, and she kept watch, complete with feather duster, in the vestibule, while Lara searched the study for her birth certificate.

While in the study, Lara couldn't resist peeking in the drawer she'd looked in before. There was no sign that Charles had been continuing to practise her signature; no papers with her name written all over them as there had been before, but she did find more bank statements. She glanced through them, noting that he was no longer in the red.

What did it mean? She struggled to think, but her brain felt flabby and unused. That he had faked her signature to take out a loan on the house perhaps and then used that money to make good his debts? She stared in front of her, at the book-case still filled with her father's books, because neither she nor her mother had wanted to get rid of them. Charles seemed to want to keep them too, as if they presented some image of him which he sought to maintain, even though, like her signature, it was fake, all fake.

She sighed. It was possible that already, she no longer owned this house that she had once loved, that had meant so much to her parents before her, but which now seemed tainted from what had happened within it. This thought was heartbreaking, but it gave her even more courage to go on.

As promised, Hester brought round a homemade salve made from daisies, for Lara to dab onto her cuts and bruises, and some dried flowers with which to make tea to help soothe the internal bruising. But nothing could ease the damage that went even deeper inside. Hester brought food too – soups and stews, to keep Charles happy and to tempt back Lara's appetite.

'You must get stronger,' Hester urged her. 'For the journey.'

And so, Lara obeyed. It wouldn't be long now. She just had to wait a few more days. Once her passport arrived, they could make more concrete plans. They could name the day.

Several times during this period, Lara suffered with nausea and stomach cramps and sometimes felt so weak and dizzy that she had to go and lie down.

Hester was concerned – she said that she'd ask her mother's advice about what to give her.

But when she returned the following day, she was hesitant.

'What is it?' Lara had suffered from the nausea again this morning. But she couldn't go to the doctor – Charles certainly wouldn't allow it – and even if he did, how could she be truthful about what had happened between them?

'Mum says . . . are you taking precautions?' Hester glanced down and a faint stain blushed her cheeks.

'Precautions? Oh. I . . .' Why hadn't she thought of that? Lara tried to remember when her last monthly had been. It was possible, she realised. She put a hand on her stomach.

Hester put her dark head to one side. 'Charles?' she whispered.

Lara had not told her about the shame of those cold nights with her husband. 'I don't think so,' she whispered back. Because how would it have been possible? He had never once finished. Apart from . . . But she didn't want to think about that time – she had been barely conscious and it wouldn't have been that night, it was far too recent, surely?

'Then . . . ?' Hester was smiling now.

'I think, David,' Lara said in a wondering voice. It seemed

like a miracle. And yet, not such a miracle, because, no, they had not taken precautions – they had made love as if every afternoon would be their last.

'Gosh.' Hester sat back on her heels. She wasn't being judgemental, though, Lara could tell. It was more as if she couldn't believe their naivety. And neither could Lara, come to think of it.

'I know,' she said.

'All the more reason then,' said Hester.

'All the more reason,' Lara agreed. She would die rather than bring a child into this house, especially a child that Charles would quite rightly suspect to be David's.

But what would David say? Would he want a child? They hadn't discussed it. He had asked her to come to Italy, but how would he feel when she turned up pregnant? It wasn't exactly an ideal situation, but nevertheless, Lara couldn't help feeling it was wonderful. She just hoped that David would think it was wonderful too.

'I won't say anything to anyone,' Hester said. 'But David will be delighted. He loves you so much, Lara. It will all work out in the end.'

Lara prayed she was right.

Once they'd applied for Lara's passport, her next task was to get to the morning post before Charles did, and not only that, but to do it without raising suspicion. This wasn't easy; once Lara had stopped waiting for news of David after the war, she hadn't shown much interest in the mail, so it would look odd for her to start now. She took to keeping an early morning watch from her bedroom window for the postman and then wandering downstairs at the right moment on the pretext of making tea. What could be more natural than for her to pick up the mail and place it on the hall-stand table for Charles? After she'd surreptitiously flipped through it, that was.

A couple of times, despite her best efforts, Charles got there first. Unfortunately for Lara, he had always been keen to see what the morning post would bring; a bit too keen since he had obviously destroyed David's last letter which would have told her that her sweetheart had survived the war and was living in Italy. But both times, as Lara drifted past, she was unable to spot any envelope bulky enough to conceivably contain a passport, so she was able to breathe again.

On the following Saturday, Lara was keeping watch as usual when she saw the postman approaching down the drive. He was early. Something told her that this might be the day and she flew down the stairs in her pyjamas and bathrobe, only slowing when she got to the bottom stair. She could see the postman close to the front door now. Any second and . . .

Where was Charles? As if that thought had summoned him, at the same moment, a door opened upstairs and Lara turned to see him emerge from the room he had begun sleeping in. He must have overslept; this was late by Charles's standards. He yawned.

And the postie rapped on the door.

Lara caught her breath. 'I'll get it.' She whipped open the door before Charles could object. He didn't want her to have any interactions with anybody, even now that her bruises were fading and her cut lip almost healed.

'Morning.' She smiled and held out her hand for the post, every second an agony as the postie sorted through the envelopes.

'Morning. Registered,' he said.

Ah, of course. They hadn't thought of that. 'Thank you.' She signed quickly, with the pen he held out to her.

She could hear Charles coming down the stairs now with a heavy tread. What could she do? The envelope she'd been waiting for was there, on top of the rest of the mail, of course it was, she could see it in the postie's hand and it was addressed to Lara. But that wouldn't stop Charles and he was still coming down the stairs. She held out her hand. Charles was at the bottom of the stairs, close behind her now. He would see it. He'd have to see it.

The postie handed her the mail. Her bathrobe was loosely tied. Quick as a flash, she tucked the envelope that she knew contained her passport to freedom into the waistband of her pyjama trousers and tightened the belt of her bathrobe. Hopefully Charles would think she was just guarding her modesty.

The postie raised an eyebrow. Lara shot him a warning look. *Please don't say anything*, she silently pleaded. *Please.*

'Morning.' Charles was right beside her now, she could feel his breath on her neck and she was conscious of the nausea rising.

The postie glanced at him. 'Morning.' He seemed to hesitate. He must be wondering what on earth was going on.

'I'll take those, my dear.' Smoothly, Charles swept the remaining post from her hands.

The postie opened his mouth as if to speak.

'Thank you.' Charles practically shut the door in his face. He wouldn't want to waste time indulging in small talk, not with the postman anyway.

Thank God for his rudeness, thought Lara. It might have saved her.

'A cup of tea, Charles?' she asked him, not so sweetly that

he might suspect her of something, keeping her voice sad and weary, the same tone she'd been using for days.

'The only decent way to start the morning.' He sounded almost jovial as he flipped through the mail.

'I'll put the kettle on.' She took a step towards the kitchen.

'Why did the idiot knock on the door?' Charles muttered to himself.

Lara froze.

'There's nothing important here. Did he say there was registered mail?' His voice changed. Lara heard the edge in it and she tried not to panic.

She thought quickly. It was pointless to deny it, since Charles had obviously heard him. 'He did say that, yes.' She turned to face him and frowned. She needed those acting skills that seemed to come so easily to Hester, more than she ever had before. 'It must be one of those letters. Can I see?' She took a step closer.

'No need.' Charles held them away from her. 'Nothing for you to worry about. You concentrate on making that tea, hmm?'

Because that, thought Lara, *is all that you're good for.*

Straight after breakfast, when Charles went into the study, Lara slipped out to the garden, the envelope now tucked safely into the waistband of her trousers. She ran straight to the window in the wall as planned. Checking behind her, looking around, she ensured she wasn't being watched. She pulled out the bulky envelope, bent down and dropped it through the hole in the wall and onto the other side, out of sight. Hester would see it, though. They'd arranged this already and Hester had promised to check every day. They'd agreed that it was too risky to keep it in the house. Hester would give it to David and he would look after it until they'd left.

David . . . Lara rested a hand on her belly. It wouldn't be long now. But she knew she must contain her excitement. If Charles noticed anything amiss, all their plans could be for nothing.

Later, Hester popped by with some soup and Charles asked her to sit with Lara for an hour or so, even though Hester wasn't supposed to be working for them that day.

'Of course, Mr Fripp,' Hester purred, looking up at him as if butter wouldn't melt.

They turned to one another as soon as he'd shut the front door behind him.

'Did you get it?' Lara asked.

'Of course. I've passed it on to David already. We can't waste any time.'

'Oh.' Lara felt a warm glow in her belly. 'You've seen him? How is he?'

'Concerned for you,' Hester told her. 'But everything's going according to plan. And it's to be Tuesday.'

'Tuesday!' Lara stared at her. She'd known it was coming, but she could still hardly believe it.

'I'll come round as usual. Here's hoping he goes out to the village as per. Otherwise, we'll have to sneak you out anyway.'

Lara tried to steady her breathing. 'Where will David be?'

'Waiting for you down the road away from the village. He'll be in a car.' Hester took her hands. 'You must run, Lara.'

'I will.' *Like the wind*, she thought.

'Pack a small bag on Tuesday,' Hester said. 'After lunch, go upstairs for a nap and do it then. Leave it somewhere safe but have it ready.'

'And when Charles comes back? After I've gone, I mean?' Lara couldn't help worrying about the repercussions, and for the first time, she thought Hester too looked anxious. Would Charles suspect their young neighbour of helping her? Would he try and follow Lara and David? She shuddered.

'You don't need to worry about that, Lara. You and David need all your energy to get away quickly. As for the rest . . .' Her voice trailed.

'What?' Did she have a plan? Lara took her by her shoulders and looked into her dark eyes. They were so black, just like her mother's eyes. Black and mysterious.

'Everything will be fine.' There was only a slight catch in Hester's voice. 'I promise. Just leave it to me.'

Tuesday eventually arrived. After lunch, Lara went up to her room to rest, aware that Charles quite liked this new habit of hers; it gave him a period of time when he knew she was safely upstairs and not about to run away, she supposed.

Quickly, alert for the sound of his footsteps on the stairs, she packed her bag. It was hard to decide what to take. In the end, she packed one change of clothes, her wash things, her identity card and a photograph of herself with her parents in the garden in happier times. Everything else, she could leave. She was leaving her entire world behind, she realised. Except for David. She put a hand to her belly. And except for this tiny life growing inside her.

Hester appeared with soup and a pie at three forty-five that afternoon looking the same as ever. For a tense thirty minutes, Lara imagined that Charles wasn't going to go out as usual – he'd been working in the study all day and was in a foul temper.

But at four fifteen p.m., he grabbed his jacket and took off.

The second he was gone, Lara ran upstairs to get her bag while Hester kept watch in case he should come back again.

'Wait here.' Hester ran down to the end of the drive to check that Charles was heading towards the village. Lara guessed that she'd wait until he was out of sight.

After a few minutes, she beckoned to Lara that the coast was clear.

Lara ran. She had said goodbye to the garden that morning. She had wandered through each little section that had given her such a sense of sanctuary over the past months, touching and smelling the plants, murmuring to them, ensuring everything was in order. She had said goodbye to the house too; silently going into each room, examining the simple lines and generous flow, the hand-crafted furnishings, the wooden floors, fat-patterned cushions with the Arts and Crafts prints in terracotta, mustard yellow and olive green, those mellow, earthy colours, every piece of local stone, every grain of the wood integral to the elegant house that her parents had created together.

But now, she ran.

When she reached Hester, they embraced quickly but with all the love in the world. 'Thank you,' Lara whispered. 'I'll write.'

Hester nodded. There were tears in her eyes. 'Now, go,' she said.

Lara didn't need telling twice. She ran, in the other direction to the village, where a black car was parked not too far away. In it, she knew that David was waiting.

As she approached, the passenger door swung open and she jumped in.

She turned to him. Took in every detail of his sweet face, put her hand to his cheek. 'David,' she said.

'My love.' He kissed her lips so briefly, but it was enough. 'We must go.'

CHAPTER 47

Bea

Dorset, July 2018

At the house that evening, after they'd had supper together and Hester and Lewis had gone back home, Bea was surprised to hear a knock at the door.

She went to answer it. Lewis was standing there holding a bottle of wine.

'Grandma's gone to bed,' he said. 'Do you want some company? If not, I can save this till another time, no worries . . .' He hovered on the threshold.

Bea smiled. He was right. As usual, she hadn't wanted the evening to end. 'Come through.'

It was still warm outside, and so Bea found two glasses, Lewis opened the wine and they sat on the veranda in the tobacco-coloured Lloyd Loom chairs to watch the sky shifting into night-time.

'It's been quite a day,' Lewis remarked as he poured the wine. 'I wanted to check you were okay – with what we found out from Dorothy earlier.'

'Yes, sort of.' Bea had certainly been mulling it over. She'd also sent a text to Dorothy's daughter, to thank them both for seeing them and to ask one simple question that had somehow, in all of this, been overlooked.

'What Dorothy told us does fit in with the theory about Lara being unhappy.' Lewis glanced across at her as if gauging her reaction.

'Hmm.' Bea took the glass of wine he was offering her. 'Thanks.' Though Hester hadn't mentioned anything about her grandmother's fragile state of mind and Bea still wasn't convinced about that part of the story. She took a sip. The wine tasted of peaches and grapefruit and was delicious.

'But what about your grandfather?' Lewis frowned. 'From what Dorothy told us, he sounds like a pretty popular guy, trying to help everyone out during the war years. Do you think he could have treated your grandmother badly?' He sat back in his chair and took a sip of wine.

Bea shook her head. 'Nonno would never have treated her badly. They were devoted to one another.' She was sure of that. Even when you were young, you sensed these things.

'So . . . ?' Lewis cocked his head to one side.

'He was not my grandfather,' Bea told him. Which made a whole lot more sense.

'Lara's husband, do you mean?' Lewis leant forwards, elbows on his knees, eyes intent. 'Who was he then?'

'His name was Charles Fripp.' Bea took another sip of the deliciously fruity wine. 'I messaged Dorothy's daughter earlier and she asked her mother. We all assumed the man Nonna married was my grandfather. But Nonno's name was not Charles, it was David, David Curtis.'

Lewis whistled. The sound echoed around the darkening garden. 'So, who was Charles Fripp?'

'He was her first husband, the man she married just after the war.' Bea could guess how this might have happened. 'David Curtis — my grandfather — was her second husband. I had no idea Nonna was married before.' Bea shifted in her seat. And no idea why Nonna had never mentioned it either.

'I see where you're going with this.' Lewis nodded.

Bea's smile was grim. 'And so, given what we now know, I think that Charles must, for some reason, have kept Nonna a prisoner in her own home.' Which explained why Nonna had always been unwilling to speak of that time. Instead, she had told Bea stories that had seemed more like fairy tales — about a girl who loved her garden but who in fact was trapped and needed to escape. But Nonna's stories had held more than a grain of truth. She had been that girl and it must have been her way of speaking of the unhappiness of her past.

Lewis swore softly. 'And the story about your grandmother having some sort of breakdown? Is that even true?'

Bea shrugged. 'Who knows?' Given what she had gone through, it was certainly possible.

'And David Curtis?' He was watching her closely. 'Where did he spring from?'

'I do not know.' Not yet, anyway. But perhaps he had rescued her grandmother? Because now that Bea knew what and who Nonna had been escaping from, she could begin to imagine who she might have been escaping *to*.

Lewis was thoughtful. 'How do you suppose we can find out more?' He poured more wine for them both.

'From Hester, do you think?' Hester, she felt sure, knew the whole story.

'Maybe.' But Lewis's expression didn't give her much hope. And he was probably right. The story would be buried somewhere in Hester's memory, but they would have no way to uncover or verify it.

'From the garden?' Bea looked out towards the Romantic Garden where she could still make out the sculptural shapes of the alliums and tall verbena, although the garden was mostly hidden under the cover of darkness now. Something told her that the Arts and Crafts garden had already yielded most of its secrets.

Secrets . . . As she sipped her wine, feeling the cool liquid slip down her throat, Bea thought of the secret garden so well concealed behind the high swathes of *Stipa gigantea* grass and bamboo. She'd gone down there a few times and something still niggled at her . . .

'From your grandmother?'

'It is possible.'

'Or Dorothy at the post office might have more to tell us?' Lewis half turned in the chair and followed the direction of her gaze.

He loved it too, Bea realised. This Arts and Crafts garden seemed to have a way of drawing people in. 'Perhaps.' Dorothy had already told them that Lara had been seen getting into an unknown car and then simply disappeared. But what had happened to Charles? Dorothy might be able to tell them that much.

Lewis seemed to be following her train of thought. 'If Lara escaped,' he said, 'wouldn't Charles Fripp have followed her and tried to bring her back?'

'I would have thought so, yes.' He didn't sound like the kind of man who would give up very easily.

Bea decided to stop thinking about it for now. Maybe she'd never find out the whole truth and maybe it was better that way. It had been a surprise to discover that Nonna had been married before, and horrific to think that Charles Fripp might have been cruel to her, but at least she'd managed to get away from him eventually, even though now, poor Nonna obviously couldn't bear to think back to that time in her life. Bea understood so much more now – about the house, about the garden. No wonder parts of the house held such a dark atmosphere. No wonder Nonna had loved the garden. She'd tried to save it, but in an important way, it had saved her.

'What are you thinking about now, Bea?' Lewis was still watching her intently. His face was in shadow, although the light of the moon had escaped the cloud cover and was falling onto the Romantic Garden, on the stone sundial in the centre. 'Are you still trying to work out the mystery?'

Bea took another sip of her wine. 'Just that I hate to think of Nonna being so unhappy.' In fact, it was hurting her more than she could say.

Lewis leant forwards and lightly brushed a strand of hair from her face. It was such a tender gesture that for a second or two, it took her breath away.

'But in the end,' he said, 'your grandmother has had a good life, don't you think?'

'Yes, I am sure she has.'

'And that's what matters.' His smile was gentle.

Bea took in the shadowy contours of his face. Out here in the deepening darkness, she felt braver. She felt that she could be more personal, she could ask him what she wanted to know.

'Why do you not exhibit your work, Lewis?' she asked softly. 'Why not approach some local galleries?'

He didn't answer for such a long time that she thought she'd upset him. She reached out and touched his arm. 'I only ask because your work is so good,' she said.

'Did you ever doubt yourself?' he asked, his voice low. 'Did you ever think you weren't good enough? At garden design? At life?'

Bea considered. It would be too easy to make a glib reply, but he deserved more. 'I have often found it hard to fit in with other people,' she admitted. 'I like to spend time alone – preferably in a garden . . .' She smiled and was relieved to catch his answering grin. 'So, it was not always easy – going to college, having the courage of my convictions when it came to the garden design world.'

'I sense a "but",' he said.

And he was right. 'But I was lucky enough to have my family behind me – especially my grandmother. She taught me to have faith in myself and my abilities. She taught me that you can make a dream come true.'

'Ah. Yes, I see.' He was toying with the stem of his wine glass.

Bea picked up the bottle and gave them both a refill. 'And there was something else . . .'

He was looking at her, waiting.

'When I am thinking about what to put in a garden, or how to arrange it, something often just seems to come over me.' It was hard, she found, to explain. She'd never told anyone this, never before been able to be so open. 'Almost,' she said hesitantly, 'as if the garden is using me to design itself.'

She waited for him to laugh and tell her she was crazy, but he remained silent, seemingly deep in contemplation. And that was one of the things she liked about him, she realised. He was relaxing to be with. He didn't always need to talk. He could do comfortable silences.

'I get it,' he said at last. He took another sip of wine. 'It's a bit like that when I'm painting. Sometimes, on a really good day, I could lose a whole hour and afterwards I get this weird feeling that someone else has painted the canvas for me. Or . . .' – he shrugged – '. . . I've been taken over.'

'Lost to inspiration,' she said. 'It is a gift.'

'It would be nice to think so.' He sighed. 'And I want to be positive, I do. But I suppose I had my confidence knocked out of me and it's hard to build it up again, you know?'

She nodded. She could certainly imagine. She thought of Matteo and the way he'd criticised her for not making more of an effort to dress up. She'd hated that. It had made her feel inadequate, and as if he was trying to make her into someone she didn't want to be.

'Who did that to you?' she asked Lewis. She had the feeling that this might be it – the story that he'd said would wait until another day.

Lewis hesitated, took another slug of wine and seemed to come to a decision. 'I was married,' he said.

'Oh, I see.' She hadn't expected that.

'It worked between us at first. But she always wanted me to get a "proper" job.' He made the quote marks in the air.

'As opposed to painting?'

'Exactly.' Lewis sat back in his chair. 'I understood the reasons why. Cathy wanted us to start a family, she wanted us to buy a house . . . And I wasn't earning enough money. In fact, I had very little stable income at all.'

'Hmm.' Bea could understand how it might have been. 'She did not see how important your art was to you?'

His laugh was harsh and devoid of humour. 'No, she didn't. Or she didn't care.'

Once again, Matteo's attitude to her work slipped into Bea's head. She supposed that plenty of people were unable to fully appreciate other people's dreams. And really, no one could blame them. Everyone had their own agenda, but those agendas didn't always match. 'So, what happened?'

He finished drinking his wine and placed the glass deliberately back on the table. 'I gave it up,' he said. 'Cathy persuaded me I wasn't much good anyway, and that I should keep it just as a hobby, so I went to work as a salesman instead.'

'A salesman?' She stared at him. Now that, she really couldn't imagine.

'I know.' He shook his head. 'Me, a salesman? Ridiculous, huh?'

'Um, how was it?' But Bea thought she already knew the answer to this question.

'I hated it. I was rubbish at it too.' His tone was matter of fact. 'It meant long hours and travelling away from home, spending half the day in a car, never being outside in the fresh air . . .'

Bea gave a little shudder. *Talk about clipping your wings.*

'But it wasn't just that.' He sighed. 'I was under pressure the whole time – to sell things I didn't even like or believe in, to make targets, to play the game . . .'

'But you kept going?'

He shrugged. 'Well, yes, I kept going, because that's what Cathy wanted.'

Very unselfish of him. Bea found herself wondering if he still would have married Cathy if he'd known what she expected of him beforehand. 'And did you still paint?'

He shook his head. 'I was too knackered, to tell the truth. Plus, I didn't believe in myself any more. Cathy said there was no point and I just accepted it.'

'You gave it up?' Bea was surprised. He wasn't a weak man. And he seemed to love painting so much. But she supposed he must have loved his wife very much too.

'Yeah.' He squared his shoulders. 'I've never had a whole lot of confidence anyway. It took me a long time afterwards to realise that it didn't matter if I wasn't successful. Plenty of decent artists aren't. What mattered was that I was doing it and surviving, fulfilling the dream.'

Bea was glad that he'd eventually come to that conclusion, but she was aware that he must have left out a big chunk of the story. 'And Cathy?'

'She ran off with my best mate.' He leant forwards, his eyes intense even in the darkness. 'It's a cliché, I know. They started meeting up when I was away for work. I was too busy and exhausted to even see it coming.'

'Oh, Lewis.' She put her hand on his. 'I am so sorry.'

'And what made it even worse,' Lewis said, 'was what he did for a living.'

Bea arched an eyebrow. 'Really? He was a . . . ?'

'A painter,' he said. 'A painter and decorator. Oh, the irony . . .' His laughter was more genuine this time.

Their eyes met and Bea laughed too. '*Mio Dio*,' she muttered.

One second, they were laughing and the next second, he'd taken her hands and pulled her closer until their faces were only centimetres apart. 'So, that's the story, Bea,' he said.

She only had to move a fraction and it wasn't a hard decision to make. A few glasses of wine, a moonlit night, the fragrance

415

of honeysuckle perfuming the air . . . And a man, a rather lovely man who had somehow become more than a friend.

She felt his hesitation, couldn't blame him for that. And then his lips were on hers, and he tasted of the wine they'd just been drinking, of grapefruit and flowers. And it was sweet, so sweet. Bea swept her mind of everything that had been occupying it – her grandmother's story, Matteo, the garden. And she gave herself up – to the moment, the longing.

CHAPTER 48

Rose

Italy, July 2018

Federico had been quiet all evening and Rose was worried. Federico was never quiet. Also, he had eaten very little at dinner and this was also unusual. He had the healthiest appetite and had always appreciated her cooking.

Since that awful argument when he had walked away, something had changed between them. They went about their usual business – Federico working in the olive grove or meeting with various business contacts, Rose looking after the guests, the *trulli*, the house and the domestic chores. And as they did so, they spoke politely to one another. *I am just going into Locorotondo – would you like me to pick up anything?* Or: *I was planning seafood pasta for dinner. Is that okay with you?*

The politeness, this was the problem. Gone was their usual banter and good-natured bickering. Gone were the quick hugs or the fleeting touch of hands. Gone were the shouting, the stomping, the gesticulation. Gone was the warmth of their long-standing companionship and the heat of lovemaking. Both kept a careful distance from the other. It seemed to be all about self-preservation now.

This had never happened before. They had always made up after every row – usually before bedtime. And they had never been polite with one another – not ever.

Still, since she had shared the truth with her mother, Rose had at least felt a little lighter. Her mother was old and frail and not as aware of her surroundings as she once was, but she was still sharp enough. And it had been a huge release for Rose to tell her, to let it out. For so long, it had been burning her up inside.

Rose had waited for the anger, the disapproval, the shock which must surely come, but this did not happen. Instead, her mother had opened her arms and stroked her hair and held Rose as if she was a young child again. Perhaps, Rose thought, they were all children forever in one vital way, which could explain why the loss of a parent would always be so great. She thought of Bea. *When her daughter came home . . .* Rose had a lot she must make up for.

'It was so long ago, Rose,' her mother had soothed. 'You were just a young girl. But now you must not let yourself be haunted by this man any longer. It is over.'

Even the sound and rhythm of her mother's voice were soothing. How had Rose forgotten that?

'But for it to be truly over, you must tell Federico.'

Rose had drawn slightly away at this. 'Tell him?' she whispered.

'You have to.' Her mother seemed very sure. 'It is only by telling him that you will ever ease this burden.' She nodded. 'Cesare Basso or no, the knowledge of what you have done will

418

continue to trouble you, my darling, until you tell the truth to your husband and try to atone.'

'Oh, Mamma.' And Rose wept all the more, because she knew she was right. She should have told Federico at the start, she should have told him everything, but of course, she had been so ashamed and she still was.

'You will find the right time.' Her mother was still stroking her hair. 'And you know it is the correct thing to do.'

'He will not understand,' Rose said. How could he? 'He will not forgive me.'

She could feel rather than see her mother shaking her head. 'Federico is a good man,' she said. 'And he loves you.'

But now, facing her husband across the dinner table, Rose was not so sure that he did still love her. There was none of the usual warmth in his brown eyes and the set of his mouth was grim.

'Shall we go for a walk?' Federico got to his feet.

Rose stared at him. 'A walk?' They never went for a walk after dinner. By then, they were both always too tired.

'There are some matters I need to discuss with you.'

Rose felt the familiar pain in her chest, the trepidation deep in her belly. What now? What things? Was now the right time? It did not feel that way. She had an awful premonition that something very bad was about to happen.

'Va bene,' she said. Rose tried to stay calm. She realised that he had suggested the walk because he did not want her mother to hear whatever it was he had to say. Which worried her even more . . . 'I will just check on Mamma.'

He nodded and she walked through the hall and into her mother's room. She was sleeping. In the last few days, she seemed to have grown wearier still, as if she was ready to soon let life slip away.

419

Rose dreaded that this might be the case. Her mother was a very old lady but Rose couldn't think of losing her. Should she tell Bea? Not yet. Rose did not want to worry her and perhaps it was as well that their daughter wasn't here at the moment to witness whatever it was that was happening here.

Gently, she touched her mother's brow at the point where her skin met the snow-white hairline and she smiled fondly. 'I love you,' she whispered. How long since she had told her that? How many chances had she missed? Hopefully, her mother could hear her in her dreams.

But Rose couldn't linger here any longer. She returned to the living room where Federico was standing by the window, hands in pockets, looking restless.

'*Andiamo*,' he said. 'Let us go.'

They walked not into the garden, but past the *trulli* and the little white chapel towards the olive grove. And why not? It was her husband's favourite place. His life.

'Have I neglected you?' he muttered as they walked. 'Is that it? For this?' He gestured towards the forest of olive trees.

'No,' she said. She had never felt neglected. Only grateful that he had wanted to share it with her.

The trees stood serene as ever, the grey-green of their leaves creating a hazy halo around them in the deepening dusk. They were planted in orderly rows an exact distance apart – to preserve the quality, Federico had once explained to her. Some people, she remembered him saying, would push the olive trees to the limit, but then you would get burnout and this was not the Romano way. He and Bruno kept to the organic principles, never using pesticide, following a line of natural production as far as possible. They had to use copper and zinc to fight the bacteria, for this was a constant battle that the olive farmer must win, even if he continually cleared the land. Rose looked down at her feet. As always, the dusty red earth was smoothed and clear. Otherwise, regular pruning kept the trees healthy, and this they did by hand every alternate year.

Rose sighed. It was calming, though, to think of the olive trees rather than what might lie ahead. Was this what it was like for Federico too?

Some of the trees were crooked and gnarled, some stood straighter; they were becoming laden with olives, their branches drooping lower to the ground. She glanced at her husband. Federico always said that he felt most at peace when he was walking through the olive grove, but he did not look peaceful now as he led the way along the path and into the grove. His back was stiff and she could sense the tension from the way he was walking, very different from his usual lazy, laid-back stroll. Rose's feeling of dread returned.

Once they were inside the shroud of the trees, Federico abruptly stopped walking. She couldn't help noticing that they were standing beside the pitted and gnarled old tree they called the 'Great-Grandfather' because of its age. It was the most ancient tree on the farm, planted by the local Messapian tribe before either the Greeks or Romans arrived in Puglia apparently. It had bent over and rotated itself three times and had to be supported by stones underneath and ropes to keep it stabilised these days – but incredibly, it was still producing, yielding about fifty kilograms of olives every two years, Federico had once told her proudly.

But he didn't look so proud now . . . Rose realised that she could no longer distract herself from the matter in hand and what her husband was about to say to her – and she knew it would not be about the olives.

He turned to face her. 'Rose,' he said. 'Please answer me honestly.'

Rose braced herself. '*Sì?*'

'Is there someone else?'

'Someone else?' she said stupidly, unable to think what he meant.

'Another man.' His voice was low and quiet as if he didn't want to disturb these olive trees he loved so much.

Another man? She almost laughed. 'No,' she said. 'Of course not.' How could he think such a thing?

At her words, his shoulders dropped with the release of tension. 'Then tell me this.'

'Yes?'

'Is it that you have decided to leave me?'

'Oh, Federico . . .' Rose could hardly believe that he was asking her these questions. And she realised two things. One was that her mother had been right. She must tell Federico the truth. And two, the time to tell him that truth was now. 'No, it is not that, never that.'

'What then?' he said. 'What is happening between us?' He tore his fingers through his hair. 'Tell me . . . because I do not know.'

'It is me.' Rose took a deep breath. She wanted to step closer towards him but she did not dare. 'Something happened – a long time ago when I was with Cesare Basso. And then . . . he came round here a month or so ago.'

'Basso?' He stared at her, uncomprehending. The name hung in the air between them, disturbing the tranquillity of the olive grove at dusk. 'That . . . thug?' He bunched his hand into a fist and slammed it into the unsuspecting trunk of the nearest olive tree – not the Great-Grandfather, but a tree they called the Tepee because of its shape.

Rose winced. She knew Federico would regret that.

But the tepee tree seemed only to shimmer softly in response.

'What have you done, Rose? Did you take up with him again? *Per favore*. Please tell me you did not.'

'Of course I did not!' She was indignant. What did he take her for?

'But the bastard was in prison,' he growled.

'He is out now.' More was the pity.

'And he came here?' Federico seemed to grow taller. 'He came here, you say?' His arms were down by his sides, his fists already bunching again as if preparing for a fight.

'*Sì*.' She nodded. 'I felt . . .' She tried to explain. 'Threatened by him.'

'What did he do?' Rose thought that Federico would explode.

'Nothing,' she said quickly. 'I sent him away. But . . .' That was when it had started – the dreadful shame, the fear. That was when it had all come back to haunt her.

'What did he want?' Federico was pacing now, up and down between the trees.

Rose could see faces in the trunks sometimes. A man grimacing or laughing; a sharp jaw, an aquiline nose. She had never told Federico this in case he laughed at her, but now she thought that maybe he saw the faces too and that this was one of the reasons he loved the trees so much. She shrugged. 'Money. A job. My help.'

'Did you give him money, Rose?'

'A little.'

'You gave him our money?' The tone of his voice . . . it scared her.

'I wanted him to go away,' she admitted. 'I wanted him to leave me alone.'

Federico hardly seemed to be listening. 'That man . . .' He muttered a low curse. 'I will go and see him. He will not do this to my family. I will—'

'I did something very wrong.' Rose interrupted him. She stepped forwards, as if she was walking up to the gallows, she found herself thinking. Around them, the olive trees were still. She had to tell him now. 'Years back, when I was under his influence.'

Federico stopped pacing and turned to stare at her once again. 'What did you do, Rose?'

'He persuaded me to go to an old lady's house.' Rose had been rehearsing how she would tell him this, but in the end, she had to just be honest and tell him how it was. 'He wanted me to chat to her, befriend her, tell her about him and persuade her that he was a fair man to do business with.'

Federico snorted.

'He asked me to tell her that he would give her a fair price for her jewellery if she wanted to sell it . . .'

Rose hadn't wanted to do it. She did not know the old lady, but the whole thing sounded dodgy and, knowing Cesare, it would be. But she was still in thrall to him at that stage. She remembered even now being scared that he would leave her, scared that if she didn't do what he asked, he would lose interest, drop her, find another girl.

'Did you know what he was planning?' Federico stuck his hands in his pockets. If Rose didn't know him better, she would imagine this to be a casual question. But she knew it was one she had to answer candidly.

'I suppose that I did,' she admitted. 'Although I did not want to think it.'

'So, he was out to cheat the woman, I suppose. We know what he was – what he still is.'

'Yes.' Rose had not been so young nor so naive. She could not pretend that she did not know.

Federico shook his head mournfully. 'Oh, Rose,' he said.

'I am not proud of it.' Rose felt the emotion swell. There was a thickness at the back of her throat and when she swallowed, the taste was bitter. 'I have relived it many times over the years, you can be sure.'

'So, you did what he asked?'

'Yes.'

'And what then?'

Rose met his stern gaze with some difficulty. Federico was a man who had been born with integrity. He would never understand the pull of the rogue, the desperation to keep a bad man happy, or that anyone could sweep their misgivings aside for an approving glance from a man such as Cesare Basso. That was the hold he'd had over her.

But she must go on. 'When I got back, he asked many questions. Not only about the woman, but about her house, the layout of the rooms, where she slept.'

Once again, Federico let out a muttered curse.

'That was when I knew for sure,' Rose said.

'And so, he went there later? He robbed the old woman of her jewels?'

'Yes.' Rose had been powerless to stop him. And yet, she had liked the old woman; she had been kind and had spirit.

You have done your bit, my love, Cesare had told her. *You have played your part.*

What could she say? That she was innocent? That she had not known she was doing wrong? No, she could not say that – not

425

to Cesare, not to Federico and not to herself. She could only watch helplessly as Cesare and his friend went off to the woman's house in the early hours of the morning and she could only know that she was responsible for what he was about to do.

Federico was standing very still, very straight. 'Did he hurt her, Rose?'

'Not directly.' *But if she had woken . . .* Rose could not say what he might have done.

Federico seemed to be considering. 'It is bad, Rose,' he said.

It was worse than he knew.

'But you were very young. He used you. But you were in so deep. And . . .'

She looked across at him. In his eyes was a warmth and understanding she knew she did not deserve.

'It was many years ago,' he said. 'It is a long time to have such a thing on your conscience.'

'It was Teresa,' said Rose.

Federico was silent for so long she almost thought he hadn't heard her. Then: 'Our Teresa? You are talking about Teresa Castello?'

'Yes.' This was the part that he would not be able to forgive. Rose had thought there was something familiar about the old lady at the time. But there were so many relatives in and out of the Romanos' house and of course she and Federico were not together then, so she had not been mindful of them all. Teresa was a cousin or a second cousin who had married into the Castello family – far enough removed for Rose not to be aware.

'You knew this? You knew it was Teresa?' His voice was so soft, it hardly broke the silence of the night.

She shook her head. Not until afterwards. When she knew, when she realised how Cesare had played her and deceived

426

her, when she understood that he had chosen Teresa Castello because she was part of the Romano family . . . That had been the tipping point for Rose. That was when she had run.

'Teresa suffered a stroke a few weeks after that burglary,' Federico said.

'I know that.' It had made Rose feel like a murderer – or an accessory at least. 'That was why,' she said. 'That was why I could not tell you what I had done.'

But Federico was not there to listen to her words. Already, he was stomping off down the path through the olive grove. And the trees . . . they seemed to gently rustle and close up behind him until she could see him no more.

Miserably, Rose turned to make her way back indoors. Well, she had told him now. She had carried the awfulness of what she had done to a member of her own husband's family alone for so many years, but now he knew.

After Teresa's death, she had gone to the funeral, taken flowers, visited the family and met Teresa's daughter Sofia and granddaughter Lucia. She knew that she could never atone for what she had done and so how could she ever forgive herself? She would always feel the shame.

Her only consolation was that she was now free of Cesare – her mother had been right about that much. She would go round to visit Lucia, and she would tell her everything, she decided – it was only right that Teresa's granddaughter knew the truth. And then Rose would continue to live with it just as she always had. But perhaps it would be without Federico. Because he was proud and family had always come first for him. How could he possibly feel the same about Rose, knowing what she had done? How could he ever forgive her now?

CHAPTER 49

Bea

Dorset, July 2018

Bea was humming as she prepared her breakfast the following morning. She loaded the coffee percolator and fetched some fruit from the bowl. She would eat outside on the veranda, she decided. It had been raining earlier but now it had cleared and there was even some weak sunshine. *The veranda . . .* She felt a delicious shiver run through her.

Perhaps she should have known that something would happen between them last night. It had been such a perfect setting and she'd felt so close to Lewis – closer still when he confided in her: about his life with Cathy, about how first his self-confidence and then his trust had been broken.

The percolator began to bubble and she put some milk on to boil for the *caffè latte*. The house didn't run to a microwave, which was hardly surprising, given that no one had lived here for such a long time.

Lewis was a kindred spirit . . . This realisation came to her

428

as she took the tray of coffee, fruit and toast outside. He loved the outdoors, just as she did. He too was a creative. Like her, he was vulnerable and had experienced what could be described as a controlling relationship that had dented his self-belief. *A kindred spirit* . . . But was that all he was?

She didn't think so. Bea helped herself to a fresh peach and bit into the furry skin. There had been a spark, a current of attraction running between them almost from the start. And last night it had intensified . . .

She closed her eyes for a moment, remembering, the sweetness of the peach juice on her tongue. The kiss between them had started tentatively, as if they were both hesitant and unsure. But seconds after they drew apart, looked into one another's faces . . . they came back for more, hungrily this time, moving into kisses that were as deep, Bea found herself thinking, as the night.

She had wanted more. It would have been so easy to go on . . .

Bea opened her eyes and gazed out into the lilac and blue haven of the Romantic Garden, which looked so different by day. Her whole body had ached for more as she held him, closer and tighter, as she felt the strength of his desire and answered it with her own, as she felt them slowly fold together into one.

But, 'Not yet,' he had whispered. 'Perhaps, not yet?'

And she knew he was right. She wanted him, but she also wanted to take her time this time. She wanted to be slow, to enjoy their developing passion, to taste every second of it in the present moment and experience it again on a slow replay, then another, then another. It was too good to rush.

Bea sipped her coffee thoughtfully. When he'd left, he'd whispered it in her ear. 'Tomorrow.' Like a promise. So, he would be here this morning, working in the garden by her side or painting in the studio, and she could hardly wait.

She spread some apricot jam onto a slice of toast and took a bite. She wouldn't think of the obvious obstacles – that this was a temporary arrangement, that she would have to return to Italy before too long and that this house would have to be sold. She wouldn't think of how many days or weeks this might last. Right now, it felt as if it could go on forever and right now that was all that Bea wanted.

A knock on the door startled her out of her reverie. Lewis. Here already. She glanced at her watch. It was still early, but perhaps, like her, he couldn't sleep, couldn't wait for the next day to begin and for whatever was growing between them to flower and bloom.

She hurried to open it. Hester would be there too. Would it be awkward between Bea and Lewis? She didn't think so. And as for Hester . . . Once or twice, she had caught a certain knowing twinkle in Hester's eye, wondered if this old lady with dementia could see more than they gave her credit for. Who knew?

Bea flung open the door. For a moment, she thought she was hallucinating. For a moment, she could make no sense of what was in front of her – or who. And then he grabbed hold of her, his hands around her waist, lifting her into the air.

'Beatrice! It is really you! Beatrice! *Cara!* My darling!' He put her down. Now, he was holding her at arm's length, then pulling her close and smothering her with kisses, and all the time, Bea remained speechless, trying to make sense of it all.

'Matteo?' Why was he here? *How* was he here? Surely she must be dreaming?

'Beatrice.'

430

She wrung her hands. She wasn't dreaming. 'What are you doing here?'

'But, naturally, I have come to see you.' He took charge, hoisted his flight bag onto his shoulder, swept past her and into the house. 'I needed to see you,' he went on, shrugging as if this was surely obvious. 'I needed to make you understand.'

'Understand what?' Bea felt sick. It was horrible, this feeling of anxiety deep in her belly.

'Understand the mistake you are making, of course.' He swung around to face her.

'What mistake?' She didn't want him here, she realised. But how could she say such a thing? How could she possibly turn him away? What could she do? 'But, Matteo, I explained everything in my voicemail . . .'

'Pah!' He dismissed this with a wave of his hand. 'Voicemail, you say? This is what I mean. This is what I am saying. I cannot talk to you on the phone about this matter. I needed to see you.' His voice softened. 'I needed to see your beautiful face.'

'But how did you know where to find me?' There were so many questions she wanted to ask him, but most of all, she wished that he hadn't come here at all. She hadn't had the chance to explain anything to Lewis – about what had happened with Matteo and how her feelings had changed. If only Matteo had answered just one of her texts, she might have had more of a clue what was going on in his head, but to simply turn up here, charging in like this after not speaking to her for over a month – it was impossible to comprehend.

'I begged your mother to tell me.' He smirked. 'I think she imagined I wanted to write you a letter or send you flowers or something.'

'Hmm.'

He turned to her and took her in his arms. 'Are you not pleased to see me, my darling?' he crooned.

Bea couldn't bring herself to even answer that. How could she tell him what she was really thinking? 'But what about the restaurant?' she asked instead. How had she got this so wrong? Hadn't he objected to her coming away? Hadn't he refused to give her time to consider his proposal? Hadn't he made it plain how he felt and what he expected of her? Hadn't he ghosted her for weeks?

He brushed this concern away with another of his expansive gestures. 'Oh, my parents will manage without me for a week or so.'

A week or so . . . ? Bea looked at her watch again. 'But it is so early.'

His eyes gleamed. 'I caught a very early flight, my darling. And I had a hire car booked.'

Of course he did.

She tried again. 'But, why did you not answer any of my messages? All of this time?'

He gave a little shrug. 'I admit I was hurt,' he said. 'I thought you loved me. I thought you would want to share your life with me.'

Bea had guessed this much was true. 'And why . . . ?'

'Why have I come over here now?' He shook his head sadly. 'Not just to see you face to face, my love, but also to see this place.' Another gesture. 'To see what can be so special to keep you away from me.'

Had he forgotten what had happened between them? Had he forgotten what he'd said?

Apparently so. He glanced around the hallway. '*Certo*, it has some history, I can see.'

'My history,' Bea said quietly. She squared her shoulders. 'And you should have told me you were coming, Matteo.' Because then, she thought, she could have stopped him.

'I wanted to surprise you.' He grinned. 'I thought that if I gave you the chance to say "no", you would have said it.'

Well, exactly . . . 'Matteo, after the way things were left between us . . .' Bea knew she had to get this straight with him and fast.

'Yes. You are right.' He hung his head. 'I put pressure on you and that was unforgiveable.'

Mio Dio . . . He certainly knew how to make a girl feel guilty. And he could turn things around in the blink of an eye. How could he make it any harder? It was difficult enough already, but if Matteo started admitting his mistakes . . . And she really, really didn't want to hurt him. Matteo was not a bad man. He was exuberant and fun and being with him when his father had been taken ill had shown her quite another side to him. But she knew now, it would never have worked between them. Matteo wasn't *her* man.

'I am not right for you, Matteo,' she said. 'I told you that in my voicemail. I am sorry you had to come all this way for nothing, but—'

'Nonsense.' He pulled her into another embrace. 'I know you did not mean what you said in that message. You are exactly right for me. I knew it the second we met.'

Bea stood her ground. 'But I could never give up my gardens.' Because that was what he had expected of her. And after that, what else? He would always be trying to make her into something he wanted her to be, rather than what she really was.

He stroked her hair. 'I would not ask you to.'

433

Only, he already had . . . 'I could not work in the restaurant.'

'You need never set foot in the place.'

'And . . .' What could she say? That she had met someone else? That she had thought they were finished and the man next door had captured her heart?

Lewis. She almost stopped breathing. He would be here any moment. She couldn't risk him bumping into Matteo – God knows how Matteo would twist the truth. She must go straight over there and explain.

'Come outside into the back garden,' she said to Matteo.

'After all this time?' He quirked an eyebrow. 'I expected you to invite me upstairs, *cara*.'

'Outside,' she said firmly. 'There is coffee.'

He considered this. '*Va bene*,' he said. 'Okay. For five minutes only.'

Oh, hellfire . . . 'We need to talk,' she told him. 'But first, I must go next door.'

'Next door?' His brow clouded.

'I need to tell . . .' – she searched for the best words to use – '. . . my gardener, not to come over today.' That sounded convincing enough.

'Ah.' His arms were around her waist again. 'Because we must be alone, *sì*?'

She extracted herself with some difficulty. 'There is a lot we have to discuss, Matteo,' she said sternly. But first, she must talk to Lewis.

'Why do you want to be here in this godforsaken place anyway?' Matteo's expression was sulky but his booming voice was now echoing around the veranda. Bea cringed.

'I told you,' she said. 'I came for Nonna. This was the place she grew up in. It is my family legacy.' And as soon as she'd

434

arrived, Bea had felt the magnetic pull of the place. She'd always known she'd been right to come.

He snorted, clearly unconvinced. 'It was raining when the plane landed.' His tone was aggrieved. 'Grey sky in summer, miserable-looking people. England is everything I thought it would be.'

Hmm. It was true the climate had taken a bit of getting used to. But Bea had already come to appreciate the freshness of the breeze, the thick and intoxicating scent of foliage after a downpour. The plants rather liked it and so did she. 'I will not be long,' she said, inching towards the French doors. 'Help yourself to breakfast.'

'You do not belong here, Beatrice.' Matteo poured himself some coffee. 'You belong in Italy. With me. You need to come back right now. With me.'

And he imagined he would be able to stop telling her what to do? 'I am not coming back.' Her voice was gentle. 'At least not yet. I need to finish what I came here for.' *And then?* But she wouldn't think about that now.

There was a knock at the front door, a familiar knock, the sound Bea had been waiting for. 'Stay here,' she told Matteo.

She rushed to the front door and pulled it open.

Lewis and Hester were standing on the front step.

'Hi.' Lewis's eyes were warm, so warm. Full of yesterday evening and what they had shared.

Instinctively, Bea took a step towards him. 'Lewis,' she said. 'Can I speak with you a minute?' She had to stop him coming in. She had to explain. She should have done it last night, but the time hadn't been right and the moment had swept them both away.

'Sure.' His expression was so open, so trusting.

Bea turned to Hester. 'Could you wait here a moment, please, Hester? We won't be long.'

Hester nodded.

Bea took Lewis's arm. 'Let us walk down the drive,' she said.

But she was too late. Naturally, Matteo would never do what she asked him to. She heard a sound from behind her, a door slam; she saw the expression in Lewis's green eyes change.

'And who is it that we have here?' Matteo was beside her. He threw a possessive arm around her shoulders. 'Introduce us, my love?'

Bea wished that the ground would open up and swallow her. 'Matteo, this is Lewis and his grandmother Hester from next door,' she said. 'Hester was a great friend of Nonna's. And Lewis . . .' Her voice trailed. She tried to catch Lewis's eye. She wanted somehow to try and tell him that this was a terrible mistake, that things weren't as they seemed, that she was not Matteo's love – at least not any more.

But Lewis gave her just one cool glance and then looked away.

Matteo stuck out a hand. 'The gardener, I presume?'

Bea winced.

Lewis shot her another glance – this time she saw his surprise. 'You could say that.'

'Lewis has been a very good friend to me,' Bea said quietly. Much more than that too. 'He's not just—'

'Really?' From Matteo's expression, she saw she had made it worse. 'I had no idea, my love,' he said, 'that you were being looked after so well.'

Lewis finally took his outstretched hand in greeting. 'And you are?' His expression was icy now. Clearly, he had come to his own conclusions – and who could blame him?

'I am Matteo Leone.' He puffed up his chest. 'Beatrice's fiancé.'

Bea could have wept. 'Matteo,' she said. 'That is not—'

'Bea was just about to come over to tell you that you were not needed today,' Matteo said grandly.

'Matteo . . .' But what was the point? Even to her own ears she sounded unconvincing. After all, here he was with her in the house, his arm around her, clearly having flown here from Italy to be by her side.

'And naturally, we would like to spend some time alone,' he went on smoothly. 'We have a lot to catch up on as you can imagine.'

'I certainly can,' said Lewis. Already he was turning away.

Bea glared at Matteo. 'We have a lot to *talk about*,' she said pointedly.

'Hmm. Whatever you say, my love.' He held her closer still. 'But the time, it will not all be used on talking, you can be sure.'

For heaven's sake. But even as Bea pulled away, Lewis had taken Hester's arm and they were walking off down the drive.

'But aren't we going in?' Poor Hester seemed more confused than ever.

'No,' said Lewis. And he threw one last look over his shoulder at Bea. 'We're not going in.'

'But is it safe? Should we leave Lara here – with him?'

Bea shook her head in despair. She was only too aware of the irony. She would go over and explain just as soon as she could. But first . . . She turned around. She must deal with Matteo.

CHAPTER 50

Rose

Italy, July 2018

The following day, Rose asked one of Federico's nieces to keep an eye on her mother for an hour or two and she drove to Locorotondo to see Lucia. She didn't hope to be forgiven – perhaps she would now be ostracised from the Romano family forever. And she could not atone, for there was a death on her conscience still. But it was the least she could do – tell Lucia the truth of what she had done. And from now on, she could try to live her life the right way. Perhaps this was the first step.

Federico had slept in the guest room last night and he'd barely spoken to her this morning. Was it over between them? Was their marriage about to come to an end? It hardly seemed possible and yet she knew her husband – she knew him only too well. He would be thinking that she was not the woman he had always taken her to be. And he was right in this. Secrets could be destructive; not only the truth of them but the hiding of the truth from the one you loved.

Lucia was, of course, surprised to see her, although she welcomed her into her house, which was neat as a pin and offered coffee which Rose was glad to accept. She needed all the fortification she could get.

The Castellos were on the outskirts of the Romano family – distant cousins, Rose assumed; there had always been so many cousins and they only met all together on big celebration days. Lucia was a bit older than Rose, mid-seventies maybe, and she lived with her husband in a skinny whitewashed house in the old town. Her father had died when she was a young girl and her mother Sofia had also died some years ago, having lived to a ripe old age. The couple had children and most of them no doubt now had children of their own. Some still lived close by, some had left to find their fortunes elsewhere in Italy and abroad. Such was the way these days; the family unit was not what it had once been. But the bond remained just as strong.

They exchanged the usual niceties as the coffee percolated on the stove, the pungent aroma filling the homely kitchen where they sat. Rose was relieved that Lucia's husband was not in; she wasn't sure she could face them both.

'And Federico?' Lucia asked. 'He is well?' Her eyes were watchful as if she guessed Federico to be the reason for Rose's visit.

'*Molto bene, grazie*. He is well.' Rose thought of the way he had looked last night. 'But . . .' Her courage almost failed.

'Let me make the coffee.' Lucia bustled around, heating milk, pouring coffee and whisked milk into cups.

Rose waited until she had finished, when a tray of coffee and *biscotti* was on the table and Lucia had sat down opposite her. 'Lucia, you must be wondering why I have come here today,' she began.

'*Sì, sì.*' She pushed a coffee cup closer to Rose. 'Is it a family matter, my dear?'

'It is.' Rose took the cup but could no longer meet Lucia's clear gaze. 'It is about something that happened a long time ago,' she said.

'Oh?' Lucia grasped her own coffee cup, blew on the top and took a small sip. 'Go on.'

Rose took a deep breath. It felt so strange that she had kept this story to herself for so long and yet now this would be the third telling in as many days. 'You may have heard that when I was much younger, I was involved with some rather nasty people . . .' she began. She imagined that it had been the talk of the family at the time, everyone no doubt sympathising with what Rose's parents had to put up with. *Rebellious teenage daughters . . .*

Lucia batted this away as it was of no consequence. 'One hears things,' she said. 'In families, there is always talk. But what does it matter now? It is the past. The past, it hangs over us and yet we are living in the present, *no*? It is the only place to be.'

Rose fervently wished that were true. If she could be rid of the past . . . *Allora*, she could imagine how good that would feel. She sipped her coffee. It was strong and bitter and almost scalded the roof of her mouth. And yet Lucia was drinking it without apparent ill effect.

'Nevertheless,' she said, 'at that time I allowed myself to be persuaded . . .' And with another big gulp of a breath, she told Lucia everything. Not making her own part in it too big or too small, but as she had tried to do with Federico, telling it how it was.

Lucia said nothing while she was talking, but her bright

440

birdlike eyes remained curious and from time to time she nodded and gave a little sigh.

'Your grandmother died soon afterwards, I know,' Rose said. She stared down at the table, at the embroidered white cloth, which was so clean, so pretty. 'I have always felt that I had a hand in her death. I have always felt haunted by that.'

'Pff.'

Rose glanced across at her in surprise. Lucia's expression was one of sympathy.

'Do not misunderstand me,' she said. 'It was a terrible thing to do to an old lady. To rob her of her precious family jewellery.'

'Yes, it was.'

'And I remember how angry we all were about it – Papà, Mamma, myself too. But . . .' – and she wagged a finger – '. . . you did not commit the burglary, Rose. You did not even know there was to be one.'

'Even so.' Rose could not accept that she was blameless. 'I played a part, you know. I visited your grandmother, I talked with her. I found out—'

'Yes, yes, you said.' Lucia waved this away. 'But you know, we all do things under . . .' – she hesitated – '. . . certain influences, is that not so? It sounds to me as if this Basso man wanted to make you feel you were more responsible than you really were.'

'Oh.' Could that be true? Rose wondered if Lucia was simply trying to make her feel better. She was very kind, but that made Rose feel worse still.

'Sometimes we simply have to accept that in retrospect we would have done things differently. We made a mistake . . .' She shrugged. 'And now, we must learn from it and let it go.'

441

'I find that I cannot let it go.' Rose's voice was ragged.

Lucia reached out and put her hand on Rose's. 'I know you are sorry,' she said. 'I know you wish it had never taken place. But you cannot change the past. It happened. It is done.'

'You are right.' Rose hung her head.' But if I had refused to visit your grandmother, then maybe—'

'Pff,' she said again. 'The burglary would still have happened. You know that, do you not?'

Rose considered. 'Yes,' she said. 'I suppose.' Cesare certainly wouldn't have let the lack of more inside information stop him from going ahead with his plan.

'And you know all that jewellery was returned?' Lucia leant back in her chair. 'Oh, yes. There was someone local – a jeweller – who had bought everything, but he suspected it to be a family collection, he did not trust the man who sold the jewellery to him and so he contacted the police straightaway.'

'I did not know.' Rose was pleased to hear that at least. 'But your grandmother . . .' Again, her voice failed. She had never known her own grandmother but she could imagine how she would feel if anything like this had happened to her mother. She would never forgive anyone who'd had a part in it.

'My grandmother was not hurt during the burglary, Rose,' Lucia said. 'I remember her being surprised that she had slept right through it.' She smiled. 'Almost regretful.'

'Regretful?' Rose stared at her. She remembered how much she'd liked Teresa. She had been so welcoming – that was the worst thing. And although elderly, she had been spirited and funny.

'She was a tough old bird.' Lucia chuckled. 'She liked to think that she might have tackled the intruder. Hit him over the head with a frying pan perhaps.'

'Goodness.' Rose's eyes widened. The image conjured by Lucia's words was so different from what she had always imagined. 'But she did have a stroke soon afterwards,' she said. 'I always thought that was a direct result of the burglary.'

'Did you?' Lucia seemed to consider this, head on one side. 'I really do not think that it was, no.'

Rose was confused. 'But the family – did they not think this?' She remembered it so well. The hushed murmurings. *How could the poor old lady survive such an experience? It was the shock. It killed her in the end, you know.*

'Her close family did not.' Lucia sounded very sure. 'And we knew her the best.'

'But your grandmother must have been . . .' – Rose searched for the right word – '. . . traumatised by the experience, Lucia?' In truth, she was finding this hard to accept. 'She must have felt that her home had been violated?'

'Oh, she did.' Lucia nodded. 'But she was angry rather than traumatised. *If I were not so old, I would go after them myself,* she used to say. And how she would shake her fist . . .' She shook her own fist to demonstrate. 'As I told you, Rose, my dear grandmother was tough, very tough.'

Rose was glad of this. 'But even so . . .'

Lucia pushed her coffee cup to one side.

Rose suspected that she too was tough; she had that same look about her as her grandmother before her.

'Rose, my dear, please believe me,' she continued. 'You may have been unknowingly involved in the planning of the burglary of my grandmother's house, but you had no hand in her death. Nonna was old. She had already experienced a small stroke a year before. It was her time.'

'I see.' Though Rose was finding it hard to see. She had been plagued by her actions and the repercussions for so many years, it was proving hard to digest this new information.

'However, I think she would appreciate you coming here to my house today,' Lucia said kindly. 'And I appreciate it too. It was very brave of you and after all these years, it could not have been easy.'

Rose's eyes filled. She did not want kindness. She did not deserve it. 'I know that it is far too late to tell you how sorry I am,' she said. 'How sorry I have always been.'

'It is never too late, my dear.' Lucia got to her feet and came round to Rose's side of the table. 'It is never too late.'

Rose got up too and they embraced, uncertainly on Rose's part, warmly on Lucia's.

'Can you ever begin to forgive me?' Rose's voice shook.

'But of course, my dear.' Lucia drew away, still gripping Rose's arms. There was such warm understanding in her brown eyes. 'It is done. Although that is not the problem here, you know. It is you who has to forgive yourself.'

Rose thought about this on the way home. Could she forgive herself? Could she move on? It helped considerably to know that Teresa had in all probability not died as a result of suffering shock after the burglary. And knowing a bit more about the old lady she had met so briefly helped too. But . . .

Federico was standing outside the house when she pulled up in the car. He looked tired and hunted. Rose sighed. She had really put him through it as well, when all he had ever done was care for her. Maybe it would be best for all concerned if she walked away from this family? Would they not be better off without her? Perhaps she would tell him now, get it over.

'Rose,' he said as she got out of the car.

'Hello, Federico.' She watched him warily.

'I have been thinking.' He looked very serious.

'About us?'

'Yes.'

She would save him the bother, the pain, Rose decided.

'Do not worry,' she said. 'I will leave. I understand that what I did is unforgivable. You do not have to explain.'

'But what about your mother?' he asked gently.

'Well, of course, I will take her too.' Although the practicalities of this were daunting. Her mother was so frail and this was her home. Even to take the time to visit Lucia had been a concern. How could she even think of moving her?

'Is it what you want, Rose?' he asked.

Numbly, she shook her head. 'No.' She took a step closer. Looked up at him, at this wonderful man who had given her so much happiness. 'But surely it is what you want?'

'It sounds as if you know better than me what is in my own head,' Federico said.

Rose glanced at him suspiciously. For a moment there, he sounded like the Federico of old. 'But after everything I have told you . . .' she began.

'*Sì, sì*, I was shocked.'

'And Cesare Basso.'

'That scoundrel.' His expression darkened. And then he shrugged. 'But all you did was give him a little money,' he said. 'What is money, after all? Whereas you . . .'

'Me?'

'You, my darling, my beautiful Rose. You cannot be replaced.'

She was silent. What was he saying? She did not dare hope.

He came closer. 'You have given me so much over the years we have been together. Life. Love. A beautiful daughter. A home.

445

You have lived with this . . . this guilt for so long. But look at all the good things you have done compared with this one bad.'

'But it is your family,' Rose said.

'You are my family, *cara*.'

Rose met his gaze. 'Lucia said I must forgive myself,' she told him.

He raised an eyebrow. 'You have been to see Lucia?'

'Yes.' She stood a little straighter. 'I had to. It has been too long.'

'And she gave you her forgiveness?'

'She did.' And Rose felt blessed by it.

He came closer still. 'So, you have told me and you have told Lucia and now it is out in the open.'

'Yes.'

He put his hands on her shoulders. 'Do you know what this means, Rose?'

She waited. She knew that he would tell her. And she knew that she was safe with him now.

He tilted her chin so that their lips were close and she was looking into his brown eyes. 'It means that because it is out in the open it can now be gone. Puff . . .' He made a gesture of brushing something away. 'Blown into the air like a dandelion seed.' He smiled. 'It means, Rose, that you are free.'

'Free . . .' She murmured the word. It tasted good. Free to live and love without restraint, without fear. She could focus on her family; give them the love and attention that they deserved. Cesare Basso could not touch her now. Now, she could perhaps begin to forgive herself, she could find some sort of acceptance, she could slowly come to terms with the shame of what she had done. And one day, as Federico had said, she might truly feel free.

446

CHAPTER 51

Bea

Dorset, July 2018

By the time Bea picked up a call from her mother at eight o'clock that evening, she was exhausted.

It had been a day of talking, remonstrations and tantrums. And more . . . Bea shook her head. Matteo had once again proved himself determined to have his own way.

It had been easy to resist his continuous efforts to pull her into bed. He tried persuasion, he tried promises. He was gentle, he was forceful – though thankfully he always stopped when she said 'no' loudly enough. He didn't listen to her and then he did listen, but refused to believe her. He lost his temper and then he was contrite. It was as if he thought that if he could only succeed in this one aim of getting Bea to respond to him physically, then everything else would go his own way – Bea would capitulate, she would return to Italy with him, all would be as he wished it to be.

But she felt nothing. *Allora*, that wasn't quite true; she felt sorrow and she felt regret. That is, she wished things could have been different between them – before. She wished that she'd made more effort to contact him in the past weeks to make her feelings plain, and she wished – oh, how she wished – that she had explained her situation to Lewis, so that at least she might not have seen that expression of hurt and surprise on his face when he first set eyes on Matteo.

Lewis . . . More than anything, Bea longed to go round there and make him listen to what she had to say. She didn't want to lose whatever it was they had between them, before it had even had a chance to grow. But she had to deal with Matteo first.

'Remember how it has always been between us?' Matteo refused to give up. 'The feelings when we make love, *cara*?'

'Of course I do.' The attraction between Bea and Matteo had been so strong that it had been the bedrock of their entire relationship, Bea realised now. But as far as she was concerned, it had died. And Bea knew exactly when her feelings had died. It was when Matteo had told her that she must give up her gardens, forget her dreams, relinquish the business she had built from nothing . . . because that was when she had fully realised the kind of man he was.

Matteo, being Matteo, would not listen when she told him their relationship was finished. Which rather proved her point. They went over it, piece by piece.

'I can change, *cara*,' he insisted. 'It is different now. And I can be a different man. You will see.'

The awful thing was that, yes, it was different now. That was the problem. 'It is too late now, Matteo,' she told him. 'I am sorry, but it is.'

Bea had never thought of herself as fickle. She had believed herself in love with Matteo, she had grieved when she thought

448

the relationship was over. And she had been more surprised than anyone when she had found herself having feelings for another man. But it had happened, and now in retrospect she could see the truth that her grandmother had tried to tell her before. Matteo was good-looking, charming and confident. He had swept her off her feet and she had responded, infatuated perhaps, certainly flattered by his attentions. There had been a strong chemistry between them – undeniably. But that was it. He had never listened to her, not really, and he had never respected her career choice. He said he was in love with her, but how well did he really know her?

Besides, Bea couldn't give Matteo what he really wanted and needed. She wasn't the woman who would stand by his side in the restaurant, who would dress up and charm his friends and clientele. She knew now that what she'd had with Matteo would never be enough for either of them.

By the time the call came through from her mother, Matteo had already walked out of the house four times and walked back in again five minutes later. But now, finally, he seemed to have come to a point of acceptance. 'I am heartbroken,' he told her. 'I never dreamt you could be so cruel.'

Bea strongly suspected that her text telling him that it was definitely and finally over had been the trigger that made him jump on the plane to come and get her. Matteo was a classic example of a man who wanted something all the more when he was told he couldn't have it. But Bea wasn't playing games – it wasn't her style.

'You can stay the night,' she told him. And then when his eyes lit up, 'In another room. But tomorrow you must book a flight and go back home.'

He had seemed to accept this, though Bea made a mental

note to lock her bedroom door. Matteo was not the kind of man you could trust – at least, not in that department.

'*Ciao, Mamma.*' Bea assumed her mother had called to apologise for giving Matteo her address in England. '*Va bene?*'

'Bea.' She sounded distraught. 'I am so sorry to have to tell you, my darling. It is Nonna.'

'Nonna?' The fear crept into Bea's belly. She hadn't spoken to her grandmother for a couple of days. 'What is it? Is she worse?' *Pray God, she was still alive . . .*

'Yes, Bea, she is worse,' her mother said. 'The doctor came a short while ago. He says that it may only be a question of a few days.'

A few days . . . Bea stared out through the French windows into the garden. She was sitting in the window seat, a place that she had grown very fond of, a good place for thinking.

'We are making sure that she is comfortable,' her mother said. 'But you know, my love, she is old. And she wants to pass away peacefully here at home.'

Nonna was dying. *Dying* . . . The word seemed to echo through Bea's head. How could her beloved grandmother die? Especially now, while Bea was here in Nonna's childhood home, putting Lime Tree House and the garden of Nonna's past to rights, bringing it back to its former glory, just as Nonna had asked her to.

'I must come back,' Bea said. 'I must see her.'

'*Sì, sì,* please, if you can.' Bea could hear the relief in her mother's voice. Of course, she would want her loved ones around her for support. It was a time for coming together as a family unit, one gaining strength from the other. 'But you must come quickly.'

'Yes, I will. I need to see her,' she said again. 'Before . . .'

'Yes.'

Before the end. Though they both knew that this might not be possible.

Before Bea had even put down the phone, Matteo had crossed the room and was holding her in his arms. 'Your grandmother?' he asked.

She nodded, mute. Right now, she was numb and she didn't want to start feeling what she knew she would soon feel. She leant her head on his shoulder.

'I am sorry, *cara*,' he said. 'I am so sorry.'

All she could do was nod as she wept into his shirt and he stroked her hair and whispered words of comfort and understanding. He might not be the right man, but he was kind and he was here, and she needed him.

While Matteo looked up flights and made the necessary arrangements, Bea went next door.

Lewis answered the door. He stood there with arms folded but his expression softened when he looked at her face. It must be obvious that she'd been crying. 'Are you all right?' he asked her. 'What's happened, Bea?' He took a step towards her.

'I am sorry. I am fine. But I have to go back to Italy. Tomorrow.'

His eyes didn't leave her face. 'I see.'

'You do not.' Bea was so wrung out it was hard to even find the words to explain. 'It is my grandmother,' she said. 'She only has a few more days to live. So, you see, I have to get back there, I must see her . . .'

'Yes, of course.' His expression had changed now. The warmth was in his eyes, the sympathy. 'Oh, Bea . . .'

But Bea couldn't cope with his sympathy. Not right now.

Matteo was one thing, but with Lewis, she sensed she would lose it completely. And she had to stay strong. She took a step back. 'Could you look after the house, Lewis?' she asked.

'Yes, of course.'

'And please, continue to paint there.'

He shook his head. 'No. It's okay. I—'

'Please.' She put a hand on his arm. 'I have no right to ask anything of you. I should have explained – before. But I want you to know . . .'

'Yes?' He was hesitant, but he was waiting.

'It was real,' she said. 'Between us, I mean. It was real.' Another step away. If she moved any closer towards him, she might not be able to walk away at all.

Slowly, he nodded. 'I'm so sorry about your grandmother, Bea,' he said. 'Will you let me know?'

'Yes, I will.' She turned away. She had his number. But now that she was going back to Italy, now that Nonna was dying . . . perhaps she would never see him again. In another time, another life, maybe something would have happened between them – something wonderful and lasting – but not now. How could that be possible now? 'Thank you, Lewis,' she said. 'For everything.'

He remained silent, watching her.

'And please say goodbye to Hester for me too.'

'I will.'

And with that, Bea made her way back next door to say goodbye to the house and garden. Her heart felt heavy with sadness. Perhaps this too would be for the last time.

CHAPTER 52

Lara

Italy, July 2018

Lara knew that the time was growing nearer and that now she was losing hours, days perhaps, half waking to find them gone. Objects, people, memories were blurred. Lara knew that it wasn't a dream. It was a fading, a cleansing. It should be confusing and yet it was not; it was restful. Something was telling her that things were falling into place.

Her loved ones were there by her bedside and then they were not. Faces swam into her sight-line and then they drifted away. The person who was there most often bathed her face and sat beside Lara holding her hand. Rose.

Ah, Rose. Lara could sense her daughter's new contentment. She saw it in her eyes, even though they were filled with tears, and she felt it like a gentle haze shimmering around her. Rose had told him. Rose was already grieving for the loss to come. But she was softer, calmer. She had found a way to move on.

'I'm sorry, Mamma,' Rose kept telling her. 'I love you. I love you.'

Did she not know that Lara had never doubted it? 'Yes, my darling,' she managed to say – though it wasn't easy to speak and it certainly sounded like the hoarse croak of an old woman about to breathe her last. 'I know. Be still. I love you too.'

Then, one day, she awoke feeling different – fresher, as if there was more she must do.

She heard Rose and the doctor talking *sotto voce* about how near the end Lara might be. And yes, she knew it to be true. So why did she feel this resurgence?

Bea. Suddenly Bea was there at her bedside, looking like a beautiful young flower. Where had she sprung from?

'Bea, you are here,' she heard herself say – in a stronger voice this time.

'Yes, Nonna.' Bea's voice was steady. 'I had to come.'

Lara heard someone whisper. *She is rallying. She is so bright today.*

Do not be deceived, she thought. *This is what can happen at the end . . .*

'The house,' Lara said. She meant the house in Dorset, of course she did. Lime Tree House. But all was well. She knew what she had done with the house. She only had to explain why.

'Yes,' said Bea. 'I understand.'

Did she, though, when Lara had never told her exactly what had happened? 'There is a story,' she said. Words were coming a little easier today. And Rose and Bea – they should both know the story, because it was theirs too; their history. It was all very well to have secrets – secrets would always be hard to tell, because if you told, you could no longer guard them, you could no longer pretend that they weren't real, that they were of no consequence, that they hadn't helped form you. And yet, as she'd tried to tell Rose some days or maybe weeks ago, secrets could stop you from living your life to the full, and that was never a good thing.

Bea was smiling her sweet smile, though Lara could see that silent tears were falling too. 'There always was a story, Nonna,' she said.

And she was right. *Even when her granddaughter was a girl* . . .

Bea leant closer. She seemed to know that now, Lara needed to tell the whole story and Lara knew that Bea would help her if she could. Lara could smell her perfume, *neroli*, she thought it was, sweet orange blossom which suited Bea so well.

'I know about your first marriage, darling Nonna,' her granddaughter whispered. 'To Charles. You must not worry about that, not now, for you know it is long gone.'

Charles. She knew about Charles. 'I thought he was a good man,' she managed to say.

'Yes, Nonna.'

'But he was not.' Neither of them needed to dwell on the darkness. Bea would glean all the information she needed from the garden. And as for the rest . . . Let it go, she thought. It was well past time.

She felt the touch of her granddaughter's hand. 'Was he cruel to you, Nonna?' she whispered. 'He was, wasn't he? Did he make it impossible for you to leave the house, the garden?'

Lara gripped her hand with a sudden strength that came from she knew not where. Bea seemed to know so much already. 'I was saved,' she said. 'David came back. You know, he came back.' It was important that her granddaughter realised this. Because Lara's life with David in Italy had been so good.

It had been hard work, yes. But they had developed the business and created something worthwhile from the kindness of the Romano family, which Federico and Rose in their turn had taken to another level. The families had – thank goodness – been truly joined. Every day, Lara had thanked God (and Hester) that she had made her escape from Charles. Because they could not have done it without Hester.

'Nonno?' Bea's voice was wondering. 'Was he your old sweetheart then? My grandfather? Was he the boy who was missing in action and presumed dead?'

So she knew that too. Lara tried to breathe more slowly, more deeply, but the breath was coming in shallow gasps as if she were clutching for more time after all. 'You have been busy, darling,' she said. 'And yes, he was.'

'Did you run away, Nonna?' Bea's voice was soft and melodic. Lara felt that she could listen to it forever. Only there was no forever – not for her. 'Did you climb over the wall and run away?'

'Yes.' Because in a way it had been as simple as that. 'Thanks to Hester.'

'And Mamma?'

Lara realised that Rose was not there with them in the room. 'Please tell her the story, Bea,' she said urgently. 'Tell her everything.' Because it was her daughter's story too.

'Yes, yes, I will.' Bea sounded more hesitant now.

Lara waited for her to say more.

'But can you tell me?' Bea was so close to Lara now that her voice was just the faintest of whispers in her ear. 'Mamma – is she Charles's daughter? Is that why you never told the story before?'

Charles's daughter . . . Lara had not been sure at first. She would have known Rose was David's daughter if not for that dreadful last time with Charles. And it was possible, yes, that her child would be one born of rape. But when Rose was born and Lara looked down at David's heart-shaped face . . . Then she knew the truth, and she had known that she must call her Rose. Because their daughter, born of love, was the sweetest thing, this wild rose of hers and she would ramble and grow, but she would always come home.

'She was always David's,' Lara said as firmly as she was able. 'In every way.'

When David was gone, Lara had not been left to grieve alone. She had her Rose, she had darling Bea, and she had Federico. She still remembered him running to their house as a little boy, always wanting to look after Rose when she was small. He doted on her. Federico had always looked after Rose; he always would.

With a start, Lara realised that Bea was still here, sitting beside the bed, holding her hand. *One more thing*, she thought. She tried to sit up.

'Nonna, Nonna, lie down.' Bea sounded agitated now.

'Go back to Dorset, won't you, darling?' Her voice was so faint now, she could barely hear it herself.

'Oh, Nonna.' Bea sighed. 'I do not know what more I can do there.'

'Who . . . ?' But Lara could not finish this sentence. Who, she wanted to know, was the man Bea had talked of?

'What, Nonna?'

Lara summoned all her remaining strength. 'Things must be finished,' she said.

'But—'

'The house will be yours. And the garden.'

'Oh.' Bea sat back. Lara was dimly aware of this. It would be a responsibility for her granddaughter. But she would manage it and it had to be done, for Lara's mother's sake if nothing else.

'You must do what you think best,' Lara told her.

'Yes, Nonna.' Bea bowed her head. Lara knew that she was weeping.

'But things must be finished. The garden was meant to last forever. Promise me.' She leant further back into her pillow. She felt her breath go and then return in a gasp. *One more time*, she thought.

'I promise, Nonna.'

The path of light seemed to open up in front of her. This was it then. Lara felt herself relax; body and mind. She looked directly into the light and it didn't hurt a bit. She could walk there. Because she knew that's where David would be.

CHAPTER 53

Lara

Italy, October 1947

She and David had finally arrived and Lara could breathe again. Here, in Puglia, she could breathe in the soft, velvet Italian air and feel the warm sun on her skin. Slowly, she was starting to feel safe at last.

It had been several weeks since she and David had arrived in Italy, since she had met Augustine and Eleanora and the rest of the Romano family (which had taken a while; there were so many of them). And although she was content, basking in the mellow heat of an Italian summer, beginning to trust that she was out of danger and that no one was following her, intent on dragging her back to England, Lara had not yet heard from Hester and so she couldn't help but feel anxious. What had happened after she and David had taken flight that afternoon? How had Charles reacted when he returned to find her gone? Had Hester managed to make her own escape from Lime Tree House without incident? Lara couldn't rest until she found out for sure.

The journey from Dorset hadn't been an easy one, not least because of Lara's continuing nausea and dizzy spells.

'What is it that he's done to you?' David demanded on that first evening. 'Is it something more serious than cuts and bruises?' His hazel eyes were full of love and concern. 'Though that's bad enough, I know.' David's fists were clenched as if he would punish the man who had hurt her. But then he tenderly kissed her lips, her eyes, as if he could make everything better again.

'It is more serious, yes.' She would tell him the rest when the time was right. But she had to tell him something now. Lara was half smiling. She hoped, oh how she hoped that he would take it well.

'What are you saying?' David frowned and then she saw him notice her expression, the way her palms rested lightly on her belly. 'Lara. You're . . .' His voice failed.

'Yes,' she said. 'I'm pregnant. Expecting a baby.' And then just so that he was sure. 'Our baby.'

'But . . . ?' He still seemed lost for words.

She shrugged. 'But nothing.' He knew as well as she that they had taken no action to prevent it from happening.

'Oh, Lara.' He held out his arms and she moved unhesitatingly into his embrace. She didn't think she could ever tire of feeling his arms wrapped around her like this.

'How do you know?' he whispered. 'That it's mine, I mean?' He pulled slightly away. 'Not that it matters,' he added. 'It makes no difference to me, to us.'

'Thank you.' For a moment she rested her head on his shoulder. Quietly, hesitantly, she told him what she hadn't told him before. How different her relations with Charles had been to what she'd experienced with David. So cold. So unfeeling.

So unfulfilling too. 'Charles had problems.' She didn't want to go into too much detail. 'And that last time . . .' The timing, surely, could not be right.

'I see.' David stroked her hair. 'My poor Lara.'

'But you don't mind?' She looked up at him. 'This is a bit more than you bargained for, isn't it?'

'No, I don't mind.' He laughed softly. 'And yes, it is, but it doesn't matter. If you're not unhappy about it, then I think it's rather wonderful.'

And Lara had to admit that she thought it was rather wonderful too.

During the journey to Italy and since then as well, Lara felt that she was getting to know the man she loved all over again. Yes, they'd had their romantic meetings in the woods, when he'd told her about his traumatic experiences during the war and how he'd found peace in Italy, and she'd spoken of her unhappiness too.

But during these past weeks, they'd both confided so much more. David had spoken frankly and emotionally and her heart went out to him all over again. And Lara had told him even more about the marriage that she could hardly bear to even call a marriage, the death of her beloved parents, the way in which she had come to feel so small, so insubstantial, such a shadow of her former self. She told him too about that awful night, the night she only wanted to forget, and she watched his dear face twist with emotion as he felt her pain. It made for hard listening on both sides, she felt. But it brought them closer.

Lara came to realise that David had been even more badly affected by the war and by seeing his comrade in arms, his pal, die right beside him, than she had appreciated at first.

And she saw his understanding of what she had gone through deepen too. They were two half-broken people, she thought, and perhaps this was why they fitted together so well, just as they'd always fitted together, each understanding the other, giving the other time, space and love.

Life was very different here in Italy. David worked very hard on the land and in the olive grove – and he warned her that the work was about to get even more intensive right up until December – and Lara helped as much as she could. She learnt from him and she learnt from the female members of the family, especially Eleanora who was only five years older than Lara herself and who she loved immediately. Augustine and Eleanora had three children and the youngest, Federico, aged three, was a particular joy. He would come and talk to Lara, his huge brown eyes watching her every move, laughing with hilarity at her efforts to speak Italian with any kind of reasonable accent.

David and Lara lived in the small agricultural cottage on the land which the Romanos had given David to do up and make into a home. It was nowhere near as grand as Lime Tree House in Dorset, but to Lara, it was everything. It was a simple but happy place where she felt at peace, and that was all that mattered. She was learning not only to speak Italian but also to understand Italian ways, and to prepare Italian food. She learnt about the *cucina povera*, food for the poor maybe, but also wonderfully simple. It was all about vegetables here: the aubergines, artichokes, tomatoes and *rapini* – bitter, green and leafy with small broccoli-like shoots – staples that grew well in this region of Italy.

And now, Lara had a ready-made family who had welcomed her into their midst. Apart from Augustine and Eleanora and their children, there were Augustine's parents, who lived in the bigger house with their son and daughter-in-law, and various aunts, uncles, cousins and grandparents who seemed to visit constantly. Meals were often shared with some or all of this large community and Lara was already feeling as if this was where she belonged.

She was starting a new life with David. They couldn't marry because officially she was still married to Charles, but they were together and they were safe and that was the most important thing.

Lara had written to Hester the day after they'd arrived in Puglia and every day she waited for news. It seemed, however, to be a long time coming.

On the day a letter from England finally arrived, Lara ripped it open and quickly scanned the contents.

Hester and Elizabeth were both well, everything was fine and Hester apologised for not writing sooner. She had some disturbing news, she wrote, and she hadn't known quite how to break it to Lara.

Lara tensed. This was it then, she thought. This was what she needed to know.

It's Charles, she read.

On the day you left – later, in the evening – he suffered a heart attack, due to the shock perhaps. As we all know, he suffered from angina and so he must have been particularly vulnerable. Unfortunately, he wasn't found straightaway, but he must have died soon after. I'm sorry, Lara. He was your husband, despite the fact that he treated you so badly. I hope this news is not too distressing for you.

Lara stared at the words on the page written in Hester's flowing script. She tried to read behind them, tried to absorb the sub-text of what Hester was telling her. He'd had a heart attack that same night, possibly brought on by the shock of her leaving. Charles was dead. She gazed out into the distance of the grey-green olive trees, unmoving and hazy in the heat of the day.

'What is it, my love?' David looked up from his food.

'It's Charles.'

He frowned. 'What about him?' He pushed his plate away, came round to her side of the table, reading the letter over her shoulder.

'He's . . . dead.' Lara realised she was shaking — though whether from relief or terror, she couldn't say.

'Dead?' David's eyes were wide. 'But how?'

She told him. 'He's dead because of me, David,' she said. 'I killed him.'

'No.' He pulled her to her feet and took her in his arms. 'You mustn't think that. And in any case . . .' — he hesitated — '. . . does a man like that even deserve to be alive?'

Lara thought of everything David had been through, all he had witnessed; the good young men who had been killed. 'No,' she said. 'Perhaps he doesn't.'

David was still holding her. 'But you see what this means, Lara?'

'Yes,' she said. 'Yes, I do.' And now the relief flooded through her. 'We're safe.'

'We're safe,' he agreed. 'And you, my darling, are free.'

They exchanged a glance. 'Yes,' she said.

'So, you'll marry me?' He hesitated. 'Am I being insensitive? It's not . . . too soon?'

She shook her head. It was what she wanted. And they had the little one to consider after all. Charles meant nothing to her — not any more. 'It can't be soon enough,' she whispered.

The remainder of Hester's letter didn't shed much more light on the matter of Charles's death. There had been no inquest since he'd died of natural causes and besides, everyone knew about his heart problems.

There were mutterings around the village, Hester wrote, about the timing of Lara's disappearance.

And his sister Marjorie added to the gossip with her juicy story about you and David in the woods, she wrote.

Lara winced at that. She could well imagine.

But apparently, Hester and Elizabeth had let it be known that Charles hadn't been quite the man he'd pretended to be and that their marriage had been so dismal that Lara had first turned to her old sweetheart and then had simply run away.

Who could blame you? Hester continued.

Lara sighed. But she trusted Hester and Elizabeth to only give as much information as they had to. And what did her reputation matter now?

In any case, people soon get bored with the same old stories, Hester added. *They've already moved on to the latest incomers and what dodgy business the man of the house does for a living. So, I wouldn't worry.*

Forgotten so soon then? Charles wouldn't have liked that.

But, Lara, what shall we do about the house? Hester went on. *The solicitor told Mum on the qt that it belonged to you and Charles jointly, so it's all yours again now. But there is money owing – I think he must have taken out a bank loan. And no one – except us, of course – knows where you are!*

Lara caught her breath. So, she'd been right – Charles had forged her signature and used it to get the property into joint names and borrow on the strength of it. That was how he had cleared his debts, she supposed. At least he'd had the grace to leave her name on the deeds, though that was probably merely to avoid suspicion. How could she mourn a man like him? A man no better than a common criminal, and a vicious one at that?

Do you want me to arrange for the house to be sold? Hester asked. *Or would it suit you to have it rented out for a while?*

Lara read on. It seemed that Elizabeth knew a family whose house had been bombed out and who were looking for somewhere to live. The husband had been a casualty of war and the wife was struggling to bring up their three children alone.

'We have all we need here, David, don't we?' Lara asked him that evening.

'I reckon so.' He smiled.

Lara told him about the house. 'I'd like to feel that someone else was making good use of it,' she said. 'Putting some happiness back in.' She leant against him. 'What do you think?'

He kissed the top of her head. 'It's an excellent idea, my love.'

'Thank you.' She exhaled. She must write to Hester immediately and tell her how things stood. Lara didn't need the house any more but neither was she ready to sell it. She still remembered the promise she'd made to her mother. And as for the garden . . . But here in Italy with David, Lara had found a place that she could call home.

CHAPTER 54

Bea

Italy, August 2018

The last few weeks hadn't been easy. Bea stayed in Puglia to support her parents and help them through the awful administrative tasks of death that had to be somehow tackled in the midst of grief. But although the family was grieving, they also all knew that Bea's beloved grandmother had, ultimately, led a long, fulfilling and happy life; one to celebrate. It struck Bea, as she talked with friends and family who came to the house to pay their condolences, how much-loved her grandmother was in this land, which she was not native to, and yet had made her home.

Matteo was one of their first visitors and it hardly surprised Bea that despite the circumstances, he still managed to pledge his love and loyalty and state his desire for them to 'start again'.

'Forget England,' he told Bea. 'Forget that old house in Dorset. Put it up for sale and be done with it.'

'Not yet,' Bea said. She remembered her grandmother's

dying words: *Things must be finished.* And Dorset, Lime Tree house, the Arts and Crafts garden and what she had begun there – it wasn't finished; there was more to do.

'Think what you could do with the money.' Matteo's eyes grew dreamy.

What was he imagining? Bea wondered. That she would invest her inheritance in the restaurant business?

'I have to go back there first,' Bea said.

'And then?' Matteo took her hands.

Bea looked down at them, and then at Matteo with his dark good looks, pleading blue eyes and commanding presence. The thing was, though, she didn't want commanding and she didn't want Matteo. He had been rather lovely on the way back from England. He had comforted her, distracted her, dealt with all the admin surrounding the trip. But that didn't mean she could snap her fingers and fall back in love with him.

'I already told you, Matteo,' she said sadly. 'It's over for us, you know. Like I said before, I care for you and I am grateful to you. I hope we will always be friends. But as for the rest – I have not changed my mind.'

'Hmm.' Matteo shook his dark head as if at a loss to understand. 'Perhaps in a few weeks,' he began.

Despite everything, Bea laughed. She had to hand it to him – he did not give up easily. 'No, Matteo,' she said. 'Do not wait for me. Just believe what I say.'

But when that few weeks was up, Bea was still in Italy and she realised that she must get on with things. Her grandmother had left her some money, as well as Lime Tree house, but ultimately, Bea still had a living to make and she had to decide what to do. She hadn't stopped thinking about the house, about the garden, about Lewis . . . She felt such a strong connection to everything in Dorset; it wasn't just Nonna's words that were pulling her back there.

'Oh, Bea.' Her mother drew her into her arms when Bea told her she was leaving. 'I hate the thought of losing you again.'

Bea hugged her back. 'You're not losing me,' she assured her. 'Wherever I go, you're never losing me.'

She wasn't sure quite what had happened to her parents in the past few months, but they seemed different somehow. They still bickered, still shouted even, but there was something new, some closeness that went much deeper. Bea was finding her mother more approachable too. She had told her Nonna's story and it had moved them both to tears. Her mother still worked hard – Bea was sure that would never change – but nowadays she always had time for a hug or a chat. She seemed more at peace with her family, with the world, with herself perhaps, and that had to be a good thing.

Bea continued to think about her grandmother and what had happened to her during her first marriage. She felt that she understood most of it now. But after Nonna had run away with her sweetheart – aided and abetted by Hester, as she had guessed and her grandmother had confirmed – what of Charles Fripp? Why hadn't he followed her and tried to make her come home? Or had he? Bea so wanted to fill in the missing gaps in her grandmother's story.

Dorothy, she thought. Might she remember? It was certainly worth a try. Bea decided to send a text.

I hope you are both well, she wrote. *I have one more question for you if you do not mind? Can you tell me – what happened to Charles Fripp after my grandmother disappeared?*

A couple of hours later, an answering text came back. *Hello Bea, how nice to hear from you again!* Dorothy's daughter wrote.

According to my mother, Charles Fripp died very soon afterwards. There was talk, as you can imagine. But of course, he died of natural causes. He had a heart attack. It was common knowledge that Charles Fripp had a heart condition, you see.

So. Charles Fripp had a heart condition and then he died soon after Bea's grandmother had made her escape. How soon afterwards? Was it the shock of losing his wife that killed him? This certainly explained why he hadn't followed them and tried to get her back. It explained how Bea's grandparents had made it to Italy.

But something was still bothering her . . .

CHAPTER 55

Bea

Dorset, September 2018

Bea waited until the morning before she went out into the garden. She had arrived in Dorset rather late and although she longed to call in next door, she had resisted the temptation. Instead, she had tried to sleep, so conscious of how close she was to Lewis. He was almost within reach and she had been thinking of him so much during these past weeks. But after what he had been through with his ex-wife, after the way he had been treated, why would he want to see Bea? She too had betrayed his trust. She too had let him down.

The following morning, she made coffee, ate some muesli left in the kitchen cupboard from before and went down the mossy stone steps into the garden. Things had changed just in these few short weeks since she had been here. She could tell from the earth that there had been a lot of rain and now it seemed summer was almost over. The hollyhocks lining the avenue were still blooming, though bedraggled from wind and rain, and the lavender drying in the late summer sunshine in the Romantic Garden was still attracting bees and butterflies although it was past its prime.

Bea walked through to the Rose Garden, ducked under the yew arch into the Wild Garden and looked around. There was still some pale-yellow honeysuckle clambering the old brick wall, though most of the blooms had gone, the later-flowering sea holly, thistles and teasels were turning blue and purple respectively, and the poppy heads holding their seeds still stood erect amongst the wild grasses. The damp, musty smell of approaching autumn already hung in the air.

Bea made her way to the secret garden. She felt that she had never quite grasped the symbolism of this garden room. It was shady and it was somewhere to hide. Was that it? Or was there more? She needed to see it again. She needed to think.

The foxgloves were still flowering, speckled purple and white. The bees loved them; even as she watched, the insects were buzzing and crawling into the tubular flowers to collect their pollen. The old-fashioned pink hydrangea was also still in flower, its huge blossoms like giant pom-poms, collecting rain water, and so soft to the touch as she ran her fingers lightly over the blooms.

Many of the other plants in the garden were now finished, though. She ran through them in her mind. The lily of the valley, the larkspur, the monkshood and the rest. All plants that you would expect to find here, next to woodland, next to a stream. Nothing strange about that. Only . . . She shook her head. Was she just imagining it, or was there more to this garden story than first met the eye?

A sound from outside the secret garden made her freeze. It was the soft rustle of the bamboo and *Stipa* grass. Not just wind. Some small mammal perhaps? Only it didn't sound like a small mammal. It sounded like . . . 'Who's that?' she called.

'It's me.'

'Lewis.' She breathed his name and just saying it out loud gave her the shivers.

'I'm coming through.'

And the next minute, there he was, looking just the same, long-limbed and clear-eyed, a head of unruly blond hair, an uncertain smile on his face. 'You're back then,' he said.

She smiled. 'I am back.'

'And . . . ?'

What was he asking? 'I do not know,' she said.

'I wanted to call you.' He stuck his hands in his pockets as if he also wanted to stop himself reaching out to her. 'After you left, I mean. But I didn't want to intrude.'

'You would not have,' she said quickly. 'Intruded, I mean.' She had almost called *him* so many times, her fingers hovering over his name on her contacts list. But she had resisted. What could she say? Whatever it was, it was best done face to face.

'And your grandmother?'

'She died.' Bea felt the tears spring up again. It had been the same almost every day. She could function quite well most of the time and then something would remind her and it would bring it all back. Nonna was gone. All the love, all the laughter – it was in the past now, at least as far as Nonna was concerned. And how Bea missed her.

'I'm so sorry.'

Bea saw the sympathy in his green eyes and she gave a little nod. 'Thank you.' She edged away from the stream where she had been standing. 'And I am sorry too.'

He raised an eyebrow.

'For what happened when Matteo turned up here. For not being more straightforward with you about my situation.' She shrugged. 'All that.'

Lewis gave her a quick searching look but he didn't respond. Instead, he glanced around the little patch of garden in which they stood. 'I realised you were here,' he said. 'Or at least I realised that someone was here. I came over to check on things and I saw some stuff . . .' His voice trailed. 'I nipped back home because there was something I wanted to give you – if it was you, I mean.'

'What was that?' she asked.

'Are you . . .' – he hesitated – '. . . on your own?'

'Very much so,' she said. Hopefully, he would get the message.

'And . . .' He ran his hands over the blossoms of the blowsy pink hydrangeas in exactly the same way as she had just done. 'Here you are in the secret garden where no one can find you.'

'But you found me,' she pointed out.

'Yes.'

They were silent for a moment, gazes locked. Lewis seemed to have forgotten that there was something he had been going to give her.

'I was thinking about my grandmother,' she said at last. 'You know, all these plants – foxglove, lily of the valley, water hemlock, even the hydrangea – they are all poisonous.'

'Sounds sinister.' But he did not seem surprised.

'It could be,' she agreed. 'But on the other hand, they are all plants that like the shade and the damp, so it is a perfect spot for them.'

'I see.' He was watching her calmly, almost as if he already knew what she was going to say next.

Bea knew that she wanted to tell him everything. Lewis was part of the story, Hester too. 'I got in touch again with Dorothy and her daughter,' she went on.

'Ah, yes,' he nodded, 'I thought you might.'

'And it seems Charles Fripp died of a heart attack soon after my grandmother made her escape.'

'A heart attack? Right.' Again, he did not seem in the least surprised.

'Everyone knew he had a heart condition,' Bea went on. 'Which could be very useful.'

'Useful?'

'And Nonna, she would have been desperate.' Tears came to her eyes once again. 'Who knows what a person is capable of when they are placed in a desperate situation?'

He took a step closer to her now. 'Bea—'

But she needed to get it all out – what she was thinking, what she was dreading. 'Several of these plants can kill a human being,' she said. 'I knew some of it but I looked the rest up. Foxgloves, for example.'

They both looked across at the white and purple spiky bell-shaped blooms.

'They contain a compound used for treating heart failure, so eating them is like taking an unregulated dose of heart medicine – it can be fatal.' Bea took a quick, shallow breath. 'I read a quote about them.'

'Oh?' Lewis reached into the pocket of his jeans and pulled out an envelope.

'It said that foxgloves can both "raise the dead and kill the living".'

'Look, Bea—'

But she wasn't done yet. 'And white hemlock.' She pointed

to the offending plant growing by the stream. 'It smells like carrot, but it can attack the central nervous system causing convulsions and cardiovascular collapse.'

'Right.' Lewis still didn't seem surprised. 'But—'

'Larkspur can slow the heartbeat and become lethal in six hours.'

'Six hours . . .' He let out a long whistle.

'And possibly worst of all is the pretty and innocent lily of the valley.' A plant associated with purity and kindness. A good luck charm. '*Convallaria majalis*,' she muttered. 'It contains at least thirty-eight known cardiac glycosides apparently.'

'Cardiac whatters?' Lewis had a very strange expression on his face.

'Cardiac glycosides,' she repeated. She had done the research but couldn't remember every detail. 'They say that lily of the valley can kill a man and make it look like a heart attack.' She paused. 'It will show up in his blood – but only if someone is looking for it.'

Lewis still didn't seem surprised. 'What conclusion have you come to then, Bea?'

'That my grandmother . . .' Bea bowed her head. She did not want to say it. She did not want to think it. But she couldn't blame her, she really couldn't blame her. Nonna loved the garden and she knew it better than anyone. She knew a lot about plants. And it would explain why she'd kept quiet, why she'd never wanted to tell the story. 'Yes,' she whispered. 'I think that Nonna probably killed her first husband, Charles Fripp.'

Around them, all was quiet. All Bea could hear was the occasional note of birdsong from the garden and the woodland beyond, the gentle trickle of the stream over the stone and the soft rustle of the bamboo in the light breeze.

'Then you should see this.'

Bea glanced at the envelope in his hand. 'What is it?'

'See for yourself.'

As she took the envelope from him, their fingers brushed together and she felt the frisson of his touch. *Oh, Lewis*, she thought.

She extracted a single sheet of paper from the envelope. It was a letter, an old letter, the paper grown stiff and brittle. She unfolded it carefully and then gave a little gasp as she recognised the handwriting. 'From my grandmother . . .' She scanned the beginning and skipped to the end. 'To Hester.' She looked up and met Lewis's gaze. His expression was grave but encouraging. Bea read on.

My dearest Hester, she read. *I know what you did.*

Bea glanced quickly up at Lewis but his expression was inscrutable now.

I understand why and I thank you from the bottom of my heart.

Bea read on.

You alone knew how trapped I was. You knew what he did to me, what he was and what I had become.

It was painful reading. Bea hated to think of her grandmother suffering. What, she wondered, had Charles Fripp done to her? She couldn't bear to think.

You have risked everything to help me. You knew that with your help I could escape, but you also knew that he would follow.

Which was exactly the train of thought that Bea and Lewis had also taken.

You know everything, dear Hester.

Bea glanced once again at Lewis. *Hester* . . . He must have read this letter. But how sad it was that Hester, his grand-mother, who once knew everything, had lost so many of her memories.

I hope you don't feel bad about what you have done. I hope that nothing lies heavy on your heart.

Bea sighed. She felt the same. Hester had helped her grand-mother, helped her much more than Bea could have guessed.

I had to write this. You saved me, Hester, and I will always be truly grateful.

But taking another human life . . . That was a big thing, a terrible thing. Bea wasn't sure what she felt about that and she did not dare to look at Lewis now.

Perhaps one day, you and I will meet again.

Bea was very sure that they had not.

Perhaps I will come back to Dorset but I am not sure that I will be able.

And so it had proved.

Burn this letter, Hester. With love, your Lara xxx

Carefully, Bea refolded the letter. It seemed clear enough. Lara, at any rate, had thought that her friend had poisoned Charles to enable her escape. 'Only she did not burn it,' Bea murmured.

'She didn't, no.' Lewis gave a little sigh. 'Grandma Hester and her mother, Elizabeth – they were the herbalists, Bea. Both of them studied the art, and Hester probably taught Lara some of what she knew. As you said yourself, many of these plants can be used medicinally in the right doses. We have all the same plants in our garden too. Up until the time she got ill, people still came to my grandmother for help with various ailments.'

Bea had to admit that it all made sense. 'Where did you find the letter, Lewis? Did your grandmother give it to you?'

He shook his head. 'I was helping her clear out some of her stuff. Her idea. I read it out of curiosity and . . .' – he hesitated – '. . . I decided not to show it to her.'

Bea could see why. Nonna had told her how much she had to be grateful to Hester for. And now Bea knew what Hester had done; this letter had filled in the missing gaps and told them the rest of the story. 'Do you think she remembers any of it?'

He shrugged. 'Probably not, but who knows? She remembers Lara was in danger. She remembers Charles.'

'You are right not to show her,' Bea said decisively. 'Because now that Charles and my grandmother are both dead, what does it even matter?' She gave a little shudder.

'But at least now we know the truth,' said Lewis. 'That matters.'

'Yes.' She held his gaze. 'But no one else ever need know. It is over. It is our secret.'

She thought for a moment that Lewis was going to take her in his arms and kiss her. He looked as if he might. But then he gave a little shake of the head like a dog coming out of water and moved slightly further away. 'Let's get out of here. This garden is freaking me out a bit.'

Bea let out a breath she hadn't even known she was holding. 'Okay.' And they edged back through the grasses and bamboo.

When they got to the other side, Lewis stayed standing very close to her. She realised that she had to say something more. 'About Matteo,' she said again.

'It was probably for the best,' Lewis cut in.

'Oh.' Bea felt the deflation deep in her belly. So that's what he'd decided. That it was for the best.

'After all, you live in Italy and I live here in Dorset.'

Lewis made a gesture that seemed to encompass the green Dorset hills and woods that he loved so much.

'Yes.' Bea's voice was small. 'But just so that you know, it is all over between us – it always was. Me and Matteo, I mean.'

'Right.' He seemed to be watching her closely. 'And what about this house?'

They both looked up at the low-roofed, gabled Arts and Crafts house made of local stone.

'What about it?'

'Well, what are you planning to do? Sell it and go back to Italy, I suppose?'

'I am not sure that I will,' she said. 'At least not right away.'

'What do you mean?'

Bea hoped she was reading him right. But her grandmother had told her that she had to finish things and this would enable her to find out at least where things really stood. Bea's legacy was the house and garden and she would see the project through. 'I've fallen in love,' she said.

'You have?'

'With the landscape of Dorset.' She was teasing him now, echoing what he had once said to her when they'd first met. 'And with this garden, of course.'

'Oh?' His eyes gleamed. He got it. 'Is that all?'

'There is someone I want to get to know a little better,' she said.

'A *little* better?' He was even closer now. In fact, his hands were on her shoulders and he was gently turning her around to face him. She felt the little jolt from their physical proximity.

'Okay, a lot better,' she said.

He cradled her face in his hands. She loved that. She loved his hands. They were real artist's hands – slim and tapered, always moving, always expressing what he was feeling whether he was talking or painting. She loved that too. 'If you will give me another chance, I mean,' she added.

His lips were close, very close. She could smell the scent of him . . . He smelt of oil paint and white spirit; sharp and dry with a hint of something warm like amber. She loved that as well. In fact, there were rather a lot of things she was coming to love about this man.

'I will,' he said. 'But I don't have much to offer you, Bea.'

Bea decided to silence him with a kiss. She put a hand to his face and drew him closer. In the lightest of touches, her lips brushed against his. There was a moment of pause, the sweetest moment, before their lips met again. Deeper this time, the kiss held exactly the sense of promise she was looking for. Bea could feel it in his touch and when they finally drew apart, she could see it in his eyes.

This might not be exactly what Nonna had been thinking of when she'd said things had to be finished – to Bea, it felt more like a beginning. But she had the feeling that her grandmother would approve. After all, there had been a bond between their two families from the start.

She would finish restoring this house and garden and then she would decide what to do with it, she decided. Whatever happened, it had to go to someone who would give it the love it deserved. Because her grandmother's story was past; the garden had given up its secrets. But as for Bea . . . Maybe she might stay in Dorset and set up her business here. The English, after all, did so love their gardens. Or maybe she would split her time between Dorset and Italy. Lewis, she guessed, would love the landscape of Puglia and find plenty of subjects to paint there.

But for now, she wouldn't look too far ahead too quickly.

She moved closer to Lewis, so close that there was nothing separating them. He interlaced his fingers with hers and she felt a contentment that was unlike anything she had ever felt before. So, he thought he didn't have much to offer her? *Interesting . . .* Bea could think of a whole lot of things. *Even so . . .*

'Lewis,' she told him. 'I want only you.'

ACKNOWLEDGEMENTS

A big thank you to my superb team at Quercus. Special love and thanks to the best editor, Stefanie Bierwerth, and my thanks also to Jon Butler, Kat Burdon, Milly Reid, Hannah Winter, David Murphy, Lorraine Green and others, who are all supportive and lovely and who listen to me. (I am very grateful for that.) Massive thanks to all at MBA, including Louisa Pritchard of LPA who works with overseas publishers. Love and thanks especially to Laura Longrigg, my agent, who gives me friendship, sound advice and understanding. I am very fortunate to have all these clever and hardworking people on my side.

This book grew from a long-standing love of gardens and I thank my late parents for that. They both enjoyed growing things – my mother was in charge of the flowers and my father tended the fruit and vegetables. This was a harmonious arrangement for all concerned – with outstanding results. Some of my earliest memories include playing hide-and-seek with an imaginary person amongst the raspberry bushes and watching my mum take cuttings of geraniums.

As for Arts and Crafts houses and gardens . . . I love this period of history and the designs of William Morris and the like and I also love the idea of reclaiming tradition, valuing craft skills and using local materials for building. I have never been one for blowsy plants – I prefer the cottage garden varieties – and so the Arts and Crafts values and styles appeal to me. We have much to thank these designers and craftspeople for.

Whilst writing this book I read a lot about and by Gertrude Jekyll (1843–1932), a gifted Arts and Crafts garden designer who worked alone and also in partnership with Sir Edwin Lutyens, the architect. She was in her time and ahead of her time and was quite brilliant in her use of plants to create different spaces for different functions; extensions of the house, encouraging outdoor living. I also took notes from *Arts and Crafts Gardens* by Wendy Hitchmough (published by the V & A) and Vivian Russell's book *Edith Wharton's Italian Gardens* (Bulfinch Press, Little, Brown).

Finding out about poisonous plants in the garden was macabre fun – hopefully no one is looking at my online search history . . . And I also made use of Margaret Robert's lovely book *100 Edible and Healing Flowers* (published by Struick Nature, Random House). Plants and nature never cease to amaze me.

Best of all was visiting some beautiful Arts and Crafts houses and gardens, notably Hestercombe, Barrington Court and Lytes Cary Manor in Somerset, in the name of research. My thanks go to the National Trust for the brilliant work they do to make these historic gems still available to us. Research is such good fun.

And then there was Puglia . . . My research trip there was postponed a few times and by almost two years thanks to Covid – a small casualty amongst many much greater ones. But when we eventually got there, it was as wonderful as I'd hoped. As always, the Italians were friendly and welcoming and I found their country as beautiful as ever. I hope that some readers will be inspired to visit this unique part of Italy after reading the book! (You will not be disappointed.)

I have a beautiful book entitled *Puglia: Between Land and Sea* (Sime Books) which has the most gorgeous photographs of the region. It brings it all back every time I look at it and I hope to visit again soon.

We are very fortunate to have made the county of West Dorset our home and I love to write about it and share it with those who also live here and others who might not know it so well. I wasn't born here but I think of this place as my soul home. Thank you, West Dorset, for being inspirational; many a time I have trudged over the cliffs in an attempt to iron out a plot problem. Thankfully the answers are always there, as the book says, somewhere between the sea and the sky.

For this book, I read a lot online about Dorset people and places during the Second World War; there are some brilliant stories on the BBC's 'Peoples' War' archives for Dorset. (And other places too.) I also very much enjoyed Philip Knott's *A Dorset Farmer's Boy* (published by Natula Publications, 2014).

All wars are brutal. David's story is apparently not unusual and I learnt a lot more about the kind of thing he might have gone through from *War in Italy* by Richard Lamb (published by John Murray) and articles online about PTSD. It is a complex subject. Any mistakes I have made about this and other things are my own.

Love and thanks to all my friends and family for being there when I need them, especially Grey who, as I have said many times before, is a perfect research partner because he is curious and fascinated by so much, and because he loves to take photographs and problem-solve. Research would be nowhere near as interesting without him. Special thanks to my daughter Alexa for Instagram and the beautiful Garden Plan. Big love to Luke, Alexa, Ana, Agata, Alex and James and to the little ones Tristan and Julian too.

Thanks to Wendy Tomlins for everything she does. And to Anita Count for making the orange and almond cake for *The Orange Grove*. Thanks to all my friends who have supported me on social media. Thank you to the lovelies from local book clubs who invited me along to chat about that book and gave me jars of marmalade and wine – especially Jo and Jacqui, two of my tennis pals. (The marmalade was delicious and I have now started making my own.)

Thank you to the stunning Finca el Cerrillo and the writing groups I have taken there. Sue, Gordon and Alison are the most welcoming hosts and they have a great team who have overcome the obstacles of the last two years and continue to offer the best possible venue for a writing holiday such as ours. I have met many wonderful people here and the holidays have been hugely enjoyable for me, providing me with the opportunity to work with other writers, something I love to do. (Special thanks to the group who helped me find the title to this novel . . .) Long-standing friendships have been formed here and long may this continue.

I would like to say a particular thank you to two very important people who have given me feedback on this book while I was writing it. Firstly, my writing buddy Maria Donovan in Bridport, who has the most perceptive eye. I love the way she thinks about things and makes me question things and I also love the way she writes. Secondly, my dear friend Meriel Powell who has gone walking with me many times over the past two years whilst this book was in the writing and discussed my characters' situations, emotions and responses with me endlessly and without complaint, adding her valuable insight. As if that wasn't enough, she then read the entire manuscript as I was editing it and made the most helpful comments. Ah, the value of an honest response given kindly . . .

Meriel – this book is dedicated to you with my grateful thanks for your understanding and much-valued friendship.

Last, but not least, big thanks to the writing and reading community at large. That's all of you . . . but especially those librarians, readers, bloggers and writers who have been so supportive on social media and in other ways too and who have got in touch to tell me how much they have enjoyed a book. It is humbling, it is wonderful, it is wildly appreciated. Please don't stop.

Rosanna

www.rosannaley.com
@RosannaLey
@rosannaleyauthor/
@RosannaLeyNovels